THE FAL

SAINTS & SINNERS

RINA VASQUEZ

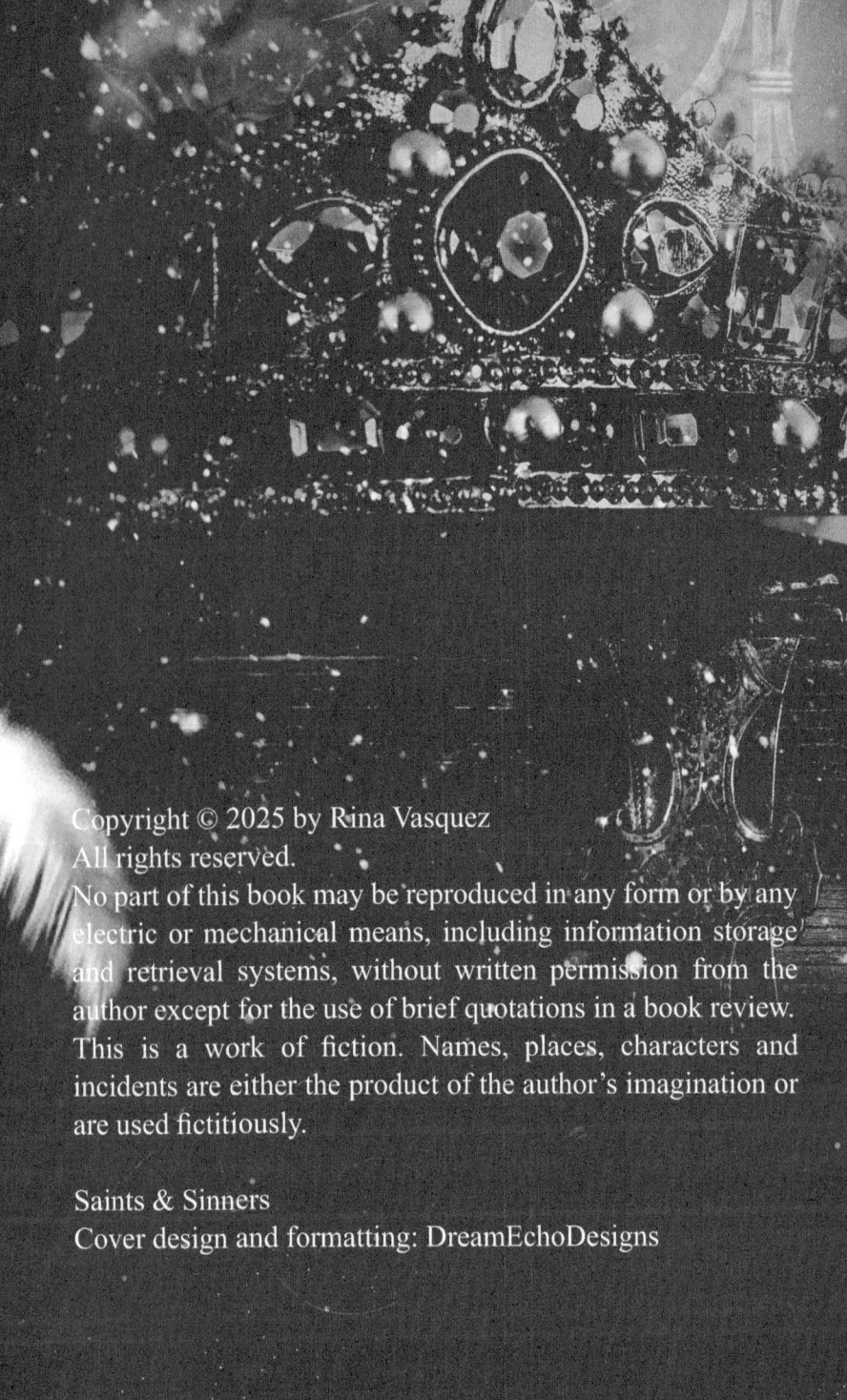

Saints & Sinners
Cover design and formatting: DreamEchoDesigns

CONTENT WARNING

Dear readers, although Saints & Sinners is a paranormal romance full of comedic and profound moments, there are still certain triggers such as violence, murder, death, panic attacks, sex scenes, explicit language, a tampon mishap (yes, I know), religious references, trauma, organised crime, SA implications, and possibly more.

PLAYLIST

Nothing's Gonna Hurt You Baby ~ Cigarettes After Sex
Your Guardian Angel ~ The Red Jumpsuit Apparatus
If You Love Her ~ Forest Blakk
Illicit Affairs ~ Taylor Swift
Angel With a Shotgun ~ The Cab
Dance With the Devil ~ Breaking Benjamin
The Power of Love ~ Frankie goes to Hollywood
How ~ The Neighbourhood
The Other Side ~ Michael Macargi
Here Without You ~ 3 Doors Down
Stay ~ Hurts
Hallelujah ~ Jeff Buckley
Look After You ~ The Fray
My Immortal ~ Evanescence
Demons ~ Imagine Dragons
One Last Breath ~ Creed
Losing My Religion ~ R.E.M.
Somebody to Die For ~ Hurts
With or Without You ~ U2
SYML ~ Where's My Love
Hurt ~ Nine Inch Nails

This is for the misfits,
the outsiders, and the ones who try
to carve their own place in a world
that tells them they don't fit.
You are not alone and for that,
I dedicate this story to you.

Ascendant Rankings

Warriors Sector
Strength, Combat, Protection

Guardians Sector
Foresight, Wisdom, protection

Messengers Sector
Communication, Speed, Telepathy

Healers Sector
Restoration, Life, Purity

GRACE

one

I wasn't suicidal. I *promised.*

That didn't mean I wasn't seriously considering launching myself out of a moving car as the wrought-iron gates groaned shut behind us, sealing me in.

My nails dug into the leather seat, and my breath was tight as the car crawled along the gravel path. Every second stretched too long, giving me far too much time to rethink every decision that led me here.

I could still jump out. I could tuck and roll, disappear into the woods before anyone even realized. But Joe would just sigh, mutter something about my dramatics and drag me right back.

Celestia Academy loomed ahead, rising from the mist like something straight out of a horror film. The kind where people go missing, and the world forgets they ever existed.

The ivy clinging to its stone walls curled like fingers, gripping onto the last traces of daylight filtering through the dense canopy of ancient oak trees. Everything about this place looked like it was designed to intimidate. To swallow people whole.

I hated it already.

And the worst part? This wasn't even my first time in an unfamiliar place with no choice but to pretend like I belonged. I'd spent my whole life adapting—running, hiding, starting over. But this felt different. More... permanent.

I swallowed hard, shifting uncomfortably as Joe steered the wheel to the left, the tires crunching over the gravel.

He sighed. "Still not talking to me?"

That was the original plan when Joe told me we were leaving *again* to come here. A four-hour drive later, I was proud I had kept up my silent treatment.

Until now.

"I'm not an Ascendant," I muttered, staring at the ivy walls. "I won't belong here."

Ascendant.

I could scoff at the title. Celestia was one of the many academies around the world for people who had been blessed by angels before birth to one day become Celestials.

"You've barely even stepped inside."

I swung my head around and cocked my brows. I was met with a pair of green eyes bordering on the color of emerald. "Easy for you to say when you're already an angel." Ever since I was left at his doorstep eighteen years ago, he's looked after me as if he were, ironically, my guardian angel—except by every law and decree written into the Angelic Code, I wasn't supposed to have one.

I wasn't supposed to be here at all.

By all accounts, I should have been just another human oblivious to this world. But instead, I was the exception. The anomaly. The human girl who an angel happened to take pity on and fought to keep me.

"I already spoke to the Angelic Council and the academy before coming here," Joe said. "Nadael says she is going to give my idea a chance."

"No offence, Joe, but I doubt you can convince everyone that a *non*-Ascendant can become a Celestial."

"That's because we haven't tried."

"No." I huffed, knowing that wasn't the reason I was here. He just wanted to protect me, like always. "It's because I'm too much of a hassle to keep around, so you dumped me here instead."

I knew that wasn't true. Of course, I didn't, but I was itching for a reaction, and I got it as Joe looked at me, appalled. He had always been a father figure to me, despite the fact that we didn't look alike. His sandy blonde hair and fair complexion differed from my curly brown locks and warm olive skin tone, but he was the only carer I had ever known.

"You really think I'm leaving you here because I don't want you anymore?"

Resigned, I slumped against the car seat. "No." But I was a lot of trouble to deal with in general.

He sighed. "You're eighteen, Grace, and people out there who know that you are aware of our kind puts you in danger. I'm just trying to keep you safe, and Celestia is the best option."

I wanted to tell him that I had better options than this, but he was right. The world was already cruel enough with demons preying on innocent souls that he feared the added danger of deranged Riftkeeper's—humans who knew of Celestial beings—would stop at nothing to bring them down.

It's not as if I was a targeted Celestial. I wasn't even one to begin with. They just believed the world should be a land for the living, not one with angels or demons added to the mix.

That, among other reasons, I assumed was why they disliked so many Celestials. And ever since they found out a Celestial took in a human—me—they have always sought me out. I was *that* unlucky.

"Will you still come visit?" I asked, my voice small as I stared down at the gold ring band on my forefinger.

"Of course." He chuckled softly. "If you need me, I'll always come to your aid."

I rested my head on the headrest and gazed at him. "Mmhmm, well, I hope you know how much I'm going to annoy you every time I do get to see you."

He rolled his eyes, amused. "You've been annoying me ever since you learnt how to talk."

My mouth dropped open, making him laugh, but I huffed and unbuckled my seatbelt instead of verbally attacking him.

"Do you have the new uniform Nadael sent over in your case?" he asked as I exited the car.

I nodded, rounding the boot where a ripped and barely contained suitcase carried all my necessities.

"Well, do you need me to go in and speak with her and make sure everything is all set?"

I shook my head and grabbed the luggage from him with strained effort. "I'll be fine. You just go and do your *thing.*"

"*Thing?*"

"Yes, *thing.* You know, the usual duties the Celestials demand of you while I stay here and settle down?"

He stopped to stare at me as concern flared across his sharp features. Same old, same old.

"I'll see you soon, Joe," I said, turning away before he could go all father mode on me.

Only when I found myself staring up at the entrance doorway, flanked by towering columns and crested angel

4

wings etched into the stone lintel, did my breath hitch, and I came back running into Joe's arms.

He had stayed in the same spot I left him, already having expected me to come to say a proper goodbye. His muscled arms wrapped around my small frame as I held onto him tightly and closed my eyes.

"I'm going to miss your terrible cooking," I whispered.

He chuckled. "I know."

We stayed like that for a minute longer before he reluctantly let go of me, and my lungs burned with unfamiliarity over seeing him leave.

"Grace?" A soft voice spoke from behind moments later as Joe drove off.

I turned as a woman came down the front stone steps of Celestia, wearing a pristine deep blue pantsuit.

"Grace Martin?" she asked, smiling once she reached me.

I nodded dumbly, and her smile stretched so wide that the most minor dimples dented the cheeks of her soft caramel skin. She was gorgeous and elegant, with long, dark ringlet curls draped over her slim shoulders.

"I'm Eden," she said with a chipper tone. "I'm in charge of taking you to your room."

Oh.

I clenched the handle of my suitcase a little too tight.

"This way, follow me." She waved me over, and I reluctantly followed close behind her. The brisk air of autumn swept my curls in different directions as Eden took me through intricate pathways. Forests and grassy fields encircled Celestia on either side of me.

A cacophony of laughter pealing through the air made me whip my head to the left, where a few children dressed in active gear wrestled one another on the ground.

"Some Ascendants are given the opportunity to come here from a young age," Eden said, and I whipped my head to where she was now standing at my side with an amused look in her dark eyes. I hadn't even realized I'd stopped walking. "Usually, the younglings will be placed in different classes and dorms until they reach the age of eighteen, when they will join the adults."

"What about others who decide not to come?" I asked, my gaze flitting back to the group that couldn't be any younger than ten.

"Depends. Some choose to have a normal life or wait until they are ready to join us."

Normal.

There would never be anything normal about that.

"Joe has told me a lot about you." Eden's change in subject snapped me from my thoughts, and I smiled, thinking about him.

"You know, Joe?"

She chuckled and resumed walking. "Many do."

I stumbled along behind her, struggling to catch my breath as she moved briskly ahead, her heels clicking confidently on the gravel pathway.

"He is one of the very few Ascendants to have become an angel within a short period," she continued as we passed a stone archway, and an old building came into view. "Most Ascendants spend years and years learning until the Council believes they are ready. But I still remember the day he was chosen to ascend."

I chuckled. "Yeah, he did once mention how when he ascended, a whole ceremony was performed with an archangel

6

appearing to grant him his official title."

Eden didn't laugh along with me, and I quickly found myself shying away at how embarrassing I must have sounded. I glanced away, focusing on the acres of trees sprawling across the land before my eyes widened as a gothic house stood sentinel up ahead, its silhouette etched against the evening sky. All I could mumble to Eden as I forced myself to stay upright was, "So, are—" I cleared my throat and shook my head as I finally tore my eyes off the engraved emblem of a flaming sword outside the doorway. "Are you an angel too or...?"

She nodded, grinning as if she loved others asking her that question. "I'm a Healer."

We entered through the doorway into the grand entrance, where footsteps echoed, and distant conversations bounced off the vaulted ceilings and brick walls.

"Oh," I said, my eyes wandering all over the bookshelves and the large stone fireplace. "I haven't met any Healers before." Glancing at Eden, I chuckled nervously. "Only Messengers or Guardians." Joe happened to be a Messenger. A great one at that.

Eden offered me a kind smile, doing a poor job of hiding the strange emotion that crossed her eyes just then. She cleared her throat, clapped her hands as she spun, and decided it was best to show me my dormitory instead of delving into another awkward conversation that she seemed to want to avoid. It had to do with Joe, I was certain. If they knew each other, then they had history, and whatever it was, I doubt Joe would ever tell me. He was a closed book, no matter how hard I tried to get any answer out of him.

"What did I say about lingering in the hallways?" Eden said as we passed a few others littering the corridors. One of them straightened off the wall as he spotted me. A copper-haired

7

boy with a petite brunette at his side.

"Sorry, Eden," he shot back, still staring at me as we walked past. He saluted me. "Won't happen again."

Eden shook her head before we bounded up another set of stairs to the second floor and stopped by the first door, numbered 104. "Here we are." She smiled, handing me a set of brass keys. "I'll let you get accommodated before bombarding you with everything there is to know about—"

"I know enough." I grimaced at how rude I sounded just then. "Joe taught me a few things here and there," I amended, but it wasn't any better.

She nodded slowly. "Right. Well, regardless, you will need someone to guide you around Celestia for the first few days. I already did the duty of assigning Marnie Lewis—one of our best—to help you."

Despite not wanting to shadow someone for the next few days, I smiled.

"This is an outstanding place to be in, Grace. You don't know how lucky you are," Eden said, seeing right through my skepticism. "I know it is not a unique academy experience that humans are accustomed to, but it is still a grand opportunity that not many get, *including* someone who is mortal."

I nodded because what else could I do?

"If you need anything, I will be downstairs, ensuring no one is messing around. Ascendant or not, they're still a nightmare to deal with." She chuckled, shot me a conspiratorial wink, and walked away.

As soon as I was alone, I stared at the key in my hand, feeling at a loss. I wasn't unfamiliar with new places—Joe and I had moved plenty—but it was always us moving into a home *together*.

I sucked in a deep breath before unlocking the dorm door.

What I hadn't expected was to walk in and have someone else in here, much less come face-to-face with a guy, naked as the day he was born.

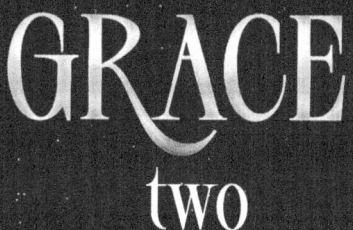

GRACE

two

"Oh my god!" I shrieked in horror and dropped my suitcase as my gaze landed on the person in front of me. He didn't seem fazed as he rolled his head to the side and smirked at me while holding a coke can in his hand.

"Oi, Tucker, Cain!" he shouted over his shoulder. "We got company!"

I panicked; I didn't know what to do. Should I run? Should I cover my eyes? Scrap that; what I needed was for the ground to open and just swallow me whole.

The light streamed through the tall, narrow windows, creating long shadows that deceived my eyes as I focused on the naked guy. He was attractive; at least there was that with his muscled and firm calves. His skin was a warm brown, similar to the color of his eyes, except they looked lighter, as if they had a hint of green and blue.

Still, that didn't excuse the current view *and* horror I'd been subjected to.

Slapping a hand over my eyes, I stumbled as I shuffled backwards. "I'm so sorry, I—"

"Woah, woah." The naked guy abruptly wrapped an arm around my waist, pulling me further into the room. "Where are you going? You just got here." He pried my hand off from my face, and I hurried to push him away when I realized I was flush up against him.

My heart was pounding so fast I almost felt like collapsing right there on the floor. Which was a dangerous choice considering I would likely end up with my head on or near his dick.

"Did you just say company?" Another male popped out from another room inside the dorm. His eyes widened when he saw me and went straight to where we were. I thanked everything and everyone in the world that he was at least fully dressed.

"Are you here for Cain?" He waggled his blonde brows suggestively, the silver eyebrow piercing moving along.

I frowned, stammering for an answer. There was none. I think I was broken.

Naked guy scoffed. "Doubtful," he said, turning his back to us and giving me a full view of his backside as he waltzed towards the leather sofa. "Cain never has anyone here. He's not a rulebreaker, you dumb fuck."

The blonde shrugged before grinning down at me. "Name's Brandon, by the way," he said, jerking his head behind him. "Over there is Silas."

I blinked.

"So, what brings you into our dorm?"

"This is—" I croaked, "—this is *my* dorm?"

"No," he drawled in confusion. "This is *our* dorm." He pointed towards the golden numbers stamped on the door.

12

"104. Warriors Sector."

Warriors Sector... Oh god. "Right, clearly this was a mistake; I'll just—"

"Put some clothes on, will you?"

A door creaked open, and the third roommate stepped into view. My gaze shot to him, and I froze. His hair, dark brown with golden streaks from the firelight, looked deliberately tousled, like he couldn't care less about his appearance. But it wasn't his looks that made my stomach twist—it was the way he carried himself, casual yet coiled, like he was waiting for an excuse to strike.

"But it's so hot in here." Silas groaned, running his hands through his shoulder-length curls. "Why must you always deprive me of my needs?" That elicited a chuckle from the other guy, and the sound resonated deeply within me, causing me to squirm in an attempt to soothe myself. It was deep, gravelly, with a hint of sarcasm.

I found my eyes glued to his every movement before he stopped beside Brandon and stared down at me. I suddenly felt so small. I *was small,* 5 ft to be precise, but this felt different, and I couldn't explain it.

He looked at me with gunmetal eyes draped in shadows. Despite how beautiful he looked from the side, from the front, he was devastating. His sharp and defined jaw moved as he rolled his lips to the side, assessing the stranger in front of him.

My pulse flickered.

"Who's this?" His voice was low and measured, like he already knew the answer but wanted to see if I'd squirm.

Brandon's brows furrowed. "That's what we're trying to figure out. She has our dorm key."

I glanced at said dorm key, which was still dangling from my fingers. "Clearly, this was a mistake." A terrible, terrible one

13

I would amend immediately. "I'll just go—" Embarrassment flooded my chest as I turned toward the exit only to stop short at the sound of his voice. "Hang on," mystery roommate number three said. I didn't turn but could hear his footsteps nearing until he was behind me. "What's your name?"

I contemplated a fake name. That is what I had been programmed to do when strangers asked me. It's what Joe had desperately tried to drill into my head in case I ran into those maniac Celestial haters, but I was at a place where I couldn't just do that.

Slowly and with unsteady feet, I twisted around. My gaze landed on his chest first, and I startled myself, thinking he was at least a good centimeter away from me. But no, he was a breadth away—close enough for me to smell an intoxicating blend of smoke and vanilla-laced cologne.

"Grace," I answered quietly, forcing my eyes to look up at him. "Martin. Grace Martin."

He continued to stare at me, but his expression gave no hint of what he was thinking except for the weight in his eyes, as if something always bothered him. "You're the one who got accepted into the academy without being an Ascendant."

I nodded shamefully. Word must have already gotten out before I even arrived.

His gaze narrowed. "Well, *Grace,* a little bit of advice since you're new here." His voice almost carried a tone of sarcasm as he lowered his head to my height. "You should probably walk back out the way you came from. You won't last a day in here. I highly doubt you would have even if you were one of us."

My brain seemed to replay those words in a painfully slow way. What I had thought to be remarkable about this person changed drastically.

He was an asshole.

Silas snickered from the sofa while Brandon raised his fist to his mouth to stifle a laugh.

Roommate number three just looked at me as if awaiting my reaction. He likely wanted me to run out of here crying. I was close to doing exactly that as my eyes burned with unshed tears. And yet, I didn't know what came over me as I raised my shin and kneed him in the groin with an extra amount of force. Immediately, he doubled over with a groan right as the other two boys began howling with laughter.

"Asshole," I spat before grabbing the handle of my suitcase and storming out of the room.

"Shit, man, are your dogs okay?"

More laughter filtered from their dorm.

"Stop calling them dogs!"

"She got you good, huh?"

"'What do you think?'"

"I'm thinking she has *balls*—ow, fuck—"

I wiped a stray tear before smiling to myself as their voices became muffled, and I made my way down the stairs.

HUNTER

three

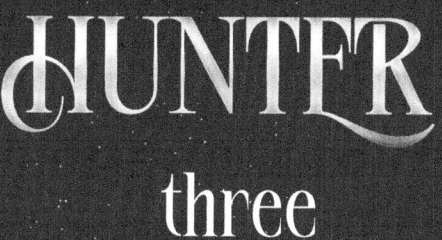

The pack of frozen peas landed straight on my balls, forcing me to double over in another fit of pain.

"Sorry," Brandon muttered, scratching the back of his head as he plopped onto the sofa beside me. As if his apology weren't hollow enough, he made it worse by slapping my back.

I saw stars. My soul left my body.

"I thought you'd catch them."

I shot him a dry look before tipping my chin up at the ceiling and settling the packet of peas between my thighs. Nausea still churned inside my gut, but thankfully, it wasn't as strong as it was minutes ago when I thought I was about to black out.

"I'm starting to think you should reconsider how you talk to women, Cain." Silas's voice came from the kitchenette. No longer stripped naked.

I sighed. "Not now, Dunn."

"Just saying, at least it wasn't me this time."

"True," Brandon mused. "Usually, those are Silas's dick

peas."

I groaned. "Did you seriously have to call them Silas's dick peas?" My nausea was back, this time tenfold.

Brandon nodded gleefully as if he hadn't traumatized me for the twentieth time this week. I hurled the cold packet towards his face, but he dodged it at the last second. "Hey! I was just trying to help the situation here."

I rose with caution and winced at the dull ache down there. Shit, that Martin girl had really done one on me. If she kicked with that much passion, she might actually be worth something at Celestia.

Not that I'd ever tell her that.

"Do you think she's left?" Silas wondered, taking out a bowl from the top cupboard and then a carton of milk from the fridge. He took a few gulps before saying, "The girl who kicked Hunter in the balls?"

"I'm well aware of who you meant."

He grinned at me. "Yeah, I know."

Prick.

"One can only hope," I muttered, thinking back to the moment I laid eyes on the petite girl by our doorway.

"Why?" Silas pushed. "Scared she'll hurt your manhood again? Not like we can have children anyway in this lifetime."

I clenched my teeth. "Silas, I'm this close to losing it with you." For emphasis, I pressed my thumb and forefinger together—not because I was close, but because I had already lost it with him years ago. I just lacked the physical strength right now to actually do something about it.

When he raised his palms in surrender, my lips curved into a smile, followed shortly by a grimace as pain shot through my balls.

"Moving on from that Grace girl," Brandon drawled, and I

rolled my eyes at him. "Do you think you'll be okay for later tonight?"

"Why? Do you need me to look after you again?"

He chuckled and shook his light blonde hair away from his eyes. Brandon Tucker, Celestia's resident nerd. He'd joined a year ago after his mom convinced him to accept the Celestials offer. On the other hand, I'd known Silas since we were thirteen. And he's had the pleasure of annoying me ever since.

"Nah," Brandon said with a smirk, "I think Silas is the one who needs looking after."

"How's that?" Silas mumbled; his words muffled by a mouthful of Cheerios.

"Because you're twenty years old with the mind of a five-year-old," I said.

Silas raised an eyebrow at me, a playful challenge in his eyes. "But could a five-year-old beat me in a fight? I don't think so."

I scoffed, shaking my head. One day, I hoped a child would knock Silas down a peg or two. When that day comes, I'm going all out.

"Shit, the corner shops outside of Celestia close soon," Brandon muttered, glancing at his phone. "I promised Sam I'd grab supplies." He hurriedly slid on his jacket and patted his pockets.

I was already holding his ID out for him. "Don't forget it this time."

Brandon grinned, then leaned over the sofa to pat my shoulder—and instead smacked me directly in the nuts.

I doubled over, wheezing.

"Thanks, Cain."

I barely managed a thumbs-up as Silas erupted into his

usual obnoxious laughter.

Grace Martin.

Her name echoed in my mind, drowning out Silas's noise. She'd get out of here while she still could if she had any sense. Because I don't forget...and I definitely don't forgive.

GRACE
four

"How did this even happen in the first place?" Joe shook his head at Nadael.

I cringed, wanting to sink into the chair and disappear. I didn't like the current attention I had on me inside Nadael's office. It reminded me too much of the times Joe had to pick me up from the head teacher's office in primary school because I was either bullied or Miss. Pollin was worried over my fascination with demons and angels.

"I assure you, I did not mean to—" Eden said but silenced herself when Joe looked her way, and she reddened.

Something thickened the air between them as Joe never dropped his gaze, leaving Nadael to clear her throat and gain his attention back to her.

"The dorms at Celestia typically accommodate two or four individuals per room within their designated ranking sector," she stated, resembling every headteacher I had encountered in my life, except for her midnight blue robe cinched at her waist and a gold belt. Her silver-white hair was slicked back into a low bun, and her office matched the color scheme of her clothes. Blue, white and minimalistic. "Room 104 was listed as not having a fourth roommate, which—" She glanced in Eden's direction. "Eden should have known it was occupied by three other *boys*."

Eden bowed her head in shame, and I instantly felt sorry for her. I had made such a bother of it as soon as I left the dorm that she didn't have the chance to sort it out herself. Instead, I rushed to call Joe. Like I always did for everything. I sought him out to fix any inconvenience I ever had. It was wrong because I was so heavily dependent on him. And it only took Joe minutes, if that, to come back. Just as he said he would. He didn't even need to use that old car of his anymore. The angels and Angelic Council had their own ways of transport. Wings, yes, but secret passageways through paintings were their preference. More... *discreet.* And now that Joe was working with the Council, he didn't need to act normal for my sake.

"Is there any other room she can stay in?" That was Joe.

Nadael pursed her pale pink lips in thought. "There should be a few spare rooms in the south wing of Celestia where Guardians stay. We can sort it out straight away for her, so she doesn't have to wait around."

Joe's sigh sounded relieved. When I turned to look at him, his smile was full of encouragement, and for some reason, it didn't settle right with me. It was the same smile he had given me for years, where, deep down, he didn't know what to do with me half the time.

Mr. Martin, I don't know what to tell you. She is scaring half the other children with her conversations about... demonic beings?

I know, I know. I'm so sorry; she is just a little misguided—

Misguided or not, that is hardly an appropriate conversation

24

for a grownup to give to a six-year-old. I would hate to have to take matters into my own hands, Mr. Martin.

I blinked out of that memory, trying to forget the expression Joe had on his face. He was still struggling to adapt to a world involving a human kid, and despite how amazing he was at playing the doting single father, I still made things difficult for him.

"If you'd like, I can take both of you to see the new dorm—"

"No," I cut Nadael off. The entire room went quiet. Nadael opened her mouth, and silver brows raised while Joe's startled gaze burnt into the side of my face. "I mean that—" I licked my lips, straightened myself against the chair and offered her a polite smile. "Moving won't be necessary. I can stay in room 104."

"What?" Both Joe and Nadael said at once.

"Grace," Nadael choked out a surprised laugh. "The reason you are here in my office is to change rooms. The Angelic Council would not be on board if they heard you were sharing the same room with three other men. It's—it's—" She seemed at a loss now, her tanned skin darkening into a deep shade of red.

I shrugged. "We all have separate bedrooms. And who is to say it wouldn't be the same if I shared with girls instead?"

Nadael's eyes widened.

"Grace," Joe said as a warning.

"Grace," Nadael sighed. "You should know that regardless of whether one is an Ascendant or not, their emotions can get the better of them."

I was aware. An Ascendant Healer could have the ability to heal someone with their own touch, but that didn't mean they didn't breathe, dream, and think the same as any other indecent human. Hell, they were still susceptible to becoming

25

corrupted souls.

"I'm sure my new roommates are good people." I lied. I could do without having to live with the guy I kicked between the legs, but I didn't want to say that. I was taught from a young age to give someone the benefit of the doubt, and besides, I wanted to prove something to Joe, no matter how stupid it might be.

Nadael opened her mouth to speak, but Eden got there before her.

"They are," she said; the smile she had given me when we first met flickered across her lips once again. "Hunter Cain is an excellent Warrior, ranking at the top of the class alongside Silas Dunn."

Hunter Cain.

That is what Brandon and Silas were saying. *Cain.*

I'm assaulted by the image of grey eyes staring down at me, then. Eyes that sparked something restless inside of me and a wave of unease.

"True," Nadael murmured, once again in thought, but my mind was now elsewhere, specifically on Hunter.

Ugh!

"Wait, wait, wait." Joe shook his head before facing me. He said in a quieter voice, "Grace, less than two hours ago, you called me in hysterics, wanting to change rooms. What's changed now?"

The fact that you look at me like I am still this naive little girl who needs you.

But you do still need him, my mind whispered.

"I was just thrown off balance." I grabbed his hand and squeezed it gently. "You know what I'm like in new situations." I chuckled, hating how the lie sounded on my tongue. "I'm sorry I created such a fuss out of nothing."

Joe glanced down at our hands and frowned. Sighing, he shook his head and ran a hand through his short hair. "I don't think I've ever worried over someone like I do with you."

I know. "I'll be fine this time. I promise no more panicked calls from me."

He smiled, but the worry was still evident in his eyes. I wanted to erase that from him, but all I seemed to do was cause more of it.

"Well then, if that is settled," Nadael blew out a breath and smiled tightly. "You can stay with Eden for the night, and tomorrow evening, you can unpack at your new... *dorm.*"

I frowned. "Why can't I move in today?"

Nadael blinked her crystal blue eyes at me as if the question surprised her. She looked sideways at Eden before saying, "I think it is best you settle somewhere else for the night after the surprise you and the boys received. Besides, tonight happens to be one of the days when the older Ascendants go out into the forests of Celestia and relax with one another, marking the end of summer. It's an excellent way to make friends and treat yourself to some snacks. I highly encourage you to attend it yourself."

A party. That's what she meant. One where I would feel like the odd one out of the bunch because, at the end of that day, that's what I was in an Ascendant's eye.

I faked a smile. Something I had mastered for years and excelled at. "Sure. I'll think about it."

HUNTER

five

"I told you not to get too close to the fire." I smirked, watching Silas as he sucked on the tip of his now burnt finger. The flames crackled and spat from the metal bins, casting flickering light over people while soft rock played in the background.

"How was I supposed to know I'd burn myself?"

"It's fire, Silas. That's kind of what it does when you get too close."

He grumbled under his breath, "Annoying prick."

I shook my head, chuckling as I took a swig of beer, the bitter taste lingering on my tongue.

"Shit." Silas nudged my shoulder, nodding toward the path ahead. "The baby maker destroyer is back."

I stilled.

No. No fucking way.

She couldn't be here. But then I saw her. Right in the middle of a group of Ascendant Healers stood Grace fucking Martin—looking as lost as a lamb in a wolf's den. Her eyes darted around, scanning the crowd, oblivious to the fact that my night was about to be ruined.

"Better hide your nutsack, Cain. She might be looking for round two."

I shot Silas a dark look, my mood souring instantly. "Keep talking, and I'll kick you in the balls myself."

He raised his hands, taking a step back. "Hey, I'm just trying to protect your goods."

I finished my drink in one gulp, tempted to throw the bottle at his head.

Instead, I put all my focus back on her.

Grace.

She was shifting from foot to foot, looking uncomfortable, like she knew she didn't want to be here but hadn't figured out how to leave yet. Part of me knew she would stay. The other part was praying she wouldn't.

And that? That pissed me off.

Because I didn't want her here.

Because I didn't want to look at her.

Because I *couldn't* stop looking at her.

She wasn't even doing anything, just standing there, being all polite and innocent, apologizing to people who bumped into her first—which, honestly, told me everything I needed to know about her.

She still hadn't noticed me as a redhead stepped into her path, blocking her view before she could turn in my direction.

GRACE

"Hi!" A freckle-faced girl suddenly appeared in front of me, waving a red cup that matched the vibrant curls of her hair. "I'm Marnie." She pointed a finger at me, squinting one eye as if trying to place me. "You're the new girl I'll be showing around. It's Grace, right?"

I chuckled awkwardly, pulling my denim jacket tighter around me. "I see my name travels fast around here."

Marnie let out a high-pitched laugh, the kind that was both endearing and a little overwhelming. "Everything at Celestia does. You'll get used to it, and soon enough, you'll fall into the same pattern as all of us."

I wasn't sure I wanted that, but it felt inevitable after Eden convinced me to come out tonight. "So, is this a usual thing around here?" I asked, glancing around at the other Ascendants mingling.

She shrugged. "The Celestials like to pretend we can have a normal boarding school experience." She gestured for me to follow her through the forest, pulling a packet of skittles from her pocket and offering it to me. I smiled and took only the green ones. "The older groups are the ones who throw these little gatherings. Usually, it's because they know that once Monday rolls around, it's back to competing against each other."

I grimaced at the thought. "Sounds more like a prison, then."

Marnie gave me a small laugh. "It's not all bad. We get sent our own food hauls, decent beds, and depending on whether you have supportive parents or not, we either get monthly spendings sent from them or from Celestials. But I suppose you already knew all of that, considering your upbringing."

I stopped in my tracks, frowning as she turned to face me.

"Joe Martin?" she asked, a little too casually, then winced at my reaction. "Sorry, I didn't mean to pry. It's just... he's kind of a big deal among Ascendants. He ascended within two weeks of being at Celestia. That's rare."

I chuckled because Joe was my norm. He couldn't cook, would always lose me inside shopping markets, and would panic whenever my period came. Yet, even with that, he still managed to be a source of hope among those who wanted to become angels.

"Except that he didn't give birth to me," I said, and she laughed, her mouth full of red-colored skittles.

For the first time today, I flashed her a bright, genuine smile. But it faded as quickly as it came when my eyes locked onto a pair of piercing grey ones staring right back at me.

My heart stopped, the sudden urge to flee tightening around my chest.

Hunter was leaning casually against a tree, his head tilted slightly as he watched me with an intensity that made my skin prickle. His expression was unreadable, but those eyes were sharp enough to cut through the distance between us like a blade.

Marnie continued talking, oblivious to the silent exchange Hunter and I were having. I barely heard her words as I struggled to maintain my composure. Hunter's gaze was relentless, and with every passing second, I doubted he would ever look away.

I forced myself to focus on Marnie and blurted out, "What do you know about Hunter Cain?"

She almost choked on her skittles before glancing around in search of him. "Hunter?" Her bright green eyes widened as they snapped back to mine. "Um, well, a few things... but he's sort of an enigma. He's been at Celestia ever since he was thirteen after his brother was taken away by the Riftkeeper's."

"Brother? Was he also an Ascendant?"

"No." She shook her head and leaned forward to whisper.

"But I doubt he's alive anymore if the Riftkeeper's took him. Apparently, they even killed his mother in front of them, too."

That knowledge made the skittles I'd had churn inside my stomach. I was no stranger to how dangerous Riftkeeper's were. I had only ever seen them a couple of times. They bore a specific brand, distinguishing them from the rest. It was one of the reasons they couldn't pass the barrier to Celestia if they found it. But... to know that happened to Hunter's family makes me wonder if he really deserved the kick I gave him.

"He's also part of the Warrior Sector," Marnie added nonchalantly, looking over her shoulder, though I refused to let my eyes roam anywhere near Hunter. "Ughhh, he's just so dreamy."

I made a face. "Who, Hunter?"

Marnie scoffed, grinning. "*Obviously*, but I'm not talking about him this time; I'm talking about Brandon."

I couldn't avoid it anymore. I had to look Marnie's way to where Brandon had joined Hunter.

"Would you look at that face?" Marnie murmured, her voice slipping into a low, playful growl that made me laugh. She grabbed a handful of skittles and shoved them into her mouth. "Too bad we could never date."

Forgetting the whole concept of where I was, I raised an eyebrow at her. "Why not?"

"Ascendants," she emphasized as if that explained everything. When I still looked confused, she sighed and continued, "If I want to become a Celestial, I can't get involved in relationships. Here at Celestia, once you join and swear that you're here to one day ascend, then any form of romantic relationship is strictly prohibited."

Ah, right, I forgot about that.

"Others might not care much about messing around for a

quick lay, but getting into something serious with someone? Say goodbye to your time at Celestia and any future of becoming an angel."

"Well, in that case... I don't think there's anything wrong with being able to have fun without having to enter a relationship for now."

Marnie shook her head. "And then what? Have my heart broken right before I ascend? No thanks. I'd rather not break the Angelic Code or have to sneak around Celestials just for a quick shag to then be caught."

She was right, but perhaps part of me found it problematic that was the life of a Celestial. Somehow, drinking alcohol and partying were fine by their norms, but to date? A treason in their eyes. "You know," I suggested with a shrug, "you could always choose not to become an angel."

Her reaction was instant, and the horrified expression on her face told me that option wasn't even remotely on the table for her. "I don't know what Joe has told you about Ascendants or how the Angelic Council works, but I'm not risking everything for love. If you decide against becoming an angel, the Council will strip you of your powers—every memory you've ever had connected to this place and as an Ascendant, including the family members that might know of your nature. So, either way, you'd lose the person you fall for."

Her words left me stunned. Joe had never mentioned any of this to me. I knew that Celestials couldn't fall in love—neither with another Celestial nor a mortal. The threat of a Nephilim being born was too great; they were seen as abominations by the entire Angelic Council. But to have your memories stripped... I couldn't even process the idea of it.

"Hey, Marns," someone called out, jolting me from my thoughts. "Already trying to drill the rules into the new girl's head?"

I looked up to see someone with copper hair sauntering over, slipping between Marnie and me as if personal space didn't matter to him.

"Grace, right?" he asked, his tone dripping with casual arrogance. I nodded reluctantly. "I saw you with Eden earlier. Never thought I'd see the day when someone without the Ascendant label joined us."

Oh, right. Now I remembered him—it was the guy who had been lurking around the hallways earlier.

"Matias," he said, pointing both thumbs at himself when I didn't respond.

"Please don't be annoying—" Marnie began, but he cut her off with a dismissive shush, his eyes fixed on me.

"Hey, let her—" I started, but he interrupted me without a second thought, laughing as he shoved his hands into his pockets.

"So, what's your plan then? Since, you know, you don't exactly have a... *gift.*"

My eyes narrowed. "And what exactly do you mean by that?"

Of course, I knew what he meant, but it was clear he wasn't picking up on my irritation.

"Well," he said with a smirk, "we've got Healers who are pretty straightforward—unless you're already dead, of course—Messengers who are telepathic. Guardians who can see all. And finally, Warriors—the ones considered greater than the rest." He tilted his head, giving me a smug smile. "So, which category do you fit into?"

He was obviously trying to rub it in that I didn't have enhanced combat skills or some type of Celestial wisdom that made me a Messenger. That I couldn't communicate telepathically or heal someone with a touch. It was like being back in secondary school, except worse—because this time, the guy in front of me clearly had a god complex.

Marnie opened her mouth, probably to defend me, but I knew if I let that happen, I'd be seen as someone who couldn't stand up for herself. Just like before.

"Are *you* a Warrior?" I asked.

He grinned, clearly pleased that I assumed so. "You didn't answer my question."

"No." I hummed thoughtfully. "But you perfectly answered mine." *Cocky prick.*

The grin slid off his face almost instantaneously, replaced by a look of confused annoyance.

Marnie let out a half-laugh, half-snort, trying—and failing—to cover it with her hand. I smiled as I reached for a skittle, and she handed me the entire bag, still chuckling.

Matias looked even more baffled, as if the whole exchange had short-circuited his brain. "Wait, hold on, I—"

"Matias."

Oh, for God's sake.

Both Marnie and Matias turned to see Hunter standing behind them with his hood down, hair tousled and catching the light from the flickering flames around us. The firelight made the golden strands even more striking than usual against the darker brown.

"Leave." Hunter's voice was calm, but it had an edge that left no room for argument. Matias stiffened, and after a tense moment, he stalked off, muttering something under his breath.

A nervous smile played on Marnie's lips before Hunter turned his attention to her and blankly stared at her.

She cleared her throat, glancing back and forth between us before walking away, saying, "I'm just—yeah—" She spun around right as I was about to tell her not to leave, but it was too late. She was already lost amongst the crowd of Ascendants.

My hands immediately became clammy, and I tried to look anywhere but at Hunter. It was impossible because my gaze kept wandering towards him and his intense stare.

I swallowed slowly and carefully. "A shame to see that you can still walk."

His eyes fell to my throat before he tipped his head to the side, not giving me enough emotion to know what was passing through his mind. "And much to my disappointment, you're still here."

Oh. I should have known it would have to do with me not running away from this place.

Clearing my throat, I said, "Surprised?"

He shrugged, now looking bored. "I give it a week."

Irritation flared up inside me, and I threw another two skittles into my mouth for good measure. "Well, a week is going to feel like a *long* time because I plan on staying." I chewed slowly as my brows rose. "In your dorm as well, or should I say ours?"

That ruined the disinterested look on his face as his expression hardened, and he took a step closer. "You—"

"Can't stay there?" I finished off for him with a perky smile to mask how on edge I felt around him. If he looked close enough, he'd see how badly my legs were shaking. "Yeah, I didn't want to, especially after the rude welcoming, but once I spoke with Nadael, I realized I shouldn't be quick to judge, although I can't help it since you seem like a real dick and if anything—" I chuckled softly. "—I've realized how badly you deserved that kick I gave you because I have no regrets—" I paused when I saw his lips twitch. "What?"

"Is this a usual habit of yours, rambling nonsense?"

My mouth dropped wide open.

How dare he be right.

How *dare* he look this amused right now.

Rambling *was* a usual habit of mine, and it tended to happen when I was flustered or overly excited. The latter clearly wasn't why this time.

Not wanting to dignify him with a response, I brushed off some imaginary lint from my denim jacket and shoved the bag of skittles against his chest. I tried to push past him, but he grabbed my arm, spinning me around to face him. My breath caught as his gaze swept over my face, intense and unyielding.

"I meant it," he said quietly, voice low and serious. "This place isn't for you."

For some reason, I didn't pull away. Instead, I met his stare with equal intensity, letting my anger simmer just beneath the surface. "Do you *want* to be kicked again?" Maybe once just wasn't enough.

His eyes flashed with a dangerous challenge. "You'll regret it."

"The kick or staying?"

"Both."

With that, he released me as if my touch had burnt him, leaving a strange tension hanging in the air between us. He stepped back, and something in the way he was staring at me told me I *would* regret it before he walked away.

Since the moment he had laid eyes on me, he hated me; the question was, why did my being here bother him so much?

GRACE

six

I was startled awake when Eden's bedroom door flew wide open. She came in with a smile on her face and a steaming mug in her hands.

"Morning!" She sang, waltzing towards the blinds. I winced as she pulled them open, and the early morning sun shone through the window. After the eventful party yesterday, I spent the night tossing and turning in bed. Every time I closed my eyes, I saw grey. Gun metal grey that pissed me off.

"I've spoken with Nadael," Eden said, her tone chipper as she straightened the crooked frames on her wall. "She'll be speaking to your dormmates today, making sure they're accommodating."

I stifled a laugh.

Right—*accommodating*. That's what they were like yesterday when one of them decided walking around naked was a normal way to greet someone.

"Marnie has also told me she will meet you by the entrance and is incredibly excited to show you around." Eden walked toward me and sat at the edge of the bed. Handing me the mug, she smiled as I thanked her despite the nausea and nerves I felt. "How was the outing last night?"

I blew the steam off my tea, contemplating whether I should tell her about Hunter or not. She spoke so highly of him in Nadael's office yesterday that she'd think I'm lying to cause a scene. *Again.* "It was good," I lied. "Thank you for letting me stay in your room, by the way. You didn't have to do that."

She waved a hand and stood. "After the mix-up yesterday, I owed it to you." She sighed as she glanced at her watch. "I should let you get ready. It's a bit of a walk from the Celestial quarters to the main building." As she went to turn and leave, she stopped. "Oh, and um, I'm sure Joe would have told you this, but it's been requested that you not go out into town when weekends come. He thinks it will be safer if you stay here at all times."

I nodded, gripping the handle of the mug a little too tight. This *was* a prison but for me only.

Once Eden left, I stripped off the beige bed linen and hurried to get ready, not even bothering to tame my curls as I placed the tailored, deep midnight blue blazer over my white shirt. I stared at the gold and silver embroidery along the lapels and cuffs before running my hands over Celestia's crest, a winged emblem embroidered in silver thread.

I sighed, shook my head, and turned to the pleated blue skirt laid out on the bed. An hour later, I was heading out of the Celestial quarters and sending Joe messages about my first night here.

Joe: I hope you've been eating - Joe Martin

I hadn't.

You:u know u don't need to add ur name at the end of

every text, right? I know it's you

Joe: It is common courtesy – Joe Martin

You: ur not in the 1920s anymore, Joe. This isn't a formal letter for ur strict old granny, lol

Joe: You still haven't told me if you have been eating or not – Joe Martin

I rolled my eyes at his message and replied with a quick, *I have*, before slipping my phone into my blazer pocket. It was still early September, so the chill in the air was mild. The leaves on the trees lining the narrow pathway had just started to fall, and after about twenty minutes of walking, I emerged onto the main road where the grand entrance to Celestia stood. Hundreds of Ascendants were streaming through the towering doors, most of them in the same attire as me, while others wore a form-fitting jacket in deep blue—like ones made for combat. Silver angelic runes adorned the sides, and a stitched Roman numeral *1* stood out against their upper arm.

Another wave of nausea hit me, no doubt thanks to the sip I took from Eden's mug earlier. As I walked, I noticed some Ascendants turning their heads to stare, their eyes lingering a little too long. They likely already knew who I was—my nerves were practically palpable, and I felt they could sense it from a mile away. Last night, most of them barely acknowledged my presence, but as Marnie said, *once Monday rolls around, it's back to competing against each other.*

I doubted they saw me as any real competition, but I could feel their judgment like a weight pressing down against my chest. My stomach churned with the uncomfortable awareness, and I dropped my head, hurrying past as many of them as possible. I was avoiding eye contact as if my life depended on it. Only when I reached the stairs did I dare to lift my chin, and there, barreling through the crowd, was Marnie.

"Move out of the way, Tom—" she huffed, pushing past a tall boy who barely moved in response. She reached me and gave me a once-over, her eyes sparkling with awe. "You look so—"

"Nope," I interrupted, shaking my head before she could finish that sentence.

Marnie grinned. "Don't you like it then?" she said, linking her arm with mine.

"I feel stupid." For more than one reason. I was tugged across the foyer, and my eyes shot to the ceilings that soared high above, supported by grand marble columns. "I thought after I turned eighteen, I wouldn't need to wear school uniforms anymore."

"Everything in the Celestial world follows orders," she chuckled. "Meaning uniforms are part of a structure that we should *all* follow."

Children younger than me darted past Marnie and me, their innocent laughs echoing across the expansive hall. My gaze drifted upwards, almost making me gasp. Golden light cascaded through towering stained-glass windows, each pane depicting Celestial scenes—angels in battles, others healing. On the left side, another window told the story of creation. It wasn't the story most of humanity believed. The first angels or lifeforms were not crafted by an all-powerful god. The origins of angels, demons, and even life stemmed from the Seraphim—the first Celestials. They were beings born from the balance of light and darkness.

Joe used to tell me they were creators, not rulers. But Joe was the only person to view them as that.

When Marnie pulled me along the halls, I saw four banners hanging from the walls far ahead. Each banner detailed the

44

sectors and what they stood for.

"And yet demons never follow orders," I murmured, my voice seeming to be elsewhere while I stared at the first banner for the Warriors. *Strength, Combat, Protection...*

I remained fixated on it until Marnie abruptly pulled me away. My gaze fell to the number IV and the Healer's emblem of a golden chalice above it stitched on her left breast pocket.

"Do you want to get us into trouble?" she whispered harshly.

"What? I—I didn't think there was anything wrong with mentioning them."

"It's not, but in a place where everyone wants to become an angel, it's hardly a topic they wish to hear. I'm surprised Joe has never spoken to you about this."

He had... in his own cryptic way. He would tell me how the Angelic Council was private, and until now, demons haven't been much of a threat other than to corrupt people into becoming one of them. It's the reason why Ascendants exist. They're chosen so that when they do become an angel, they can protect others and help grow the angelic hierarchy.

"Anyway," Marnie sighed. "I should probably take you to Nadael's office. She said she wanted to see you first thing in the morning."

I swallowed my nerves, not necessarily liking the idea that Nadael wanted to see me. The sensation in my stomach was the same whenever I would wait to be seen by the headmistress in school. What was worse this time around was that Nadael was an immortal angel. Not a regular human trying to do their 9-to-5 job.

Marnie led me up the spiraling staircases adjacent to the ones on the right. We both kept quiet, our minds still on the subject of demons, before she dropped me off by Nadael's office. Twice in a row, I was here, and it didn't make me feel

45

any better.

"Come in," Nadael's voice called out when Marnie knocked. We stepped inside, and Nadael glanced up from her desk, offering a polite smile. "Thank you, Marnie, for bringing her. You can report to the Healers Sector now—a Warrior's already in bay one."

Marnie gave a sharp nod, then flashed me a wide-eyed look, mouthing good luck before slipping out the door. The click of it closing behind her left the room in an awkward silence.

I shifted on my feet, but Nadael gestured toward the chair in front of her desk. I obliged, keeping my gaze low and my backpack squeezed tightly between my legs.

"How was your first night at Celestia?" she asked, her tone neutral but probing. "I wanted to apologize again for the... dorm situation."

"It was fine," I said quickly, though the lie sat sourly on my tongue. *It wasn't fine. I felt like an outsider here. I knew it. Everyone knew it.* "It's definitely different from what I'm used to."

Nadael didn't laugh or offer a light-hearted comment, which only deepened the tension between us. She folded her hands neatly on the desk and studied me briefly before continuing. "Grace... I wanted to discuss your classes. The Celestials here are all aware of your unique situation and we've decided it would be best if you shadowed Marnie for the time being."

Disappointment sunk into my stomach like an anchor. It wasn't that I didn't like Marnie—she was kind, after all—but the look of pity in Nadael's eyes made it clear she didn't see me capable of much more.

"She's a Healer, which involves treating injured Warriors and—"

"Can I not choose where to go?" I cut her off with a pensive

46

frown.

She blinked at me and almost chuckled at the idiocy of my words. "Grace, this place revolves around an Ascendant's specific ability. Everyone has a future to pick. A Warrior, once ascended, will become an Authority in the angelic hierarchy—"

"And a human falls nowhere, right?" I looked away and sighed deeply. My thoughts tangled with those of my childhood—the ones where I would move homes each time and where, even in a school full of humans, I still felt like I did not belong. "Why did you accept Joe's offer for me to come here?"

I was met with silence, so I faced her again.

Nadael's gaze dropped to her hands, fingers tightly intertwined on the desk as if she couldn't bring herself to look at me. "I've known Joe for over a century, and more importantly, I have watched you grow up. I felt it was my duty to give you a chance."

I wanted to shake my head and tell her I didn't believe a word she said, to challenge her and question her morals as a Celestial. But the words stuck in my throat, locked behind fear of what consequences it would give me or Joe.

"He thinks you'd be excellent in the Healers' Sector," she spoke softly. I bit the inside of my cheek, unsure if it was out of irritation or just a desperate need to feel something other than helplessness. "I know that you enjoy that side of—"

"I want to join the Warriors," I admitted, the words spilling out before I could second-guess myself.

Nadael's fingers tightened briefly, and she finally lifted her gaze to meet mine. There was a flicker of something in her eyes—worry, perhaps, or frustration—but it quickly disappeared behind the usual veil of professionalism. "Grace, the Warriors... it's not like the other sectors. It's brutal. And you—" She paused as if carefully considering her words. "You don't have the same advantages as the others here. The Ascendants are born with abilities for a reason. The physical demands of a Warrior are not a question of willpower. It's survival."

Her words struck a nerve, as I knew she was right in every sense of the world. "I know that," I replied. "But if I'm trying to protect myself from Riftkeeper's. Involving myself with the Healers won't help me with that."

Nadael sighed, but I decided I wasn't done just yet.

"I don't want to stay here hiding forever, and if the Riftkeeper's were so dangerous to me that I *had* to come here, then Joe should never have taken me in as if I were one of you." My heart pounded in my chest, resenting the fact that I had spoken those words aloud—*that* part of me detested growing up with too much knowledge. "I don't want to spend the rest of my life scared of everything out there."

Nadael studied me for a long moment, her expression unreadable. The silence between us stretched until it felt like the room itself was closing in, and I had no way of escaping.

She leaned back in her chair, inhaling slowly through her nose. Her eyes narrowed as if there was more to it all. She stared off to the side momentarily before shaking her head slightly. Without a word, she reached for the phone on her desk, punched in a few numbers and brought it to her ear.

"I need a fresh set of rank 1 clothes sent to room 104," she said briskly.

A flicker of relief passed through me, but I kept my face neutral as Nadael's gaze shifted toward me, her eyes assessing me.

"Small," she muttered, her eyes drifting over my uniform.

I frowned, glancing down at my outfit, wondering if she was making a jab or simply stating a fact.

She gave a curt nod into the phone before slamming it back into its handset. Without missing a beat, her gaze shifted to me. "You can start unpacking in your new dorm if you wish."

The thought of living with Hunter made a jolt of nerves race through me. "No training?" I asked, trying to steady my voice. I had to remember that I was the one who chose to stay in that dorm.

"Tomorrow," she clipped as she handed me a piece of paper. "Today, you can sit in on a Guardian lesson. Here's your timetable and the Celestial you'll report to. Other than that, all Ascendants are usually required to attend certain lessons, which you will see on that sheet. Now, go. Don't make me regret this more than I already do."

I glanced at the timetable, and then the name scribbled at the bottom—Azrael. My stomach tightened as I mumbled a quiet *thank you* and stood up.

Just as I reached the door, her voice made me halt. "Oh, and Grace?"

I paused, glancing over my shoulder as she wrote something on her notepad.

"I trust you're already aware," she began, her tone clipped, though her gaze flickered up to meet mine as if searching for any sign of defiance. "But it bears repeating: we have a strict policy regarding... romantic entanglements."

I remained silent.

"The life of an Ascendant demands' sacrifices, the same for any Celestial. And while these rules may not concern humans outside of these walls; we prefer to avoid *complications*. If you wish to form friendships, then by all means. But it can never go beyond that." Her eyes narrowed. "Do not jeopardize yourself or the path of an Ascendant to Celestialhood for the sake of fleeting emotions. Remember the Angelic Code states: To love is to fall and to fall is to be forgotten."

Her warning hung in the air, and I felt the weight of her words press down against my chest, forcing me to take a deep breath.

She didn't want me distracting anyone.

As if *I* were the problem here.

Then why do I have to stay here if you're so worried? Is what I wanted to say. Instead, I forced a smile and nodded, not giving her a verbal response as I walked out of her office with the words playing on a loop inside my head.

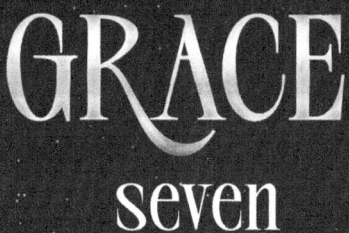

GRACE
seven

The Guardians Hall exuded an otherworldly presence. Constellations shimmered faintly across the vaulted ceiling, mimicking the night sky. Ancient runes etched along the walls pulsed gently with a silvery glow, like veins carrying life through the building. A faint hum filled the air—not sound exactly, but a vibration that prickled along my skin.

According to my timetable, Sariel was the head Guardian. She stood at the center of the class as her silver-white robe shimmered as if woven from starlight itself. "Name?"

I swallowed, feeling every eye in the room on me. "Grace… Martin?"

Her gaze lingered on me for a moment, and I wondered if she could sense I didn't belong here before she nodded, motioning for me to take a seat among the other trainees. As I moved to the back, I couldn't help but glance at the massive moving mural spanning one wall—a depiction of who I assumed were Guardians standing shoulder-to-shoulder with other Celestials, their glowing shields raised against a sea of darkness. Beneath the mural, words were carved into the stone in the angelic language of Enochian.

The class was already full of people as I made my way to the last bench, where nobody was, and even then, I felt the many stares of people as I sat down. On the left of me was another girl—a pale blonde with a mullet—sitting on another lonely bench. She didn't hide the fact she was staring at me. No one did. But something about her seemed extra frightening. She nibbled on her darkly painted lips and narrowed her eyes, forcing me to look away.

It was just in time for me to see Sariel writing on the chalkboard in bold letters:

THE LINK BETWEEN POWER AND CORRUPTION

"As I have mentioned prior to our lessons," she began, her voice cold and precise, not one I imagined her to have. "None of you are safe."

A redheaded guy leaned forward, smirking, his arms draped over his knees. "Don't worry, Sariel, the school wards won't let anything get to us."

Sariel's dark eyes narrowed on him. "And what about when you are outside of these wards, where *nothing* can protect you or your family?"

The redheaded guy's smirk faded slightly, and the girl beside him nudged him as if he should have just kept his mouth shut.

"Ascendants are just as susceptible to being corrupted as humans are," Sariel went on, the sound of her shoes clicking beneath the floorboards as she slowly made her way around the class. "Power doesn't matter in that instance. You're all still in the process of becoming full-fledged angels—"

"Except for the human," someone snickered, and others chuckled under their breaths, looking in my direction.

Yep, not even in a school where one is supposed to become

an angel will I be safe from snide comments.

I cowered in my seated position, unable to help it. I could stand up for myself in front of Hunter, but somehow, right now, I felt infinitely small.

"You're all desperate to prove your worth." Sariel's gaze didn't waver; neither did she seem to tell the person who made the comment off. "You're ambitious," she added, then stood in front of someone. "But also, *babies*."

The whole class erupted with 'Oooh's' and laughter, but that didn't bother Sariel as she made it back to the board.

"You can see why demons and, most of all, Riftkeeper's love to take advantage of that."

The blonde girl on the lonely bench suddenly said, "That's why Guardians should be at the top of the rankings, instead of Warriors," she said, her tone inviting a challenge. "I mean, we're supposed to see things coming from a mile away. I don't get why we have these lessons when we could be out there preventing things already."

I frowned at that, knowing that although many had the same ability as a Guardian, they would always tell Joe how, most of the time, it was a curse rather than a gift.

I didn't realize I had started talking until everyone had turned to look at me. "When a Guardian has the ability to see all, that doesn't mean it's literal. You can't figure out what someone will have for dinner a week from now or if a corrupted soul is really just one of us already." When the girl opened her mouth to argue, I spoke up before she could. "Your gift is unpredictable, as is the world and its people."

My eyes widened as soon as the class went silent, and the blonde girl staring at me looked as though she was ready to knock out my teeth. But it was Sariel who turned to me and smiled in surprise.

"You're right," she said before glancing at the blonde. "And sometimes knowing the right things—rather than simply seeing what is to come—is far more powerful than you think."

I shifted in my seat, uncomfortable with the realization that my rambling led me to be right, and although that was the case, I didn't think the class agreed with my outburst. Glancing down at my lap, I bobbed my knees up and down, drowning out the voices of everyone around me. Sariel continued on with her class, sending some of them up to the front to try and zone in on their gift. I was glad once the lesson was over, and I waited until all Ascendants left the room before I got up and made my way down the rows of benches.

"Grace," Sariel said, and I almost cursed at myself. I slowly turned and tripped when I saw how close she was standing in front of me. She smiled despite my clumsiness. "I understand you may not be here of your own will, but you are always welcome to come by my classes as many times as you want. I believe it would be beneficial for you."

"I'm not sure anyone would want that. I'm already going to give certain people a heart attack when I join the Warriors tomorrow."

Her smile turned sympathetic, and for a moment, I felt embarrassed. "Well, either way, my door is always open," she said.

I didn't answer her because I didn't know what to say in the first place. I couldn't deny and be rude, but I also didn't feel confident enough yet to agree and say I would consider it as much as I wanted to.

Nodding, I left the room, my chest heavy as I made it down the stairs and never looked back.

The long, dark corridors stretched out before me, eerily

silent and empty of Ascendants. I glanced down at the map Eden had given me, but the Enochian lines and symbols were too hard to decipher.

As I turned the corner, my steps slowed, and I found myself standing before one of the countless paintings lining the walls of Celestia. This one, though, caught my attention. Glancing left, then right, I made sure I was alone before focusing on the moving painting again.

It was of a statue bathed in light, standing tall in the center of a gleaming marble room. Wings enclosed the statue, hiding the angel behind it, and for a moment, I wondered if that was where the Council held meetings. A veil between the human world and the Celestial world—not quite heaven, but not relatively humane.

A door on the right swung open, and I stumbled away from the painting. When people started emerging from a class, I turned the other way and sprinted before they could see me.

GRACE
eight

I stood outside room 104, clutching the packet of fresh clothes and combat boots in one hand that was left outside the doorstep and the key in the other. My fingers twitched nervously, but I hadn't moved for ten minutes. The hallway was empty, and the light streaming through the windows hinted that it wasn't even evening yet. No one would be in the room, right? Why would they be?

Fuck it.

I shoved the key into the lock and swung the door open with more force than necessary. The room was completely empty, and a wave of relief washed over me, loosening the tension in my chest. But I knew it wouldn't last long—soon enough, the boys would return, and peace would be a distant memory.

I stepped into the dorm, where there was a hallway past the kitchenette and a door to my right. You could tell men occupied this place—clothes and shoes scattered the floorboards, and I could smell the faint earthy cologne that no doubt belonged to one of them.

I walked down the hallway, jiggling doorknobs to see which was my room. Instead, I almost gagged when I entered a room with hundreds of leftover foods on top of a desk. Another room had posters of Star Wars and action figures, while the last room was entirely locked.

I huffed, knowing the other door led to the bathroom. "I am *not* sharing a room with one of them," I muttered to myself and stalked back into the main living room toward the last remaining door.

When it opened, I had never felt such joy to see an almost barren room. A single bed, a simple wooden desk and a wardrobe where all my clothes had already been stashed–thanks to Eden–stood waiting for me. I sighed, dropping the new uniform packet onto my bed.

I suppose this was home now. I wasn't sure if the gnawing feeling in my stomach was dread or anticipation. Maybe both. I hadn't felt this before, not even when Joe would move us to a new town.

Just as I was about to lie down, my phone buzzed inside my pocket, and I noticed it was Joe calling.

I grimaced before answering. "You know, this is the most you've used a phone that wasn't decades old. I'm proud."

He chuckled. "Have you eaten?"

I sighed, making my way towards the window and pulling the curtain aside. The view wasn't much—just the stretch of forestry sprawling under the dull light of the afternoon. "Yes, Joe, I have. Do you also want me to tell you if I showered, brushed my teeth and tidied Eden's room before I left?" I couldn't help the snarky tone behind my words. I couldn't even tell him that I had joined the Warriors yet. I knew sooner or later he would find out because of Nadael, but I just wasn't ready for him to scold me. To tell me I was too much of a dreamer or that I was reaching for something that was beyond me because that's all I ever did.

"Did you?"

I shook my head at the teasing tone in his voice. Clearly, he hadn't picked up on my frustration yet. "You're annoying."

He chuckled again, unfazed. "What about classes? Did Nadael stick you with the Healers? Thought you might love it there."

I nearly choked as I swallowed. I was thankful he couldn't see the color drain from my face as I faced the mirror beside the desk. "Oh, yeah... it's perfect," I said, forcing a smile into my voice.

There was a brief pause on the other end of the line, and I winced. I should've felt guilty, maybe even ashamed, for lying to him. But they never surfaced, no matter how hard I tried to summon those feelings.

Licking my lips, I exhaled slowly, "Joe?"

Before he could respond, I heard the distinct sound of the door locks turning.

"I've got to go," I blurted out. "I'll talk to you later, okay?"

"Wait, Grace—"

I didn't give him the chance to finish. I tossed my phone on the bed and dashed toward the bedroom door, positioning myself just out of sight. From the crack between the door and the frame, I saw Brandon, Silas, and Hunter walking into the dorm. All three wearing the Warriors' uniform.

"I swear Azrael has an agenda set out to just kill me with his drills," Silas said, throwing his jacket onto the sofa and revealing silver arm guards engraved with runes against a tight-fitted black shirt.

Brandon walked past him, chuckling. "You don't pay

61

attention; that's why."

"Says the one who was flirting with that girl from the Healers Sector. Let's hope none of the Celestials caught on."

"Fuck off. I was just trying to be nice."

Silas burst into laughter, collapsing onto the sofa with his legs sprawled out and arms lazily tucked behind his head. He said something else, but the words barely registered as my attention drifted toward Hunter by the kitchenette.

I took in the sight of him, his hair a tousled mess, the dried mud clinging to his neck, and how his uniform effortlessly fitted his muscular frame. The sight of him, rugged and unbothered, made it impossible to focus on anything else.

Damn him.

"You're real quiet over there, Cain." Brandon's voice was cautious but clear as he sat beside Silas. "Did Azrael get to you too?"

My eyes went back to Hunter as he grunted in response, a noncommittal sound that could have meant anything. He was awfully hard to read, not that I was any good at reading people.

"Did you hear about the new girl speaking out in Sariel's class?" Brandon said, and my stomach immediately twisted into knots.

Silas frowned. "Grace?"

"Yeah, apparently, she spoke up after Veronica made a comment or something."

Silas sat up a little straighter at that, his brown eyes narrowing. "Really?" A smirk crept onto his face. "Bet Veronica's pissed."

Hunter's voice cut through the conversation, flat and unimpressed. "Since when do you two girls' gossip?"

Silas grinned up at him. "Well—"

"Go shower. You stink," Hunter muttered, brushing past

them without giving either Brandon or Silas a chance to respond.

"It's called musk," Silas replied, puffing out his chest in mock offense.

Hunter leaned in and took a sniff, his expression unchanging. "Pretty sure it's called shit. Now go take shower."

I fought hard not to smile at the exchange as I watched Brandon give Silas a playful tap on the back. Their footsteps faded into the hallway, and I let out a slow breath, closing my eyes as I leaned my head forward in relief.

"You know, if you're going to eavesdrop, you should probably learn to hide better."

My eyes snapped open, and through the small gap in the doorway, my gaze locked with Hunter's across the room. He stood by the sofa, hands pressed against the edge as he leaned forward with his head tilted slightly.

"I hear a glass to the door works just as well."

Heat flashed through my cheeks, and I hoped that it wouldn't be visible in all that was mighty as I stepped out from behind the door. "I'll keep that in mind."

His lips twitched into a faint smirk as he stood upright. "So, that you're willing to do."

I raised an eyebrow, trying to ignore how his presence seemed to dominate the room. I was a mouse stuck in his trap. "Usually, I like to make my own decisions."

He hummed softly, pushing away from the sofa and strolling toward me. His eyes locked onto mine even as the distant sound of the shower filled the air, followed by the muffled shouts of Brandon and Silas arguing somewhere down the hall.

I swallowed hard as Hunter stopped just a few feet away. The height difference wasn't so noticeable from a distance, but it was impossible to ignore up close as he towered over me.

He reached for one of my curls without warning, and I had to fight the urge to flinch. His fingers gently tucked it behind my ear, and I could feel the goosebumps prickling across my skin. My body betrayed me with a slight shudder, and his lips tugged into a knowing smirk before he turned to walk away.

Frustrated, I blurted out, "I know a lot more about this world than you think."

He paused mid-step, glancing back over his shoulder. "And? Do I look like a man who cares? Because if so, that's wildly misleading."

Glaring, I ignored that and took a few steps deeper into the room, trying to hide the fact my legs were shaking. "Look, I may not be an Ascendant, but I grew up around this life. If knowing that hell exists doesn't scare me, then why should you?"

Hunter's gaze roamed over me, sending a spike through my pulse. "I'm not trying to scare you," he said, his voice low and deliberate. "Though your Bambi-eyed look makes it seem like you are." He tilted his chin slightly and a dimple carved into his cheek as his smirk deepened. "Goodnight, *Grace*." And with that, he turned and disappeared into the hallway, vanishing just as effortlessly as he had the night we were in the forest.

GRACE
nine

I was late.
    Unbelievably late.
    I stumbled out of my room, desperately trying to tie the laces of my combat boots while awkwardly hopping around the empty dorm. The boys were long gone, and of course, in their infinite kindness, they'd forgotten to wake me up. Silas and Brandon already knew I was staying here. After last night's tiff with Hunter, they ended up coming out of the shower to find me in the center of the room, still trying to understand what had happened between Hunter and me.

Two hours later, I was listening to Silas and Brandon list their rules on door locks and leaving girl *stuff* in the bathroom.

"Fucking great," I muttered to myself when I opened the fridge and found the carton of orange juice empty. Slamming the fridge door closed, I settled on no breakfast for the second day in a row and left the dorm with my hair in a mess, the map of the academy upside down and my tactical trousers loose on my hips.

The academy grounds were already full of Ascendants walking through pathways and the forest coating each inch of this place. The map crinkled in my hand as I sped up and rounded the corner to where Ascendants clad in blue combat jackets stood in the middle of the muddy training grounds, either sparring or working out.

I dragged back a sharp inhale and made my way towards everyone. There was no sign of Celestial or the so-called Azrael, as it was written on my timetable, but there was a dozen weapons scattered on the ground. They looked like your standard swords, bows, and arrows, but I knew they were more than that. The silver engraving of wings and ethereal shapes on some of the blades made me believe that they were angelic blades, the ones I would always overhear Joe speak about.

"You look like you're about to pass out, and we haven't even started training yet."

I spun around, startled to find a blonde guy in a Warrior's uniform, chuckling as his eyes fell on the crumpled map, I was clutching onto like a lifeline. He was a few good feet taller, with classic good looks—sharp features, cropped hair and striking blue eyes that gave him an air of familiarity, though I couldn't quite place who exactly.

"I—" *Was too flustered to form a proper sentence.*

"Lucas James," he introduced himself, extending a hand.

I hesitated, then reluctantly took it. "Grace... Martin."

His eyes lit up with recognition as he released my hand. "Ah, so you're the one who left my sister rattled after her class."

Sister—?

It clicked. I suddenly realized why he looked so familiar,

and my eyes widened. "Oh my God—I'm—"

"Relax," he laughed, waving it off. "My sister finds an excuse to hate on everyone."

That didn't make me feel better.

"She's just thrown off by someone who isn't an Ascendant being here," he added with a shrug.

I nodded, feeling the familiar weight of that fact settle on me. It wasn't just his sister who felt that way—nearly everyone had made it clear since I first arrived.

"But don't let it get to you," he added quickly, noticing the shift in my expression. "She'll eventually get over it. They all will."

"And you?" I asked. "Are you thrown off by it?"

He shook his head. "There are worse things to worry about than a human at Celestia."

I frowned, mulling over his words. He wasn't wrong, but I wasn't so sure everyone else shared his perspective.

Before I could ask another question, someone shouted, "Cain!"

My shoulders tensed, and my gaze snapped towards everyone else, searching for him in the crowd. There he was with his familiar figure in sight as he slapped Brandon on the back of his head, and Silas laughed hysterically alongside them. The air shifted as I swallowed hard, and almost as if he could feel my stare on him, he turned his head, his eyes locking on mine. He froze, and I saw a flicker of anger ignite within him when he noticed I was dressed in the same uniform as him. Without a word, he cut off whatever Brandon was saying and strode toward me.

I thought about running, but what good would that do? It would just paint me as a coward.

Before Lucas could even help me, Hunter was already

grabbing my arm as he pulled me to the side and away from everyone else, where no one could hear us.

"What the hell are you doing here?" he growled.

I tried yanking free from his hold, but there was no give. "I'm here—" I pulled again, glaring up at him. "To—" Another yank, and at last, I was free. "*Train.*"

His gaze turned cold. "Right, and I'm here to sit back and relax beneath the lovely English weather."

I gazed at the cloudy sky and its grey color, darkening the morning.

Hunter swore under his breath before grabbing my wrist and dragging me along with him. "Come on."

"What? No!" I pulled against him, seeing that he was trying to take me back to where the dorm was. "I'm not leaving this class. I was put in here, and I plan on staying." I'm not, of course, telling him that I *made* Nadael place me here.

He stopped, and I almost stumbled into him as he turned to face me. His jaw tensed as his eyes scanned the training grounds. "You know you're really doing a great job at giving me headaches."

I smiled up at him. "Thank you! Joe tells me it's a gift, and I like to think it's better than what an Ascendant has to offer in terms of powers—"

"What will it take for you to get out of this place?"

It went silent between us, and I could feel the stares of people watching, but it didn't seem to matter.

My lips pursed as I stared at his face and the anger brimming on the surface of his grey eyes. It almost looked like smoke. "You can't make me leave."

He grew more frustrated; his jaw about to pop. "Trust me, I can make you do anything. Just give me a couple of days, and you'll see."

My pulse thundered in my ears, and I thought about slapping him this time around, but before I could act on the impulse, a sharp voice cut through the tension, stopping both of us cold.

"I didn't expect one of my best trainees to be such a talker." Hunter stepped away from me as we both snapped our heads to the side. Standing there was who I assumed was Azrael. Unlike the rest of the Celestials, he didn't wear a robe or any combat gear. Instead, he wore a perfectly tailored charcoal grey suit as if he had stepped out of a high-powered meeting rather than an academy for wannabe angels. The suit jacket hugged his broad shoulders while his high cheekbones and dark, slicked-back hair added to the intimidating aura that practically emanated from him.

"I was just informing the new girl that she is in the wrong class," Hunter said while Azrael watched me. There was something unsettling in his green gaze, as though he was constantly assessing... constantly one step ahead.

"No," he said slowly, his eyes narrowing and his voice a deepening sound of curiosity. "According to Nadael... she's in the right class." His gaze slid towards Hunter, and it lingered on him for a few seconds before he turned and walked through the mud as if he didn't care whether it messed up his slacks or not.

It felt like I hadn't breathed at all during that interaction, and as I looked up at Hunter, I could tell he was even more pissed than before.

71

HUNTER

ten

S he was a test. She had to be.

One I was failing at fast.

I watched as Lucas strode over, throwing me a glare as he took Grace by the arm and led her away. She glanced over her shoulder, looking as timid and unsure as she was the first time I saw her. But I knew better. Beneath that hesitant exterior was a fire—a spark that ignited every time she argued with me.

I doubted anyone had seen that side of her yet.

"First, she takes over our dorm, and now the Warriors?" Silas comes to stand at my side along with Brandon. Everyone is already starting to gather around Azrael, yet I keep my arms crossed, and my eyes locked on every movement Grace makes as she follows Lucas. "Man, the Celestials are growing weak."

I didn't respond. Neither did Brandon, as Azrael stood at the center, watching us all as if wishing to pick each of us apart or deciding who was worth his time and who wasn't.

The murmurs of other Ascendants stopped, and all eyes

were soon on him.

Azrael clasped his hands behind his back, his voice calm and steady, yet it carried across the field like a thunderclap, making Grace jump.

I smirked at that.

"As many of you know, the Ascension competition is approaching."

Silas and I quickly exchanged glances, preparing ourselves for another competition. The Ascension was held every three years, with the winner receiving goods and prizes. Silas won it last; I won it before that.

"The Ascension competition is a tradition," Azrael continued, "A test of skill, endurance and morality. Nadael calls it a way to measure your dedication. I call it something far simpler: a reckoning. The competition separates the capable from the weak."

I glanced at the other Ascendants. Some stood straighter, eyes gleaming with determination. Others shifted nervously, their hands fidgeting at their sides.

Azrael's gaze swept over us, pausing briefly on me. "This competition is rooted in Celestia's history. It was first established to honor the angels who fought to restore balance to the realms. Those who prove themselves will earn not just glory but the Council's favor. And this time..." He let the words linger for a moment, his sharp green eyes narrowing. "The stakes are higher. One among you may be granted early ascension."

A collective gasp ran through the crowd, but it was I who felt the strange twist in my chest. Unwillingly, my eyes went to Grace. She was the smallest in the crowd, and her uniform barely fitted her.

"As per usual, only five from each sector will be chosen to

participate. Meaning, from here on out, each and every one of you will not only be training for a spot in the competition, but you will be competing for the one thing you all desire." His gaze was like ice, cutting through the bravado of most Ascendants standing here. "You have less than four months to win your spot." He stood still and glanced at everyone who was closest to him. Some Ascendants were already casting side glances at each other, calculating their odds. "Your training starts now."

With that, he walked off the pit, and everyone immediately began rushing to get their weapons and training in gear.

I glanced at Silas, who was shaking his head, his usual grin replaced with something more serious. "This is just going to cause more rifts between Ascendants, you know that, right?"

"Maybe I'll be the one who wins it this time," Brandon snickered, and I just nodded, my mind elsewhere. I didn't need them all telling me how this would go down. The Ascendants at the academy were already competitive, but things were about to get worse now that the stakes were higher.

"Cain! Williams!" Azrael barked, his voice slicing through the other Ascendants already sparring. "Pair off in the middle and use your powers. No holding back."

I shot a look over at Matias, who rolled his shoulders and grinned. My fists clenched, knowing that Azrael chose him on purpose. Matias was an arrogant prick who got on my nerves a hundred times a day. He had decent combat ability, but he lacked the brains for control.

Shrugging off my jacket, I passed it off to Silas and made my way past Grace. She was still next to Lucas, her eyes wide as she stared at everything new around her. After this, I hoped she would realize the Warriors Sector wasn't for her.

I stepped into the center of the training grounds, my gaze

narrowing on Matias as he mirrored my movements with that cocky grin still plastered on his face. Someone threw me a weapon, and I caught it with my right hand. My lips tugged when I saw it was the blade of an archangel—a dagger crafted from Celestial steel that blinded anyone with the right skill applied.

"Sure, you want to do this today, Cain?" Matias called out, his grin widening as the other Ascendants around us stilled. "I would hate for the new girl to see the top student get knocked flat on his ass."

My fists clenched tighter, and he laughed when I didn't respond.

Azrael's voice rang out from the side, clear and commanding. "Begin."

Matias didn't hesitate. He charged forward with twin daggers, his muscles tensing as he activated his enhanced strength. The ground beneath him cracked as he closed the distance between us in a blur. His first strike came in fast, but I was faster as I sidestepped the blow. Without wasting time, I felt the rippling power of enhanced strength rushing to my fingertips as I swung my leg up and landed a solid kick to his ribs. He grunted, staggering back. He clenched his fists, and I saw the familiar glow of power—a shimmering aura that radiated from his skin, amplifying his strength even further. It was predictable. Matias fought with brute force, relying too much on raw power. That was always his mistake.

He lunged again, summoning more force as he aimed the twin blades toward my torso. I knew better than to take it head-on. Instead, I used the momentum of his charge to my advantage and grabbed hold of his arm. I twisted, throwing him off balance and sending him crashing to the ground. The impact shook the muddied pit, but Matias was back

76

on his feet in seconds; a flash of irritation crossed his eyes. "Not bad." He wiped the mud off his mouth and spat out blood onto the ground. "But you're still lacking, Cain." His blades cleaved through the air with terrifying speed, and I dodged, feeling the force of the weapons whistle past my ear before I countered each strike with one of my own. The archangel's blade connected with his, and the clashes sent sparks flying.

We traded blows, each strike heavier than the last. Matias's strength made him a powerhouse, but with every swing, he grew sloppier. I stayed calm, my blade a blur of light as I parried and dodged.

Behind me, I could feel Azrael's eyes on us. He wanted to see us push ourselves to the brink, and I was fine with delivering that to him.

Matias's frustration cracked through his composure. He lunged, and I sidestepped easily, waiting for the exact moment he'd overcommit. As I raised my hand, the archangel blade ignited in a bright light, causing Matias to wince and slip onto the ground. He was blinking furiously, trying to get his sight to catch up, but I didn't wait as I charged toward him, aiming the blade at his exposed side.

But just as my blade was about to connect, Matias's powers absorbed the impact, the Warrior powers rippling out in a protective barrier. He grinned, thinking he had me, until I twisted the blade mid-strike, redirecting the energy into a sharp upward arc. The energy pulsed outward as Matias fell back, his eyes wide with shock as the shield dissipated. He hadn't expected me to use his own energy against him.

"Still think you've got some fight left in you?" I muttered, stepping forward and pressing the blade against his neck. The light from the archangel blade flared as Matias's chest heaved and his hands raised in reluctant surrender.

"Enough," Azrael's voice sliced through the air, and with it, a shadow of his wings flared out, engulfing the space. They weren't solid, nor were they ever fully tangible. Instead, Azrael's wings—among other Celestials—flickered in and out of existence at will.

Azrael's gaze shifted. "Good control, Cain." His sharp eyes moved to Matias. "Williams, work on your restraint. Power is nothing without control."

Matias's jaw clenched as the feeling of satisfaction surged through me.

"Everyone else," Azrael called out. "Back to training."

As I turned to leave, my eyes caught Grace's. She was still watching, but I could see a flicker of doubt in her eyes. Maybe now she'd understand.

I walked towards her, my shoulder brushing against hers before I leaned and whispered against her ear, "You heard him. Get back to training."

GRACE
eleven

On the second day of officially joining the Warriors, I stood there, hiding behind Lucas, as Azrael paced in front of us. His suit was once again immaculate, with his hands clasped behind his back as his gaze swept over the rows of Warriors standing before him.

"You should all know by now that a Warrior doesn't just train to ascend," he said and paused in front of a girl. "A Warrior trains to become an Authority—a Celestial soldier in the *Second Order* of the angelic hierarchy."

I shifted uncomfortably on my feet. There were four orders in the angelic hierarchy I knew of. Authorities happened to be part of a group up there with Seraphim's.

"Their purpose is to prevent the destruction of life, to protect the Celestial realm," he continued, pacing once again. "And all of you that were born with the gifts of a Warrior are given this opportunity to train for more than just power—you are here once again to become Authorities."

As he walked past us, his gaze briefly fell on me, failing to use Lucas as my personal hiding spot. My throat tightened as he gave me a cold, assessing look, and the Warriors around me snickered quietly.

Luckily, Azrael moved on and addressed the group. "Now, the upcoming competition is not just about the brute strength that you Warriors possess. I will be analyzing each and every one of you. And those who do well will see their names posted in the common room of their sector every two weeks."

The anticipation among the Warriors was palpable. They were all buzzing in hopes of being selected now that the role of ascending was on the line. Even Lucas straightened up and puffed out his chest as if he'd been preparing himself for this very moment.

"Cain." Azrael's voice rang out across the muddy pit, cutting through the hum of sparring Ascendants. "Dunn, step forward."

Silas grinned, his cocky swagger on full display as he stepped forward. Hunter followed reluctantly as his sharp grey eyes scanned the crowd briefly, pausing just long enough to land on me.

I froze under his gaze, unsure whether the flicker of emotion I saw was irritation, a warning, or something else entirely. Whatever it was, it was gone before I could name it.

"Demonstrate to the rest the use of shielding," Azrael ordered. "Show me how you can absorb the force of an attack and convert it into energy for a counterstrike."

Hunter and Silas nodded, positioning themselves opposite eadhleahed into Lucas, whispering, "Is Azrael an Authority?"

"He used to be."

I frowned. "Used to be?"

"He left that position to teach Warriors on Earth instead."

That only left me with more questions than answers, considering how important it seemed to be if one became an Authority.

I sighed, focusing on what Silas and Hunter were doing instead. Silas was the first to attack, his power surging toward Hunter like a wave of heat. Hunter moved seamlessly, raising a shield of energy. The force of Silas's power seemed to absorb into the makeshift shield, glowing briefly before Hunter pushed it right back at Silas.

Silas barely blocked it in time as the energy from the shield sent him flying back. He groaned as he landed on the muddy ground and rolled onto his side.

I was suddenly annoyed, wishing that could have been Hunter on the ground instead. I wasn't sure why his lack of reaction to winning or demonstrating how good he was at the counterattack infuriated me. I wanted him to be smug so that I could have another reason to dislike him, but he just stood there like he wanted to leave already. Like it all meant nothing to him.

Azrael turned to everyone else and began instructing others to practice.

I glanced at Lucas and smiled. He didn't return that smile.

He scratched the back of his head, not meeting my gaze. "Um, I—" he stuttered, and my face fell. I understood what he was trying to get across without even needing him to explain it.

"It's okay," I said softly. "You can partner up with someone else. I think I'll just go and practice my hits."

"You sure?" He grimaced. "I'm sorry, Grace. If I wasn't terrible at shielding, I would go with you and practice other stuff, but—"

"I know." I offered him a weak smile. "Now go, find a

83

partner before you get stuck with Matias."

Lucas looked over his shoulder before giving me an apologetic glance. "As soon as I'm done, I'll come help you."

A lump tugged at my throat, making me unable to speak as I nodded and watched him run off to someone else. I sighed inwardly and made my way toward a practice dummy, far from all the Warriors in the pit.

I felt utterly humiliated as I snuck a glance over my shoulder. Azrael's instructions echoed in my mind, but all I could hear was the sound of barely concealed laughter from the others. I punched the dummy half-heartedly, the impact sending a dull vibration up my arm.

I had to remember that I asked for this. *I* wanted to join the Warriors, and it was all *my* doing.

"That's all wrong, you know."

I froze, my knuckles resting on the dummy as Hunter strolled over, his expression flat and intense as always.

"Wow." Sarcasm dripped from my voice. "Thanks for telling me. I hadn't noticed. Have anything else to say about what I'm doing wrong?"

He smirked, crossing his arms as he leaned against the wooden post next to the dummy. "Plenty. Like how you're placing your thumb wrong."

I huffed, took a step back and placed my hands against my hips. "Shouldn't you be practicing?"

"Brandon's with someone else, and Silas wanted a break."
Already?

"Besides." He tilted his head, strands of brown hair falling across his forehead. "Watching you punch the dummy like that is far more entertaining. I wonder how long it will take for you to break your hand before you land a decent hit."

I rolled my eyes and aimed a punch straight for his chest,

letting my annoyance fuel the swing so I could prove him wrong. But before my fist could connect, Hunter caught my punch easily. His hand wrapped around my knuckles, practically making my whole hand disappear beneath his.

His eyes locked on mine as he shifted my hand, fixing the position of my thumb. His grip was firm but not painful, and the heat of his hand sent an unwanted shiver down my spine. "This way, you won't shatter your bones."

I ground my teeth, trying to ignore the warmth of his touch and the way the rough feel of his skin made my pulse spike. "Why do you even care if I break my hand or not?"

He shrugged. "I don't. Just hate watching bad technique."

My eyes narrowed, and I pulled my hand away from his. He stepped back, and without saying another word, he turned and strolled away.

Staring after him, my frustration grew into something else— something confusing. An annoyed groan left my lips, and I punched the dummy again, this time with the proper form, which didn't seem to aid whatever nonsense I was feeling.

"Dickhead," I mumbled, unsure if I meant it about Hunter or myself.

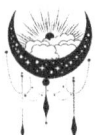

It was late.

My feet dragged along the empty corridors of Celestia, with the weight of the day pressing heavily on my shoulders. I had barely done anything other than punch a dummy, and yet my muscles screamed in protest.

I turned the corner, my thoughts muddled with all sorts of things, before I collided hard with someone. Looking up, I scowled when I saw it was Hunter.

He was the last person I needed to deal with right now. My plan had been to head back to the dorm and avoid him at all costs by locking myself in my room.

"Excuse me," I snapped, shoving past him with more force than necessary.

Hunter didn't budge and leaned against the wall, blocking my pathway. "Careful, Grace. You might actually hurt yourself with that attitude."

"Good," I said, trying to sidestep him. It didn't work.

"Still bitter about helping you earlier?"

"I am *not* bitter. For all I know, you helped me just to gain an upper hand for one of your schemes to get me out of here."

His lips twitched as though he found that idea amusing. "That does sound more like me."

I bit the inside of my cheek. "I don't need this right now. Could you please move out of the way so that I don't have to keep looking at your face?"

Yes, I was annoyed. By everything and especially by him. Though the Warriors laughing at me earlier when I was just there by the dummy might have been the final straw.

When he didn't make any movement to let me go, I blew out an exasperated breath. "I'm really trying my best here." At what? I didn't know.

He hummed. "At surviving?"

That... sounded like the right answer I was searching for.

"Because that's all you seem to be doing." He pushed himself off the wall, allowing me to run past him, but I didn't. I just stood frozen in place as his presence suddenly became suffocating. "You're not fighting. You're not trying to win. You're just waiting for that angel of yours to come save you."

The truth of those words hit me like a punch to the gut and

before I knew it, I was stepping forward, closing the space between us until I was staring up into those cold, unreadable eyes of his.

"I don't need anyone to save me," I hissed, my voice low and trembling with barely contained anger. "Least of all, Joe."

Hunter let out a dry laugh. "Right. Because you've done such a great job on your own so far."

I felt my chest squeeze, and for a moment, the hallway was silent as I refused to say anything else. The air between us cracked with a current of electricity, and I could hear my pulse pounding in my ears. Each beat was louder than the last, and our proximity became suffocating.

"Whatever you're trying to prove by joining the Warriors," he said quietly, though his voice was low and rough, heating my skin. "You're going about it the wrong way."

"I don't need your help," I whispered, though even I could hear the uncertainty in my voice.

Hunter's gaze flickered to my lips and then back to my eyes. "I'm not offering it."

"Then what is your problem with me!"

I was frustrated. I was practically shaking from it.

Hunter's eyes darkened, and something dangerous flickered behind the storm in them. He leaned down, his lips dangerously close to my ear as he whispered, "*You*. You're my problem."

The sharpness of his voice twisted something inside me. I turned my head to look at him, our noses almost touching.

"Why?" I whispered, my head spinning at how intoxicating having him this close felt. When he pulled back slightly, my chest heaved as I stared at him.

His stare was empty yet cold. He looked down at me and spoke monotonically as if repeating a phrase someone had told him to say: "Because humans are useless to us in this place."

87

We stood there for what felt like forever, neither of us moving nor daring to speak another word. I feared if I said something, I would crack, and it would give him every reason as to why I *was* useless.

Forcing myself to find some semblance of strength, I pushed my legs forward and stormed past him without looking back.

If being human was my biggest flaw, then what was his?

GRACE
twelve

"**I** really don't get why you joined the Warriors; even my mum was shocked when I told her," Marnie said, popping a chip into her mouth as I groaned, rubbing my temples. The dull ache from the hit I took earlier in Azrael's class still lingered. No thanks to everyone finally insisting that, human or not, I should be trained the same as the Ascendants. Azrael ended up listening to them, and ever since, I'd been tossed around like a ragdoll by a girl named Norah.

"At least I'll get to visit you often in the Healers Sector," I said, injecting a little optimism.

Marnie shot me an unimpressed look. Well, it was worth a try.

"How's Joe taking it?" Lucas asked as he sat down beside me in the canteen. He'd become my closest friend within the Warriors Sector and the only one who didn't treat me like some fragile outsider.

I made a face, my appetite fading as I pushed away the plate of shared chips. "He's not yelling anymore, if that's what you mean."

When Joe found out I'd joined the Warriors, he had marched into the middle of a training session and humiliated me in front of everyone, making it painfully clear that the Warriors Sector wasn't for me.

Marnie chuckled, shaking her head. "Oh, Grace, you've really got a rebellious streak under that cute, innocent exterior, don't you? First, you room with three guys—including Brandon, of all people—and then you decide you want to join the Warriors. What's next? You're hoping to get picked for the competition?"

I let out a dry laugh. "Pretty sure Joe would have a heart attack if I did that."

Marnie grinned, waving a ketchup-stained finger at me. "Celestials can't have heart attacks, Grace, so you're in the clear."

I smiled, and for a brief moment, my appetite started to return. That was until Hunter walked through the double doors of the canteen with Silas trailing behind him. My body tensed instinctively, and my muscles—what little I had—tightened as I shrank back into the bench, trying to disappear.

Living with them hadn't been the nightmare I initially imagined, but it hadn't exactly been great either. Hunter ignored me entirely after I bumped into him that evening in the hallways, and Silas only occasionally threw me a glance. Brandon, at least, seemed to feel bad for me, though it didn't make things any less awkward.

Lucas nudged my shoulder. "You're staring."

"Hard not to," Marnie chimed in, running her chip over her ketchup fingers. "But hey, look on the bright side—they haven't kicked you out yet. Or done anything to mess with you."

Somehow, the fact that Hunter hadn't followed through on his threats didn't make me feel much better. His silence was more unnerving than anything.

"Please don't jinx it," I muttered, watching Hunter and Silas grab drinks from the display fridges.

Lucas chuckled, standing up and brushing off his hands. "There's Ver," he said, nodding toward the doors. "She needs my help with something in her dorm. Probably scaring off another roommate—it's like the hundredth one she's done that to."

I believed him.

Veronica, standing near the entrance, was sucking on a lollipop, her mullet pulled into two low pigtails. The contrast between how innocent that looked and the sharp glare she shot in my direction was almost laughable.

Yeah, she definitely still didn't like me.

"I'll see you guys later," Lucas added, giving us a quick wave before heading over to join Veronica. Marnie and I muttered our goodbyes, watching as they left the canteen together.

I let out a sigh, my attention drifting back to Hunter and Silas. They seemed engrossed in a conversation, Silas more than Hunter.

Marnie looked over her shoulder and gave me a comforting smile. "You know you're always welcome to stay in my dorm. We even have a spare bed if you want it."

"It's fine. I've made too much of a fuss about it already. Hunter just has to learn how to deal with it."

Marnie raised an eyebrow, clearly unconvinced. The look on her face told me she thought I was way in over my head, and perhaps, deep down, I was.

Living with the boys was like walking on the edge of a cliff—you never knew when you'd slip into the abyss.

Just then, Hunter turned his head, scanning the room. Like a magnet, his eyes found mine. I froze, yet his expression didn't change.

I quickly tried to look away, focusing on the half-eaten plate of chips in front of me. But the weight of his stare lingered, and I knew then that I was screwed.

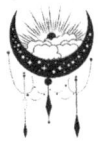

Marnie had jinxed it.

Hunter Cain was finally out to get me.

No—scratch that. Hunter Cain was on a mission to make my life a living hell. Every day that passed, I regretted every single second of my decision to bite my tongue and stay in his dorm. And he knew it. He thrived on it.

For example, the other morning, I was half-asleep when I walked into the bathroom, grabbed my toothbrush, and started brushing my teeth.

Then I froze.

The bristles tasted... off.

Slowly. Very slowly, I turned my head, and there he was. Hunter leaning against the doorframe, arms crossed, smirk locked and loaded.

"How's the taste, Bambi?"

No. *No.*

I spat into the sink, gagging before pointing an accusing

finger at him. "What did you do?"

He shrugged, all innocent-like. The audacity. "Nothing. Just figured you should know Silas used that last night... to clean his shoes."

My mouth dropped wide open, and his reaction was to simply walk away laughing.

I had never felt more homicidal in my entire life.

Then there was yesterday morning.

At 5:00 AM sharp, my world exploded with the shrillest ungodly alarm known to mankind.

I shot straight up, blinking blearily before groaning and slamming a pillow over my face.

"Someone turn it off!"

No one did.

Because Hunter's alarm went off three more times.

And this morning? Oh, Hunter had upped his game. He brought reinforcements. Enter Silas, another menace of my existence.

I woke up to chaos. All my clothes were strewn across the floor, and my curling products were scattered like crime scene debris all over my bed covers.

All of that had led to now, where my patience had finally hit an all-time low as soon as I got into my room, wanting to collapse on my *recently* cleaned bed only to pull back the blanket and witness, sitting right there in the middle of my bed, like it had full ownership, the biggest spider I'd ever seen. Not just any spider but one easily the size of my hand, with long hair and legs, twitching as it slowly crawled across the bed.

"Nope." I shook my head. "Nope. Nope." I wasn't dealing with this, *nope.*

I spun on my heel and marched down the hall, heading straight to the usually shut and locked room. Only one person would pull something like this, and I knew exactly who. I should have known that these past few weeks of silence were leading up to something.

"Hey!" I yelled, banging on Hunter's door like a mad woman. It took approximately ten more seconds for me to keep knocking before he opened the door, wearing a plain grey t-shirt and sweats. He leaned against the doorframe and raised an eyebrow.

"Yes?"

"Get your damn tarantula out of my room!"

Hunter stared at me, blinking slowly as if he would rather not deal with my outburst right now. "That's not mine."

I scoffed. "Please, a spider on my bed has you written all over it. Do you really think that's going to make me quit? I happen to like spiders!" A lie clearly not masked well enough.

He tilted his head slightly, giving me that infuriating blank look. "Like I said, Grace. It's not mine."

I folded my arms, glowering up at him, but my eyes snagged on something.

A flicker of gold right there on his pinky finger.

My gold band ring.

I blinked. What the hell? When did he get that?

"Wait—" My accusation about the spider invasion died on my tongue as I grabbed his wrist, dragging his hand up. "Is that my ring?"

Hunter, completely unfazed, barely spared it a glance. "Yeah."

"Yeah?" I was dumbfounded. "Since when did you start stealing my jewellery?"

He sighed like I was the exhausting one here. "Since you left it on the windowsill last week and never picked it up.

96

Finders keepers."

My lips parted. "Give it back!"

He smirked but said nothing.

I tried snatching it back, but his reflexes were too quick for me, and something sharpened in his smirk—like he was enjoying watching me spiral.

Grabbing the front of his shirt instead, I leaned up against him and gritted my teeth. "Get that tarantula out of my room and give me my ring back or—"

"Did you say spider?"

I turned to see Silas strolling toward us with a wide grin on his face. *Oh no.*

"Grace found your spider," Hunter added nonchalantly, and I just stood there gaping at him.

"Jerry?" Silas asked as if I would even know.

"Jerry?" I practically shrieked. "Since when do you own a tarantula?"

"Since always." He shrugged. "Don't worry, she's completely harmless. She actually has a thing for the ladies, so I'm not surprised she decided to go into your room."

I blinked at him.

God, I really hated the male species.

Hunter was still standing there, his lips twitching with the necessity to laugh at me. When I whipped my head back to face Silas, I could see the grin growing wider as he and Hunter shared a look that told me they had done it all on purpose.

"I'll go grab her," Silas said. "She's probably already missing me. Tarantulas are sensitive creatures, you know." He sauntered off to get his precious pet while I shot one final glare at Hunter. He was smirking at me, and I could practically feel the amusement radiating off him.

"You should learn not to accuse people so easily of

97

something they didn't do." His voice dripped with sarcasm. "Not very virtuous of you."

I scowled at him, pivoted on my heel, and raised my middle finger in the air for him to see.

As I stormed toward the living room, I made a mental note to check every corner of my room from now on.

"Who calls a tarantula Jerry?" I muttered to myself, still in disbelief.

"Silas calls all his pet animals Jerry," Brandon's voice floated over from behind me.

I spun around to where he was leaning against the kitchen counter and narrowed my eyes. "Really?"

"Yeah, I think it's because he's too lazy to come up with anything else."

I crossed my arms, still annoyed, but couldn't help the slight grin peeling at my lips over the ridiculousness of it all.

"If it helps." Brandon nibbled on his lip piercing, his tone softening. "I don't think it's so bad that you're here."

I let out a short laugh, but there was no humor behind it. "Yeah, well, according to your friend, I'm going to regret it."

Brandon's expression tightened slightly. "Cain's just... complicated."

I snorted. "That's what everyone says when they're trying to defend their friends' actions."

"I wish that was the case," he muttered, leaving us in a void of silence.

I cleared my throat and started making my way toward my room, thinking there was nothing left to say.

"Word of advice?" he said, and I looked back at him. His eyes flickered toward the hallway where all the boys' rooms were. "Play his game. He's always one for a challenge."

I stood there, taken aback by his words. Unsure of how

to respond, I gave him a slow nod. "I'll keep that in mind...
thanks."

He offered me a small, genuine smile, then casually grabbed
his mug from the counter before heading down the hallway
and leaving me there to brainstorm ideas.

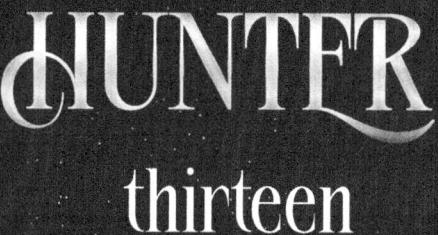

HUNTER

thirteen

I woke up to muffled voices outside my door, punctuated by Silas's loud, exaggerated groan. Pulling the pillow over my head, I rolled over, but it did nothing to block out the noise.

"It's been an hour!" Silas's voice echoed down the hall, his tone bordering on whining. "An *hour*, man!"

I sat up, ran a hand through my hair and debated whether it was worth getting involved. Something told me I shouldn't, but it was too late as I swung my legs off the bed and dragged myself to the door. As soon as I stepped into the hallway, I saw Silas pacing in front of the bathroom while Brandon stood nearby, leaning against the wall with an amused grin.

"She's not coming out," Silas continued and paused by the door to the bathroom. "Come on, Grace! I need to piss badly!"

"What's going on?" I asked, my voice still rough with sleep.

Silas turned to me. "She's been in there for an hour, Cain! I haven't even had a chance to shower, and I'm five seconds from pissing in one of my drawers if she doesn't come out."

Brandon chuckled from his spot against the wall. "Not like you haven't done so before."

Silas glared at him. "I'll piss on you in a second—"

I sighed, rubbing the back of my neck and strode toward the bathroom door. "Grace," I called, knocking on the door. I was too tired for this bullshit. "You're not the only one who lives here. Get out, or I'm knocking the door down, with or without your permission."

For a moment, there was nothing but silence. Then, slowly, the door unlocked, and Grace stood there, hair freshly done up and her Warrior uniform already on.

"All yours," she said. her voice sounded innocent, but those Bambi eyes lit up with mischief. "You're out of hot water, by the way."

Silas gasped dramatically from behind. "You used up all the hot water?"

Grace shrugged, completely unapologetic, and Brandon let out a low laugh. I just stared at her; my expression blank. I didn't know whether to be mad or amused.

I stepped forward, towering over her, but she didn't flinch. There was a glimmer of challenge in her eyes as if she wanted to see how I would react. This was her side that I unwillingly admired, and right now, she was making the competitive part of me light up. "You really want to start off the day like this?"

She gave me one of her bright smiles, which infuriated me. "You should probably get a new toothbrush. I stepped on bird poop yesterday and yours was the closest thing nearby to clean it with." Her smile never faltered as she brushed past me, the scent of strawberries infiltrating my nose. I watched her walk down the hall, and my jaw clenched.

"She's used up all the hot water, Cain," Silas kept saying

even as my stare lingered from where she had just disappeared off to. "All the hot water! Do you know what this means?"

"That you'll have to take a cold shower?" Brandon snickered.

"I don't know what you're laughing about. You're the one who's obsessed with having bubble baths."

Brandon lifted his palms in self-defense. "Hey, I'm not the one that put Jerry on her bed."

"Cain told me to do that!"

I tuned out both of them, my attention fixed on the hallway, hoping—no, definitely dreading—that Grace would reappear. She was a whirlwind of chaos wrapped up in an infuriatingly irresistible package. And the worst part? I hated how much it thrilled me.

GRACE

"You look happy," Lucas said, gesturing to the wide grin I couldn't hide as I wrapped my knuckles in white tape. The sun was still low, casting long shadows across the field, and best of all, Hunter was nowhere in sight.

"I am," I replied, tying the tape off with a satisfied tug.

"Care to share why?"

I shrugged, trying to play it off. "No reason."

I loosened my ponytail before gathering it into a plait, and leaving a few loose strands to frame my face. I didn't expect much to do today—probably just work on technique with Lucas, which would inevitably end in me failing and coming out bruised over nothing.

My eyes soon caught movement, and I couldn't help but let

my smile stretch a little wider. Hunter, Silas and Brandon had finally made it onto the grounds, and from the looks of it, they weren't exactly in peak condition. Silas, in particular, looked like he'd been dragged through five rounds of combat already, with his long hair a disheveled mess and hardly placed combat boots on.

Hunter, of course, wore his usual scowl, while Brandon appeared equally worn out, though more amused by it all. When he spotted me, he winked, and I chuckled.

Lucas followed my gaze, and the corner of his mouth quirked up. "Now that smile makes sense."

Yes, it did.

"Care to explain why the three of you are late?" Azrael's voice was frighteningly calm as he stood at the center.

Silas kicked at the mud as he passed him and muttered something under his breath while Brandon kept up his pace behind him.

Hunter, however, stopped. His nonchalant stance differed from the cold stare he gave me over his shoulder. I could hear Matias laughing with some of his friends on the other side of the field, enjoying this a little more than he should. "No excuse, sir. Won't happen again," Hunter said, and Azrael kept silent, which was damning enough. His eyes narrowed on Hunter and my stomach churned at the disapproval. before he brushed past Hunter, undoing his cufflinks as he scanned the gathered students.

"Pair off. We have visitors today."The group shifted as people began searching for a partner, but Hunter's voice cut through the conversation before I could turn to Lucas.

"I have a suggestion, sir."

Azrael turned. "And that is?"

Hunter's gaze slid over to me as he sunk his hands in the

pocket of his combat jacket. "Grace and I should spar. She's been practicing all week and mentioned it this morning, in fact."

My heart dropped in my stomach.

I could feel the eyes of other Ascendants land on me, and whispers started to ripple through the group. My stomach twisted.

Azrael's gaze flickered to me, and I straightened as if that would help me look any less weak. "Is that right, Martin?"

My eyes shifted toward Hunter at the spark of challenge in his expression. If I said no, would that mean I had lost whatever power play this all was?

I swallowed but my mouth was suddenly dry as I locked my gaze on Hunter. "Yes."

"Grace," Lucas scolded me before directing his attention to Azrael. "Sir, she can't—"

"Oh, come on, James," Hunter called out. "I'll go easy on her." He raised his palms. 'No weapons or powers."

Prick.

Azrael sighed in annoyance. "Martin, center. Now."

Lucas grabbed my arm and shook his head at me, not to go. I yanked free from his hold and smiled as if that would ease his mind. I could barely calm mine down.

Hunter stepped forward, his eyes never leaving mine as we met at the center of the pit. Ascendants gathered around us, snickering while my focus was locked on Hunter until I saw Nadael and a group of other Celestials approaching from the corner of my eye.

"Bambi," he acknowledged, his voice low and taunting.

I gritted my teeth as I raised my fists.

"Begin," Azrael said, and Hunter wasted no time. He lunged at me, his movements swift and precise, like how he fought against Matias. I could barely keep up as I blocked one of his hits. The force sent a shockwave up my arm, and I clenched my eyes shut, staggering back, as I tried to regain my balance.

When I peeled my eyes open, he stood there, unmoving, his fists lowered, and his lips pressed into a thin line. Laughter erupted around us, sharp and cutting.

"You're not even trying," he muttered, his voice low enough that only I could hear. "Prove me wrong, Grace. Show me you deserve to be here."

I glared at him, and without a word, I swung at him. I tried to land a hit, but he sidestepped easily, grabbing my wrist and twisting it behind me so that my back was against his front. I gasped as pain shot through my arm. He tightened his grip before letting go and shoving me back with enough force to send me sprawling to the ground.

Everyone was watching, and my cheeks flamed. When I turned to look toward Azrael, embarrassment flooded me at the view of Nadael and the other Celestials beside her taking notes.

Nadael shook her head, giving me a rueful look as if she knew how right she was about me joining the Warriors. She didn't want this. Joe didn't want this. No one did.

"Looks as if you might need another shower, Grace," Hunter taunted, circling me like a predator. "Pity you keep proving me right. Like I've said before, this place isn't meant for a mortal."

I glared at him, wiping the dirt from my trousers as the weight of everyone's eyes landed on me. He was doing this on purpose, making a spectacle of me in front of others— especially in front of Nadael.

Rising to my feet, I felt rage crackling through my veins like thunder, readying to break through the clouds. "Would you have said that to your brother if he were here?"

The second the words left my mouth, I knew I'd hit a nerve. Hunter's expression fell, his eyes darkening in a way that I had never seen before. I should have regretted it and swallowed the words back, but it was too late. The look in Hunter's eyes wasn't just angry. It was something else, something far more... punishing.

Before I could react, he moved. In a blur of motion, he swept my legs out from under me. I hit the ground hard—the breath knocked out of me as my head spun and my ears rang with the impact.

I struggled to push myself up, but he was already on top of me, pinning me down. My hands shot up to slap at him, but he grabbed my wrists, slamming them above my head with ease.

"What do you know about my brother?" he growled, his voice so low it barely sounded like him. "What the fuck do *you* know?"

I clenched my fists, but I couldn't move. He had me completely trapped, and the worst part was that he wasn't even trying.

"*Enough.*"

Azrael's voice sliced through the tension, and Hunter immediately pulled away and rose to his feet with barely controlled fury.

I sat up, my hands trembling, not from fear but from the overwhelming anger and humiliation I'd been subjected to.

Azrael placed a calming hand on Hunter's shoulder, whispering something I couldn't hear, but Hunter's eyes never left mine. His gaze burnt into me even as Lucas hurried over to help me up. We were locked in that stare, Hunter's anger still simmering beneath the surface and mine boiling over. Lucas was saying something and brushing dirt off me, but I

107

couldn't hear anything. The pounding in my head drowned out everything else.

"Grace?" Lucas shook me gently, and his voice finally broke through to me. "Are you okay? Do we need to go see Marnie?"

"I—" I stammered, my eyes flickering toward Hunter, who stormed past us without another glance. Silas and Brandon stood nearby, looking equally tense. "No." I shook my head. "I'm—okay."

"Grace," Nadael said from where she stood with the other Celestials, her gaze sharpening with concern. "My office. *Now.*"

I swallowed hard at the firmness in her voice and followed her as she turned, strolling towards the academy.

GRACE
fourteen

I sat stiffly in the chair across from Nadael. My wrists still ached from where Hunter had grabbed me, and my head only kept spinning, the longer I sat here.

Nadael leaned forward, her fingers clasped together as she gave me a measured look. I was starting to despise this office. "Grace." She sighed. "Do you understand what happened today?"

Not really, no. But that wasn't the answer she was looking for. "Yes."

She studied me for a moment longer. "I want you to know something... the people there today, watching the training—they weren't just Celestials from the academy. Some of them were members of the Angelic Council."

My eyes widened on their own accord. Just when I thought I couldn't embarrass myself any further, I realized I had done it in front of the most important figures.

"And it's a good thing," Nadael added with a sigh, "that Joe wasn't there to witness what happened."

Shame washed over me as I lowered my eyes to the desk. The thought of Joe seeing me made my chest tighten. He would have been furious, maybe even disappointed.

"What I said... I didn't..."

"You need to remember your place here," Nadael told me. "You are already under intense scrutiny as a human staying at Celestia. I'm trying my best here to help Joe by keeping you away from the outside world, but incidents like today only reinforce the Council's doubts about you."

I nodded, my throat tight with the need to plead my case, but I had none.

"And another thing," she continued, her voice much gentler now. "It is in your best interest that you apologize to Mr Cain."

My head snapped up. "What?"

"You provoked him." She raised a brow. "And whether or not his reaction was justified, you share a dorm together. So, I suggest you find him and make amends."

I wanted to argue, to tell her that Hunter had pushed me first and that this whole thing was his fault. He wanted me gone, and granted, mentioning his brother had crossed a line, but he was just as much in the wrong.

With a resigned nod, I stood up. "If that is what you wish, then I will. Sorry for the display I caused."

Nadael seemed content with that answer, which was far from what I felt when I left her office and returned to the dorm.

When I walked through the doorway, I found Silas lounging on the sofa, his feet kicked up on the coffee table. Brandon wasn't back from training, but I assumed Silas had made an excuse to come up here earlier.

I approached him cautiously and asked, "Where's Hunter?"

Silas glanced up at me, then shrugged lazily. "No idea."

That clearly meant he did have an idea of his whereabouts. "You always know where he is."

He smirked. "Not today, Gracie. And even if I did, I wouldn't tell you."

I scowled at the new nickname I had been given and crossed my arms over my chest. "Fine then. I'll find him myself."

Leaving Silas behind, I stormed out of the dorm and down the hallways until I found myself in the common room. I paused by one of the dark sofas, wanting to scream out of frustration. I hated this place—everything about it. I wanted to call Joe and tell him to move me somewhere else. I didn't care about all the towns we'd end up living in—I was used to that. But this? I wasn't used to this.

"Well, you look like shit," someone drawled from behind, and I spun to find Matias leaning against the doorway.

I ignored the sudden unease that crawled up my spine as he stared at me. "I'm not in the mood, Matias. Have you seen Hunter?"

"Why?" He smirked. "After today, I'd say you need a new sparring partner to teach you to fight."

I crossed my arms, covering my chest. "I don't need a partner."

"Oh, come on," Matias said, pushing himself off the doorway as he walked toward me. I staggered back before hitting a bookshelf. "It's not like Lucas can teach you anything. If you ask me, it should have been his sister in the Warriors Sector, not him. Besides, I could show you a few moves. You know, to stop you from getting pinned down so easily."

My pulse quickened, but before I could respond, another voice—one I seemed to attract wherever I went, cut us off.

"If she wanted help, you'd be the last person she'd go to." Hunter stepped into the room, his expression dark and his hair

113

a tousled mess as if he had run his hand through it one too many times.

Matias glanced at him, his smirk faltering for a second before he raised his hands in mock surrender. "Was just offering a little help, that's all." He started backing away. "I'll leave you two to it." The smugness never left his eyes. "I'll see you on the field, Cain."

As Matias disappeared from the common room, the tension didn't ease one bit. If anything, it grew thicker, more suffocating, more... *dangerous.*

"I was looking for you," I said, my voice hoarse.

Hunter hummed, his finger brushing against one of the sofas as if checking for dust. "Was that Nadael's doing?"

I swallowed my nerves. "I didn't... I didn't mean to—"

"Bring up my brother?" He asked, puncturing each word he spoke.

"It was a mistake," I whispered.

There was a beat of silence. His jaw tightened, and I just watched him—watched how his thoughts consumed him.

Brother? Was he also an Ascendant?

No, but I doubt he's alive anymore if the Riftkeeper's took him.

The memory of what Marnie told me faded in the back of my mind, and I frowned more at myself than at him. "Is that why you hate me?"

It all made sense now as Hunter's eyes flashed with something I couldn't quite place. I took a step closer, wondering if what I was about to say would fuel my curiosity or not. "Because I got a chance? Because I'm here, and he isn't?"

His hands clenched into fists, and for a moment, I thought we would be heading for another round in combat.

"Do you want me gone from here so that the Riftkeeper's

can kill me?"

"No."

"Or are you just that spiteful that I was given the opportunity—"

Hunter closed the distance between us in one swift motion before I could finish. His hands shot out, grabbing my arms as he pinned me against the wall with a force that made my breath hitch.

For a heartbeat, neither of us moved. His face was inches from mine, strands of his hair brushing against my forehead. I was breathless, taking in the intensity of his grey eyes.

"You don't understand," he whispered, his voice raw with frustration. "You never will."

I stared up at him, my body trembling under the weight of his hold. It felt like everything else had disappeared for a moment—the academy, the fight, even the anger between us. It was just us two on the precipice of something dangerous. And then, just as quickly as it had started, Hunter pulled back. His grip loosened, and he stepped away, leaving me standing there with my heart in my throat.

Without another word, he turned and walked out of the common room towards the dormitories. *Our* dorm.

GRACE
fifteen

The crisp air bit my cheeks as I crouched low behind a cluster of ferns, my heart pounding in time with the distant shouts echoing through the woods. The so-called *Ecliptic hunt* challenge wasn't exactly what I envisioned for Warrior training, but Azrael believed it was a 'necessary exercise to refine agility and strategy.' I called it the worst type of paintball to exist.

Next to me, Lucas was leaning against a tree, looking far too calm for someone who could get tagged out at any moment.

"Do they make you guys do this often?" I whispered, scanning the forest for any movement.

He shrugged. "Every few weeks, depending on how close we are to the competition. It's supposed to help us think on our feet. You'll get used to it."

"Used to it?" I muttered, brushing dirt off my knees. Dodging Celestial energy beams in the woods wasn't my idea of fun. "What do the other sectors do to prepare for the competition?"

"Guardians and Messengers have these intense tests. Think

high-stakes puzzles that test their minds and reflexes at the same time. Healers? They've got it easy—they basically get to play pretend doctor all day."

At least Marnie would be fine.

"Do you think anyone's out yet?"

"Definitely," Lucas replied, peeking around the tree. "I saw Silas nail Brandon earlier. Poor guy didn't even see it coming."

I snorted. "That's what they do on a regular basis back at the dorms."

A rustling sound came from our left and I froze. Lucas looked down at me as I tugged my jacket closer. Lucas peered past the tree before whispering, "It's Norah."

I grimaced.

"Split up," he said. "I'll draw her attention while you go left."

"Lucas, wait—" I started, but he was already stepping out from behind the tree. I hesitated, torn between staying and following his lead, when I heard Norah's voice.

"Found you, Martin."

I bit my lip as I turned toward Norah. An orb, almost blinding to the eye, lay in one of her pale hands as she smiled at me. She was ready to fire it in my direction when a rock smacked against her cheek, and she grunted, stumbling with the beam in her hand. My head whipped to see Lucas had been the one to throw it as a form of distraction.

"Grace, go!" he yelled, and I didn't even give it a second thought as I darted off, weaving through the trees. The sound of another beam firing was followed by Lucas' grunt of frustration, and my stomach twisted for a moment before a root on the ground caught my foot, sending me lurching forward. I barely caught myself as I slammed into a solid chest.

"Well, well, what do we have here?" Matias's voice slithered into my ear, smooth and taunting. I staggered back, meeting his predatory grin head-on and tried to pull away, but his grip only tightened, fingers digging into my arms like a vice.

"We were hoping to run into you. See, Norah and I made a bet to see who could get the mortal out first."

"Let go," I hissed.

Matias ignored me, exchanging glances with his friends. "Looks like I'll be winning the bet today."

All three laughed when a sharp crackling sound cut through the air. A beam of Celestial energy shot one of Matias's friends before the other was shortly sent to the floor by another. Matias released me, and I stumbled, watching as he whirled around. The third orb struck Matias straight in the chest, causing him to fall on his back against a mass of leaves.

"What the fuck, Cain?" he snarled.

I blinked as my gaze snapped to Hunter, who stood a few feet away, his arm still raised from firing the beams. His expression was calm—too calm—as he watched Matias, who looked like he was on the verge of losing it.

"We're on the same team, you prick!" Matias snarled.

Hunter gave an indifferent shrug. "Are we? Must've slipped my mind when Azrael was droning on and on about it."

Matias huffed, rolling his shoulder back as he stood. The bright blue stain of Celestial energy glowed on his shirt, matching the ones marking his friends, who stood beside him, muttering curse words under their breath.

"Guess you're out either way," Hunter said, unfazed.

One of Matias's friends took a threatening step toward him, but Matias shot out an arm, stopping him. His lethal glare was locked on Hunter, and after a beat, Matias muttered something to his friends, his jaw tight before they turned and stalked off.

A shaky breath fell from my lips as I turned to Hunter. I

wanted to feel grateful—he had just saved me from Matias's taunts—but the way he was now looking at me, as if I was a puzzle he couldn't solve, made my chest tighten.

His words from a while ago echoed in my mind. *You don't belong here.* And yet, he kept stepping in when no one else would.

He strode toward me and my heart began to hammer as he stopped just a foot away from me.

His imposing presence made the air around us feel charged with energy—nothing like the Celestial beams that were supposed to be full of it.

I opened my mouth, the hesitant "thank you" lingering on the edge of my tongue, but it vanished as soon as his hand wrapped around my waist and drew me close to his chest.

My breath escaped me in a surprised oomph as I tilted my head back to meet his gaze. His eyes held mine, and before I could demand an explanation, something firm was pressed against the small of my back. There was a sudden burst of heat, and a faint crackling sound followed. The impact wasn't painful, but it sent a ripple of energy through me, leaving me stunned. Hunter held me steady with one arm while raising the other, revealing his hand alight with blue, glowing Celestial energy.

Oh. My. Fuck.

"What the hell!" I yelled, shoving at his chest with both hands. He stumbled back slightly, his smirk only deepening as I stared at him in disbelief.

"Rule number one, Bambi," he said, his voice laced with infuriating amusement. "Never trust someone on the opposing team, even if you believe they're on your side for just that one split second."

My fists clenched as I glared at him, but before I could

deliver the scathing retort clawing its way up my throat, the sharp sound of a whistle echoed through the woods, signaling the end of training.

Hunter's smirk widened, showing off a set of dimples as he took a few steps back. "Think of it like gravity. Even the smallest things can pull you under if you're not paying attention."

"What the hell does that mean!"

He chuckled and without saying another word, he turned on his heel and disappeared into the trees.

Asshole.

GRACE

sixteen

Today was different than usual. It wasn't just Warriors outside training this time. Everyone was here. The massive open space had been divided into sections as if it were an exhibition for Ascendants.

The rising sun bathed the grounds in gold light, and the sound of murmured chants, bursts of Celestial energy and weapons clashing fi lled the air.

I stood near the edge of the pit, arms crossed and feeling small amidst the crowd.

The Warriors, of course, were hard to miss. Their section dominated the center of the grounds, where Ascendants were sparring with brutal intensity. Hunter was there with Silas as they both moved with skill and precision, their Celestial blades colliding with sharp metallic clangs.

I watched as Hunter ducked under Silas's swing, pivoting with an ease that made it look effortless. It was terrible of me to want him to fail, but it was all I could think of as Silas lunged forward, and Hunter sidestepped, spinning his blade until the tip hovered at Silas's throat.

I almost rolled my eyes before glancing towards the other sections.

To the right of the Warriors, the Healers were gathered in a quieter circle, their hands glowing faintly as they worked. Marnie was among them, kneeling beside a volunteer with a nasty gash on his arm. Her brows furrowed in concentration as she pressed her hands to the wound, and a soft golden light spilt from her palms, weaving itself into the torn skin. Slowly, the tear closed, leaving only smooth skin behind.

"That's incredible," I whispered, unable to hide the awe in my voice.

"It's amazing, alright." Lucas came to stand by my side, and I nodded.

Farther down, the Guardians trained in a more shadowed part of the grounds. I watched as one of them—a tall girl with dark hair—closed her eyes, her hands moving in slow, fluid motions. It was honestly ethereal—all of it.

The Warriors.

The Healers.

The Guardians.

Even the Messengers worked in pairs, communicating telepathically, sending and receiving messages without a single spoken word.

I wrapped my arms tighter around myself, and every bit of negativity swirled across my mind. All I had to show these Celestials were my instincts. My will to fight.

But was that even enough?

"What are you two doing just standing there!" Marnie called out as she jogged over. Brushing a stray copper lock of hair from her face, she added, "Did you see what I did?"

I nodded with a smile.

"Impressive, Lewis," Lucas admitted. "Hey, whenever I get ill, can you come over and heal me?"

Marnie chuckled, lightly slamming her fist against his shoulder, but her smile faltered when she glanced at me. "You're doing that thing again."

I balked. "What thing?"

"The thing where you compare yourself to everyone else and decide you're not good enough. I may not read minds, but it's written all over your face."

I sighed, kicking at the dirt. "It's hard not to when... look around, Marnie. Everyone here is extraordinary. It's technically unfair. Why was I just cursed with endless clumsiness and the inability to sing?"

Marnie threw her head back with a laugh before coming to my side and wrapping an arm around my shoulder. "You have great taste in sweets if that helps."

I shrugged, not entirely convinced. But before Marnie could say more, a loud clang echoed through the grounds as one of the Warrior's swords hit the ground.

"Break's over," she said, nudging me lightly. "Come on, let's see what else is happening." I hesitated, glancing over at Lucas, who simply gave me an encouraging nod as I followed him and Marnie toward the other areas.

HUNTER

I rolled my shoulders, gripping the hilt of my sword tightly as Silas squared off with me again.

A cocky grin tugged at the corner of his mouth. "I swear, I'll beat you this time."

Which is what he always said.

I chuckled as he charged towards me. Our blades collided with a sharp ring, its force reverberating through my arms. He came at me again, this time energy circling his weapon as he aimed for my ribs. I parried, twisting my wrist and sending his blade off course.

"Huh," I teased. "Not bad."

He grunted in response, backing up for another attempt. But my focus wasn't entirely on Silas anymore.

It was on *her*.

Out of the corner of my eye, I saw Grace lingering near Lucas and that Healer girl. Arms crossed, her gaze darted between different groups, looking... lost.

I frowned, nearly missing Silas's next wing.

"Oi! Eyes on me, pretty boy," Silas said, puckering his lips in a mock kiss.

I blocked him again, this time with more force, sending him stumbling back. "Maybe if you were quicker, it wouldn't matter where my eyes are."

Silas smirked. "Ouch. Someone's testy today—too soon?"

I ignored him, glancing back toward Grace. She wasn't moving; she was just standing there like she didn't know what to do with herself. She always looked like that, no matter where we were.

Silas sighed. "This is no fun when you're not trying."

I struggled to look back at him, and when I did, he pouted like a five-year-old. "You should practice using your enhanced strength," I said, ignoring his previous tantrum. "Maybe then, you might win for once."

Brandon scoffed, passing us by with thin daggers called Aetherion's. Its purpose was that it remembered the movements of past wielders and guided the current person in combat.

"What enhanced strength? The only thing he has to show for it is that six-pack, nothing else."

"You fucker—" Silas lunged at him, grabbing Brandon in a headlock. "I won the last competition; what about you, huh? You haven't even competed in any yet."

Brandon couldn't stop laughing as he tripped Silas up, and they landed on the ground. They were idiots. Idiots that I was sadly friends with.

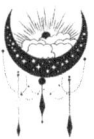

Later, after Brandon and Silas had finally managed to stop bickering, I found Grace near the Healer's circle, watching Marnie work her magic on others.

"Still just watching others do all the work?" I called out as I approached.

Grace turned sharply, her eyes narrowing as soon as she saw me. "I'm *observing*."

"Right," I said, crossing my arms. "Because standing on the sidelines is going to prepare you for what's coming."

She expelled a frustrated breath. "Why are you here? Don't you already bother me enough back at the dorm?"

I shrugged, unwillingly enjoying how she became this other person when I was around. I aggravated her. She angered me. Yet, I couldn't stop. "I'm just making sure you're not planning to sit the whole of training out. Wouldn't want you to break your perfect record of doing absolutely nothing."

Her lips pressed into a thin line, and for a moment, I thought she might actually swing at me. "You're insufferable."

"And you're defensive," I countered, taking a step closer. I didn't care about the Healers suddenly watching us.

Grace's eyes flared. It almost made me grin. *Almost.* "I don't need to prove myself to you. I'm here for a reason. Deal with it."

I blinked, surprised by her confidence. The smirk slipped from my face, but even as I was about to respond, I couldn't. Marnie glanced over at us, wiping her glowing hands on a cloth.

She came to Grace's aid, linking arms with her. Her eyes didn't leave mine as she said to Grace, "Shall we go?"

"Yes, please," Grace said quickly, and Marnie wasted no time leading her away.

It was only for a second that Grace seemed to hesitate, glancing back at me before giving me one raging look and a middle finger that caused my smirk to lock back into place.

GRACE
seventeen

Grey clouds scattered the sky, casting shadows through the arched windows of the classroom as I tried to keep my focus on what Sariel was saying. A few days had passed since the training exhibition, but I still couldn't shake any of it off. Every time I closed my eyes, I either saw how the Celestials looked at me or how Hunter did with that never-relenting stare.

"Today, you'll be pairing off to practice controlling visions," Sariel announced, and the room instantly buzzed with excited whispers. "As a pair, one of you will be the guide, controlling the vision, while the other anchors them back to reality. This isn't just about tuning into your sights but also about trust. Something Celestials admire."

I glanced around the room, watching as everyone stood from their benches and began to pair off. Sariel continued speaking while I shifted in my seat, unsure of what to do or where to go. I knew I should have avoided this class; instead, I'd listened to Sariel's advice and attended it because I was curious... and stupid.

"Veronica," Sariel called out, her sharp eyes narrowing. "Where's your partner?"

Veronica shrugged. "Don't have one."

Sariel's gaze drifted towards where I was, and I froze. *Please don't choose me. Please don't choose me. Please don't—* "Then Grace can be your anchor."

The universe hated me.

Veronica's icy gaze landed on me. I could practically feel the disdain radiating off her as she folded her arms across her chest.

I bit the inside of my cheek to keep from huffing. Of all people, why her? The last thing I wanted was to be responsible for anchoring her during a vision. But there was no way I could argue with Sariel. I was already on a thin line with the Angelic Council. So, swallowing my frustration, I nodded and made my way over to Veronica.

Veronica didn't say a word as I stood in front of her, but the way her black-painted lips curled into a tight, unimpressed frown said everything.

"This should be fun," she muttered under her breath, and I forced a neutral expression as we sat down, cross-legged, facing each other.

Sariel walked between the pairs, giving us the instructions we needed. It was quite simple, really. Veronica would reach a state that could trigger a vision, and I would be responsible for keeping her tethered to reality. But the way she was glaring at me told me this wasn't going to be *that* easy.

"Visionaries, close your eyes," Sariel instructed. "Anchors, remain as you are."

Veronica gave me an eyeroll before doing as she was told, and I tried to steady my breathing as I mentally prepared myself.

"Now," Sariel said, "Anchors. You may touch the visionary."

Then it started—a subtle shift in the air, as people grabbed each other's hands or arms. I watched, mesmerized, as faint golden threads began to shimmer around the pairs. They danced and twisted, stretching into infinity, some as thin as spider silk, others thick as ropes.

"Futures," Sariel murmured from the front of the room, her voice low but resonant. "Possibilities. This is the gift of Guardians—to see and to guide the world accordingly. *But*... futures are never fixed. They can change. In fact, they are always changing."

One pair, a girl with a sleek braid, seemed caught in an argument with herself. The threads around her shimmered erratically, flashing from gold to silver to a dull grey. The Guardian frowned, muttering under her breath as her anchor steadied her with a firm grip.

"The harder the choice," Sariel continued, "the more volatile the threads. It is the duty of Guardians to weigh these futures, to find the path that serves the greater balance."

I hesitated, my fingers hovering over Veronica's hand. She already looked annoyed, her sharp green eyes narrowing as if daring me to mess this up.

"Just do it," she snapped, her voice low enough for only me to hear. I swallowed hard and clasped her hand, bracing myself for whatever might happen.

As soon as I did, her body jerked, and her face twisted in pain for several seconds.

"Veronica?" I whispered, unsure if I was supposed to speak or not.

She fell silent for a moment, the threads around us darkening into an inky black—then, without warning, she screamed.

I jumped as her panicked voice echoed through the room. "Something's happening to my brother! I can't change it— I—I can't stop it. No!"

My blood ran cold. "Ver—"

"This is all your fault!" she cried, her eyes snapping open but still glassy as if she were lost in the vision. "You did this!" I stumbled back, the accusation slamming into me with full force. "What—"

"You shouldn't even be here!" Her voice was filled with rage as her fingers clawed at the floorboards, drawing blood. "You're just as bad as a Riftkeeper!"

I looked around the room, panicked about what to do. Sariel was moving toward us, her usual calm demeanor replaced with urgency.

"Leave the classroom," she said to me, kneeling in front of Veronica.

"What? But—"

"Now!" Sariel repeated in a way that left no room for argument.

Veronica continued to scream with tears streaming down her face as she cried out for her brother. My stomach sank as I stood and stumbled toward the door, barely able to breathe past the agonizing sounds.

I ran across Celestia's hallways, the words, '*this is all your fault*' repeating in my mind like a curse I couldn't shake off.

I didn't know where exactly I was going, but I just wanted to get out of here. I wanted—

Stumbling to a stop, I blinked as I almost crashed into someone. I stared at a crisp, clean blue suit before my eyes slid to Azrael's face.

"Sorry," I mumbled, a pathetic apology. My head was

throbbing.

"It seems you lack spatial awareness as much as you lack the skills to be a Warrior."

I didn't care for the insult, at least not at that moment.

"Perhaps," he continued, straightening the collar of his shirt. "You should watch where you're going. Would hate for you to get lost one of these days."

My brows furrowed at the meaning behind that, but when I went to ask, Eden appeared.

"Grace." She smiled from behind Azrael, though her smile quickly morphed into concern. "Are you alright?"

I wasn't sure if I had nodded or not.

She looked at Azrael and cleared her throat. "How is she settling in with the Warriors?" Her question seemed innocent, something to ease the tension from the air, but it didn't work.

Azrael turned to face her properly, giving me his back. "You already know what my opinions are, Eden. No need to start meaningless conversations." He shouldered past her, and she shook her head, before plastering on a wide smile as she focused on me. She cleared her throat and changed subjects. "So... have you been to the library yet?"

I shook my head.

"Oh," she said, suddenly beaming. "Well, then you'll absolutely love it." She hooked her arm through mine and started dragging me across the corridors. "Come, let me show you. It's the perfect place to unwind; hardly anyone goes there, and I can tell it is exactly what you need right now."

HUNTER

eighteen

I pushed the door to the dorm and found Brandon sprawled out on the sofa, his eyes glued to the screen. I raised an eyebrow as the flicker of blue light from the TV illuminated the familiar glow of lightsabers battling on screen.

I cleared my throat, and Brandon shot up, attempting to turn the TV off and failing. "I wasn't watching anything—I wasn't—oh, it's you."

I chuckled, closing the door behind me. "You sound like someone who got caught watching porn."

Brandon flashed me a lazy grin before dropping onto the sofa again. "I thought you were Silas. He made a bet that I couldn't go through an entire week watching Star Wars. Obviously, I'm failing, but he doesn't need to know that."

I shook my head, amused, and my gaze naturally drifted to Grace's room on the right. "Is she in?" I asked, jerking my head toward her door.

Is she in so that I can annoy her and see how flustered she gets around me? Is more so the question I wanted to ask.

Brandon frowned, leaning forward. "Dunno. Haven't seen her since she left this morning." He shook his head and chuckled. "Silas practically chased her out the door when he asked her if she could shave his chest."

I grunted in response. I thought irritating her during the Ecliptic hunt challenge and training sessions would work in my favor. Instead, I came out of it all feeling shit and annoyed at myself. All I seemed to do instead was search for her even when I didn't mean to.

The door swung open behind me, and Silas came in, looking like he'd been through hell. His hair was a mess, his face slightly flushed, and his usual carefree expression was nowhere to be found.

"Azrael?" Brandon suggested, quickly turning the TV off.

Silas shook his head, his gaze flicking between me and Brandon. He seemed on edge, which immediately made my mind drift to Grace, and I hated that.

"What happened?" I asked, way too eager to know when, usually, I didn't care much about what went on.

Silas ran a hand through his messy hair and leaned against the back of the door, letting out a harsh breath. "Something happened in Sariel's class."

Brandon sat up at that. "What do you care? You're not a Guardian."

Silas rubbed the back of his neck, clearly uncomfortable. "Veronica... she freaked out. She had a vision or something."

I narrowed my eyes, watching Silas carefully. He was never one to care, especially when it came to someone who wasn't him, Brandon, or me. But Veronica... he'd known her since they were six years old, and whatever it was, he always seemed at his most vulnerable whenever she was brought up.

"Veronica?" Brandon repeated, cocking an eyebrow as he looked at me. He knew little about Veronica and Silas's strange relationship.

"Yeah, she—she was paired with Grace—"

I felt a sharp twist in my gut at the mention of Grace's name. *Shit.*

"Started screaming about her brother and went off on Grace. Like, really went off. Saying it was all her fault. I don't know much else other than Veronica was taken to the Healers, and they wouldn't let anyone other than Lucas see her."

The room went quiet, and I forced myself to stay still. Horrible visions from the Guardians were typical, but anything that involved Grace wasn't.

"So, where is Grace now?" Brandon asked, sitting forward with a concerned look.

"I don't know. Sariel sent her out of the classroom, and no one's seen her since."

"I'll go look for her."

At that, Brandon and Silas turned their heads in my direction. I swore I heard the sound of crickets chirping.

"What?"

Silas narrowed his eyes. 'Since when do you care where Grace is or not?'

I shrugged. "I don't. Couldn't care less, in fact." Now where the fuck was she?

Both my idiotic friends looked less than convinced but I ignored them, feeling suddenly frustrated as I headed toward the door without saying a word.

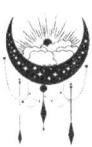

I wasn't sure why I felt the sudden need to find Grace, but the urge was there, telling me to do it. Maybe it was because I wanted to know more about why Veronica lashed out at her, or perhaps I just wanted to see how she felt. I shook my head at that last ridiculous thought.

The academy halls were almost empty, except for some younger kids heading to their next class. I walked and walked, making sure to investigate every empty room, including the canteen.

She wasn't in any of them.

My last resort was the library on the fifth floor of the main building at Celestia. I pushed open the heavy doors and stepped inside. My eyes immediately scanned the rows of shelves for any sign of her. The place was practically deserted as I made my way through the book aisles. Right there, beneath the soft glow of a lamp, I saw her petite figure as she held onto a book, her eyes engrossed in whatever was inside of it.

She hadn't noticed me yet, and for a moment, I hesitated. I watched her flip each page. Her curls were up in a bun, and she was still wearing the Warriors uniform.

I took a deep breath, pushing down the unfamiliar tightness in my chest, and walked over to her. She didn't look up until I was standing right in front of her, my shadow falling across the pages of the book.

GRACE
nineteen

Eden was right. The library at Celestia was beautiful in its own intricate ways. It was hard to believe no one else was there except me. The high arched ceilings were adorned with Celestial figures, and the walls—each were lined with tall, built-in bookshelves that stretched up to a second level. The combination of the ornate ceilings and the gleaming gold accents against the blue archways and shelves made it all feel like I was in a palace.

I took my phone out, texting Marnie about how she should have taken me here ages ago before my finger hovered over Lucas's incoming message. Sighing, I opened it.

Lucas: Hey, heard about what happened between you and Ver. U okay?

You: I think u should be asking that to Veronica. How is she?

I bit my lip, waiting for his response but nothing came, so I typed:

You: Can we meet later?

Three dots appeared.

Lucas: Sure, I'm just walking out of the Healers Sector. We can meet in the canteen, say, at 4pm?

I replied with a thumbs up before pocketing my phone away and navigating myself through the library.

As I walked through each aisle, names such as angelology and lore stood out, and I felt like I was in my element for once. I ran my fingertips across each book, searching for something I wasn't so sure of when something flickered from behind me. I turned and frowned.

When I whirled my head back around, I jumped as I saw a small figure appear in front of me.

I pressed a hand to my racing heart and shook my head as the creature hovered a few feet above the ground, his small, childlike form crowned with a faint golden halo that glowed softly in the dim light of the library.

"Hello!" it spoke in a surprisingly deep and melodic voice.

Oh.

A cherub.

He looked exactly as the paintings depicted him, with his petite wings, large and silver eyes, and innocent appearance that seemed both young and ancient at once.

"Aren't you supposed to be guarding the Garden of Eden?" I asked, half-joking

The cherub tilted his head. "Why, there are far more than just a few cherubs in the angelic realm, Miss Martin."

I frowned, a bit thrown off. "How do you know my last name?"

"Cherubs are omniscient deities." His eyes gleamed. "We hold the knowledge of every book in this library and of any human we first meet. Ask me anything, and I shall provide the

144

adequate answer."

I stared at him for a long moment. It felt strange to speak to this small, ethereal creature, but I also felt comforted in its presence. After all, it had been the first I'd witnessed a cherub in front of me. That was a once-in-a-lifetime opportunity.

I decided to test his words. "Alright," I said slowly. "Tell me something interesting about the Celestials."

"Celestials are beings divided by a distinct hierarchy." The cherub smiled as he spoke, almost as if he enjoyed the chance to share his knowledge. "They operate within different orders: First, Second, Third and finally Fourth. Each one holds unique power and influence over the cosmos. The Demonic Celestials, however, have a hierarchy of six levels, each one ascending into darker corruption, such as the Ruler, the Overlords, the Archfiends, the Hellbound Knights, the Lesser demons and finally the corrupted souls."

I was captivated by his words. Suddenly, I wanted to ask him every little thing as if I were speaking with someone claiming to be a fortune teller. I might as well have been.

"What are some of their powers like? Are they... similar to an Ascendant?" I doubted it.

"Demonic powers range from who and what they are. A lesser demon can possess one signature power, such as shadow manipulation, blood and soul magic, hellfire conjuration, or mind corruption based on their emotions. An overlord may hold all of those powers and more. The ruler—"

"Will have everything. Got it." I chuckled. "Why don't you tell me more about the Riftkeeper's?" I asked, pushing a little further.

"Riftkeeper's," he replied, a note of caution creeping into his voice. "They are an organisation born from the ancient wars between angels and demons. They may be protectors of humanity, but their methods are often... ruthless, skirting the edge of cruelty. They believe the ends justify the means, which is why they are sometimes considered worse than the biblical monsters."

I lifted a brow. "Worse?"

"It is a hypothesis, Miss Martin. Most have not had to encounter a Leviathan or the first beast, but they have Riftkeeper's."

I hummed. "Okay... and what about the Grand War?"

The cherub's tone dropped, and his silvery eyes darkened just slightly. "The Grand War," he spoke as though the words were sacred, "occurred after Lucifer's fall, a declaration of war on all Celestial beings. It was a brutal clash between light and dark, ravaging humanity until the Seraphims established a truce to preserve mankind."

"And do you have any books detailing the war?"

"Why, of course!" With a click of his fingers, a book materialised and fell into my hands. "The Remnants of the Grand War, written by the Archangel Gabriel in the year 803. Will that be all, Miss Martin, or do you require any more information?"

I shook my head, slightly dazed. "No—um—that will be all, thank you."

"You are welcome, Miss Martin," he replied, his head dipping in a small bow before he vanished in a faint puff of simmering smoke.

I blinked and glanced behind me as if someone else was there to see all of that. Although they probably wouldn't be as stunned as I was right now. Puffing out a soft sigh, I looked back at the book in my hands. It was heavy, with leather bindings and silver accents running along the spine.

I flipped the book onto its first page, scanning the inked

writing and sketches that resembled weapons.

Fascinated, I was just about to dive into the text when a shadow loomed over me, and I jumped once again, though this time nearly dropping the book on my feet. "Oh fu—" I started, only to stop when I looked up and saw it was Hunter, standing there, his head tilted as he watched me with that usual unreadable expression of his. I instantly frowned. "Is it a habit of yours to suddenly appear when I would prefer not to see your face for the millionth time?" I asked.

There was a slight smirk on his lips. "Depends. Does it make you want to quit?"

I glowered. "Hardly."

His eyes landed on the book in my hand, causing me to quickly close it so he didn't read into it. "The Grand War?" He lifted a brow, and I huffed.

"I was bored," I said, plopping the book down on a random shelf.

"Right."

He didn't believe me. I didn't care. Well, I didn't *want* to.

There was a moment of silence between us before he said, "I heard about what happened in Sariel's class."

I blinked, taken aback. "You did?"

He nodded, leaning against one of the shelves, his eyes narrowing slightly. "Veronica had some kind of vision. She blamed you."

My hands clammed up, and the uneasy feeling of what happened in Sariel's class began creeping up inside me. "Is that why you're here then? To rub it in my face that someone else doesn't want me here just as much as you do."

He looked away, his jaw straining. "Not exactly."

"Then what is it?"

Hunter's expression shifted as he looked back at me. He

147

seemed... worried. But I refused to believe that was for my benefit. "Do you know what the vision was about?"

I was suddenly uncomfortable. I didn't want to mention the part about Lucas. That felt too... personal. "No," I lied, though not entirely. All I knew was that it involved Lucas. "She just... blamed me, I guess."

Hunter stared at me for a long moment, his eyes searching mine like he was trying to decide whether or not to believe that lie, too. I knew he didn't, but it didn't stop me from holding his gaze, refusing to back down, and when he didn't push further, I let out a small breath of relief until my stupid mind decided I had a question for him.

"Do all the visions that Guardians have come true?"

He gave me that look again, the one that felt like he was peeling back every one of my layers and studying them in depth. It unnerved me, yet it thrilled me all at once.

"No," he said after a pause, and I held my breath. "Ascendant Guardians are still learning, so their visions aren't always... accurate."

"What do you mean?"

"When you're learning to harness the power of a Guardian, sometimes your fears and worries can get mixed up with the different visionary pathways." He shrugged, sliding his hands into his pockets. "It creates scenes that feel real, but they just reflect what you're afraid of."

I mulled over his words, feeling a sense of relief that perhaps what Veronica saw was just her fears manifesting into one.

Before I could ask him more, the shrill wail of an alarm shattered the quiet atmosphere of the library. The sound wasn't just loud—it felt alive, vibrating through the walls, the floor, and into my chest.

"What the hell is that?" I gasped, pressing my hands over

my ears.

Hunter's expression hardened instantly, his entire body tensing. "The barriers."

"What about them?" I demanded, panic clawing its way into my throat.

He turned to me. "It means the barriers to Celestia have been compromised, and someone that is not one of us has managed to get in."

My stomach dropped before he grabbed my hand and yanked me to a nearby window.

"Do you see that?" he said, pointing to where a shimmering barrier stretched across the horizon, its surface flickering. "That's not supposed to happen."

I frowned, wrapping my arms tightly around myself. 'What's causing it?'

He hesitated, his gaze fixed on the barriers. "The barriers are alive in their own way. They're woven from Celestial energy, tied to the balance of our realms. When that balance shifts— when demons gain too much power, or there is corruption within Celestials and Ascendants—the barriers weaken."

I swallowed hard, my chest tightening as the blaring of alarms increased. "So why now? What's changed?"

"I don't know." Hunter's jaw clenched. "Just stay here." He changed subjects and started toward the exit. I hesitated for only a few seconds before deciding to follow. He turned to me, making me almost bump into him. "Grace," he warned.

'I'm not staying here. I'm not a dog that you can—'

"Then what are you, Grace? Because you seem awfully eager to disobey."

I glowered. "I'll disobey if I want—"

He didn't stay to listen as he began to walk away before pausing and turning to look at me. There was something so fierce and promising in his words as he spoke, "I'll come back for you." And with that, he disappeared through the doors of the library.

I stood there frozen for a moment, trying to gather myself. The library suddenly felt small, too distracting, too exposed. The alarms had quieted into a distant sound, but the eerie feeling that followed was somehow worse. I bit down on my lip as I backed up into the shadows between two towering shelves.

"Cherub?" I whispered as if he would appear and protect me, but the little deity never came. The minutes crawled by, each one more excruciating than the last. All I could think was, who had breached the barriers? Would the Riftkeeper's know we're here? Was it demons?

My mind was on overdrive, thinking of the worst possible scenarios involving Hunter not coming back. Why would he, after all? If he was so adamant about wanting me to leave this place, maybe he'll make sure I do after today.

Then, I heard it. The soft creak of the library doors opening. I'd spoken too soon. He did come back.

Relief washed over me briefly as I peered around the edge of the bookshelf, but when I saw a scrawny figure moving quietly through the aisles, I realized it wasn't Hunter, and panic consumed me instead.

I dared not breathe as the man, with his face hidden beneath the hood of his jacket, made precise movements as if searching for something or someone.

My pulse pounded louder, and I tried to think. I started to creep through the stacks, keeping my body low. My fingers brushed the spine of old heavy books as I manoeuvred my way around the library. There was an opening for the entrance. I could run quick before he caught me, or I could—

Stop running, Grace. That's all you do. You always run and wait for someone else to save you.

My hands trembled as that voice spoke inside my head, the same one that would tell me I was worthless.

I closed my eyes, knowing that what I was doing was just as foolish either way. I backed up onto another shelf and reached for a heavy book. The footsteps of the intruder seemed to get louder, and I took a deep breath before I lunged out, the book raised high and ready to slam it down on the person's head—

"Grace!"

I froze, my body stiffening as the book hovered inches above Hunter's head.

"What the fuck are you doing?" he asked, his voice sounding exasperated.

"I—" I lowered the book as my face flushed bright red from embarrassment. "There was someone here, I thought—" I stopped myself, my hands still shaking.

His eyes narrowed, processing my words. He glanced around us, checking the front and then behind him. "What did you see?"

I shook my head, feeling ridiculous, yet my chest was heaving. "A man. He was wearing a jacket, but I couldn't see his face. I just knew it wasn't you—"

Before I could say more, a scream echoed outside the library, and my knees buckled at the shrilling sound. I looked up at Hunter, wide-eyed. His shoulders tensed before he grabbed my arm and pulled me toward the door.

We sprinted down the stairs, the sound of our footsteps swallowed by the growing chaos outside Nadael's office. My chest tightened as we rounded the corner where a small crowd had gathered, their faces pale.

And that was when I saw him.

Lucas.

He lay crumpled on the cold stone floor, his body bent at unnatural angles. Blood pooled beneath him, dark and viscous, spreading in thick rivers. My breath caught, and for a moment, the world tilted.

"No," I whispered, the word barely audible over the panicked voices around me. My legs refused to move, rooting me to the spot as the image of Lucas's lifeless body burned into my mind.

Something's happening to my brother!

This is all your fault!

You did this!

Hunter's hand clamped on my arm, steadying me before I could collapse. "We need to go."

"I can't—"

"Now, Grace," he snapped, his grip tightening as he pulled me away. The world blurred around me, but Lucas's broken form stayed vivid, etched into the darkness behind my eyelids.

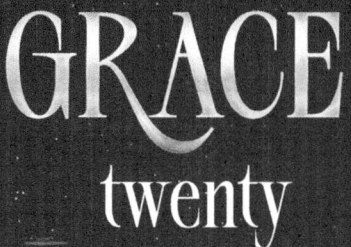

GRACE
twenty

The courtyard buzzed with movement and whispers, but it all felt muted, like I was hearing everything through water as I stood beside Hunter. My feet felt rooted to the ground; my breath shallow as I thought about the blood. The way Lucas's body had been twisted and broken. The image wouldn't leave my mind, no matter how tightly I closed my eyes.

"Grace!" Marnie's voice broke through the haze as she threw her arms around me, and for a moment, I let her warmth anchor me. But even her embrace couldn't drown out the whispers around us.

"She was there."

"Maybe the intruder was after her."

"Told you humans don't belong here. They ruin everything."

Each word stabbed deeper, and I pulled away, unable to meet Marnie's concerned gaze. I wanted to tell her that I wasn't okay, that I wasn't fine, but then I saw Joe.

He was standing with a group of Celestials near the back

doors that led to all those paintings I'd seen. My heart sank into my chest when his gaze locked on mine, and his steps quickened as he pushed through the crowd to reach me.

"Grace," he breathed, his hands landing on my shoulders as his gaze frantically searched me for any possible injuries. "Are you hurt? Did you have anyone with you?"

I shook my head, but the words wouldn't come. The shock of everything that had happened buried itself deep inside me. Lucas—oh god, did Veronica know?

Joe's hands tightened on my shoulders, his brows furrowing in concern as I began to breathe fast and shallow.

I *couldn't* breathe.

Someone help me.

I couldn't—I couldn't—

"She's having a panic attack," Hunter said, forcing Joe to finally look his way. Hunter pulled me away from Joe and sat me down on the staircase. He bent down to meet me at eye level, and I clutched my chest as if I could somehow pry it open and let some air in to breathe. "Hey?" he said, but it sounded so distant.

"Grace?" I think that was Marnie.

I knew people were staring, but it didn't matter. I could do the most embarrassing thing in front of everyone right now, and I wouldn't care, just as long as I could breathe again.

Hunter muttered something to Marnie, and she came over. She sat beside me as I struggled to speak, and nausea crawled up my throat like an unwanted guest.

She placed her hand over mine, which was pressed against my chest. Her eyes closed, and a glow emanated from her palm as it radiated onto me. A surge of energy pulsed between us. The tightness in my chest eased, and an overwhelming sense of peacefulness filled me.

My breathing gradually slowed, and my eyes locked on Marnie as the soft glow around her faded, leaving her looking tired but steady. She took a deep breath, and I blinked, exhaustion sweeping over me now that the intensity had passed.

Marnie gave me a small, sheepish smile, shrugging slightly. "I can also do emotional healing."

Tears welled up in my eyes with a sense of gratitude I couldn't contain. I hugged her tightly, my voice barely a whisper, "Thank you."

As I held her, my gaze drifted toward Hunter, still kneeling in the same spot, watching us silently. Something flickered in my chest, and I couldn't quite place whether it was finally a truce between us or what, but I think he felt it himself as he looked away from me.

"Grace... what—" Joe was staring down at me, his face twisted with worry, but he didn't have time to finish as the sound of Nadael's voice filled the entrance.

Marnie and I rose to our feet, though it felt as if my legs had fallen asleep. My knees almost buckled, but Hunter caught me upright as I placed my palm flat against his chest.

"Ascendants," Nadael called out, and I pushed myself away from Hunter, looking up to the first-floor balcony where Nadael was staring down at us. "I am sure you are all concerned about the events that took place today. After an immense search, we were unable to locate the attacker. This has sadly led to one fatality—" Her eyes flickered for the briefest moment, landing on Joe and other Celestials before continuing. "For now, everyone is to return to their dorms immediately," Nadael commanded, but I barely heard her. My mind was still trapped in the image of Lucas's broken body, the blood pooling beneath

157

him...

"It was a demon," someone murmured.

"How did it get through?" another replied.

"The barriers must be failing."

Nadael raised her hands, silencing the crowd. "The *demon* that infiltrated our grounds was nothing of the ordinary. It knew exactly where to strike and when. This was deliberate." Her gaze swept over us, sharp and unyielding. 'Rest assured the Angelic Council will investigate. Until then, the barriers have been reinforced. No one enters or leaves Celestia without our permission."

My stomach churned, and I felt the familiar panic rise again.

Nadael didn't give any further explanation or offer any comfort. She was all business-like, and her focus was entirely on containing the situation as the crowd began to disperse, adults and children moving back toward the dorms in hushed whispers.

I stood there, as did Marnie and Hunter. When Joe turned to face me, I couldn't help but blurt out, "I want to leave with you."

I didn't want to be here anymore, not after seeing Lucas, not after everything.

All it took was for this to happen and for Hunter to get his wish of me begging to leave this place.

For a brief moment, Joe's face tightened, revealing a strange flicker within his emerald eyes. He hesitated like he was holding something back. 'Grace... I can't." He sighed. "Just go back to your dorm."

I frowned, hating that answer. "Why can't I leave with you? Didn't you see what happened today? This place is just as dangerous, if not more than, the Riftkeeper's."

He pressed his lips into a thin line, and the usual warmth in

158

his eyes was now replaced by something colder. "It's best if you stay here with the others. I'll be nearby for the investigation. But please, for now, just stay in your room."

Frustration flared inside me, but I didn't have the energy to argue. In fact, I didn't have the energy for anything at all.

I nodded reluctantly as Marnie, and I hooked arms, and she led me away. I cast one last glance at Joe before following Hunter out the door.

HUNTER

twenty one

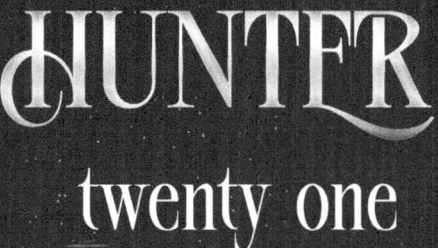

The dorm was quiet, the kind you could feel pulsing with unresolved tension. Grace sat quietly on the sofa, her knees drawn up close to her chest while Silas paced back and forth across the room. You could sense his frustration erupting in waves. It was unsettling and also fucking annoying.

"Would you stop moving around so much?" Brandon came over to Grace with a cup of tea, setting it down gently in front of her. He shot Silas a glance. "You're starting to piss us off."

Silas ignored him, his agitation only growing as he muttered. "I don't get how you're all so calm. Veronica just lost her brother, and we're sitting here... doing fuck all."

I could tell where this was headed. It wasn't the first time Silas had lashed out after something went wrong. He ticked like a bomb and exploded like one when provoked.

He stopped pacing, his eyes drifting over to Grace, who sat silently staring at the floor. "And don't think for a second I don't know why Veronica's vision went to shit." His voice dripped with anger, making me straighten up from the doorway. "She blamed you; you were in her vision. So, somehow, you're at the center of it all. It wouldn't surprise me if the barriers came down because of you."

"Silas," I warned, watching as Grace flinched at Silas's words. "Pack it in."

Silas's eyes flashed with anger as he looked at me. "What? Don't act like you care now, Cain." His lips curled into a bitter sneer. "You hated her not long ago, remember? Or has that suddenly changed from one day to the next?"

His words hit me sharper than I expected. Grace glanced over at me, defeated, as if she knew all of this and didn't want to hear it again. She was used to it. She was always used to people disliking her.

I swallowed hard, trying to keep my temper from rising as I went over to Silas, placing a hand over his chest. "Take a breather, alright?" I said, keeping my voice as calm and as level as I could. "Go to your room and do whatever you must but just calm down before you say anything else you'll regret."

Silas's jaw clenched, and his body was still wound tight as we stared each other down. After a minute or so, he shoved his hands into his pocket and stormed off down the hall, the door to his room slamming shut behind him, rattling the walls.

I exhaled slowly, turning to face Brandon and Grace as she sat there, looking smaller than I'd ever seen her be before.

"I didn't—" Her voice trembled as she glanced between me and Brandon. "I swear, I had nothing to do with it; you were there in the library with me when it happened. I—"

I looked at her, feeling the strong urge to wrap her in my arms and tell her that she didn't need to worry. But that wasn't the case. People were scared, and when they were scared, they needed someone to blame. And in this case, it would likely fall on her.

"I know," I whispered. "But that doesn't mean anyone else will believe it."

Her eyes met mine, wide and full of that devastating look that made me want to fix everything, even though I knew I couldn't. Brandon reached over, giving her a reassuring pat on the shoulder as if to lift the mood.

"The Council will investigate," I continued. "Until they find out what actually happened, the Ascendants here are going to look for someone to blame. And right now, you're the easiest target."

Grace looked down and sighed. I didn't know Lucas as well as others did. He was always in his own world, getting through Azrael's classes and spending time with his twin sister. When he befriended Grace, I thought how disgustingly irritating it was that she found a friend. Now, she'd lost him in the time she'd spent here, and I felt like absolute shit.

"You didn't do anything, Grace," I added as if that would make things better between us. "And that's what matters. Let them think what they want, but it won't change the truth."

Grace nodded slowly, but the uncertainty was still there, lingering in her eyes. "I thought... you'd be happy right now."

I frowned.

She looked up, her eyes glossed over with tears. "I asked Joe to take me away from here. That's what you wanted, right?"

Brandon glanced at me, and a pang of guilt hit my chest.

Yes, I did. I wanted her gone, and, in many ways, I still did. But maybe, just maybe, I should give her the chance that my brother didn't get to have.

I found myself crouching beside her, wanting to comfort the shit out of her. "Turns out I've changed my mind."

Her brows drew in together. She was confused. So was I.

"I want you to stay here," Brandon said, taking the brunt of

163

my words with him as both Grace and I looked over at him. "I also know that you would never willingly hurt someone. I mean, I wasn't with you at the time, but you're Grace." He chuckled. "The worst you've done so far is take too long in the shower."

I smirked at the memory, and Grace gave him a shaky smile that never quite reached her eyes.

"I didn't actually shower for that long," she whispered, making Brandon frown. "I just got out and let the water keep on running while I got ready. It worked though, huh?"

Brandon blinked at her and then he started to laugh. His eyes creased with unkept humor, and I watched as that smile on Grace finally reached her Bambi eyes.

165

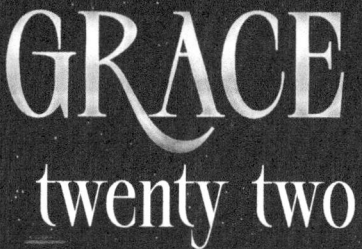

GRACE
twenty two

"Lucas!" My breath came in quick gasps as I shot up from the bed and glanced around my bedroom. I ran a hand through my damp curls, the image of Lucas's lifeless body still vivid behind my eyelids. I swallowed, trying to calm the pounding in my chest. A nightmare wasn't the best way to wake up to, especially one that involved your recently deceased friend.

I shook my head, blinking away the tears threatening to push through and swung my legs over the bed. It was barely 7 o'clock in the morning, but the kitchen light was already on. As I padded barefoot toward it, the unmistakable sizzle of something frying filled the air before a waft of bacon hit my nose.

Hunter stood at the stove, spatula in one hand while moving with the kind of focus he had on everything else. He was shirtless, his combat jacket tossed over a nearby chair, and the muscles in his back flexed as he shifted.

My chest began pounding again.

"You're cooking?" My voice came out squeakier than I had intended it to, and I mentally wanted to hit myself.

"Morning to you too, Bambi," he said without turning around. "Figured someone should make sure we didn't starve."

I crossed my arms, looking at a stack of plates sitting on the counter. The smell of eggs and toast lingered in the air. "Any updates from the Celestials?"

His movements faltered for a fraction of a second before he flipped the eggs as if he were on an episode of MasterChef. "Nothing yet," he said quietly.

I nodded, swallowing the lump that had formed in my throat. I'd hoped I would wake up today and for my nightmare to just be that. A nightmare. But I wasn't so fortunate in that department.

"How are you holding up?" he asked, glancing at me. His grey eyes locked on mine, searching, and I immediately stiffened under his gaze.

"I'm doing fine." A lie if he ever saw one.

He raised an eyebrow. "Sure, you are."

We stared at each other, the silence stretching longer than it should. I think he was waiting for me to fess up and tell him that I was far from *fine*, but just as I was about to do that, Brandon burst into the kitchen, his blonde hair looking like a bird's nest.

"It smells so fucking good out here." He clapped his hands and rubbed them together as he peered at the breakfast buffet Hunter had cooked up.

Hunter shot him an annoyed look. "Here's your vegetarian breakfast," he grumbled, pushing a plate of grilled tomatoes and mushrooms toward Brandon.

Brandon squinted at it. "You call this a fry-up? Where are

168

the hash browns? The beans? The brown sauce!"

"I'm not your personal chef. You want your hash browns? Get Silas to buy the food next time."

"Silas would just spend our monthly allowance within the first five minutes if he went shopping."

Hunter shrugged. "Not my problem. Now, if you don't want it, I'll eat it."

Brandon snatched the plate before Hunter could take it back. "I didn't say I wasn't eating it. Hey, are those eggs runny by any chance?"

Hunter rolled his eyes as Brandon scooped up some eggs and took a bite out of his toast. I wanted to smile for a moment but the light-heartedness of it all shattered when Silas appeared in the doorway. His long dark hair was unkempt, and his expression was too cold not to go unnoticed.

Silas's gaze landed on me, and his jaw clenched. "What's she still doing here?"

Brandon's smile disappeared as he dropped the plate back on the counter and walked up to Silas.

"Look," I began, trying to ease the situation, "I know you're angry. And about Veronica—"

Silas scoffed, cutting me off. "I'm not angry."

I frowned.

"I'm just pissed."

Now, I blinked, feeling as though I had missed something here.

"Pissed is the same as being angry, my guy," Brandon said, but I didn't think Silas was in the mood to be educated on what those words meant.

Silas ignored him and took a few steps forward until he was standing over me. Brandon followed closely behind, while Hunter's grip tightened against the counter. "Listen, I don't

169

care if you're not an Ascendant or how you were brought up; what I do care about is that Veronica saw you in that vision of hers, and it hurt her. That's my problem."

The way he said Veronica's name—it was raw, like it clawed its way out of his throat, leaving behind something jagged and broken. It wasn't just a simple name to him. It was a wound he couldn't hide, and the dark circles under his eyes told me he hadn't slept. That made two of us. But I couldn't bring myself to ask what it was between him and Veronica. Not when his gaze locked on me as if he were silently weighing the reasons to keep hating me.

"I wasn't the only one there when it happened," I said quietly, almost like my voice didn't believe me either. "I just want to make things right."

Silas let out a dry laugh. "Oh, you want to make it right, do you? Fine." He took a step back and looked me up and down. "Get naked for me. Go on, you've seen all of me; it's only fair I see some of you."

My stomach dropped.

"Silas," Hunter warned, but if I knew anything about Silas by now, it was that he enjoyed pushing people too far.

Unfortunately for him, I was in no mood to play any of his games as I raised my hand and slapped him clean across the face.

Silas's head snapped to the side and the room went completely still.

Brandon blinked. "Holy shit—"

But before he could finish, Silas calmly turned and slapped Brandon across the face.

I jumped.

"What the fuck, man?!" Brandon clutched his cheek, looking all confused. He then turned toward Hunter, his hand twitching like he was about to run over to him and retaliate, but Hunter just raised a brow in warning. Brandon hesitated before turning back and slapping Silas again.

What the hell just happened here?

Silas didn't even flinch this time. He rubbed his jaw thoughtfully and let out a low chuckle. "Okay," he muttered, giving me a slow, considering nod. "I respect you a little more now... I needed that wakeup call, although I was never going to actually let you get naked in front of me."

I rolled my eyes. It was hard to believe him. Ever.

"I would say we do that behind closed doors, since I am a gentleman after all—"

"Silas," Hunter snapped, causing Silas to raise his palms. At least he seemed back to his usual aggravating self.

"Great slap, by the way," he said, then pointed a finger at me. "Still not a hundred percent sold on you, though."

"Yeah, well, I'm not exactly here wanting to collect any approval ratings from you," I shot back.

"Good. Saves me the trouble."

Hunter let out an exasperated sigh, dragging a hand down his face while Brandon still looked offended, rubbing his reddened cheek.

"I'm just saying," Brandon huffed. "Why did *I* get slapped?"

Silas grinned at his friend. "Collateral damage."

"You're both fucking idiots," Hunter muttered under his breath, and somehow, that all felt like progress.

I was about to say something else, but before I could, a loud pounding sounded at the door. Everyone froze, glancing at one another.

"What the fuck?" Brandon asked.

Hunter strode to the door, peering through the peephole before opening it cautiously. He glanced around the hallway, then bent down and picked up a piece of paper off the floor. As he unfolded it, his expression darkened.

"What does it say?" I asked, my stomach twisting as if part of me already knew it would be directed at me.

He turned it around, and the word *KILLER* was scrawled in bold, black letters.

My heart sank.

Hunter crumpled the note and tossed it into the bin. "Ignore it. They're just cowards who won't say it to your face."

Brandon nodded in agreement, but his easy going demeanor couldn't mask the concern and pity in his eyes. Despite Hunter's words, the sting from the note lingered, and I knew I was once again a pariah in a school environment. Not like I ever got out of that title.

"Hey," Brandon said softly, stepping closer and brushing a hand lightly against my arm. I blinked, looking up at him as my vision blurred. "You're fine, okay?" he assured me. "Right, Silas? She's *fine* isn't she?" He turned toward Silas, his brows raised in an unspoken challenge.

Silas hesitated, his gaze shifting between Brandon and me before exhaling slowly. "Yeah, I guess," he mumbled.

Even with their reassurances, a small part of me still wavered. I'm not sure what Hunter and I were, and while Silas looked less resentful than before, I was still their unwanted roommate.

Hunter's phone buzzed, and he pulled it out of his pocket. His brows furrowed as he read the message, and tension settled into his shoulders. "I've got to go and meet with Azrael," he said, slipping the phone back into his pocket.

"Wait." I frowned. "I thought that we weren't supposed to leave our sectors after what happened?"

"It's just something about training," he dismissed, grabbing

172

a shirt from one of the stools. Brandon and Silas exchanged glances but said nothing, and something about their silence made me uneasy.

As Hunter grabbed his jacket and headed for the door, I suddenly couldn't help but call after him, "Be careful."

He paused, looking back at me, and I felt my cheeks burn. "Always," he said before disappearing into the hallway.

GRACE
twenty three

I was going insane.

It had been six days since I last left the dorm or breathed in fresh air that didn't reek of male body spray and unwashed dishes.

Nadael had given strict instructions: I was to be excused from training following the loss of Lucas.

Meanwhile, Brandon had taken it upon himself to visit me every day, casually dropping updates like, *"Hunter beat the crap out of Matias in training again."* That was the only thing that made me smile.

Joe had come by once too, checking in on me, though his answers were vague anytime I asked how the investigation was going.

To top it off, my hair had gone full rebellion mode without my curling cream, and sleep had become a myth.

By Sunday, I decided enough was enough.

I flung my bedroom door open—only to have Brandon and Silas collapse into the room, landing flat on their backs with startled groans. They must've been leaning against my door the entire time.

Silas clutched his head like he'd just been assaulted by reality, while Brandon blinked up at the ceiling, barely able to keep his eyes open.

"What are you guys doing outside my room?"

Brandon was the first to rise to his feet, letting out a yawn. "Making sure no one tries to come for you."

A single brow rose. "Why would they come for me? You said I would fine and besides, aren't they all meant to be righteous and... whatnot?" Though after the 'KILLER' note, I doubted that.

He sighed. "Some Ascendants won't care, or at least they are trying to scare you. Plus, there's been... a few more rumors going around the Warriors Sector that you are working with the Riftkeeper's and killed Lucas yourself."

I frowned. "How does that even make sense?"

"It doesn't." Silas grunted, still rubbing the side of his head.

My gaze went to him, and I wondered why he was here with Brandon in the first place. "I thought you still didn't trust me?" At least that is what I overheard from his conversation with Brandon the other night.

"Look." He rubbed a hand down his face. "Just because I still find you somewhat guilty, I also trust in Cain. If he says you didn't do it, then maybe you didn't."

I nodded in suspicion. That didn't sound like Silas to be reasonable.

"And also, I was threatened by both of these numpties into protecting you, so—ow!" he shouted as Brandon kicked him.

I chuckled for the first time this week, but I couldn't help but wonder where Hunter was. It was definitely insanity taking over my mind if I was questioning why he wasn't here once

176

again.

A knock at the door interrupted the strange encounter with the boys, and they pushed me back into the room in a ridiculous protective stance.

I rolled my eyes, squeezing past them. "Relax, it's Marnie. I texted her to try and sneak out so she could come over."

"Marnie?" I heard Brandon ask from behind before I opened the door.

Marnie shot past me, wearing earmuffs over her copper hair and a fluffy white coat. "You will not believe the looks I've been getting just by coming up here. They all looked like they either wanted to punch me in the face or stab me in the stomach!" She faced me as I closed the door behind me. "I swear, since everyone knows I'm your friend, they think I'm your minion or something."

I cleared my throat, looking past her shoulder.

She turned and almost jumped when she saw a shirtless Brandon and a partially nude Silas standing there. "Oh." Her voice took on a timid tone. "Hi."

Brandon raised his hand to the back of his neck, equally looking just as shy. "Hey."

She instantly spun around again and mouthed the word *WOW* at me.

I held back a chuckle before grabbing her hand and whizzing past the boys into my bedroom. Shutting the door, I let Marnie take her coat and earmuffs off as she stared at the lack of decoration I had in there. After a minute or two, she turned around and smacked her lips. "You know, when you messaged me to come round, I didn't expect to see Brandon and Silas. I thought they'd be out training."

"It's a Sunday," I deadpanned. "Besides, no one is allowed to leave Celestia's grounds until the matter is resolved." Not that I could leave, even if it *was* resolved.

"And? Have you not seen them? They look like they're always training with all those muscles; also, let's not forget the abs on Silas. I mean, did you see them?"

I've seen a lot more, unfortunately.

I passed her, pulling the blinds open and letting what little sun we had into my room. "They said they're *protecting* me."

"Really?" she mused. "Wow, who would have thought, huh?"

Not me, apparently.

Huffing out a breath, I turned to see she was already sitting on my bed. She patted the free space beside her, and I came over and settled onto the springy mattress.

"So..." she said. "Is everything okay? Well, I know it probably isn't; I mean, I've hardly been able to sleep since it happened."

"Me neither." I sighed, resting my head on her shoulder. The only other thing I had resorted to was researching and wallowing. Otherwise, I would picture Lucas on the floor, lifeless, every time I even so much as blinked.

Marnie's head tipped against mine, and we stayed like that for a few minutes before I couldn't hold it any longer.

"Marnie?"

She hummed.

"What do you know about the Grand War?"

She straightened and looked at me like I had gone insane. I basically had. "The Grand War? Grace, why—"

"Just enlighten me, will you?"

Since I hadn't gone back to the library after that day, the only other thing on my mind was what the cherub said.

Marnie let out a resigned breath. "I just know that it happened way before our time."

"Yeah, but after it ended," I prodded. "There was a treaty formed, right? Angels and demons could remain on earth as long as they didn't kill one another."

She looked at me, confused. "Okay?"

"A demon killed Lucas," I stated. "He was an Ascendant; wouldn't that mean the treaty is broken?"

At that, her expression fell into a pitiful look. "Grace, that treaty was forged a long time ago. Demons have still been killing other Celestials for a while now, as have angels in return, making that treaty null."

Oh.

I glanced down at the ground in disappointment. "I just thought—"

"Thought, what? That another war could start just because of Lucas? We're not the first this has happened to."

Right. Things had changed over the centuries, and even Joe hadn't mentioned anything about the Grand War. It was likely just that. The past.

I nodded, then looked at my hands and nibbled on my bottom lip. Marnie watched me carefully as I expelled a breath and glanced her way. "I think I saw him."

"Who?"

"The one who killed Lucas."

Her lips parted in confusion, but I spoke before she could.

"He was there when I was in the library." I retraced my steps from that day and shook my head. "I thought I could get to him with a bloody book. Can you believe that? A book."

"Anyone would have done the same—"

"No. A Warrior would have fought him, and maybe that's what Lucas did before he…" I didn't finish what I was about to say and heaved out another heavy sigh instead. "I just don't want to be weak anymore, Marnie."

She placed a hand on my upper back. "But Grace, you're not weak."

"I feel like I am." And I wanted it to stop. "We haven't got much left until the competition. I have until then to change the Council's mind on why I should be given the chance that every Ascendant has."

Marnie jumped up from my bed. "You're kidding, right? Grace, not even a week ago did you want to participate in something like that. I mean, I would still support you if you wanted to do it but—"

"I don't want to do the competition," I was quick to add. "I just want..."

Marnie sat back down. "To prove yourself?" She suggested softly, and I shook my head.

"No," I said. "I want... others to see me as a threat. I want angels and demons to know my name and realize that a human can do both."

"But Grace—"

"I don't want to be protected all my life. So far, that's all it's ever been for me. I want to be able to do it for myself... for others."

Marnie pursed her lips and nodded. "Okay," she whispered. "Then if that is what you want, maybe you should learn from the best." Her eyes drifted towards the closed door.

The boys.

"Would they even want to help me?"

She shrugged. "I think the one who would go above and beyond to physically improve someone's skills would be Hunter. He's the best of the class. Azrael's prodigy, if you will. If he doesn't get chosen for the competition or win it, then I bet he'll still be Ascended sooner or later. He's been here for years now."

180

I mulled that over, but I doubted he would willingly help me. Things were still off between us. Lucas's death hadn't changed that. Him asking the boys to protect me was likely to save face. "Maybe", I said, giving her a tight-lipped smile and resting my head on her shoulder again.

GRACE

twenty four

L ater that same night, I sat at my desk, with my chin resting against my arm, as I drew random things on a piece of paper. It had been hours since Marnie left that I was beginning to think I had found a new talent in drawing. *I hadn't.*

Eventually, I heard a noise. It was faint, but it sounded like the boys were talking.

I sat up, frowning. It wasn't the usual banter I would hear from them. This was something different.

Standing, I cracked open my door, peering into our small living room. Brandon and Silas were awkwardly carrying someone between them—someone slumped, their feet dragging against the floor. I cleared my throat, and as soon as they heard me, they panicked, dropping the person behind the sofa.

Both Brandon and Silas were the picture of fake innocence as I crossed my arms and raised an eyebrow.

"What did you just drop behind there?"

"Nothing," Brandon and Silas said at the same time, a little too quickly.

Brandon cleared his throat. "You're up late. That's no good if you want enough beauty sleep."

I narrowed my eyes, walking towards them. When I glanced behind the sofa, my eyes widened. "Oh my god!" The words left me in a gasp as I saw that the person they'd dropped so carelessly was Hunter, bloodied, battered, and barely conscious.

I dropped to my knees beside him, my hands hovering over him, unsure of where to even start. "What happened?"

"He went into town," Silas said, to which Brandon slapped the back of his head.

"What?" I shot back. Concern and, most of all, anger seeped into my chest. "How did he even get into town if there were no buses this weekend? H—how did he not get caught? Actually, scratch that. Who the hell did *this*?"

Brandon and Silas exchanged a look.

Silas sighed first. "Well..."

"Well, what?"

"There's this car," he admitted. "It's a rusty old thing, really. We found it years ago in the woods, and Hunter taught himself how to drive it. I'm surprised it still even works."

I stared at him, then at Brandon, nodding along. "How were you guys ever chosen to be Ascendants?"

"Um, we were chosen before birth?" Silas shrugged and made a face. "So, that's not really our fault."

I scowled, feeling a rush of frustration run through my veins. "Why didn't you take him to the Healers Sector?"

"No one's allowed out of their designated dorms after nine." Silas scoffed. "Plus, it'd just be too risky."

Unbelievable.

"You allowed Hunter to leave the academy when there's a whole ban set in place and didn't think that was risky enough?"

I always questioned where Hunter was at times, but I believed him when he said he was meeting Azrael for extra training. I didn't expect *this*.

Brandon grimaced. "Grace—"

"Aaron," Hunter mumbled.

I frowned, glancing back at Brandon. "Aaron?"

Brandon sighed, a heavy look passing between him and Silas. "That's his brother's name."

"His brother?" I said slowly, not understanding anything.

"Yeah," Silas said, his voice suddenly quiet. "Hunter's been searching for him."

I stared at Hunter, at the pain etched on his bruised face. "I thought his brother died?"

"That's what Cain thought, too," Silas explained. "But then he got a letter that seemed to be from Aaron, telling Cain he was still alive and needed help."

"And he believed it?"

"He was so sure that it was Aaron's handwriting," Brandon said. "But ever since then, he's risked himself and his position at the academy by looking for him."

My heart broke then. Everything I had said to Hunter—the day out in the pit, the moment we were together in the common room... he had been looking for his brother all along.

"Do you think this could be a Riftkeeper's doing, then?" I asked, glancing at the slash across his chest.

"If it was, I don't know why they'd keep him alive," Silas said, and I shook my head at the thought. "It doesn't make sense, really. It doesn't even make sense that his brother would still be alive."

It was hope. Hunter was willing to take the risk if there was even the slightest possibility of his brother being alive. Anyone would.

"Come on," I said as I stood up. "Help me at least get him to his room."

The boys gently lifted Hunter by the arms and carried him into his room. We laid him down on the bed, and I quickly turned to Brandon.

"Grab me a bowl of water, disinfectants and some clean cloths."

Brandon nodded and hurried off while Silas lingered by the doorway, looking torn between wanting to help and feeling guilty.

I sat down beside Hunter, my hands shaking slightly as I began to rip his t-shirt, revealing cuts and skin glistening with sweat and blood. I blew out a shaky breath just as Brandon came back with the bowl of water and a cloth. I began to clean the blood from his face, wiping away the dirt and grime. His injuries weren't as many as I thought, but whoever had done this had given him a gash that seemed borderline punishing.

His chest rose with every deep breath he took, and I watched as he stirred and winced whenever I touched an injured spot. For once, he looked vulnerable. One could almost assume that he wasn't the temperamental person I'd seen him be.

I squeezed the excess water into the bowl and dabbed at his skin. He felt warm under my fingers, and I contemplated texting Marnie. I didn't want to get her in trouble, but something like this should be healed by an actual Healer with abilities, not someone pressing a damp cloth to his body.

His eyes fluttered open for a brief moment, unfocused but soft, like he was barely there. When his hand twitched, it brushed against mine, and I froze.

But it wasn't the contact that made me stop—it was the glint of gold.

I slowly turned his hand over, and there it was. My ring still wrapped around his pinky.

My throat tightened.

He hadn't thrown it away like I thought he would have.

"Do you need us to get anything else?" Brandon whispered.

I blinked from my stupor and glanced over my shoulder. "No, it's fine. I'll take care of it."

He seemed skeptical. "You sure?"

I nodded. It wasn't the first time I had to tend to someone. Often, Joe had gotten into a tiff with a Riftkeeper, prompting us to move from place to place.

Brandon didn't say another word as he slipped out of Hunter's room, leaving the door to creak shut behind him. I stayed for a few minutes, perched silently at Hunter's side, listening to the steady rhythm of his breathing as it evened out. Knowing he was in less pain was a strange kind of comfort.

Eventually, I stood, hesitant to leave. My gaze wandered around his room, caught between the urge to stay and the feeling that I might be overstaying.

The walls were painted a cool grey, the exact shade of his eyes when they darkened with thought. I turned slowly, taking in the small, unassuming details such as posters of old classic cars and bands, until a neatly stacked pile of CDs by his desk caught my attention. My fingers drifted over the covers, lingering on one with Bon Jovi across it. Beneath it was a collection of soul music and alternative rock.

A quiet laugh escaped me.

Of course, this was his musical taste.

On the left side of the desk, a CD player stood out among the otherwise sparse space. I grabbed a CD from the stack, slipping the disc into the player and pressing play. A familiar melody began to fill the room, and I checked the back of the CD cover to see it was the song Power of Love by Frankie Goes to Hollywood.

A smile tugged at my lips as I closed my eyes, letting the music seep into my chest. The rhythm swayed through me, gentle and steady. Without thinking, I let myself move to it, my body rocking softly to the sound.

"Grace?"

My eyes widened as I spun around, almost knocking my back into Hunter's desk. He was there on his bed, his eyes half-lidded, staring at me.

Panic embedded itself in my chest, and I rushed toward him, pressing the back of my hand to his forehead. "Shit, you're burning up. I think I have painkillers in my room, or if you want, I can text Marnie. She might still be awake, and maybe I could try to sneak out and get her to come—"

He shook his head, pulling me towards him. I fell onto the bed, my hands landing on his chest as my curls went all over my face. He brushed a few strands behind my ear. "You *stayed*." His voice was a mixture of anger and something else—something weakening as his thumb lingered on my cheek. "You stayed even when I didn't want you to. You *keep* staying, Grace, and I wish you wouldn't."

Even in a feverish state, he continued to want me gone. "You need to rest."

His jaw tensed. "I will after I find Aaron."

I huffed, knowing there would be no point in arguing with him. Not when he was like this.

His fingers brushed against my temple, and I froze, caught in the intensity of his gaze. His eyes, usually so guarded, softened as he murmured, "He would've liked you, you know.

My brother." A shiver ran down my spine at the touch of his hand. "The way you challenge me, make me smile when all I want is to despise you... it's maddening. *Infuriating.*"

I let out a startled laugh—more of a snort, really.

His brows furrowed. "What's so funny?"

I licked my lips, the smile still tugging at them. "Nothing, it's just... in the morning, you'll realize everything you've said and regret it."

He shook his head, a faint smile curling at the edges of his mouth as his teeth grazed his bottom lip. "I won't."

I tilted my head, my smile fading into something softer... maybe even sadder. "You will," I whispered, and when I went to stand, his hand shot out, catching mine with a gentle but firm grip.

"Stay with me," he whispered, his voice breaking just enough to make my heart clench. He wasn't fully aware of what he was asking, or maybe he was, but the way he looked at me as if me leaving would shatter him left me no choice but to say yes.

Slowly, I nodded, my heart racing. "Okay," I whispered, squeezing his hand gently. "I'll stay."

He exhaled a soft, relieved sound, and I carefully lay down beside him. My body was tense at first, unsure of where to position myself, but it became clear that space was nothing but a myth to him as his arm wrapped around my waist, pulling my back flush against his chest.

I swallowed hard, feeling the steady rise and fall of his breathing against my neck. His warmth seeped into my skin, and I was afraid of moving and grazing one of his wounds, but it didn't seem to matter to him. He held me with a consuming and comforting fierceness, as if letting go wasn't an option.

"Bambi?" he murmured against my hair.

"Yeah?" I breathed.

His lips brushed lightly against my temple, and he whispered, "You've done the impossible. You made the huntsman put down his bow."

The irony was not lost on me even as my heart went up in flames, leaving me completely and utterly undone.

It was quiet now, and I knew Hunter had fallen asleep within seconds of saying that to me. Still, I stayed there, heart racing against the steady rhythm of his.

HUNTER

twenty five

I woke up to warmth—a soft, steady warmth I hadn't felt for a long time. For a moment, I didn't know where the hell I was. My body ached, and my head felt heavy, yet everything around me seemed too quiet.

And then I felt someone stir against me.

I glanced down at Grace. Her body was curled into mine, her head resting against my chest while one of her legs draped over my thigh. My arm was still wrapped around her waist, holding her close like she belonged there.

It all hit me worse than the beating I had taken last night.

Fuck.

Panic flared in my chest, and I felt my entire body tense. I wasn't sure how we'd ended up like this. Everything was still a blur of pain and exhaustion, but I knew it was wrong.

I jerked upright in bed, with Grace groaning softly as the movement woke her. She blinked, her eyes heavy with sleep as she slowly came to and looked up at me in confusion.

"What—" Her voice was soft, but I cut her off as I rushed

to get out of bed, shaking my head.

"This... we shouldn't have..." I muttered, running a dried, bloodied hand through my hair. "This was a mistake. You shouldn't be in here."

Grace blinked again, sitting up more fully now. "I shouldn't be in here?" Her face twisted as her eyes hardened into something colder, angrier. The same way she looked at me often, except this time, it sounded as if I'd wounded her. "You asked me to stay with you! Here! In *your* bed."

"I didn't mean it!" I shot back, pacing across the room. My head was still foggy, trying to piece together the things after I'd—

"You were hurt." She pushed herself out of the bed. "I was trying to help, and even through all that, you act like it's my fault?"

"I never said that," I growled, but the implication had already been set in stone. She thought it. She believed it. "Look, I shouldn't have let you—"

"Let me?" she interrupted, her posture tense. "I chose to stay with you, Hunter, because you were hurt. Because you did something stupid by going out when there's a ban up, all because you received a supposed letter from your brother."

My jaw twitched, annoyed that she knew that now. Not even Brandon and Silas knew all the details. They understood not to get in the way, even when I could tell they were worried.

"You don't get it," I snapped.

"Yeah, you've said that before, and I think it's bullshit."

Surprise flashed across my face, seeing how she marched towards me with no sense of fear or timidity in her eyes.

"I'm not stupid, Hunter." She stepped closer. "Unlike you, who went in search of someone straight away over the slightest bit of evidence. What if it was a trap? What if whatever

194

happened to you last night didn't just endanger the rest of the Ascendants?"

I clenched my fists because there was so much more to it all. So much that I couldn't tell her—that I couldn't tell anyone.

"Sometimes, I fear for this world," she added after a long pause. "I fear for the next generation of angels—Ascendants like you being the ones guiding and protecting every bit of lifeform because right now, you're behaving selfishly."

I kept to myself, forcing my expression to be neutral even when I knew how much truth was in those words.

She shook her head bitterly at how I was deliberately shutting down in front of her. She stormed past me, slamming the door behind her as she left. The sound echoed through the room, leaving me standing there in silence as I stared at the bed.

GRACE

I was still fuming after this morning's argument with Hunter. Granted, I was horrible to him before I left his room, but I couldn't help it. He angered me more than anyone, even when I knew and told him he would forget he'd ever asked me to stay with him.

My original plan had been to sneak out once he fell into a deep sleep, but that didn't end up happening. I'd grown so comfortable beside him that I didn't want to leave. Truthfully, I wanted to stay like that for a while longer, and it made me want to kick myself just to snap out of that idiotic thought.

My hands were balled into fists as I walked through Celestia, trying to shake off the irritation that clung onto me like a second skin.

As I turned the corner, I nearly collided with Joe and Nadael, who were already in deep conversation. I froze, trying to gather myself before they noticed—especially Joe. Nadael was the first to look up, her sharp eyes softening slightly as they landed on me.

"Grace," Nadael said as she and Joe stopped in front of me. "How are you holding up?"

I forced a smile, though it felt weak. "Better," I replied, trying to convince myself, but even my own mind wasn't buying it. I cleared my throat. "Though I am wondering if I could return to classes as soon as possible – preferably *now.*"

Nadael nodded, glancing towards Joe as if she didn't seem convinced. "Very well. I would imagine it'd be great to get back into a routine. Am I correct to assume so, Joe?"

I looked at Joe, who was watching me with the usual concern mixed with something else I could never quite read.

"Joseph?" Nadael repeated his name.

He blinked, shaking his head. "Apologies, Nadael. You're right; I think Grace would hate to be cooped up in her dorm for another week." He shot me a knowing smile. "Although I do still wish she would participate in the Healers Sector rather than the Warriors."

I wanted to roll my eyes. "Joe, can I talk to you for a second... in private?"

He frowned for a second, then nodded. Nadael seemed to get the hint as she excused herself so she could go and find Eden.

When Joe and I stood in the empty hallway, I crossed my

arms over my chest, hesitant about where to begin, but the words just ended up tumbling out of me: "Do you know how Veronica is doing? She hasn't left her dorm since everything happened, has she?"

Joe sighed, rubbing the back of his neck, and by that, I already knew the answer to my question. "No. She won't talk to anyone. She won't even let a Healer anywhere near her to at least try and help."

I looked down, guilt gnawing at me. I knew Veronica blamed me for Lucas's death. She had her vision, and for whatever reason it may be, she only focused on me.

"And Lucas," I started, swallowing the lump in my throat. 'Why can't he be... resurrected? I mean, you're all angels, right? Surely there is a way around it."

Joe's face hardened. "There are rules, Grace. Strict ones. We can't just—" He sighed. "Look, there are consequences for that kind of interference. The Council wouldn't allow it. Besides, we've spoken about this before. Life should never be tampered with, whether a soul is in heaven, purgatory or even hell."

I refused that answer, even when Joe first told me about it. "What about the Hollow?" I regretted saying the name out loud. I could see it in Joe's eyes as they became a door open to fear and worries. He grabbed my arm and took me further down the hallway to another empty and even quieter corner.

His gaze searched up and down the hallway before settling back on me. "What have I told you about the Hollow, Grace?"

I was silent for a moment.

And then I whispered, "That it is forbidden to talk about."

He nodded as if he was reprimanding me, just as he had when I turned nine years old and found out about it. Nadael had come to visit us, and I spent the evening listening outside the kitchen door to how they spoke of this *place*. A place that was deep within the confines of hell where every Celestial that died in any realm was sent.

I spent nights dreaming about what it could look like. I couldn't shake it out of my head, so I went searching. In libraries, in anything that Joe might have had in his room. It wasn't until he caught me that he finally told me about the Hollow. Every angel and demon were afraid of the Hollow. And whenever I'd ask Joe why these Celestials couldn't return to their homes, he would tell me that their deaths would disrupt the delicate balance between realms.

Perhaps that was where many Celestials ended up after the Grand War.

"Sorry for bringing it up," I mumbled, and I fought to keep my disappointment from showing too much. I had been clinging to some small, impossible hope, but no, life was cruel, even with the existence of Celestials. "I should probably go catch up with the Warriors. I'll talk to you when you're... less busy."

Joe reached out, grabbing my arm gently as his eyes softened in a way that stirred a sense of guilt in my chest. "Grace... I really do wish I could take you away from all of this. Give you the life you deserve away from *here*."

I pulled my arm away, biting back my tongue on the fact that if he wanted that, then why did he take me in when he knew the Celestial world was beyond reach for me? But I also knew that I couldn't see myself in a world where Joe never took care of me. It was all too conflicting.

"I know," I said. "But this has been my life for a long while now, Joe." I didn't want to deal with any more well-meaning reassurances. "Maybe it would be better for me to accept the situation and deal with it, right?"

Without waiting for a reply, I turned and walked away with my heart racing and my mind spinning as I made my way out towards the training grounds. The moment I stepped onto the field, I could feel the eyes of other Ascendants on me, their judgmental glances cutting through the brisk air. Some whispered, others snickered. I didn't need to hear what they were saying to know what it was already.

Azrael was standing at the pit, watching two trainees go up against each other with his usual calculated gaze. When his eyes landed on me, they narrowed, and a wisp of disappointment passed over his face. "Martin," he said. "If you're going to return to my classes, make sure you are early, not the latter."

I didn't respond. I just held my chin up and walked past him, ignoring the looks I was getting from others, including Matias, as the murmurs grew louder as I passed. Words like 'trouble' slipped through the cracks in the conversations around me, making it hurt more than I wanted to admit. It always did.

My eyes then swept over the training grounds until they landed on him—Hunter, standing across the field. The moment our eyes locked, everything else melted away. The argument from this morning, the Ascendant's whispers and lingering stares—all of it disappeared. What only lingered was the memory of last night, the comfort I found in his arms. It was a mess of emotions, tangled and raw, and everything I had tried to suppress crushed into me at once.

Neither of us moved. We just stood there with the weight of unspoken words stretching between us like a fragile thread ready to snap.

I tore my eyes away from his and made my way to the weapons rack. My fingers grazed the weathered wood, the cool metal edges rough beneath my touch. I tried to focus, to calm the whirlwind in my mind, but the sleek blades and polished handles meant nothing to me then. All I wanted was for the chaos inside of my mind to be quiet.

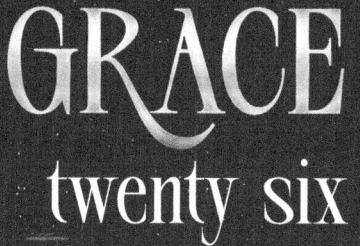

GRACE
twenty six

"This is a terrible idea," Marnie whispered beside me, her face scrunched with actual genuine concern.

I gave her a reassuring smile that I wasn't entirely sure I believed in myself. "I just need to talk to her. Stay out here, okay?"

Marnie's eyes widened, and she stepped back reluctantly. "Okay, but if you scream, I'm coming in."

I shook my head, suppressing a laugh, and with a deep breath, I turned toward Veronica's dorm door in the Guardians Sector. My heart ricocheted against my chest as I knocked lightly. When no sound came from inside, I hesitated and reached for the handle. To my surprise, the door creaked open.

It wasn't locked.

I pushed it open, stepping cautiously into the room. The inside felt heavy, and I immediately spotted Veronica by the small kitchenette. She was hunched over, carving something into the wooden tabletop with a knife. The rhythmic scrape of the blade filled the silence, and for a moment, I wasn't sure if

I should say anything at all.

"Bold move of you, coming inside." Veronica's voice broke the silence. "*Alone.*"

I swallowed, nerves prickling my skin. "I just... wanted to check on you."

She stopped carving, her hand still gripping the knife. She looked up at me, her eyes dark and tired. "Funny, you're the last person I expected to check up on me."

I wasn't sure how to respond, so I stood awkwardly, watching as she pushed away from the counter and walked toward her bedroom. Her movements were slow and deliberate, as if she was waiting to see if I would follow. I did, reluctantly.

As I stepped inside her room, I couldn't help but glance around at the decor. The walls were painted a deep, gothic black with splashes of dark purple and crimson. Some candles melted down to almost nothing. There were also posters of punk bands I didn't recognize and artwork that looked both beautiful and haunting.

I cleared my throat, tearing my eyes away from the walls. "I'm... I'm really sorry about Lucas."

Veronica didn't respond at first. She just sat down on the edge of her bed, her fingers brushing over the worn fabric of her comforter.

"And... I also wanted to say that I never had anything to do with it," I added quietly, not sure how else to say it. "I swear, Veronica. I would never do anything to hurt someone."

Her icy gaze shifted toward me, but then she surprised me by sighing, her voice coming out softer than I expected. "I know."

I blinked. "You do?"

"In the vision, it was all about Lucas. I saw him there lying on the floor dead, and then you... you were standing there, and

I just—" She sighed. "I needed someone to blame."

Though I was relieved, this still meant everyone believed I had something to do with his death, coincidentally after Veronica had a vision in front of the whole class.

"I didn't come to Celestia to cause trouble or hurt anyone. I only knew Lucas for a little while, but I cared about him. Other than Marnie, he was the only person who wanted to be my friend."

Veronica didn't say anything, and I took it as a sign that she wanted me to leave. I had pushed my luck already.

I turned to go, but before I could reach the door, the rasp in her voice stopped me.

"My mother abandoned us."

I turned slowly, uncertain whether I'd heard right or not.

Veronica's eyes were distant as she stared at the wall. "She left Lucas and me when we were young. Obviously, she was human. Bitter about it, too. We ended up growing up at Celestia and I..." she trailed off. "I've been angry about it for a long time, and Lucas was all I had left. That's why I took it out on you when you first got here. You reminded me too much of her."

Her words hit me hard. All of the tension between us, all of the hostility... it made sense.

"I get it," I said softly, stepping back toward her. "My mother left me too... except that I was never able to find out why." I blew out a slow breath. "I'm sorry for everything that's happened to you. Truly."

She had been quiet for a long time, but there was something softer in her eyes now. It was not quite acceptance, but it was not rejection either. I took that as a win.

"Lucas," she began, her voice breaking slightly, "he liked you. A lot. So, I guess... I can dislike you a little less. For him.

But that doesn't mean I'm entirely fond of you yet."

I chuckled softly. "That's okay. I don't like myself much sometimes, so I think we can both agree on some level there."

She glanced at me, and it was the first time I had seen her give me somewhat of a laugh mixed with a half-hearted smile.

As my eyes drifted to the paintings on her wall, I saw a drawing of a spider almost hidden behind one of the posters.

"Do you like spiders?" I asked out of curiosity and somewhat—well, mostly—because I was just plain nosy.

Her gaze snapped towards the drawing. She played with her cross necklace before she said, "They've always been my favorite."

I nodded, feeling the tension finally begin to ease and decided it was best to leave certain things unsaid. "Well, thank you," I whispered. "For everything." As I turned to leave, I briefly paused to look at her. "Oh! Um, one other thing."

She raised her brows.

"I know I'm overstepping here but... is it possible to maybe get people off my back, considering they keep blaming me?"

Her eyes narrowed at that, and I figured I was *really* pushing my luck.

"I mean, I get it," I continued quickly. "People want someone to blame, and I just happen to be the easiest target but—"

Veronica scoffed, cutting me off. "You think people are still blaming you?"

I frowned. "They are, aren't they?"

She let out a short laugh, shaking her head. "Not after Hunter got involved."

I blinked. "What?"

Veronica leaned her back against the bed, her expression torn between exasperation and amusement. "You seriously don't know? Hunter's been shutting down anyone who even thinks about blaming you for Lucas. And I don't mean with *kind words*."

My stomach flipped. "What do you mean?"

She tilted her head. "You think the whispers just... stopped? That people just decided to let it go?" She let out a dry laugh. "No. Cain made them."

My mouth suddenly went dry.

She pushed off the bed and began ticking things off her fingers. "Elias? Got cornered outside the canteen last week and hasn't spoken a word about you since. Chris? Nearly got thrown off the roof—allegedly. And don't even me started on Leon, because I heard Cain grabbed him by the collar so hard, the guy could barely breathe before he got the message."

I swallowed hard. "He—wouldn't—"

"Wouldn't he?"

I had no words. No defense. I was utterly speechless.

Veronica sighed and shook her head. "Don't forget to close the door on your way out."

I opened my mouth, but nothing came out as she turned her back to me and flipped through some of her sketchbooks.

I stood there, staring at her while my pulse thudded in my ears. Hunter had been threatening people for me? Silencing them? I should have been furious. I should have been storming to our dorm, demanding answers. But all I could think about was—why wouldn't he tell me?

Veronica didn't say anything else so, I left the dorm, closing the door softly behind me. Marnie was waiting outside, eyes wide and full of questions, but I waved her off with a slight smile. There was still so much to figure out, so much left unresolved, but for now, I felt a spark light up in my chest, thinking about what Hunter had done.

GRACE
twenty seven

The following few days, I was nonstop training. Except I was making no improvements. I should've been focusing on bettering myself, but my mind was elsewhere. Hunter had barely spent time in the dorm and when he did, he'd lock himself in his room. I had contemplated whether to tell him I knew about him threatening others for me, but things were still tense between us, and I was too stubborn to apologize.

Sighing, I threw a weak punch at the padded dummy in front of me.

"Hey, Grace." Matias sauntered past, his smug grin making my skin crawl. "How's Lucas? Oh—wait. I forgot. He's no longer here. My bad."

My heart twisted in my chest, and he may as well have driven one of the angelic weapons into me. I turned toward him, my fists clenched. "What did you just say?"

Matias chuckled, along with a few others beside him. "Nothing. Just stating facts. Must be strange for you, though. Your friend is dead, and his twin sister is probably wishing it was you instead."

Rage surged through me like an electric current, and I stepped forward. Matias's eyes dipped to where my fists were turning white, and smirked.

"Woah, careful, guys." He glanced at his friends. "I think we might have angered the little beast."

Obnoxious laughter broke out between the group, and I practically growled as I raised my fist to hit him. But before I could, a strong hand gripped my wrist, pulling me back.

I glanced up into a set of piercing grey eyes.

"Trying to be the next Rocky, Bambi?"

I shot him a glare, yanking my arm free from his grip. He barely seemed to notice as his focus shifted entirely to Matias, and the moment their eyes met, Matias stiffened. His face drained of color, his confidence withering under the weight of Hunter's stare. Without a word he took a cautious step back, grabbing his friends and pulling them along with him.

Had Hunter *threatened* him too?

I wanted to ask, but I didn't get the chance to when I noticed a group approaching from afar. A few familiar Celestial faces arrived alongside Council members, with Eden, Joe, and Nadael walking in the front. Her usual serene expression was in place as the attention of everyone in the training grounds turned toward them.

I leaned closer to Hunter, enough to smell his aftershave and that blend of smoke and vanilla.

A woman—who I presumed was part of the Council—in a grey pantsuit stepped forward, harsh eyes scanning us all. "Warriors," she began, her voice echoing across the field. "As per our investigation into the incident that occurred on the 23rd of October, we have finally caught the demon responsible for the breach."

I froze as blood rushed to my ears.

"Thanks to Eden." The Council turned to a smiling Eden. "He was found outside the academy, where we presume he was planning another attack. She managed to subdue him with an angelic weapon and is now awaiting trial. As for the upcoming competition, it will proceed as scheduled—"

What?

My jaw clenched in disbelief. How could they just move on? Lucas was dead, and they were acting like it was just another obstacle to brush aside.

Before I knew it, I was storming over, my blood boiling. "That's it?" I called out, ignoring the whispers around me. "You're just going to go forward like nothing happened? Lucas didn't even get a proper burial! How is that fair?"

One of the Council members shot me a withering look, then turned to Joe, who stood at the side, trying to remain composed. "Keep your human in check," he said coldly, dismissing me like I was an annoyance.

"With all due respect, Cael," Joe said. "Grace isn't just *my human.* She is someone I have taken care of since her birth, and I believe she has every right to demand answers."

The Council member's gaze cut to Joe, his expression calm, but I could see the flicker of annoyance beyond it. "Answers?" Cael repeated, his voice dripping with condescension as he looked at me. "What answers do you seek? That death is a part of this? That sacrifices are necessary? Or perhaps you think the world should stop spinning every time one of you falls."

My fists curled so tight that my nails bit into my palms. "It's not about the world stopping; it's about respect. Lucas James deserved better than this—better than everyone dismissing him like he didn't matter!"

Cael's expression darkened to the point where I thought he

211

might actually retaliate. His sharp blue gaze bore into mine. "Careful, Miss Martin. You're treading dangerously close to insubordination."

I barked out a bitter laugh, unable to stop myself. Nadael's eyes widened, and she looked over at Joe as if pleading for him to stop this.

But it wasn't Joe who spoke up again this time. It was Hunter. He'd stepped in front of me, his body partly hiding me away from Cael's wrathful gaze.

"Insubordination?" he said, his grey eyes staring down Cael. "You call it insubordination, but all I see is someone demanding basic decency. Lucas fought for us, and now you expect us to stand here and pretend his sacrifice meant nothing?" He stepped closer, his posture rigid, shielding me even more as his voice dropped lower, deadlier. "You want to throw around words like loyalty and obedience in order to preserve the Angelic Code? Fine. But respect goes both ways. And if you can't give that to people, then maybe you're the one who's forgotten your place."

Cael's gaze narrowed dangerously, but Hunter didn't back down. His broad shoulders were squared, and his jaw was set like he dared Cael to challenge him.

Silence followed before Eden cleared her throat. "I think Mr Cain is trying to say that they have all had a tiresome few weeks, and Lucas was such a good friend to them. It is normal to feel all these emotions, especially in their case."

Hunter glanced at Eden like he knew what she was saying was utter bullshit. That was not what he meant at all.

"Yes, exactly," Nadael chuckled nervously. "Come, Cael, let us head to my office, and we can discuss the upcoming competition in more detail."

Cael hummed, ignoring Nadael as he glanced back at me

212

and Hunter. He leaned forward, his cold smile firing my anger again. "Do you know what your problem is, Mr Cain? You think this is about justice, about fairness. But fairness is a luxury in this world, and justice... justice is for those who serve. It is a pity you haven't still learnt that after what happened to your brother."

The words sent a shot of anger to my chest. I could only stare at him, my breath coming in short, sharp bursts as Hunter's jaw twitched in response.

I was practically trembling with rage for him, refusing for the fire in my chest to be extinguished.

"Remember, Mr Cain," Cael said smoothly, "the second rule of the Angelic Code: 'To question is to rebel. To rebel is to fall.'"

I stepped forward before I could stop myself, fists clenched at my sides—but Joe caught the movement instantly.

"That's enough," he said, voice taut with warning.
"You've made your point, Cael. I say we head back now."

Cael smirked as if he'd already won. "Of course. It's always a pleasure, though, to hear the passionate rambles of a mortal."

I wanted to argue, then scream, but the crushing weight of Joe's gaze stopped me. With one last glare at Cael, I watched as they all left the training grounds.

As soon as we were out of earshot, I turned to Hunter. "Are you okay?" It was a rubbish question to ask. I knew he wasn't okay.

He didn't look at me right away. His jaw was still tight, and his eyes were fixed at some distant point ahead of him.

"That asshole," I muttered, unable to contain it any longer. "He had no right to bring your brother into this. None."

Hunter finally turned to me, and for a moment, I wasn't sure what to expect. But when our eyes met, the depth of emotion

213

there—the anger, the pain, the guilt—was enough to take my breath away.

"It's what they do," he said in quiet rage. "They twist the knife wherever it'll hurt the most. That's how they keep people like us in line."

"But that doesn't make it right, and it doesn't mean we just have to take it."

"And what do you think happens when we fight back, Grace? Huh? You saw what just happened in there. If I push too hard, if *we* push too hard—" He broke off, running a hand through his hair, his frustration palpable. "They don't care," he finally said, voice rough. "They only want control, and they'll destroy anyone and anything who steps out of line."

There was something in his tone, something darker that was just out of reach, but it was there, waiting... anticipating. For the first time, I noticed how his hands trembled slightly as if he was trying to hold himself together but barely succeeding.

I didn't know what to do, and the only thing that I thought could distract him was turning his attention on me. "I want you to train me," I blurted out.

Hunter raised an eyebrow as he looked down at me, his posture easing. "Train you?"

"Yes, train me. Teach me how to be a Celestial Warrior – just anything."

He chuckled at that, the sound low and gruff. "I'm going to pass on that."

"Look, you're the best Warrior, and whether I like it or not, I'd benefit from you teaching me."

Hunter stared at me for a few silencing seconds before turning and walking away from me. "Ask Azrael for private lessons," he said without looking back as if he knew I was following behind him like an idiot. "Or Silas. I'm sure he'd be happy to teach you something—if you don't mind his spider crawling up your arm or him walking around naked."

I rolled my eyes, trying to match his long strides across the field. "Azrael would rather see me fail than give me private lessons, and Silas spends half his time shirtless, chasing Jerry around. I know we're not on the best of terms but... you're skilled, Hunter. I need that."

He stopped and turned to face me. His eyes narrowed. "And you don't think I'd also rather see you fail?"

I swallowed nervously, aware that our complicated relationship was hardly sunshine and rainbows. "I figured it's worth a risk."

Hunter shook his head, his jaw set. "Find someone else." He was turning away again when desperation kicked in, and before I could stop myself, I was blurting out the very words that could make or break this moment.

"I'll help you look for your brother."

That made him pause. His back was still to me, but I saw the tension rise on his shoulders. Slowly, he turned around, his eyes hard. "What?"

"I'll help you find A aron." T he n erves t wisted i n my stomach as we stared at each other.

"And how exactly are you going to help? You know as little as I do."

"I'm strategic," I shot back, refusing to back down. "I can talk to people, unlike you, and above all, a Riftkeeper is no different than a human; maybe I can relate to them... in a way."

He laughed at that—a short, dry laugh that did nothing to help the situation. "So, you think charm and words are going to help me find my brother?"

"It's better than you doing it alone."

Hunter was quiet, and that flicker of desperation in me grew.

215

I took a step closer. "I'm not saying I can fix anything, but I can help you."

His gaze locked on mine, and for a moment, his expression shifted vulnerably. But then it was gone, replaced by that cold, infuriating mask he always wore.

He didn't say anything else. He gave me one last unreadable look before turning and walking away. I watched his back disappear into the distance, and frustration simmered in my veins. I hated him for always making me feel this way—for pushing me away when I knew deep down we could actually help each other.

I looked around the training grounds, the other Ascendants sparring and practicing with ease, while I stood there again on the outside, watching.

I couldn't decide what was more frustrating—how badly I wanted his help or how much I cared that he didn't even consider mine.

HUNTER
twenty eight

I lay in bed, staring at the ceiling as Losing My Religion by R.E.M. quietly played from my computer. My thoughts consumed me as Grace's offer kept circling back, refusing to let me sleep. She said she wanted to help me find my brother, and the sincerity in her eyes made me believe her. But she was stepping into a territory that I'd guarded for years. Even Brandon and Silas knew not to get involved, but Grace... those boundaries didn't matter to her.

A faint noise outside my door broke the stillness, and I slid out of bed, moving quietly toward the hallway. When I reached the kitchen, I found Grace searching through the cupboards like she was trying to rob the place.

I leaned against the doorframe, arms crossed as I watched her. "If you're looking for the last packet of biscuits, let me save you time. Brandon ate them."

She spun around, hand on her chest, looking startled. I bit back a grin at the annoyance flashing in her eyes when she realized it was me. "Ever heard of announcing your presence instead of scaring someone half to death?"

"Didn't know I needed to. You're the one raiding the kitchen in the middle of the night."

She shook her head, turning back around and sighing as she searched the top cupboard.

"Looking for something specific?" I asked, taking a step toward her.

"Hot chocolate," she muttered, sounding almost defeated.

I neared her until my front was touching her back, and she tensed. Reaching above her, I slowly grabbed the tub of cocoa powder she hadn't seen and placed it in front of her. My hand lingered against the counter for a few seconds, and I heard her breathing pick up.

She whispered, "Thank you."

I shook my head, taking a step back as she turned. She looked tired, her usual fire dimmed. For some reason, I wanted to see it come back.

Clearing my throat, I walked toward the fridge and grabbed the milk."Didn't Joe ever teach you where he kept this stuff?"

"No," she said quietly. "But he used to make it for me whenever I couldn't sleep. He'd sit with me, listening to me ramble about whatever was bothering me until I fell asleep with the hot chocolate in my hands."

As I warmed the milk up, I glanced at her. "So, you kept him up too, huh? Nice habit you've got going on there, Bambi."

She rolled her eyes, but I caught a glimpse of a smile. "Do you always have to be so sarcastic, hm... huntsman?"

"Only when it's this easy to rile you up." I smiled.

She came by with the cocoa powder, and I grabbed two mugs for her. Before we settled at the counter, she stirred the powder and milk into her cup while I did mine. Silence stretched between us, and I watched her take a sip. My eyes

220

went to her mouth as she licked her lower lip, and something inside of me almost shattered.

She wasn't mine to touch. Wasn't mine to want. But then why the hell couldn't I stop staring at her lips?

I cleared my throat, forcing myself to look at her actual face, not her lips, not the way her curls cloaked her features and not the way she swallowed each drop of hot chocolate. "So... what's the real reason you're up so late?"

She tilted her head, eyeing me like she was trying to decide whether to answer me or not. "You're up too."

"I asked first."

Her gaze dropped to the mug, her fingers curling around it. "I keep having nightmares," she said, her voice so soft, I had to lean closer to catch it. "About Lucas, about what happened. About... demons."

I felt my chest tighten. I knew what it was like to carry that kind of loss, the way it clawed at you when no one was around. The choices you would make just to stop yourself from going insane.

"Can I ask you a question?" she murmured, her eyes still on the mug.

I knew if I said no, she would likely ask me either way.

"Sure," I whispered, and she hesitated, her brows knitting together as though she was searching for the right words. Finally, she looked up at me.

"What does it mean exactly for someone to be corrupted?"

The question stopped me cold, like all the air had been knocked out of my lungs.

My hand clenched around the mug, so hard it cracked. I dropped it onto the table, as hot chocolate started to slowly spill from the gaps. "Why would you ask me that?"

"Because I want to understand," she said as I grabbed at tea towels and wiped down the surface. "No one talks about it—I mean, not really. But I want to know more, not just from what they teach us in angelic history lessons or what Joe tells me. I just..." she faltered, shaking her head.

"Grace," I started, but she cut me off.

"How does it happen?"

I realized she wanted to know because she was afraid, that she would be a target for corruption. Leaning back, I ran a hand through my hair as I wrestled with how much to say.

She stared at me, unrelenting, and I knew then she wouldn't back down until I told her.

I sighed. "I heard it starts small," I said finally. "A crack. A moment of weakness, of anger, of desperation. That's all it takes for them to find you."

"Them?"

"Demons." The word tasted bitter on my tongue. "They don't just show up out of nowhere, Grace. They look for people who are always breaking and offer..." I trailed off, my throat tightening.

"What?" she pressed. "What do they offer?"

"Whatever you think you need. Vengeance, power, freedom, a way to stop pain—whatever it is to pull someone in."

Her eyes searched mine, fearfully. "And then what happens?"

"They take a piece of you," I said quietly. "Your soul. Not all at once—just enough to start. And the more you use what they give you, the more they take. It's slow, subtle. You don't even realize how much of yourself you've lost until it's too late."

She swallowed. "And when it's too late?"

"Then I suppose, you become one of them. A demon, someone fallen..." I shrugged.

"And you?' she whispered. 'Have you ever experienced something like that or close to it?"

I tensed. I should have stayed in my room, stayed far away from her. "Let's just say it's not the first time that I've heard of this happening."

The silence that followed was suffocating. I could feel her staring at me, but I couldn't bring myself to look back. My instinct was to reach out to her and tell her not to worry about it, that it would never happen to her because I wouldn't let it, but then a shuffle of feet broke the tension, and I turned to see Silas stumbling into the kitchen, scratching his head and, of course, completely naked.

"Fuck's sake, Silas," I groaned, the tension dissipating as he stopped in front of us. "Put some damn clothes on. No one wants to see that."

Silas blinked, half-asleep, squinting at us as if he'd just realized he wasn't alone. "What?" he muttered, grabbing a banana from the counter and shooting me a lazy grin as he made his way back to his room. "You weren't saying that to me the other night."

Bastard.

Grace tried to stifle a laugh, her face turning pink as she shook her head. "Well, on that note," she said, setting the mug down. "I think it's time I head to bed. Hopefully, this will help me sleep."

"Grace—wait."

She stopped and glanced back at me.

"Were you serious before?" I asked, the words leaving my mouth before I could second-guess myself. "About helping me find my brother?"

She held my gaze, the warmth in her brown eyes easing the tension within me. "I was," she said. "I want to help. I... want to try."

I nodded, feeling that resolve settle over me. "Alright, then if you mean it. Meet me tomorrow at seven. Canteen. I'll train you."

A small smile played on her lips. "Really?"

Unapologetically, I smiled down at her. "Yes, really."

There was a spark in her eyes again that made me want to go back on this, on everything I have done over the last few weeks.

"I'll see you then," she said, pausing outside her door. But instead of going in right away, she lingered. "Also... thank you," she murmured. "For getting people off my back."

I didn't say anything. Didn't need to. She gave me a small smile, one of the rare ones that didn't quite reach her eyes and disappeared into her room.

I stood there in the quiet, a slow smile tugging at my lips.

So... she knew.

I glanced down at my hand and twisted the gold ring on my pinky.

I was so fucked.

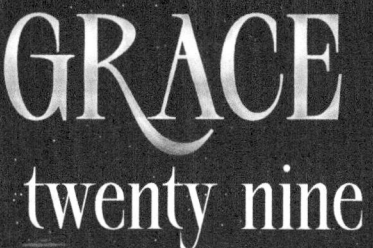

GRACE
twenty nine

I arrived at the canteen precisely at seven o'clock. Empty chairs and tables sat scattered in the dim lighting, and for a second, I thought I'd beaten Hunter here, but as soon as I stepped further in, his voice cut through the quiet.

"You're late," he said, arms crossed as he leaned casually against one of the tables.

"By, like, thirty seconds."

He smirked, pushing off the table as he motioned for me to follow. "You just cut your training time in half, but I'll be gracious."

I snorted, falling into step beside him as he led me toward the back of the kitchen. We were both in our Warrior attires, save for the jacket and my hair was no longer up in a ponytail or plait. The lights flickered dimly as we moved through stacks of crates and shelves. "So, where exactly are we going? The canteen hardly screams 'training ground' unless we're having a few snacks first before I start learning. I wouldn't mind that;

I quite like the canteen's apple crumble."

He glanced down at me with an amused glint in his eyes. "There's a passageway here. It leads to the armory."

I blinked, a rush of excitement and confusion bubbling up. "There's an armory here? Like where they keep every single weapon ever used?"

Hunter chuckled at my reaction and nodded. "The armory is pretty strictly controlled by the angels, but I figured out a way to it years ago."

We stopped at a wall of cabinets that looked like they held stacks of canned goods. With a swift glance to make sure no one was watching, Hunter reached up and twisted one of the handles. The wall shifted with a low mechanical groan, sliding open to reveal a narrow, shadowed corridor.

"What in the haunted mansion..." I muttered as Hunter walked past me. His lips curved into a half-smile, and it shocked me because this was the most I had seen him smile in the space of two minutes.

"Why are we here?" I whispered as we made our way through the dark corridor. "I thought we'd be training—oh, I don't know—outside?"

"This is your training."

I laughed, waiting for him to crack another smile, but he didn't. "Oh, you're serious? You're just going to throw me into the armory?"

We both stopped, and he turned halfway, studying me like I was missing the obvious. "If you're going to train to a Warriors standard, you need to know each weapon inside and out. What it does, how it feels in your hand, and, most importantly, how it reacts to you."

I opened my mouth to argue, then paused, realizing he was right. It was more than just holding a sword or swinging daggers left and right.

"Alright, fine, but what if I already know all about angelic weapons?"

Hunter's mouth twitched as he took me down the steps into a vast dungeon-like room with thousands of weapons dotting the place. He led me to a rack and held up a strange, curved blade. "What's this called, then?"

I stared at the weapon, racking my brain. It looked familiar, but I couldn't name it to save my life. "That?" I pointed at it. "Well, that's a—" I started making gestures with my hand as if I were digging at the ground. "Fling...flinger?"

"Thought so," he said.

I scowled, feeling a blush rise. "Fine. Educate me then, since you're obviously the expert."

"I am, thanks for acknowledging that."

I fought not to roll my eyes, and for the next hour or so, he guided me through each weapon—naming them, explaining their strengths and drawbacks, and how they were meant to be used. He was thorough, his voice low and smooth as he spoke. There was a surprising passion in the way he talked about each one, and it was shocking to see him so animated.

After a while, he stepped back, watching me. "Alright, now pick one."

I looked over the selection, my eyes trailing across the various blades, staffs and bows. After a moment, I reached for a dagger with a jagged, obsidian blade. It felt cold and smooth in my hand as I studied it. The dagger was called a Nightsteel. According to Hunter, it was forged from the nightmares demons inflicted on souls in hell. It could render someone in a nightmare-like state if injured with it.

"Good choice," Hunter murmured. "Now show me how

you'd use it on me."

I laughed, glancing up at him. "What, you want me to just... attack you with this?"

He didn't blink, didn't so much as even flinch. "If you're serious about training, you've got to go all in. So, what are you waiting for?" He took a step back, giving me enough space to lunge at him.

I gripped the dagger tighter. This was probably the only time I'd get a free shot at him, and I was more than willing to take it. I rushed toward him, aiming for his side, but he sidestepped effortlessly, his hand snapping out to grab my wrist and twisting it just enough that the dagger clattered from my grip.

"Again," he said, and I huffed in annoyance.

Picking the dagger up, I went for him again, but he moved faster than I could react, and before I knew it, he spun me around, pressing me back against the wall. My breath hitched, the adrenaline thrumming through me as his dark gaze held mine.

"Not bad." His voice was barely a whisper. "But you're still too predictable. Did you know that in this position, I could quite easily knock you out?"

I swallowed, feeling my pulse race. His hold on me made my skin tingle with every inch of distance he wasn't giving me.

"All I would need to do is place my thumb and forefinger behind your neck and press..."

Just as he leaned in, the sound of footsteps echoed down the corridor, and we both froze.

Hunter's head snapped toward the noise, his hand slowly releasing my wrist as he listened.

"What is it?" I whispered in anticipation.

"Celestials." Hunter's gaze met mine, and without saying another word, he grabbed my hand and pulled me behind a set of pillars. He pressed his fingers to his lips, and I held my breath, praying we wouldn't get caught.

Heavy footsteps echoed off the stone walls, and through a narrow gap, I caught a glimpse of Nadael and Joe walking into the armory. Their voices were hushed, and something about how they moved—guarded, almost conspiratorial—made me tense up.

"The Riftkeeper's are getting too close," Joe muttered. "If they discover where she is..."

"Then we need to ensure it doesn't happen. Grace's location must be kept a secret, no matter the cost."

My location?

"Hiding her won't be enough forever. The Riftkeeper's are relentless; you know that."

I felt my heart pound. What the hell did they mean?

I wanted to speak, but Hunter held onto me so closely I could hardly breathe.

"I'll make sure to keep an eye on her," Nadael said, and I gasped as Hunter's grip around my waist tightened. He quickly smothered any noise I made with the palm of his hand, and both Nadael and Joe turned in our direction as if they'd heard me.

"No," Joe said, his eyes narrowing as he stared at the pillars. "That will only cause her to feel suffocated, and we both know—" His gaze met Nadael's. "She already feels that way."

"Then we will do what is necessary for now to protect her," Nadael said quietly, and their voices faded as they began making their way up the stairs.

Hunter shifted beside me, gently releasing his hand from

my mouth.

My chest heaved as he let go of me, and I shook my head. "You were hurting me."

His eyes softened into regret. "I didn't mean to."

I exhaled, knowing there was so much to unpack from what we'd heard. From what *I'd* heard.

I knew Joe had been protecting me from the Riftkeeper's ever since he took me into his care, but why were they going to all these lengths to protect me?

"Grace—" Hunter started, but I stopped him.

"I think I have an idea," I whispered, needing to focus on something else. "For finding Aaron."

Hunter's eyes flickered, cautious. "Are you basing this off what you just heard? Because believe me, Grace, I've been searching—"

"Joe said the Riftkeeper's are getting close," I cut him off. "Maybe we can find out more about that and go to—"

"You're not going out looking for a Riftkeeper hideout when they just said they are trying to protect you from them."

"You said I could help you."

"It's risky," he admitted and shook his head. "I shouldn't have agreed to this. I'm putting you in danger—"

"Since when has that ever mattered to you?"

He didn't like that. His sharp eyes snapped at me, challenging me to say another word. He confused me more than anyone ever has.

Did he hate me?

Did he want me gone?

Did he want to protect me?

Or did he not want to carry another person's blood on his hands?

"Let's just go before someone sees us," he said at last in

232

defeat.

I frowned internally, knowing that was the last thing I wanted to do. Leave.

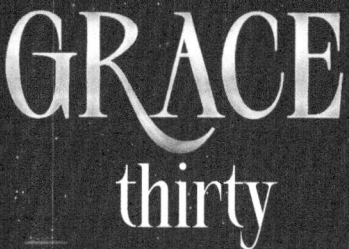

GRACE
thirty

In Rael's class—a Celestial lecture on angelic history—he droned on, barely scratching the surface of what I'd actually learned from Joe growing up. Instead, my mind drifted, fixated on what I'd overheard last night in the armory.

Marnie leaned over. "Are you sure about what you heard?"

I nodded, doodling a sunflower on the wooden desk. "Everyone here is keeping something from me—especially Joe. It's like some big secret and I'm the last to know about it."

As I spoke, I glanced over my shoulder and saw Hunter sitting beside Brandon. His gaze was already on me, and my pulse skittered as I quickly looked away. I leaned into Marnie and whispered, "At least on the bright side, Hunter's helping me to train."

"What?" Marnie yelped, having missed out on the crucial information of how Hunter and I had ended up in the armory last night.

I grimaced as Rael's gaze landed sharply on us from the front of the class. "Marnie Lewis, care to enlighten the class on what's so shocking?"

Marnie straightened up, her cheeks turning pink. "Well, actually, I was just explaining that according to ancient records, the Seraphim have always held a position of jurisdiction since the beginning of time."

Rael frowned, having hoped Marnie would crack under his scrutiny. A few stifled chuckles rippled through the room before Rael resumed his lecture.

Marnie leaned in again. "I thought you weren't going to ask him to train you?"

"It's... complicated."

Marnie scoffed. "Nothing's complicated. We just like to pretend it is."

"Miss Martin," Rael interrupted. "Given your apparent fondness for conversation, perhaps you could answer this. What was the reasoning behind the Grand War?"

My mind flashed to the endless information Joe had drilled into me from a young age. None, though, dealt with the Grand War. "I—" I stammered for an answer, wishing I could retrieve that book from the library that the cherub gave me about the war. I'd completely gone blank.

Rael raised an eyebrow, waiting for a response, but I had none.

"It was Lucifer." That was Hunter speaking. I sheepishly looked over my shoulder, and our eyes met. "When Lucifer started to rebel, he was the first Celestial to create the Nephilim using mortals. From there, the four horsemen of the apocalypse were born, and when the first order destroyed his first-born children, he declared war."

I nibbled on my bottom lip, unable to look away from him. I didn't know whether he had just saved my ass or was showing off just how much he knew. If Rael asked me where Lucifer was now, I could happily tell him that he was locked away. Where and why? Joe wouldn't tell me, but at least I knew he wasn't reigning over hell at the moment.

"Thank you, *Mr Cain*," Rael said, enunciating his words as he knocked a fist down onto my table to get my attention. He returned to the front, explaining the orders and how the forces of light and dark are what shaped our world.

When class wrapped up, we all shuffled out, and I half-ran, half-walked before Marnie or, worse, Hunter, could catch up to me. The corridors were busy with a few children in their training gear, and I assumed they were young Warriors. I smiled before nearly running straight into Eden.

"Oh, sorry!" I said, trying to regain my balance.

Eden offered a small smile, her gaze warm and knowing. "Don't apologise, Grace. I'm the one walking in the opposite direction."

I hesitated as she laughed, and the crowds dispersed until only Eden and I stood in the middle of the corridors. "Eden..." I sighed, wanting to confide in her but unsure how. "If you don't mind me asking, how long has it been since you Ascended?"

Eden's expression softened, oblivious to the fact I wanted to somehow gain information from her. "A few decades now. It's strange how fast time passes around here."

"And..." I said slowly. "During all those years, did you ever encounter Riftkeeper's?"

Her smile faded just a little, and she glanced around, clearly guarded. "A few times, yes. Their influence... is everywhere you go."

I nodded. "I have as well. Except Joe always kept that hidden from me as much as possible."

Eden cast a quick glance down the hallway. "So has Joe never mentioned their hideouts to you?"

That piqued my interest. "No, never."

She sighed. "Might as well be a good thing. They are dangerous people, Grace. They don't care whether you're innocent or not; if you get involved with them, there's never any going back. You could end up in their dark markets, underground—" She paused, knowing she had said too much. Cursing under her breath, she shook her head and plastered on her usual bright smile. "You should head to the training grounds. I would hate for Azrael to tell you off for being late."

She moved to go past me, but I turned and blurted out, "What about the demon you captured recently? Did he give any information?"

She paused. "No," she said, casting a glance over her shoulder but not necessarily meeting my eyes. "He made sure we wouldn't get anything useful out of him. He'll likely be sentenced soon."

Like to the Hollow.

The thought of it made me nauseous.

"I hope you keep this information to yourself, Grace," Eden said. "It's not something you should have to worry about." She walked off at that, and all I could think was how I couldn't help *but* worry about all of it.

Instead of training, my mind went to what I could do, and rather than take the stairs down to the fields, I went up to the library in search of the cherub.

HUNTER

thirty one

Brandon and Silas were going at it in the sparring pit, each testing the other's patience with every swing and jab. I stood by, arms crossed, watching them with half an eye while my attention drifted to the far side of the grounds, where Grace sat on the ground, tying her combat laces up. She was trying to look confident, but I could still see how nervous she was.

"Looks like you're getting close to her," Brandon called out between breaths, dodging Silas's punch.

I kept my expression flat, not giving them anything. If I so much as agreed, that would just give them an opening to annoy me. Fuck that. "She's learning to defend herself, that's all."

Silas let out a low chuckle, shifting his stance as he prepared for Brandon's next move. "Sure, because teaching someone how to fight is your style, right? We thought you'd still want her gone by now."

I shrugged, keeping my gaze trained on Grace. They didn't know Grace had offered to help me find Aaron yet or that, in some fucked-up way, I wanted to be near her.

"Martin." Azrael made his way over to her as she jumped to her feet. "Pair off with Fulcher."

My jaw clenched. Norah Fulcher was part of Matias's clique, a grade-A ass with a tendency to use underhanded moves to get her way. Grace had fought her a few times before, but it was different this time. It *felt* different.

Brandon shot me a look, noticing the tension in my stance. "What are you gonna do?"

Ignoring him, I approached Azrael, who raised an eyebrow as I pulled him aside.

"What is it, Cain?" he asked, clearly unimpressed.

"There's no point in having Grace fight Norah," I said, forcing away the hint of irritation in my voice. "We all know how that'll end. Just pit Norah against someone on her level."

"Everyone trains here, Cain, including your new friend. You said so yourself the day you decided to challenge her."

A muscle in my jaw ticked, but Azrael's expression didn't waver. He turned back to Grace and Norah, dismissing me with a curt nod. I clenched my fists as I stalked back to the edge of the training pit. Grace stood across from Norah, who was grinning in that smug way she always did, clearly relishing the idea of having Grace as her opponent.

They both squared off, and Azrael's voice boomed across the field, calling for their match to begin. Grace immediately shifted her stance, but I could see how her hands trembled slightly as she took tentative steps forward. Norah, on the other hand, radiated the predatory type of confidence.

Grace moved first, a quick jab towards Norah's side, but Norah dodged it effortlessly. I hadn't trained Grace enough for her to actually fight. We'd had less than two lessons, for fuck's sake.

From the edge of the pit, I felt my pulse hammering as Grace tried again, throwing a series of weak strikes. Norah evaded each attempt with ease until she lunged, her fist connecting with Grace's shoulder and sending her stumbling back.

I hissed as if I'd received the hit.

Norah geared up for another jab, but luckily, Grace recovered quickly, attempting a kick to ward Norah off. Just as she aimed for her stomach, Norah grabbed Grace's ankle, twisting it just enough to unbalance her before letting go. Grace hit the ground hard, her face showing a flash of pain before she pushed herself back up.

I hadn't realized I'd taken a step forward to intervene until Brandon clasped a hand over my shoulder and pulled me back.

Each blow Grace received made me want to step in. I knew she had guts; she'd gone up against me the first few weeks of being here, but Norah was merciless. She wasn't fighting to prove something; she was fighting for herself.

When Grace tried to dodge, Norah was faster, managing to land a sharp jab to Grace's ribs. Grace's face contorted in pain as Norah's knuckles dug in, winding her. Everyone else let out a mix of cheers and taunts, fuelling Norah's grin.

"At least she's not using any Warrior strength on Grace," Brandon said, and I shot him a look that made him regret saying that in the first place.

I focused on Grace again as her eyes narrowed with determination. I knew that look—she wasn't about to back down. She squared her shoulders, gritted her teeth and readied herself, managing to duck under Norah's next strike. I could see the flicker of surprise in Norah's eyes just for a second, but it wasn't enough. She swept Grace's legs from under her with a brutal kick that sent Grace crashing to the ground. Before Grace could fully get her bearings, Norah was already on top

243

of her, pinning her down with one arm around her neck.

My fists clenched, seeing Azrael wasn't going to do anything and shrugged Brandon off. I stepped forward when I noticed someone with the Nightsteel blade in their hand.

I grabbed the guy's wrist, and he looked up at me with a frown as I glanced at the dagger.

He didn't even get a say as I snatched it from his grip and flung it towards Grace. It landed right beside her as she fought to get Norah off her.

Grace's eyes darted toward it, her fingers twitching with the need to grab it.

"Come on, Bambi," I muttered under my breath, my eyes fixed on her every move as she managed to twist her body enough to escape Norah's hold and make a dash toward the blade.

She lunged for it, but Norah grabbed her ankle before she could reach the Nightsteel, yanking her back with enough force to send her sprawling. Gritting her teeth, Grace used her free leg to kick out, finally breaking Norah's hold. She pushed herself forward, her hand finally wrapping around the hilt of the dagger before she spun, swinging the blade just as Norah lunged at her again. The edge of the blade slashed Norah's cheek, drawing a line of blood.

Norah shrieked, stumbling back as her eyes widened, turning milky white and unfocused.

The crowd went silent, watching as the effects of the Nightsteel took over Norah and a surge of pride shot through my veins.

But before anyone else could take in what had just happened, Azrael stormed into the pit, pushing past people trying to attend to Norah's needs.

"That's enough! Martin, get out. Not only did you seek aid

from another Warrior—" His eyes went to mine, but I challenged him back with my own. "But you fought with a weapon that shouldn't be used by a human without authorisation. Are you a Riftkeeper, Martin?"

Grace shook her head, the fight draining out of her in an instant.

"Then you do not use these weapons on any of the Warriors unless I tell you to." The words were final, and as she looked over at me, I saw that it was as if the toll of the fight had finally caught up with her. She swayed and collapsed to the ground, but not before I was by her side in an instant.

Her skin was pale, her body limp as she heaved out shallow breaths. Anger seethed inside of me as I looked up at Azrael, whose expression remained impassive.

"Take her to the Healer's wing," he said, dismissing her with the usual detachment in his voice. "Let's see if she's still eager to train when she wakes up."

My teeth gnashed together. Every nerve in me was ready to snap back at him, but Silas and Brandon stepped forward, placing a steady hand on my shoulder, grounding me. I knew better than to give Azrael the satisfaction of a reaction, but seeing Grace like this—defeated, hurt and still so determined struck something in me that I hadn't felt in a long time.

Scooping her up, I felt her head rest against my shoulder as I carried her away from the pit and away from the stares of every other Warrior here.

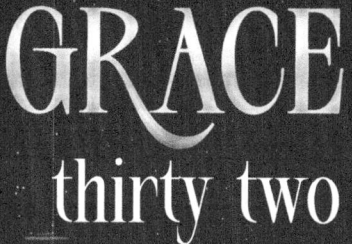

GRACE
thirty two

My eyes cracked open at the soft glow of lights and the unmistakable scent of herbs. Marnie's face hovered above mine, her eyes wide and worried as she tilted my chin to examine me.

"Thank god, you're awake," she said. "You had me scared, you know. Luckily, it was only a mild concussion, but still."

I winced, feeling a few dull aches here and there.

"I healed some of your cuts and bruises, but you should take it easy. Just a little rest and—"

"How did I end up here?" I looked around. The last thing I remember was Norah sending me to the ground with one of her brutal punches.

"Hunter brought you here. Well, he practically carried you in like he was Superman. You should have seen how worried he was; he was making a whole scene telling everyone to heal you first, which—"

The shock of what she was telling me made me jolt upright, and Marnie quickly pressed a hand to my shoulder to steady me.

"Hunter brought me here?"

"Yeah." She nodded. "And refused to leave your side. That is until Nadael stopped by and told him to get back to training."

Refused to leave your side.

I couldn't stop repeating that inside my head.

Maybe Marnie hadn't healed me enough. I needed another round to quell this strange feeling that swelled in my chest.

"And... Nadael, did she—"

"She said that you're lucky you didn't get struck with the Nightsteel instead." Joe appeared by the doorway, his face paler than usual. "Your opponent, on the other hand, will need a few hours to recover."

I grimaced, not from the pain but from the fact Joe had been called in because of me.

He sighed and walked over to the side of the cot, letting Marnie get up from the bed so that he could sit down. "Grace," he said, his voice tinged with what sounded like both relief and frustration. "Maybe this is a sign you should reconsider the Warriors Sector. You could just stick to Sariel's lessons —"

I shook my head before he could say anything else. "I'm not quitting." I didn't want to. At all.

"You shouldn't even be fighting with any of them. I should talk to Azrael, tell him that you—"

"It's not your choice to make," I snapped, the sharpness in my tone surprising me.

The thought of walking away now over something that was happening regardless since I joined the Warriors seemed like a silly idea.

"It *is* my choice," Joe pushed. "I've taken care of you for the past eighteen years; why should I stop now?"

"Because I'm exactly that, Joe. *Eighteen*. Right now, I

248

should be at a university, studying philosophy or something that would give me a headache, not here at a Celestial academy where I won't even receive a title in the end."

Joe didn't say anything; he just looked at me with that familiar resentment and worry he always wore whenever I gave him a reason.

I grabbed Joe's hand. His was so big compared to mine that it barely covered his palm. "I'll be fine, I promise." My eyes flitted towards Marnie. "I'm in the hands of the best company."

She smiled, and Joe finally nodded, though the concern in his gaze never left.

"If I were still mortal, I'd have the greyest hairs because of you."

A laugh tore through my cracked lips. "You already have grey hairs despite the age you Ascended."

He frowned. "They're not grey, they're blonde."

"Grey with a hint of blonde."

He was glaring at me now, and I couldn't stop laughing.

Marnie cleared her throat and leaned forward. "In my personal opinion, Mr Martin, your hair is definitely *not* grey."

"Thank you, Marnie," Joe said over his shoulder, then raised his eyebrows at me. "See."

I glanced at Marnie, mouthing the words 'kiss ass', and she shrugged unapologetically.

Joe chuckled before we ended up spending a few hours together in the Healers Sector, talking while he allowed me to draw sunflowers on his arm with a Sharpie pen.

Later, when I'd finally been cleared to leave, I headed back to the dorm with one thing on my mind. *Hunter.* But when I got there, he was nowhere in sight except for Brandon and Silas sitting on the sofa.

"Grace!" Brandon got up, his eyes scanning me whole to

see if I was okay. He rubbed the back of his neck and sighed in relief. "Do you maybe want to watch some Star Wars with us? Silas agreed to sit through it in silence."

I laughed, grateful he wasn't dousing me with concerns over whether I was still hurting or about the fight with Norah. I knew Norah was still in the Healers Sector, since the Nightsteel might have worked a *little* too well. "Do you really believe that he'll sit through it in silence?"

Silas gave me an exaggerated scowl, crossing his arms as I joined them on the sofa. "Your lack of faith disturbs me."

Brandon gasped so loudly and dramatically that it made me burst out laughing. "He said the quote! See, I fucking told you, you're a secret Star Wars fan."

"Used to be. Ever since I met you, you've made me hate it."

The three of us settled in, and though my mind often drifted to where Hunter could be, the worry gnawing at me began to ease. Silas and Brandon bickered over the films while I had no idea what was happening half the time, and finally, I invited Marnie around for backup.

I was letting myself relax for once in a place that was out of my comfort, and I didn't even mind it. Not one bit.

HUNTER

thirty three

The first thing I hadn't expected to walk into when I arrived at the dorm was for me to see Brandon explaining Star Wars lore, complete with grand hand gestures and sound effects.

Grace sat on the edge of the sofa, captivated by the gun noises Brandon had just demonstrated. Marnie was beside her, and Silas was sprawled out, looking like he was enduring torture.

"Lightsaber mechanics just make no sense." Silas muttered. "And don't get me started on the Jedi code."

"Um, the Jedi code is far more intriguing than our own Angelic Code," Marnie stated.

"Exactly!" Brandon shot Silas a mocking glare, but I doubted he even cared.

"It's basically the same thing! *A Jedi cannot fall in love. Oh, where have I heard that shit before? We're practically living it in real time.*"

"Yeah," Brandon muttered. "Just without lightsabers and a

Millennium Falcon."

I glanced at the table where a packet of skittles lay, mostly emptied with the greens picked clean. Typical. Grace always went for those.

I let the door close with a soft click, and all four of them looked up, but it was Grace who held my attention. She glanced at me—free of bruises and blood—and her face shone with relief.

"Thank fuck," Silas dropped his head back, and I cocked an eyebrow at him. "I was being bullied by these lot. I needed you here on my side, Cain. Tell them you hate Star Wars just as much as I do."

"I like Star Wars."

"No, Cain, you don't. Otherwise, we aren't friends."

"Then we're not friends."

Silas pouted. "You're lashing out. I get it. It's fine; we can kiss and make up later, preferably in my room. Jerry misses you holding her."

I rolled my eyes and walked over to them, stopping a couple of feet away from Grace. The only object in our way was the table.

Brandon stretched, yawning like he hadn't just been on an enthusiastic Star Wars rant. "Well, I think that's enough education for one night," he said, standing and patting Grace on the shoulder. "Glad you're feeling better, at least."

Marnie stood, too, almost colliding with Brandon. They awkwardly exchanged looks before she held her hand out. "Thank you for tonight. I learnt a lot about lightsabers and that little green sensei who speaks funny."

I raised an eyebrow, watching how they interacted. It was like witnessing two shy puppies meet for the first time.

"Yeah," Brandon's voice went high before he cleared it and

shook Marnie's hand. "Yeah, no problem."

"Um, well, okay, bye then!" Marnie rushed to leave but not before saying, "I'll see you tomorrow, Grace. Don't forget to text me later tonight."

Silas groaned but got up and nudged Brandon along, muttering something about how they should go before the prequels started playing. The two of them shuffled to their rooms, leaving Grace and me alone. Her eyes darted up to mine, hesitant but curious, as she slowly got up from the sofa and tucked a curl behind her ear.

"Where were you?" she asked.

"It doesn't matter," I said, shrugging it off.

She looked down, fiddling with the sleeves of her shirt. Her cheeks faintly flushed, and I found myself wanting to smile. "Thank you, by the way... for bringing me to the Healers Sector. I know I was probably a mess."

She wasn't. I was.

"I'm glad you used the weapon," I said, keeping my tone even despite how helpless I had felt, seeing her unconscious. "Didn't think you'd get that far."

She narrowed her eyes in amusement, but then she bit her lip and glanced around the living room. "Anyway I... I wanted to talk to you about the Riftkeeper's," she whispered. "I discovered a few things the other day that might interest you."

She led me to her room, where we would have more privacy. When she closed the door, her nerves were more visible.

"What is it then?"

She bit her lip and gestured to a spread of images—crime scenes with marks on the bodies that made my blood go cold. The Riftkeeper mark burned into their skin of two arrows facing opposite directions, encased in a thorny circle. Their mark was to signify the divide between Celestial realms and earth, that there was never an escape for their targets.

As I stared at the photos, my fingers twitched with unkempt rage, but Grace covered them with a notepad, making me look at her instead.

"The other day," she said, "I was told that Riftkeeper's hideouts could be linked to black markets and underground areas."

I was about to question who had told her that when she clicked through a few images on her computer and showed me articles about different murders in towns nearby.

"See, these were all dismissed as cult killings, but then I went to the library again and spoke to the cherub—" Her voice faltered, like being in the library after Lucas's death unsettled her. "He confirmed that Riftkeeper's operate mostly in hidden places, you know, underground clubs, drug dens—places off-grid." She glanced up at me. "I looked up closed warehouses nearby and found a few that could be it."

A sense of pride stirred in my chest as I took in her handiwork. She'd been thorough, down to the last detail. "Impressive," I murmured. "I'll check it out this weekend, now that the ban's been lifted."

Grace immediately straightened. "I'm coming with you."

I chuckled. Cute joke. "Not a chance."

Her jaw tightened, and I knew that look of hers all too well. She wasn't going to back down. "I'll be careful. Besides, I'm the one helping you remember?"

I shook my head. "We're talking about Riftkeeper's, Grace. Fucked-up people who will take one look at you and know you don't belong there."

"Oh, and you don't think they'll figure out what you are? You got attacked not so long ago, remember?"

I didn't tell her that it wasn't the Riftkeeper's who had done that. No one needed to know. No one should. "Grace—"

"No," she interrupted, her voice unyielding. "I said I was helping you, and I'm not going to do that by staying here, giving you directions like some sidekick. Everyone keeps saying I need to be safe, that I should always be hiding from the Riftkeeper's. I've been running from them for years now. I'm tired of it."

Silence stretched between us, and the way her eyes burned with stubborn determination, I knew I wasn't winning this argument. I let out a frustrated exhale. "Fine. Fine! But you always follow my lead, and if anything goes wrong, you're out. You understand?"

A hint of satisfaction softened her expression, and she nodded. "Deal."

Fuck, me. This girl.

HUNTER

thirty four

The forest was quiet except for the crunch of damp leaves underfoot. Grace followed me, sticking close as we navigated through the trees. When we finally reached the car, I pulled back the tarp that was covering it, and she hesitated, looking at the rusted exterior with a mixture of doubt and, if I wasn't mistaken, a bit of fear.

I tapped the hood and smirked in hopes of making light of this. "It's reliable... most of the time."

She frowned.

Guess, I failed.

"How did you ever learn in this thing?"

"By trial and error... I had Silas as my instructor."

She frowned... again and pried open the car door before sliding into the passenger seat, tightly gripping her coat. I couldn't help but notice how her hands flexed, fidgeting as she tapped her fingers against her knee. I could tell she was starting to regret coming with me, and if anything, I didn't want her accompanying me this weekend when it involved being near Riftkeeper's.

After a few minutes of silence, I glanced over at her. "Do you want to go back?"

She took a deep breath and then shook her head. "No, I don't." Her eyes snapped in my direction, the hint of sunset brightening her doe eyes. "Marnie is with Brandon and Silas covering for us, so that means I'm going with you, even if that means I'm risking my life by being in this god-awful car."

I smirked to myself, turning the engine on. "You're going to be fine, Bambi. Nothing's going to happen to you." I looked at her as I placed the car into first gear. "You're tougher than you look. Though with those eyes of yours, you'd likely have half the world ready to step in before anyone even tried to hurt you. Including this car."

She raised a brow at me, but the hint of a smile softened her expression just as I stepped on the gas.

The tires screeched as the old Nissan Micra lurched forward like it had just awakened from the dead.

Grace let out a noise—somewhere between a gasp and a strangled scream—as she clutched the dashboard. "Hunter! What the hell!"

I grinned, shifting into second gear. "Relax, Bambi. I know what I'm doing."

"That's exactly what someone says before something bad happens!"

She barely had time to finish her sentence before we hit a small ditch, sending her bouncing in her seat. Her head smacked against the roof with an audible thud, and she whirled toward me, brown eyes wide with pure, unfiltered horror.

I grimaced.

Shit.

"Sorry—"

"Just drive slower!"

My grip tightened around the wheel as we took a sharp turn onto a dirt road, and I listened to her, slowing down at a pace she was comfortable with.

The second we hit a slightly smoother road; she exhaled a breath so deep it was like she had just survived a plane crash. Dramatic, but fair.

"I swear," she muttered, fixing me with a deadpan stare, "if I ever agree to get in a car with you again, just assume I'm under duress."

I chuckled, stretching one arm lazily over the steering wheel. "Maybe one day you'll be the one driving instead."

She hummed skeptically, staring out the window and for a while, we drove in complete silence. I tried not to look at her as the hum of the engine and swish of wet tires made their way through country roads but that was proving to be difficult.

"Do you ever wonder what it'd be like if things were... different?" she asked after a while, her voice soft but thoughtful as I glanced at her. She was still looking out the window, fascinated by just... trees.

"Different how?"

"Like if you weren't tied to Celestia and all the rules." She shrugged. "I know you were born an Ascendant, and I just happened to be raised by an angel, but... I just wonder what it would be like to not know this side of the world."

I let out a low chuckle, shaking my head. "It's a question that I don't think we'll ever know."

She hummed, having hoped for another answer. Truthfully, I thought about it a lot, but I also knew that it was a life I was not given.

"So," she asked, changing subjects. "When did you start

sneaking out like this?"

"Long enough to know the shortcuts." I reached a long, narrow road. "It feels good to break the rules sometimes."

"Some angel-to-be you are."

I chuckled, but it fell flat when I took in that word. *Angel.*

Shaking away the oncoming thoughts, I reached into my pocket and took out a packet of skittles. "Here. I don't want you dying from starvation while on the road."

"Gee, thanks," she mumbled, but there was a pause after she grabbed it off me and opened the packet.

"There's only the green ones in here?"

I slid a glance her way before focusing on the road again. "They're the only ones you eat."

"Did you... did you eat the others or did you pick out all the other colors just so I was left with the green ones?"

I hadn't eaten any skittles since I was five years old.

Regrettably, I looked over at her and saw she was smiling with a certain warmth and amusement in her eyes.

I huffed out a deep breath, not liking how that made me feel. "Don't give me that look."

She popped a skittle into her mouth. "What look?" she teased.

I shifted against the seat and swore under my breath. When she reached for another skittle, I said, "How can you even like that flavour?"

"What?" She said around a mouthful of skittles. "I like apple-flavoured stuff. If you ever want to get on my good side? Just hand me anything apple-related, like apple pie or apple muffins. That's a good one. What about you? What flavour do you like?"

I shrugged. "None of them."

"Well, aren't you just a ray of sunshine?"

262

I felt my lips hitch into a smile as I looked at the rearview mirror.

"To be honest, you're probably the type to not even have a favorite color," she went on, and I couldn't help but glance her way again. She was an intoxicating sight, and it wasn't helping the discomfort I felt right now.

"What's yours?" I asked her.

She mulled it over, her eyes skimming the trees that passed us before she smiled. "Yellow... like sunflowers."

Another smile tugged at my lips as I focused back on the road, letting her favorite color sink in. When Silas first asked mine years ago, I didn't have one—I hadn't really thought about it even before then. But when she told me hers, with that smile she always wore, her light brown eyes glinting, I thought, yeah, I do have a favorite color. Her.

Her rose-colored lips.

The color of her warm olive skin.

The hint of caramel that ran through her dark curls.

Her eyes.

My smile faded as I realized just how much trouble I was getting myself into.

Her brows drew together. "What's wrong?"

Everything. "Nothing."

She smiled, taking a deep breath. "We'll find your brother, Hunter; I know we will. If not today, then someday soon. Trust me on it."

It wasn't that, that I was thinking about.

"I'm holding you to that," I muttered instead.

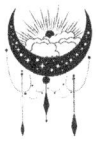

Half an hour later, we'd finally reached the nearest town away from Celestia. I parked near a side street and led Grace through the winding roads until we found a small cafe in the corner of an alleyway. Inside, it was quiet and dim, with the smell of coffee and baked goods filling the air. She looked more relaxed now, sliding into a booth by the window as she watched the drizzle outside.

A waitress came by and asked us what we'd like. When Grace said she wasn't hungry, I dismissed that after her stomach grumbled, and I ordered us both a fry-up.

She blew one of her curls out of her face and sank her back into the booth. "I'd rather not have had a full stomach before we went in search of Riftkeeper's."

'Those few skittles you had weren't enough. Besides, nothing wrong with a good old fry-up."

She rolled her eyes just as the waitress approached us with two plates and coke cans.

Grace eyed her food with undeterred hunger, and before I could say a word, she was already digging in, ravaging her sausages and beans.

I chuckled. "Slow down there, Bambi. Don't want you getting sick in my car afterwards."

She glared at me and took a sip of coke. "That car isn't even a car. It's a death machine that rattles. I don't understand how you haven't been caught when you don't even have a license."

I bit into my toast. "It also got us here in one piece, so you're welcome."

"Shocker."

I couldn't help but grin. "I get it. You're jealous I can drive. It's okay, Grace. You can admit it. This is a safe space."

"Why would I be jealous? I'd like to see you drive a *real* car. One that doesn't sound like it's going to fall apart every time you take a turn."

That's the plan... someday. I doubt it would happen, though. "Who knows, maybe I'll own a 67 Mustang and use it to drive away from here."

Her brows drew together at that. "You want to leave? But—"

I'd said too much. "You should hurry up and eat the rest of your food before it gets cold." My walls were back in place, and she could clearly see that.

It disappointed her.

She shook her head and sighed. A few minutes of silence passed by as we ate our fry-ups before, she decided to speak up again. "So, what's the plan then? Head to the abandoned lots here and scout each one for strange activity?"

If only it were that easy. "If it's a place run by Riftkeeper's, they won't just let anyone in."

"What if we snuck in?"

"Won't work."

She crossed her arms and huffed. This was another reason why I didn't want her to come with me. My idea to get into any place where Riftkeeper's hang out wasn't strictly orthodox. "Then what do we do?"

"I'll tell you once you finish your food."

Begrudgingly, she picked apart at her bacon before she continued eating until there was nothing left on that plate. When we left the cafe, the rain picked up as we walked through a nearby park that was empty except for the quiet shuffle of our footsteps.

I still hadn't answered her question, and I felt it was because she no longer wanted to know.

She shivered slightly.

I frowned and shrugged off my jacket before handing it to

her.

She pouted. "I don't need this."

"Cool. Then consider it a fashion statement."

Rolling her eyes, she tossed me my jacket back. "I can handle being cold. In fact, I can handle anything, including you."

I stopped and looked around the empty park. Holding my hand up, I said, "Alright, then. Show me what you've got."

She looked at me, mouth agape. "You're serious?"

"Come on, you said you can handle anything."

Her eyes narrowed, a playful glint flashing as she brought her fists up, mirroring the stance I'd taught her the past week. She surprised me by making the first move, her steps light on the rain-soaked grass.

I laughed, and her teeth clenched as she lunged towards me once more. She'd retained some of the basics, and I could tell she was trying everything possible to get to me, but whenever she thought she'd pinned me down, I slipped out of reach.

She launched her fist towards my face, but I managed to catch it just in time. She was getting better, and her frustration only gave way to her fierce determination since day one.

I looked down at her, unable to stop myself from smiling. "Close," I said and chuckled when she tried to free her hand from my hold. Just as I was about to release my grip, I caught a glimpse of a figure moving across the park. A man in a dark coat, hood hanging low over his face, but the length of his sleeves was pulled back ever so slightly, revealing the edges of a mark.

Grace followed my gaze, her body tensing when she saw the man disappear into the trees. "Is he—"

"Most likely," I murmured. "Come on, there's a place we

can stay at in the meantime."

Grace nodded, already matching my pace as we crossed the park and onto another road with barely a shop in sight and only a rundown motel in the distance.

GRACE
thirty five

Hunter's hand was warm against my lower back as we walked into the motel. It was a rundown place with dim lighting and a musky smell that made me want to wrinkle my nose in disgust, but I managed to keep my expression neutral. Hunter stepped up to the counter with me in tow as he requested a room.

We weren't staying the night, but like Hunter said, we needed a place to rest for a bit and get our bearing.

The receptionist barely glanced at us. She was too focused on a small TV playing above the counter. "Name and card?"

Hunter handed the receptionist everything she needed. When she finally looked away from the TV, she stared at us for a minute too long while chewing her gum loudly.

"Single or double?"

"Excuse me?" I spoke.

She rolled her eyes. "Single bed or a double."

Oh.

As I was about to say single, Hunter spoke up and said

double.

I blinked, looking up at him, but he hadn't even glanced my way.

The receptionist blew out a huff before handing us a key. Hunter then guided me down the hallway, his hand lingering a bit longer than necessary as if playing the devoted partner. It oddly felt natural, which only made the nerves in my stomach flicker.

The illusion of whatever Hunter was faking with me inside our motel room dissolved as he clicked the door shut and immediately got to work. I watched, half-amused, as he pulled two different Celestial daggers from beneath his jacket, followed by a Nightsteel I hadn't noticed was in his pocket.

"Are you always this well-armed?"

"Precaution," he said, setting the weapons on the nightstand. I was disappointed by his lack of a sarcastic response. Instead, his face was calm, but the way his jaw tightened told me otherwise.

I watched him closely; how his movements around the room were focused but tense. It reminded me of our first encounter, the darkness that lurked behind those grey eyes. "Why did you ask for a double bed?" I asked quietly.

He paused by the bed, his fingers trailing the thin covers. "You never know what a place like this could be hiding. I thought it would be best if they saw us acting like a... regular couple."

Right. Regular couple.

I found myself feeling cold again. "And, um, so, last time... was it a Riftkeeper who attacked you then? Was it this exact town too?"

He seemed to know what he was doing, so my assumption led to that but as Hunter's face shifted and a brief flash of

270

something unreadable passed him, I began to think I was wrong. "That's not important right now."

"Not important? If we're going to get anywhere close to finding your brother, I think I deserve to know what we're dealing with, don't you? Like, where were you the last time you were attacked? Was it near here? Was it close to the academy like we overheard Nadael and Joe say or—"

"Just leave it, Grace."

Frustration bubbled up my throat. "Well, you're not exactly giving me a reason to trust you right now, *Cain*."

He sighed, raking a hand through his hair; gone were the snippets of jokes and teases with him. "I don't owe you every answer."

Silence swept over us, and I huffed as he turned away, grabbing a towel from the bathroom cabinet.

"I'll be back in a few," he muttered, stepping into the bathroom.

As soon as the bathroom door clicked shut, I felt a surge of resolve. If he wasn't going to share information, I'd find it myself then.

I slipped out of the room, shutting the door behind me as quietly as I could, then made my way down the hall, retracing our steps to the lobby.

A few leaflets and a wall full of news posts were by the entrance. I went over and looked for anything that might seem out of the ordinary, but there was nothing except a few posters about a Christmas football event and a grandma who'd won the national lottery.

I sighed, turning toward the front desk, when I spotted the same man who'd been at the park sitting at the bar, deep in conversation with another guy.

I stilled, unsure whether to bolt out of there and find Hunter or do something stupid and brave on my own.

Naturally, I went with the stupid and brave option.

Inhaling slowly, I forced my legs to move and slid into a stool a few seats down from him, my fingers drumming an erratic rhythm against the bar top. I kept my head low, pretending to scan the menu like I wasn't internally freaking out. When the bartender asked for ID, I panicked and muttered, "Just a coke," like that made me sound casual and not like a fraud about to blow her own cover.

Out of the corner of my eye, I watched the two men. The second one scribbled something on a notepad, then tore the page cleanly and slid it toward the guy from the park.

My pulse kicked up a notch. They shook hands—too formal, too intentional—and stood to leave. As they passed by, I turned my face away, pretending to study the dusty drink menu like it held the meaning of life. Only when their footsteps faded did I slide off the stool and dart across the bar.

"Do you have a pencil?" I asked the bartender.

He blinked at me.

"I just need to jot something down," I added, throwing in a sheepish smile for good measure.

After a beat, he handed one over. I snatched it and flipped to the notepad the guy had written on, dragging the pencil sideways across the next blank sheet, shading fast.

"Come on, come on—yes!" I whispered in triumph, though I immediately winced and glanced up at the bartender. He stared at me like I might be mildly unhinged.

But I didn't care. A faint address had appeared through the graphite, and I scribbled it down quickly.

I had just turned to leave when I slammed directly into a solid chest. H*unter's* solid chest, to be precise.

My eyes widened.

272

He looked pissed as his eyes scanned my face. "What the hell were you thinking?" he hissed, gripping my arm as he pulled me a few steps away from the bar and out of earshot.

"I was following a lead," I said, trying to shake off his grip, but he held onto me firmly. "Why do you never take me seriously when I say I can help?"

Hunter scoffed. "Oh, I'm sorry, *queen* of questionable life choices."He then shook his head. "I thought something had happened. Do you have any idea—" He stopped himself, breathing hard as if trying to regain control.

It was strange to see him this worried about me, and I contemplated whether to dig further and ask if it was because he cared or because I would be a liability if something happened to me.In ways, I was afraid to find out, but I also *wanted* to know.

My mind had been full of contradictions lately.

"Well." I cleared my throat. "I'm okay, see? Not a scratch." I waved a hand over myself. "And guess what? I got something that might help."

His anger faltered, as his gaze dropped to the note in my hand. "You're unbelievable," he muttered, this time more resigned as his grip on my arm relaxed and his thumb brushed against my skin absentmindedly.

"Yeah? Well, maybe if you didn't keep so many secrets, I wouldn't have to be."

He was still glaring at me, but it lacked the intensity from a moment ago as he took the note from me. "Secrets are safer than the truth, Grace."

I raised an eyebrow, wondering what he meant by that. "Safe for who, exactly?"

He didn't answer as his gaze drifted to the address I'd scribbled on the paper. His jaw was set, and I could see him wrestling with his thoughts before he pocketed the note and looked back at me. "If you ever pull something like that again..." he started, his voice low, but he didn't finish. Instead, he just shook his head.

"I knew what I was doing."

He huffed a quiet laugh. "That's the problem."

Our eyes locked, and the air between us grew heady with something far heavier than anger or frustration. It was the same pull I'd felt before, that confused mixture of defiance and attraction that seemed to appear every time we were close like this. It made my body weak—made my heart beat a little faster that it would force me to panic, and from the way Hunter's fingers tightened slightly on my arm, I could tell he felt it, too.

Before either of us could say anything more, the bartender cleared his throat, casting us a wary look. I was the first to pull away, feeling suddenly exposed.

"We should go," Hunter said, his voice rough. "I have a map in the car we can use."

He turned toward the door, but as he did, his hand hovered at my back, guiding me forward like he couldn't quite bring himself to break contact. Outside, the rain had started again, falling softly as we made our way down the street. The motel sign flickered above us, and we passed it as we headed toward the car. I glanced over at Hunter, who was already staring at me. He never stopped, even as we got into the car and closed the doors.

"So, what now?" I said, breaking the silence.

His expression was unreadable, like a brick wall I couldn't knock down. "We go, we observe, and we don't get caught. That simple enough for you?"

That wasn't all, though; I knew it wasn't.

He sighed like he knew I was waiting for the extra *but.*

It didn't come. Instead, he reached into his pocket and fished out one of the weapons he'd brought with him. It was a slender blade, this one, with black leather wrapped around its handle and charred in places.

"This... is a Seraph blade," Hunter said. "It's a weapon that only Ascendants and Celestials can hold without getting burnt. See, it doesn't cut like a normal blade. It sears through flesh, marking the skin and drawing both heat and life from the person."

I didn't like where this was going. At all.

My pulse hammered against my neck as I stared at the weapon and then up at Hunter's face. "You're going to carve the Riftkeeper mark onto our skins, aren't you?"

His jaw worked back and forth as if he were reconsidering this whole night—this whole plan even. He was ready to back out, I could see. He would rather send me back and do this alone.

I looked away from him, closed my eyes and started regretting my life choices before I shimmied out of my jacket and raised my sleeve to my elbow. "Just... make it quick, please." I braced myself for the sting of the blade, but when nothing happened, I peeked up at Hunter. He was staring at me so fiercely—like he was seeing me for the first time, completely captivated.

Before I could catch my breath, his arm slipped around my waist, and in one smooth motion, he lifted me onto his lap, so close that my knees rested on either side of him.

As I was about to ask him what he was doing, his attention shifted to his arm. He started cutting into the flesh of his skin, carving the Riftkeeper's mark of arrows and a circle of thorns as if he'd remembered it off by heart. There was no ounce of pain on his face, and I swallowed nervously.

"Very artistic." It was hardly a whisper of a joke to try and

275

calm myself.

He looked up at me once he was finished, his stormy grey eyes searing into mine. "Put your mouth against my shoulder."

"What?"

"Just trust me."

I wish I didn't.

Instead, I found myself nodding as he guided my head towards his shoulder. His skin was warm even through his shirt, but I barely had time to take a breath before he apologized, and the blade tip touched my arm. The burn seared through me like a white-hot flame, stealing the air from my lungs as the pain erupted along my arm. I started to pull back, but Hunter's grip tightened on my waist, keeping me steady.

"Bite down, Grace," he said, but I could hardly function straight. "It'll help."

Desperate to muffle the scream building in my throat, I sank my teeth into his shoulder, clamping down as the burn intensified and tears were pushed to the edges of my vision. I could feel him tense beneath me, his body going rigid, but he didn't waver as his hand guided the blade path over my skin.

I clung to him, teeth pressed into his shoulder, trying to find something to ground myself as the pain became sharper. He was breathing against me, low and ragged, his own body straining beneath my movements.

"Almost done," he murmured, his voice a whisper against my ear.

I bit down harder, fighting to stay silent as he completed the last part of the mark. Then, finally, the blade pulled away, and the burn faded to a throbbing heat.

I leaned back, gasping for breath, and met his gaze. I felt hot and cold and weak at that moment. My head was spinning, and I was sure if Hunter wasn't holding onto me, I'd have passed out from the sheer pain. Yet somehow, being on top of him, knowing I had control of where I was, grounded me.

Hunter didn't look away. His eyes searched mine, lingering for a second on my lips. I could feel the warmth of his breath, see the way his jaw tensed and released, and for a moment, we just stayed there.

"You're tougher than I thought."

I managed a shaky laugh despite the ache in my arm. "Not sure if that's a compliment or an insult."

His mouth twitched in response, but his gaze didn't soften. "Take it how you want," he replied, voice quiet.

He reached out, brushing a stray tear from my cheek I hadn't even noticed had fallen. His thumb lingered there on my skin just a second longer than necessary, making me forget about the pain, forget the reason we were here, just for *one* moment.

I pulled my gaze away from his, glancing down at the fresh mark on my arm. The lines of the Riftkeeper brand burned faintly.

"Now you know what it feels like," Hunter said in the most vulnerable voice I'd ever heard. I didn't understand what he meant by that. Was it that I now knew the pain of the Seraph blade? Or that it was as if that brand made me feel different.

He shifted, his hand slipping from my waist, and I felt a strange pang of loss. I pulled myself back, realising the closeness had left me breathless. "We should get going." His voice was hoarse.

I nodded, sliding off his lap and onto my seat, feeling the heat of his gaze on me even as I moved away.

"Once we're back at the dorm, we'll get Marnie to heal them." He glanced at both our marks, and I nodded again, this time quite numbly.

HUNTER
thirty six

T his all felt too easy.

I'd been searching for ages, coming up empty-handed every time, and now, with a single lead, we were here following an address scribbled on a scrap piece of paper while trailing behind the fog-choked streets of England.

Beside me, Grace was clutching the note tightly to her chest, her eyes scanning the darkened streets after we'd parked somewhere far enough. The streetlights here barely worked, casting only the faintest glow against the cracked sidewalks, and the factories around us looked deserted. Fitting, I supposed, that places like this would house Riftkeeper's.

A low building ahead of us emerged, its steel doors adorned with faded paint, leading to what appeared to be an abandoned factory. I stopped in my tracks, putting an arm out to stop Grace as my eyes trained on the door. People were trickling in—rough types, the kind who looked like they'd gone through a thing or two. None of them hesitated either as they approached the camera by the door, and each one rolled up a sleeve or pulled back the collar of their shirts, flashing something at it.

I caught Grace's eye, her gaze mirroring the same wariness I felt. "Remember what I said. Keep by my side at all times, yeah?"

She nodded, and together, we made our way to the door, the weight of everything riding on this filling my chest like iron.

As we got closer, I rolled up my sleeve, revealing the fresh, faintly pulsing brand. Grace followed suit, lifting her own sleeve to show off the mark I'd given her.

The camera whirred, a soft click breaking the silence as it scanned us both. Then, just like that, the door unlocked, creaking open with an ominous groan. We stepped inside, greeted by a dimly lit corridor that led down a narrow flight of stairs while the air was thick and stale, carrying a scent that was equal parts damp earth and metal.

Grace stayed close, her hand brushing against mine as we descended the stairs. I thought about holding her but opted out at the last second, knowing that wouldn't look so good in front of psychotic bastards.

"Everything okay?" I asked, even though she was already glancing around, wide-eyed and quiet, taking in everything like she didn't trust a single brick of the place.

She gave me a small nod, drawing in a deep breath. At the end of the corridor, a steel door waited, guarded by a guy who looked like he bench-pressed demons for fun. His beady eyes zeroed in on our brands, then flickered to our faces, lingering just a second too long on Grace.

I felt her shift closer to me—barely but enough. Instinct kicked in, and I tilted my head just slightly, locking eyes with him. No smile. No blink. Just a silent promise that if he so much as breathed wrong, he was done.

He must've gotten the message because, after a tense pause,

he stepped aside with a grunt and a nod.

GRACE

The reality of this place struck me immediately as we stepped inside. It was darker and more twisted than anything I could have imagined. Rows and rows of cages lined the walls, each one holding whom I assumed were Celestials. Their faces were beaten, eyes hollowed while some Riftkeeper's stood by cages, sneering as they poked them with makeshift weapons. Others had actual Celestial weapons, shining dully in the dim light like they were trophies of their victories.

My stomach turned, and I fought the repeat of my fry-up from coming up my throat. Nearby, a crowd cheered as two Celestials were forced to fight each other, while around the corner, someone was using a red-hot iron to brand the Celestials with their Riftkeeper mark.

Hunter must have sensed my shock because he leaned into me and murmured, "You're fine; don't worry. Just stay close."

I nodded, swallowing hard and trying to keep my expression neutral, but it was impossible to hide the horror twisting my guts into knots. Everywhere I looked, there was suffering, all orchestrated by people who seemed to take joy in it.

We pushed through the crowd, glancing at the cages as if, somehow, we'd find Aaron here among them. But with every step I took, believing a human could survive a place like this became that much harder.

A few Riftkeeper's glanced suspiciously our way, but we kept moving, pretending we belonged when we didn't. One man in particular—a tall figure with a scar across his cheek—

watched me, his gaze unnervingly sharp as I forced myself to look away.

Then, just ahead, I saw it. Not Aaron but a cherub trapped in a small cage, his wings bound with barbed wire. A group of Riftkeeper's stood around him, laughing as one of them poked at him with the end of a spear and taunted him with threats.

I took a step forward, instinct driving me to desperately help. Hunter quickly tugged me back, but it was too late; one of the sellers had spotted my reaction and grinned.

"You want this one?" he sneered at me. "A cherub's fun for a while, but I'll tell you what—I'll get you an even better one if you kill this little prick." He nodded toward the weakened cherub. "Go on."

I froze, horrified, and my gaze flickered to Hunter. He shook his head at me right as the seller's grin faltered. Hunter didn't give me a chance to respond before he grabbed my arm and dragged me away. He steered us deeper into the crowd, brushing past a few young people and others much older.

I felt sick. Utterly sick.

The cherub's frightened face was now etched into my brain, and I struggled to keep up with Hunter's pace. The factory was a never-ending place; everywhere we turned, there was something going on. Torture, drinking, more torture and screams.

"Help me," someone croaked from one of the cages; she was missing an eye and an arm. "Help me, please."

I was *helpless*, blinking away tears as we went past her. Her working eye followed us in despair, and I turned to Hunter. "Why can't they fight back?"

Hunter's jaw tightened as he looked ahead, taking me through busy sections. "The cages are made out of something that weakens them."

"And what's that?"

"Umbra Alloy. It's a dark metal that comes from hell itself and is a weakening substance to demons and any other Celestial being, including Ascendants."

So, it was like kryptonite but for Celestials...

"That doesn't make sense," I said. "How would Riftkeeper's be able to acquire something from hell?"

"The same way, they also have Celestial weapons. Some demons will provide it for them in hopes of something in return."

I swallowed the acidic taste in my mouth. "Like protection?"

He didn't give me a proper response right away, but eventually, he nodded before we passed another row of cages and came to a stumbling stop as a wiry man with beady eyes blocked our path.

His eyes went from Hunter's to mine, making Hunter push me into a protective stance behind him. "I've never seen you two around here before," the Riftkeeper said, the suspicion in his voice practically palpable.

Hunter kept his expression impassive. "We're new," he replied. "We're just here to look around. See what there is to fuck around with."

The Riftkeeper didn't look convinced; in fact, he sized me up once more, almost like he saw something in me that he recognized. He tilted his head and made a whistling sound with his lips, summoning a few more Riftkeeper's who were now closing in around us.

A glacial fear settled in my chest, its coldness pressing down until every breath felt like I was inhaling shards of ice.

Hunter looked over his shoulder at me. "Bambi?" His voice was so low that only I could hear it. "Duck."

I didn't need him to tell me again as I dropped to the floor without hesitation, and he sprang into action. His fist connected with the nearest Riftkeeper, sending him stumbling backwards before he swiftly took a dagger from behind his waistband and used that to stab another. Chaos erupted around us as Riftkeeper's shouted, some lunging toward Hunter, others going for the prisoners.

I scrambled to my feet, dodging a Riftkeeper's grasp as I tried to get back to Hunter. But bodies crowded around us, and before I knew it, I was shoved to the side, my vision blurring as I was pulled deeper into the crowd.

"Hunter!" I shouted, but my voice was swallowed by the uproar. Panic clawed at my throat as I fought my way through, desperate to get back to him, but everywhere I turned, there were more Riftkeeper's, more cages and more eyes that looked all too eager to find out who or what I was.

GRACE
thirty seven

I searched for Hunter's familiar figure in the mess of faces, but I didn't get far as rough hands grabbed my arm, and I spun around to see a man looking at me with a predatory gleam in his eyes.

"What do we have here then, a wannabe Rifter?" He held onto me as I tried to yank myself free and struggled. He pulled my sleeve up, revealing the Riftkeeper mark, before giving me a crooked grin. My stomach churned with dread and disgust. "Or a Celestial?"

I mashed my teeth together, his touch burning my skin. "No," I hissed. "Human." I spat at him then, making him let go of me as his hands went up to cover his face. I didn't wait to see what would happen as I turned and legged it.

But I was only able to get so far before I was pulled back by my hair. A ragged scream tore from my lips as the man from before came into view. He looked pissed, my spit still gleaming across his face. He threw me to the ground, and I coughed and gagged as my hair got in my mouth. A throbbing sting radiated through my head at where he'd roughly grabbed me from, and I tried to force myself to stand, but the Riftkeeper was already on top of me, grinning.

I screamed a grunted sound as I pounded my fists against his chest, but all he did was laugh in the most horrific way imaginable.

He stopped when he yanked me closer and got a good look at my face. Time seemed to pause for him, and I seized the moment before he could utter a word or act, swiftly retrieving a dagger from his waistband and thrusting it into his throat. A surge of anger and survival flooded inside my chest as he gasped a wet, ragged sound. My own scream ripped through me as I stabbed him again with a lack of control I couldn't fathom. Blood splattered against my hands, hot and slick, and I kept stabbing over and over again, even as he slumped over me and I couldn't breathe.

A metallic scent filled the air, mixed with the frenzy of others around me and then... and then I felt hands around me, pulling me from beneath the Riftkeeper's body. I went to use the dagger on said person, but luckily my vision cleared, and I realized it wasn't a Riftkeeper, it was Hunter. His face was so sharp and focused that his voice—a low mumble of reassurance barely registered through the fog of panic.

I couldn't even feel my feet as he half-carried, half-dragged me through the factory. We passed by cages, the trapped Celestials and demons cheering and banging against their own prison bars, fueling a fire within me that I didn't know I had left.

"Wait," I panted as we made it towards where the cherub was locked up. His small frame was barely visible in the shadows of his cramped cage.

Hunter looked at me, brows knitting together with

impatience, but something in my face must've changed his mind as he glanced at the cherub and then back at me. He nodded, releasing my arm, and I stumbled over to the cherub's cage, gripping the cold, rusted bars. The Riftkeeper who had told me to kill it luckily wasn't around, and I took deep breaths, watching as the cherub's eyes lifted slowly. His once-bright face was streaked with dried blood, and the sight filled me with determination to get him out of here.

"Hold on." I looked for something to break the lock or maybe some hidden release mechanism, but there was nothing.

Just then, Hunter shouted my name right as a Riftkeeper came at me with a blade. I dodged in time for Hunter to lunge at him with the force of his power, sending the Riftkeeper flying back.

Hunter turned to me and eyed the cage. "Stand back."

"What?"

He didn't answer me as he walked toward the cage and a weird hum vibrated once Hunter touched the bars.

"No, don't!" I shouted, grabbing his arm but he didn't let go; his fingers were already turning white as he wrenched at the metal. He muttered under his breath a string of curses and pulled, but each time he did, a ripple of resistance hit him, like an electric shock sparking up his arm.

He grunted in pain, and worry raced frantically through me as his face paled.

"Hunter." His name fell from my lips, but he didn't look at me; he only tightened his grip, straining against the metal with every ounce of strength he had. But I could see it—the flicker of weakness that passed through him, the barely noticeable tremor in his arms as his powers began to waver. "It won't work; you'll just grow weak, like you said. Let me try and find a key or something—I'm not a Celestial, and I know I don't have super strength like you, but I could—"

"Grace?" He cut me a swift glance. "Stop talking."

My lips smacked shut before I could ramble further on. I looked around and saw a broken piece of wood on the floor. I ran for it, grabbing it in time for when a girl with wild hair came screaming at me. My eyes widened, and I did the first thing I thought of as I whacked the ply of wood over her head, sending her to the floor.

"I..." The words inside my mouth practically froze as I stared at her unconscious body. But when I heard Hunter's struggling grunts, I refocused, staggering back to him and placing the now bent piece of wood against the cage.

His jaw clenched tight. "Fuck," he hissed, his voice rasping as he leaned into the bars, his muscles tensing visibly with effort.

"Hunter, just stop," I whispered urgently. "It's draining you."

He shook his head. "Not... leaving him," he ground out, fingers still curled around the bars. With a final desperate push, he let out a grunt, and the metal gave way with a screech. But even as the bars were wide enough for the cherub to escape, Hunter's hands slipped, and he stumbled back, his knees almost buckling beneath him.

I instantly reached out to steady him, my hand gripping his arm as he took a shaky breath.

"Get him out," he managed, his voice low and strained as his chest rose and fell with effort. When his gaze found mine, there was a flicker of pain behind his usual steel-like resolve. Something I didn't think I'd ever see after he used the Seraph blade on himself like it was nothing.

He placed a dagger into my hands, and I barely nodded before I reached out toward the cherub. The fragile creature's gaze shifted between us, its eyes wide with hope.

"It's okay," I whispered, gently reaching out to cut the barbed wire tangled around his wings. "You're free."

The cherub lowered his head, a quiet reverence in his posture. "Thank you. Your bravery will not be forgotten."

He glanced once at Hunter—not with gratitude or acknowledgement but something more... unreadable. A flicker of recognition, maybe even a warning, passed through his eyes before he vanished into a puff of silver smoke.

"Wait!" I called after him, stepping forward. Maybe he knew something about Aaron. Maybe he could've helped.

A sigh slipped from my lips as I backed into Hunter's arms. His grip steadied me; his strength slowly returning along with the color in his face.

Together we stumbled toward the exit, half leaning on each other as we climbed the worn steps out of the Riftkeeper's hideout.

And then—finally—fresh air. Cold and sharp against my skin, but real.

We'd made it out.

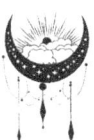

We managed to make it back to the motel somehow intact, though the details blurred together in a haze of shadows, and I felt more as though I was falling apart. Hunter checked the door, his strength fully back now as his eyes scanned the empty hallway, making sure we hadn't been followed. As his gaze settled on me, he looked at the dried blood all over my jacket, my shirt, my hair... "Get out of those clothes, wash yourself and then we'll leave, okay?"

"Okay," I whispered, like a broken doll.

My fingers shook as I ran into the bathroom and stepped in front of the mirror. I almost blacked out once I saw how much blood had splattered all over me and my white top. I was thankful this motel was that god-awful that no one had dared look up at us as we made our way through the front desk, but even so... this... I didn't recognize myself.

I tried to steady my breathing as I turned on the tap, scrubbing my hands with frantic urgency. I scrubbed so hard I couldn't tell if the blood swirling down the drain was mine or the Riftkeeper's. My eyes burned, tears blurring my vision as everything crashed down on me at once. A sob tore from my throat before I could stop it, raw and aching, shattering the silence.

The blood wasn't coming off. It was branded to my skin just as the Riftkeeper mark was, and I desperately needed it gone.

All I could think was if I was just one and the same as the Riftkeeper's. I killed that man with no remorse. Hell, this was the first I had *ever* killed someone.

What would Joe think?

What would Nadael, Eden, and every other angel at Celestia think of me?

Panic swelled in my chest, making it hard for me to breathe. "Why won't you just fucking come off!" I sobbed in frustration.

"Grace," Hunter's voice came from behind. I ignored him as I smeared the blood all over my arms, the water doing nothing to help. "Grace." My name sounded closer, but I couldn't talk. I couldn't think.

I wanted it to stop. I wanted this panic to just let me go, but it only seemed to tighten its hold on me.

Hands clasped my shoulders as I was spun around. Hunter

was there, his grey eyes searching mine, but all I could see was *red, red, red.*

"It won't come off." I sobbed. "It—it—"

He grabbed my face gently, but I couldn't stop the violent tears racking my body. "Hey," he said softly. "Look at me."

I couldn't. All I saw was blood everywhere. On me, on him, on the walls.

Red, red, red.

"Grace," he said more firmly, and I shook my head. He was now moving me towards the shower, pulling his shirt over his head and turning the tap on as the cold water came down on us. I gasped and shuddered at the impact, but Hunter didn't release me from his arms as he turned my back to his chest and slid us down until we were both sitting beneath the shower spray.

I clung to him as I broke down in his arms. It was no longer the blood; it was the Riftkeeper's, Lucas, being a Warrior when I wasn't supposed to be one and so much more blended into one giant mess.

Yet through it all, Hunter stayed with me, never once telling me to stop crying or anything. He rocked us back and forth, his chin pressed against the top of my head as he lulled me into a sense of security that I did not want to end.

I wasn't sure how long we stayed like that, letting the water soak through us but all I knew was that the longer I was in his arms, the less the world seemed to stop spinning.

GRACE
thirty eight

I stood inside the bathroom, the soft patter of water fading as I ran a towel through my damp hair. Hunter's shirt hung loosely on me, the fabric warmed from his scent even as my mind still raced with thoughts of the Riftkeeper's and the horrific things I'd seen. I didn't want to keep thinking about it, and I didn't want the panic to creep back in, but it was hard and draining.

Taking a deep breath, I opened the bathroom door and entered the bedroom. Hunter was sitting at the edge of the bed, shoulders hunched, staring intently at the ground. His jeans were damp as they hung low on his hips, but his chest was bare, the muscles in his back and arms tensing as if he was holding something back.

I took a step closer, uncertain but drawn in by the heaviness of his silence.

"Hey," I whispered like an absolute fool. He looked up, and something raw and unguarded flickered across his eyes, almost as if darkness lurked behind them.

I frowned, and without another word, I crossed the space between us and sat beside him, close enough that our knees touched. "Thank you, by the way," I said. "For what you did back there."

He kept silent as he reached for me, his touch gentle as he tucked a damp curl of hair behind my ear. My breath hitched as I felt his finger brush against my cheek, and I shivered in response.

"How—" I licked my lips. "How did you know how to calm me down?" I tried to keep on the topic of conversation. It wasn't the first time he had witnessed me in full panic mode, but this time it was different. Marnie wasn't here to emotionally heal me; it was Hunter who took the lead without a fault.

"I used to have panic attacks when I was younger," he finally said, and my heart instantly ached for him. "At first, my powers used to scare me. I'd break everything with my strength and accidentally hurt people, so... my brother, to calm me down, would sit with me in the shower. The cold water used to help."

"And now?" I said. "Do you no longer get them?"

He shook his head. "I haven't had one since you joined Celestia."

My heart cracked wide open at his admission. I didn't even think he realized the impact those words just had on me.

"Was it because you were too busy trying to make me quit?" I tried joking. It was terrible timing.

Though it somehow worked when he chuckled softly. "Maybe," he said. "Or maybe you just... I don't know. You made things feel different."

My breath hitched slightly. "Different how?"

He hesitated, his gaze flicking away for a moment before

296

finding mine again. "Like you being here reminded me that maybe not everything has to be so dark and twisted. Maybe there's... still a way to hold onto something good."

My heart stumbled in my chest. Hunter, the one who rarely let anyone in, who wanted me to quit on the first day, had just said something that stripped away at every wall he'd built around himself.

"So does that make us... friends now?" I asked softly, trying to ignore the flutter of nerves in my chest.

He stared at me for a moment, then, he shook his head, and a quiet, almost resigned chuckle escaped his lips. "No," he said. "I don't think we could ever *be* just friends."

I supposed he was right. But then, what were we?

We became quiet for a minute, and then my hand lifted, almost of its own accord, brushing against his shoulder. "I'm sorry by the way—about tonight. I know it didn't work out how you'd hoped," I said quietly, "maybe we could try again next week—"

He hushed me, shaking his head as he leaned in, and our foreheads touched. Suddenly, all the tension and confusion of the night faded, replaced by this moment only. I was a solid being yet melting from his warmth, and just as I started whispering his name, he pressed his lips to mine.

The kiss was soft and tentative at first, but it quickly deepened with a fire sparking to life as our hands tangled in each other's hair, pulling each other closer.

Hunter's hands found my waist, pulling me into his lap as he kissed me with a hunger that mirrored my own. His touch was rough yet careful, forbidden yet so unlawfully right. His fingers moved along my back as if he needed to feel every inch of me to know I was real. I let my fingers trace the lines of his shoulders, neck, and toned chest until his warmth seeped into

297

me, making everything else disappear.

He tugged my shirt up, and I lifted my arms, letting him slide it off. My skin tingled as his eyes roamed over me. My chest wasn't on the big side, and I had never done anything with a boy before, yet the way Hunter's gaze filled with something deep, something lustful, I felt alive.

Yeah... we could never be friends.

But I also knew deep down that this was a mistake—that there were heavy reasons why this shouldn't happen. I could see the same war in Hunter's eyes as he pulled back for only a second, but neither of us stopped.

Our breaths grew ragged with each kiss, with each touch and caress, but just as I began to unbuckle his belt, he froze. His hand stilled, his grip loosening as he pulled back. His forehead pressed against mine, and his eyes remained closed as he fought to regain control. "Grace," he breathed, voice thick with restraint. "We can't—"

I nodded, though I felt drawn for just one more kiss. No, a thousand more.

I leaned in again, and he took my mouth in his like it belonged to him and only him. His hands ran up my back and into my damp curls, pulling me towards him like there was still too much space between us.

"Grace," he said again but to me it sounded like a painful plea. When I went in again, he shook his head. "We can't do this. I shouldn't have..."

The words hung in the air as I kept my eyes closed, knowing that if I opened them, this moment would disappear. Maybe forever.

"I know," I whispered thickly, like a lump had formed in my throat, and I couldn't swallow it.

He stood, gently lifting me off him, and I blinked the sting out of my eyes as I finally came to. He reached for my shirt, his eyes soft but distant as he handed it to me. "Get dressed," he said quietly. "I'll wait for you downstairs."

I nodded again, feeling hollow, as he zipped up his hoodie and left the room. Staring at the door, I clung to the shirt he had given me, wishing he would have rejected me completely rather than tell me we couldn't do this with the known fact that it would ruin his chances as an Ascendant.

GRACE
thirty nine

I sniffled as I stepped into the dorm, feeling the flood of relief when I saw Brandon and Silas sitting on the sofa. Marnie was perched on the armrest as the three looked worried sick before their eyes landed on us.

Marnie stood, and I was about to run to her when someone else came out of my room.

Joe.

My heart dropped.

His expression was livid. The only time I saw this look on him was when we had to leave or whenever he encountered Riftkeeper's.

"Grace," he said, his voice low and tight like the calm before a storm.

Marnie looked at me with guilt written all over her freckled face. "I'm so sorry. He—he came by to check on you, and then I got nervous, and I—" She didn't finish what she had to say as Joe stepped closer and grabbed my arm, his fingers tightening around my wrist as he pulled the sleeve of my jacket up to reveal the Riftkeeper mark etched on my skin.

"Is this what you are now? One of them?"

I flinched, but before I could respond, Hunter stepped forward. "It's my fault—"

"Don't," Joe snapped at Hunter. "Don't even try to defend her. This—this is beyond reckless of you, Grace." He turned his full anger back on me, his grip on my wrist loosening only slightly. "You're branded with a Riftkeeper mark. Do you even understand what that means? What you've done to yourself? I can't—" He broke off, his voice trembling with something that wasn't just anger. It was fear.

Hunter took a step forward again. "I was the one who gave her that mark. Blame me all you want, but she had nothing to do with this."

Joe glanced at him and his anger refocused. "Don't worry. I'll make sure Nadael deals with you later."

My eyes widened. "Joe, no! I wanted to—" My words caught in my throat as Joe dragged me towards the door, and Hunter stepped between us, blocking Joe from taking me away.

"Get out of the way."

"She stays." Hunter's tone would make anyone flinch, but Joe was too wired, too angry to see past the sudden protectiveness in Hunter's voice.

"You're not the one who gets to decide here. Let's go, Grace—"

"No." My body trembled with the remnants of what happened today: the Riftkeeper's, the kiss, and Joe. I snatched my wrist free from his grip, and he spun to face me. "You don't get to do that to me, Joe. You don't get to decide for *me* anymore." My voice began to rise. "I've spent my whole life hiding. I've spent every single day running, looking over my shoulder, because of you! I never asked for this, and I

especially never asked for Celestia."

Joe's face hardened, his lips pressing into a thin line. "I'm trying to protect you."

"Protect me?" I laughed bitterly, the sound sharp and odd even to my own ears. "All you do is hide things from me, control me and look where it's gotten us."

"Grace—"

"You're not my father, Joe!" The words came out before I could stop them, raw, jagged, and full of everything I'd been holding back for years. "You never were, and you never will be."

The silence that followed was deafening. Joe stared at me, his face pale and drawn as his expression fell beneath the weight of my words. For a moment, I thought he might say something. I thought *I* would say something—that I'd apologize and regret it. But I couldn't because I meant it in so many ways.

He nodded, a slow, defeated movement. "You're right," he said quietly... broken. "You're right," he said again and glanced at all of us before he turned, shouldering past Hunter.

The door clicked shut behind him, leaving the remaining silence to stretch out. I stood there, my chest heaving and my hands trembling at the sides.

"Grace," Hunter said softly, but I couldn't bring myself to look at him because something inside me had already cracked open and spilt out, leaving me empty.

I shook my head and withdrew a few steps back before heading towards my room with Marnie in tow.

HUNTER

I stalked across my room and toward the window, gripping the edge of the frame so tightly that my knuckles turned white. Silas and Brandon filed in after me, their voices cutting through the calmness I was desperately trying to maintain and failing.

"What the fuck just happened out there?" Silas said. "I thought Joe was about to start throwing hands at you or something."

Brandon leaned against the wall. "We knew you were taking Grace out of Celestia, but I didn't think you'd go as far as getting branded with the Riftkeeper mark. This is getting out of hand, Cain."

I clenched my teeth and faced away from them. I didn't want to talk about it. I didn't even think about it. And I sure as fuck wasn't going to admit what was swirling through my mind. That kiss. Her lips on mine. Or the way she melted into me even though she knew it was a mistake. Hell, I knew it was a mistake. And yet—

"Something happened with Grace, didn't it?" Brandon went on, reading me like a goddamn sonogram.

"Yeah, ya dipshit," Silas said. "They went to find Aaron and encountered Riftkeeper's. That's what."

"You clearly didn't catch the vibe that Cain and Grace were giving each other when we were in the—"

"I kissed her," I said abruptly, my voice harsher than I intended. It was not something I had wanted to say in the first place.

The admission hung heavy in the air, and I could feel their

eyes on me.

"What, now?" Silas asked, off guard.

"So, you kissed..." Brandon started, and I shook my head. "Wait, let me get this straight. You kissed—"

"It doesn't matter anymore," I snapped. "It won't happen again."

Silas let out a low whistle. "It better not. You know how much trouble you'd get into? I mean, there is a reason why everyone blames Eve. She was the sole cause of the fifth angelic rule being put into place."

Brandon and I shot a questioning look at Silas. "What are you even talking about?"

"Uh, you know the first woman slash human and the ultimate betrayer? She literally had a relationship with Lucifer that led to the war."

"What does this have to do with anything?" Brandon asked. I also wanted to know myself. "And since when do you pay attention in Rael's classes?"

"I always pay attention," Silas said defensively. "I'm just stating that Eve messed up, and I would hate for Cain over here to do the same."

Brandon snorted. "You do realize she's not the only one to blame, right?"

"Yeah, but Eve's the one everyone remembers for screwing up. Like I said, she caused all of this."

I sighed, running a hand through my hair. "She's more than just that, you know."

"Oh, right. Forgot you had all the insider knowledge, Cain."

I shot him a glare, but Brandon cut in before I could respond. "What's your problem with her anyway? It's not like she ruined *your* life."

Silas smirked. "Oh, I don't have a problem with her. I just

think it's hilarious how one bad choice can screw over billions of people. Makes you wonder what other Celestial screw-ups are hiding in history."

His words hit a little too close to home, and I clenched my jaw. Silas was just being Silas, running his mouth without a care in the world. But I couldn't help thinking about how one choice—one mistake—could ripple out and destroy everything.

My chest felt too tight, and I ran a hand over my jaw to regain some semblance of control. "Either way, like I told you both. What happened between me and Grace won't happen again."

Brandon tilted his head, studying me. He rolled his lip piercing between his teeth before he said, "Are you sure about that? Because it sure as hell looks like you'd do it again in a heartbeat."

I didn't answer. I didn't want to when he was right.

"Even if that is the case, Cain will restrain himself, right?" Silas cocked his brows. "Just like we all have to."

I stared at him, knowing there was more to that than he was letting on. He didn't just mean me, but he would never admit that himself.

"Now," he said. "What about your brother? Did you find anything?"

I shook my head, and the room went silent. Brandon and Silas exchanged a glance, but neither of them pressed further. They wouldn't understand why I couldn't afford to let myself get close to Grace—or anyone. It wasn't just the rules. It was so much more than that.

GRACE

forty

Marnie's hands hovered over my arm, a faint golden glow radiating from her fingertips as she worked to heal the angry Riftkeeper mark. The burn still throbbed, but the pain was at least dulling with each passing second.

"You shouldn't have done this, Grace," she said with a shake of her head. "I told you this wasn't a good idea. Why don't you ever listen?"

I stared at the mark as it began to fade under her touch, and my thoughts drifted back to the motel, Hunter's hands on me, his lips against mine. The kiss had been a mistake—one we both knew—but that didn't stop me from missing the way he held me, as if I was the only thing grounding him amidst the chaos.

"Are you even listening to me right now?" Marnie's voice snapped me back to the present.

"Yeah," I lied, my voice quieter than usual. "Thank you...

for doing this."

She sighed, shaking her head but not saying anything more. The golden glow dimmed as she finished, and the mark was now just a faint bruise on my skin that would eventually go away. She sat back against the bed, studying me with those perceptive green eyes, and I crawled towards her, resting my head against her shoulder.

"Marnie?"

She hummed.

"Have you ever thought about... not doing this?"

"What do you mean?"

I tilted my head to look up at her. "I mean, if you were given the chance to be with someone, to live a normal life—even if it meant forgetting everything about Celestia, the Ascendants, the angels—would you take it?"

She hesitated for a second. "No," she said with a frown, but it wasn't the answer I had hoped for. She straightened against the wall, and I sat up. "I've always wanted to ascend. I don't think anything has ever made me change my mind, not my parents, nor the Ascendants around me..." Her expression softened as she glanced at me. "It's what I was born to be. I want to help people. I want to protect and heal our world, even if that means I won't ever have a normal life. *This* is my dream. It always has been, and I intend to follow it through."

Her words hit me harder than I expected. I'd never really let myself consider that possibility. Joe's life wasn't normal, even with me in it, and now I'd said something to him I could never take back.

"What about you, Grace? What would you do if you could choose anything?"

I blinked at her. What did I want? The truth was, I didn't know. I'd spent so long just trying to survive, wanting to become stronger, that the dreams I once had were now a myth.

"When I was little, I used to want to be a doctor," I said and smiled when I remembered how I'd dress up as a doctor and pretend to heal Joe. "I guess that is why I was supposed to join the Healers Sector. Joe knew I would like it. Heal people the way you do, just without the powers, I guess."

Marnie smiled. "You'd be good at that." She then nudged my shoulder. "But you'd also be good as a Warrior, Guardian and a Messenger."

I let out a shaky breath. "You just always know what to say, don't you?"

She laughed. "Only sometimes." She reached into my drawer and picked out a packet of skittles. Handing me some of the green ones while she picked at the reds, she added, "Just don't push Joe away. Father or not, he still loves you like one."

I nodded, my heart squeezing with shame as I allowed her words to linger inside my mind.

"And be careful, okay?" she said. "Because whatever you're also doing with Hunter to help him find his brother, it's not just him who's at risk."

The skittles began to melt in my hand, and I couldn't find the strength to even eat a simple sweet. She was right; whatever *was* happening between me and Hunter was a mess and not just from helping him. But for the first time, I wasn't sure I could walk away from it.

Not after tonight.

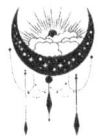

The following day, my mind was still far from calm, and the morning sun did little to lift my spirits. I was scared Joe had gone to see Nadael, that he'd told her everything from the Riftkeeper mark to what I yelled at him before he left. Maybe that was why I hadn't eaten any breakfast, left at the crack of dawn and was now making my way towards Nadael's office. I was trying to think of ways I could start the conversation with her. Most were utterly terrible, ranging from '*I snuck out... by mistake*' to '*I was sleepwalking, and they say not to disturb you when that happens, so Hunter followed me to keep an eye on me, and we just so happened to encounter Riftkeeper's!*' That one was surprisingly the least bad of them all.

"Grace!" Eden's voice called out from behind me, and I slowed down, turning reluctantly. Her expression wasn't the usual smile and dimples as she approached, which already meant something was wrong. "I am so glad I found you. You weren't in room 104?"

"I—" I hitched a thumb over my shoulder. "I was just heading towards Nadael's office."

She gave me a tight-lipped smile. "No need. She is currently overseeing the Messengers Sector in time for the competition. I wanted to let you know in person that you've been reassigned a new accommodation."

I froze. "What? Why?"

"It was Joe's request," she replied matter-of-factly, as if she just hadn't ruined my morning with that announcement. "You'll be rooming with Marnie Lewis."

My frustration wavered for a moment. As much as I loved Marnie, being moved without warning was infuriating. I knew the reason, but it only made me more inclined to be angry with Joe. "Do the boys know?"

"Yes, I believe Hunter is the one who also said it was for the best."

Those words shot through my chest, shattering the last bit

of resolve I had left in me.

I swallowed, trying to steady myself, but I couldn't. My throat felt tight, and suddenly, all I wanted was to go back to last night in that motel. "And Joe?" I said, my voice breaking. "Where is he?"

"He's with the Council."

"Of *course*, he is."

Eden observed me, then placed a hand on my shoulder that did nothing to soothe me. "Are you okay?" A soft glow leaked from her hand, and I shoved her away, knowing she was trying to heal whatever emotional damage I had going on right now. I didn't want to be tricked into a false sense of security. Despite it all, I wanted to *feel* every bit of emotion I had in me. "Do you want to go and see him?" She asked after a moment, and I froze, so she prompted. "Joe, that is."

I narrowed my eyes at her. Was this some sort of test? "I thought the Council chambers were off-limits to us?"

Her glossed lips curved into a faint smile before her gaze drifted toward a nearby painting of a Celestial battlefield. Without saying a word, she extended her hand toward it, her fingers brushing the edges of the frame as the painting shimmered and rippled like a river.

"Before I came to Celestia, Joe and I had grown up together. We were raised in the same orphanage, and funny enough, we were both Ascendants. You can imagine we were close."

"What happened?"

"He ascended. And then he had his duties to do, and I had mine." She sighed, closing her eyes and putting on her cheerful smile. "Whatever he is trying to do, Grace, by having you here, it is only because he cares. You'll see."

I still felt unsure as I glanced at the painting. "Won't you get in trouble for this?"

Eden released a breathless chuckle as she leaned forward. "Oh, I hope so. I would love a bit of thrill, wouldn't you?"

I'd lived enough thrill so far to last me a lifetime, but Eden didn't need to know that.

I smiled at her and murmured, "Thank you." As I took a step toward the painting.

"Grace?"

I turned.

"Try not to get caught."

I nodded, though my heart was already pounding like a war drum by the time I stepped into the painting. The world rippled around me, bending and reshaping until my boots landed silently on polished marble. I glanced around me, the air humming with energy so dense it pressed against my skin.

The Council headquarters looked otherworldly; a place designed to intimidate. That much I knew. Massive pillars stretched toward the impossibly high ceiling; each one wrapped in glowing runes that pulsed faintly. Enormous stained-glass windows lined the hall, their colors muted in the silvery light that bathed the place. They looked like the ones inside Celestia, but these felt older, more sacred.

I soon heard voices and ducked behind a column. The headquarters was never-ending yet wide, with nowhere to hide but the slender shadows cast by the pillars. Ahead in the center of the room, I caught sight of the dais. It was circular, carved with Enochian symbols. Farther in, at the end of the hall, there were spiked thrones cloaked in radiance, and I assumed even from a distance that they belonged to the lead Council members.

I leaned against the pillar, forcing my breathing to slow. I had no idea where Joe was, but if anyone caught me here, it wouldn't matter. I'd be in trouble; so, would Eden.

Keeping low, I slipped from one column to the next, scanning the room for any sign of movement. There were smaller doors lining the far walls, and my best guess was that they led to private chambers or worse cells where they kept prisoners before judgment.

A shudder wracked through me, and I thought about the demon that killed Lucas. My palms were slick with sweat, and I was so tempted, so, so tempted, to head in a different direction until I caught a glimpse of movement to the right, near one of the smaller doors.

Air snagged in my lungs, forcing me to be still.

It was Joe.

He was standing in the shadow of one of the doorways, his head tilted slightly as he listened to someone else speak. He looked tired, his shoulders slumped in a way I wasn't used to seeing. I couldn't help but blame myself for that.

Just then, the Celestial he was speaking with turned her head and I dipped back against the pillar, pressing myself as flat as I possibly could against it.

"Something... feels strange," the Celestial said, and I held my breath.

"Everything feels strange, lately, Mikael," Joe said. There was a brief pause before Mikael chuckled.

"I suppose you are right."

They both slipped into a new conversation, one I couldn't fully hear—though it didn't matter. I was focused on their footsteps, waiting. After a few minutes, I heard the familiar cadence of a goodbye and soon enough, Mikael strolled off in the opposite direction.

I could no longer wait. As soon as Mikael was far gone, I slipped through the shadows, my heart pounding so loudly I could barely hear my own footsteps.

The corridor was dimly lit with flickering celestial runes, and as I rounded a corner, a slab of gold-lined stone caught my eye. It stood tall, etched in angelic script that practically glowed.

The Angelic Code.

I swallowed, stepping closer and letting my fingers brush the carvings. I scanned the rules, already familiar with the first few due to Joe's influence. But it was the fifth and final one that hit me the hardest.

V. The Heart is the Weakest Flesh

No Celestial shall pledge their heart to another, form romantic ties, nor pledge themselves to a mortal, a Nephilim, or even a fellow Celestial. To do so is to forsake the divine order.

To love is to fall. To fall is to be forgotten.

My breath stilled.

I read it again. And again.

A part of me wanted to laugh at the cruelty of it all. The timing. The irony. I stepped back; the words burned into my mind.

"Grace?"

Shit.

I turned slowly to find Joe standing at the end of the corridor, his jaw clenched, and his eyes shadowed with frustration.

"What are you doing here?"

I forgot the rules. I ignored his question. I was here for one thing. Planting myself firmly in his path, I demanded, "Why did you move me to another dorm?"

He took a few sharp glances around the halls before

grabbing my arm and pulling me into a nearby empty room. Inside, shelves lined the walls with ancient-looking books. Some even glowed faintly, and I shivered at the energy they radiated. It was as if pulling at something inhumane. My gaze swiftly caught on a dagger with a mark eerily similar to the Riftkeeper symbol and the initials D.S. carved on the handle.

"Whose is that?" I asked, but Joe didn't answer me as I turned to him.

"You shouldn't be here."

"Why don't you answer me for once?" I snapped. "Why did you move me? Why do you keep doing this?"

"You shouldn't have been put in that dorm in the first place," he said, his tone clipped, but even I could see through him and how much emotion was behind each of those words. "And you know that."

"But it was *my* choice," I said weakly, pressing the tips of my fingers to my chest. Ever since Joe left me at Celestia, nothing has been the same. At least when we were constantly moving towns, cities, schools and all, we stayed the same. United. Celestia had placed a barrier between us, and I didn't know how to go back to before.

"Go back, Grace. If a Council member sees you here without having been authorized, you could face consequences."

Consequences be damned.

Joe went to open the door, but my voice stopped him short.

"Do you know why I went out in search of Riftkeeper's?"

Joe's knuckles whitened as he tightened his grip on the door handle.

I took a step forward despite facing his back. "I wanted to prove I was strong enough to go against one." It was the partial truth. I couldn't mention Hunter's brother, not after everything that had happened. "I don't know if that makes me a hero or a fool, but I did it, and I would do it again if I had to."

My chest was heavy with the memory of that night. I could still smell the blood on my hands. The sickening iron scent wouldn't leave from beneath my bed of nails, no matter how many times I'd wash them.

"Grace," Joe sighed. "All of this isn't to punish you. I just—" He paused, but I shook my head, knowing there was no reasoning with him.

"I'm the one who told Hunter about finding a Riftkeeper hideout, not him. I dragged him into it. He didn't even want me to go in the first place, so please, for my sake, don't let him get in trouble."

Joe kept quiet.

Sighing, I walked towards the door and past him. I stepped out into the hall, my eyes stinging with frustration, anger, and misery.

"I still think you should steer away from that Cain boy, Grace."

My shoulders hitched, and I stilled. Slowly, I turned to the side. Joe was by the doorway, his expression conflicted. "Why?"

"I would hate to see you get hurt over something that can never happen."

Something that can never happen.

I blinked, once. Twice.

He could tell. In some way or another.

I swallowed hard, pushing the heat in my throat back down.

"There is nothing there to get hurt by in the first place," I said before turning on my heel and making my way back to the painting.

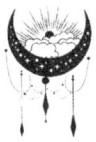

Eden was waiting for me on the other side as I pushed through the painting and landed back on Celestia's grounds. She was leaning her shoulder against the wall and smiled once she saw I'd made it back in one piece. Physically, but perhaps not mentally.

Her expression turned thoughtful when she saw mine. No doubt, I must have looked worse than before I went to see Joe. "Is everything alright?"

I nodded. "Never been better," I lied, not caring if she could see right through me as I thanked her once more and brushed past her before she could ask me another question.

Later that evening, I was officially moved into Marnie's dorm. She practically squealed when she saw me, pulling me into one of her tight hugs. And whatever suitcases and personal items I had from room 104 had been moved by Celestials to the Healer's quarters while I was in Sariel's class. I should have known that would be the case. Hunter likely packed it all away for me and yelled good riddance as soon as they came to pick it all up.

"I'm so glad you're here with me," Marnie gushed, dragging me inside. Her enthusiasm was always contagious, but her two other roommates didn't seem nearly as thrilled as she was. They were behind the kitchenette tabletop, exchanging sceptical looks as I sheepishly waved at them.

I couldn't focus on much else as Marnie showed me my new room because all I wanted to do was cry, sleep and forget everything.

GRACE
forty one

I awoke to the sound of Marnie humming the words to an eighties pop song and groaned, feeling as if I had the flu. Which, in ways, I would rather have it. It'd be easier than dealing with Celestials.

"Morning to you, too." She chuckled, tying her hair into two French braids. Once she finished, she came over and jumped onto my bed. "So, I wrote down a list of things we could do now that we are officially roommates."

One of my brows rose. "Is one of them karaoke?"

She blinked. "Yes, but—"

I chuckled, sliding out of bed to get ready, but my stomach dropped when my mind immediately went to Hunter. I hadn't seen him since that night we kissed, and worse, today, we were supposed to train outside of academy hours. It bothered me that he hadn't spoken to me before deciding that the best plan was for me to leave his dorm. I knew he wanted to steer away from me, that our kiss was a mistake, but I so wished it wasn't.

"You know, I'm starting to think you're not happy to be

rooming with me anymore," Marnie said from where she was sitting cross-legged on the bed.

I grabbed my trousers and shot her a look. "You know that's not true. It's just..."

"You miss the boys?"

Yes. Who would have ever thought that would be the case?

"I do strangely miss Brandon making lightsaber noises in the morning." What I did *not* miss was Silas telling us all that his dick was better than a lightsaber and that he could prove it if we didn't believe him.

"And Hunter?"

I went rigid, and the shoelaces of my combat boots slipped through my fingertips. "What about Hunter?"

"Do you miss him?"

Yes. "No."

"Hm, well, do you think he'll stop training you?"

"Who knows?" I shrugged, trying to sound indifferent, but my voice cracked slightly, betraying me. "Hunter does what he wants. Maybe I should do the same." But I didn't want to. I *really* didn't want to.

Marnie hummed in agreement but as I tightened the knot in my laces and stood, there was an ache in my chest that I wasn't sure if I was ready to find out what it was.

Marnie tilted her head, her lips curving into a knowing hum. She didn't press further, but her silence was heavy, as though she could see right through me.

I exhaled deeply, tightening the knot in my laces as I stood. I hoped to shake off the weight in my chest, but it lingered— almost like an ache, deep and insistent, that I could not rid myself of no matter what.

I had a feeling it would stay with me for the remainder of the day.

322

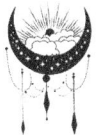

When I stepped onto the training grounds, my eyes scanned the space, searching for Hunter's familiar silhouette. Instead, I saw Silas by the weapons rack, his hair tied into a bun behind him, and Brandon standing beside him, stretching his arms out.

He smiled when he caught sight of me and jogged over. "There she is," he greeted. "Missed you this morning. Had to deal with Silas's nudity all alone."

Alone?

Silas seemed to have heard Brandon from the racks and shouted, "Oh, fuck off!"

Brandon laughed, sneering at him, but all I could concentrate on was Hunter's absence. And if he hadn't been at the dorm this morning, then where was he?

"Where's Hunter?"

Brandon's face fell. He crossed his arms over his shoulders before shrugging, "I don't know, we haven't seen him since this morning. He's not really spoken to us lately."

"Right," I said, all my resolve crumbling before me.

"I can fill in if you want," Brandon suggested with a shrug, "It'll be a lot better than having Azrael yell at you for not doing anything."

Disappointment simmered in my chest, and Brandon could see it himself, but he didn't dig for more. He understood, and he was always more understanding of the three.

After a minute, I nodded, and he steered me towards the other side of the field where fewer people were.

Brandon was patient for the remainder of training as he walked me through the basic maneuvers I'd first learned with

323

Lucas and Hunter. But it wasn't the same. His critiques lacked the sharp edge Hunter's always carried, and no matter how hard I tried to focus, my frustration grew with each swing of my fist.

Azrael watched us from afar, and his eyes narrowed on me, which only made me more tense. After training was over, I decided I didn't want to head back to the Healer's quarters. Instead, I searched for Hunter when I knew I shouldn't.

He wasn't in his dorm, and Brandon had mentioned he hadn't seen him since this morning, so my last resort was to wait until the canteen was shut and sneak into the same place Hunter took me to where the armory entrance was.

It didn't take long to find him after that. He was there, standing over a table as he sharpened a dagger under the dim light of an overhead lamp. The armory smelled just as it had before. Metal and oil mixed with the sound of the blade against the echoes of the whetstone.

I made my way down the stairs. "Busy?"

Hunter didn't look up, but his jaw tightened. "What do you want, Grace?"

"You've been avoiding me."

He finally glanced up, but his grey eyes were cool and detached. The look he normally gave anyone he wanted to hide his true self from. "I'm not avoiding you. I'm doing you a favor."

I scoffed. Some kind of favor that was. "By pretending I don't exist?"

His silence was infuriating as he went back to sharpen his blade. I gritted my teeth, grabbed a blade from a nearby rack, and held it up.

"You owe me a lesson."

His lips curved into a humorless smile. "Put it down,

Grace."

Stubbornly, I refused.

He sighed when he realized that I wouldn't do as he said and set his blade down on the table beside him. "If you wanted a blade that would do actual harm, you should have chosen another."

I frowned, glancing at the golden dagger in my hands. The blade was zigzagged but hardly sharpened at the end.

"The most damage that can be done with that is putting someone to sleep. You should know that by now from your second lesson."

I straightened, holding my chin up high as if choosing that blade was on purpose all along. "Like I said. You. Owe. Me a lesson."

He didn't say anything. He just stared at me in complete silence like he was daring me to go ahead with it.

I lunged first, my frustration fueling every swing, but he blocked each attack effortlessly like he usually would. It only spurred me on, and I fought harder, putting as much effort as I could into each of my movements—into each thrust of the dagger I'd learned from him.

"Again," he instructed, his voice steady, almost bored.

I huffed, closing my eyes and drawing a deep breath before my gaze locked on his. With all the force I could muster, I struck quickly. The fluidity of the motion felt right, but Hunter dodged at the last second, eyeing me like he was a predator playing with his prey.

A huntsman and his fawn.

"Use your legs," he taunted, ducking as I complied, and anger surged in my chest. I closed my eyes again, steadying my breath. Joe. The Riftkeeper's. Our kiss. All of it flashed in my mind, feeding that frustration just a bit more each time.

Without thinking, I gripped the dagger in my hand tighter and aimed it directly at Hunter's throat.

His hand clamped down on my wrist, stopping me before I could make contact. Our chests matched the upheaval of each breath as our eyes met. His expression softened, and something a lot like pride flickered in his gaze just for one moment. "Not bad, Bambi," he breathed, his eyes tracking the movement of my tongue darting out to lick my lips.

The space between us was suddenly too small. We both knew that, yet we didn't let go or step away from each other.

"Why did you let me leave?" I whispered.

He knew what I meant. He could even crush me with just one look if he wanted to, yet he was staring back at me like I was the one who might break him. "You know why."

"Maybe I don't care." There was a whole different meaning to those words. I cared enough not to ruin him, but I also just wanted to be near him. "You want me just as much as I want you."

He shook his head. "You don't get it, do you?" His voice was raw and desperate. "I don't just want you, Grace—I fucking need you. And that scares the shit out of me."

I blinked, my chest heaving with his admission. It was all I wanted—*needed* to hear.

"You make me want to be something better," he whispered, voice rough at the edges, sending me almost into oblivion. "And I don't know how to be that."

"Then don't be."

Hunter's gaze darkened, and before I could think, his hands were on my waist, pulling me closer as the dagger dropped out of my hand. Everything after that was a blur of heat and desperation as his lips found mine. The kiss was nothing like the other night. It was rough and consuming, as if he was trying

326

to erase every line we'd drawn between us.

He couldn't get enough of me, and neither could I get enough of him. I molded perfectly into his hold, his touch, and his warmth. I didn't want this to stop, not like it did last time. I wanted it to continue until neither of us could breathe.

I was lifted onto a nearby table, his hands roaming over my body as mine clung to him, desperate for more.

"This is a mistake," he murmured against my skin, his voice strained as his bottom lip trailed my neck.

I tilted my head back, giving him easier access, his hands exploring every inch of me. "A terrible mistake."

"We should stop."

I shook my head, breathless. "Please don't."

He didn't.

I felt the strength in his grip tighten as he lifted me higher against the table, his body pressing against mine in a way that left no space between us. He slid his hand under the hem of my training shirt, the roughness of his palms setting every nerve in my body ablaze. I gasped as he pulled the fabric over my head and tossed it aside. The cool air from the armory hit my skin, but it was nothing compared to the warmth that radiated from him.

"Grace," he said, his voice barely audible as his grey eyes locked onto mine, searching for something—permission, assurance, I wasn't sure. Either way, I answered him with a kiss, pouring every emotion I couldn't put into words with the press of my lips against his. I lifted his shirt over his head, and my hands immediately went to his chest, feeling the taut muscles contract beneath my touch.

His fingers skimmed along my sides, sending shivers down my spine as they slid beneath the waistband of my trousers. He paused for a fraction of a second, his forehead resting against mine before he claimed my lips again, deeper this time.

We were crossing a path we knew we couldn't come back from. A kiss was a kiss, but this was more to us. Everything was.

"You're so damn beautiful," he murmured, his thumb brushing against my cheek.

The words sent a jolt to my heart, and I pulled him closer, needing to feel and drown in him. His hands guided me as he unbuckled his belt and pressed himself against me. His cock jutted out from his boxers, and I inhaled a deep breath at the size... at the veins running along it.

But then, a thought struck me like a bucket of ice water. "Hunter," I whispered, pulling back slightly.

He stilled, his grey eyes narrowing in concern. "What is it?" His voice was rough and husky, filled with the same longing that coursed through me.

"Do you have...?" My voice faltered as I tried to find the right words. "I mean, we don't have—"

He closed his eyes briefly, and I saw his jaw tighten. "No," he admitted in frustration.

Of course, he didn't. He was an Ascendant. I should have expected him not to have any form of protection.

My cheeks burned, but another thought slipped out before I could say anything else. "But have you ever..." I didn't even want to finish the words.

Hunter's jaw ticked, his teeth clenching for a moment before he said gruffly, "Yes."

My mind reeled. "But—"

His expression darkened before he kissed me again, harder this time, as though he was trying to erase the weight of the past and the questions that still lingered between us. His lips moved with a desperate intensity that I could no longer think straight.

Whatever secrets he held, whatever his past entailed, I knew one thing for certain—I still wanted this. I still wanted him. Hunter Cain, in all his complexity and contradictions.

"We should really stop before—"

I shook my head, tightening my hold on him. "I don't care."

That unleashed something within him as a low groan fell from his lips and he lost all resistance.

"Do you trust me?" he whispered against my lips.

I was a virgin, through and through. And I believed he knew that already. He could tell, but the reassurance I was giving him with just one look told him everything I wanted from him. "Yes."

"I'll be gentle," he assured me, and I nodded like a lost puppy, waiting for what was to come. "As long as you don't kick me in the balls again."

A breathless chuckle burst from my lips, and he smiled, causing my stomach to dip. "I won't."

He nuzzled his nose against mine, whispering, "Good."

I bit my lip, shaking with nerves and anticipation as I lay back against the table and felt how hard he already was without having to look. My shaking legs parted, letting him have full access to me. He positioned himself by my entrance, and my heart raced as he leaned above me, his hands finding mine above my head.

The world outside faded away, and it was just us in that moment.

"Just keep looking at me. Don't look anywhere else," he breathed, and I nodded, too lost for words to speak yet.

Seconds later, I breathed in, and what was once a barrier gave way as he pushed the tip of his cock into me, and a gasp escaped my lips. He stilled, his gaze never leaving mine as he slowly moved all the way into me. I clenched my eyes shut, biting the inside of my cheek as the tight sting overwhelmed me. It felt full and warm, like a hot knife gliding through butter, until I was whimpering as that sting became a throbbing delight.

His hand came up to cradle my face, his thumb brushing away a stray tear I hadn't realized had fallen. "Are you okay?"

I nodded, opening my eyes as I released a shaky breath. "Yes," I whispered. "Don't stop."

He didn't.

His thrusts moved in rhythm with my body, his thumb running circles against the inner part of my wrist. I arched my back, and he pushed his hips forward, stretching me even more.

"Hey," he said gently, trying to capture my attention as my eyes became heavy. "Keep looking at me, Bambi. It's just us, no one else."

I nodded again, gasping as our bodies rocked against each other and the table beneath me creaked under our weight. At any moment, we could be caught. A Celestial could come down those steps and see us or, worse, the Council. But it didn't matter, not then, *not* when it was us two.

He kissed me, and I sucked in a ragged breath as his moves grew faster. Pain mixed with pleasure, and I bit my lip, hoping he wouldn't back down. I clenched my thighs around his hips right as his lips moved to my breasts, and he took one into his mouth. The sensation rocked me into euphoria as I gasped, and spots clouded my vision. I didn't understand what was happening; all I knew was that I didn't want it to end.

My skin began tingling as sweat broke out across my chest and his. He lowered his forehead against mine, our breaths becoming one as he rocked back and forth.

I was losing myself to him, and I didn't care. I would gladly lose myself over and over to feel like this with him again.

Hunter groaned, his thrusts growing faster. I tried to reach for him, but his hands held onto my wrists, keeping me at bay as I felt myself clench around him. His breath hitched, and for a moment, he stilled, his forehead still pressed to mine. I could feel the rapid thud of his heart in his chest, pounding in time with mine. His grip on my wrists tightened, not painfully, but like he was grounding himself—like if he let go, he'd lose control.

"Fuck," he muttered.

I blinked up at him, dazed, my body thrumming with heat and pressure from having him still inside me. "Hunter..."

His jaw clenched, and he pulled back slightly, his thrusts slowing. "I—I need to stop," he panted, grey eyes dark and conflicted.

The fog in my mind cleared just enough for his words to settle in. "What?"

He closed his eyes briefly, swallowing hard. "If I don't stop now, I won't be able to hold it in."

I could barely think past the way my body still ached for him, but I heard the strain in his voice and slowly, achingly, he pulled out. I bit my lip at the sudden emptiness, a soft whimper escaping before I could stop it.

Hunter leaned his weight on his arms above me, chest heaving. His face was flushed, damp with sweat, and yet his eyes never left mine. "I want you," he whispered, voice hoarse. "But not like this. Not here. Not when I can't be sure..."

My body buzzed with frustration and need. I knew he could see it too as I reached up, my fingertips brushing along his jaw and used my other hand to grab his. I lowered his hand to my stomach, then lower and lower. I didn't say a word the entire time; only my eyes spoke a million things.

Hunter's breath caught, his jaw tightening. For a moment, it seemed like he might pull away completely, but instead something shifted in his gaze—an intensity that sent heat pooling low in my stomach.

He leaned down, capturing my mouth in a slow, deliberate kiss as his fingers traced along my inner thigh, slow and teasing, before he returned to the spot where I ached for him most. At first, his touch was delicate, barely brushing over me and causing me to squirm.

"Relax," he breathed, kissing the corner of my mouth.

But I couldn't relax—not with the way his fingers moved, exploring... coaxing.

He pressed a finger into me, slow and steady. I gasped, gripping his shoulders, nails digging in and all. At first, he moved carefully, letting me adjust before adding another finger, stretching me just enough to make my back arch.

"Hunter—"

"I know," he whispered, lips brushing my neck. "Just feel me and nothing else."

His thumb moved to circle that sensitive spot, slow and deliberate, like he always was. My hips moved on instinct, chasing the pressure, and he matched my pace perfectly. Every movement of his fingers was calculated, pushing me closer, deeper into that overwhelming edge.

My breath came in shallow gasps, my entire body tensing, coiling tighter and tighter.

I had never felt this way before.

It was as though the world around me no longer existed, and it was just me and Hunter. I was shaking—no, convulsing. I couldn't stop it.

"That's it, Bambi," he murmured, his lips ghosting over

mine. "Let go."

And I did.

I shattered around him, trembling and barely holding back the broken sounds in my throat until I was left limp and breathless beneath him.

When I finally opened my eyes, his face was close, watching me like I was something fragile and precious.

His lips brushed mine in the softest kiss, his fingers slowly slipping away, leaving me sated.

"Better?" he whispered, voice smug but tender.

I let out a shaky breath and nodded with eagerness.

Hunter's smirk softened as he brought his hand up to my face, his fingertips brushing my cheek with a gentleness that made my heart stutter. It wasn't until then that I noticed the faint streaks of red staining his fingers.

My blood.

His eyes flicked to it, and I watched the smirk fade. He inhaled slowly, the weight of what had just happened grounding us both back into reality.

He had taken my virginity.

An Ascendant.

I couldn't read the thoughts flickering behind his eyes, but poignant fear coiled in my chest at the thought of losing him. Not now. Not like this.

I didn't know what we were now. We'd crossed a barrier that we could no longer recover from.

Without thinking, I reached up and cupped his face, guiding him to meet my gaze. His eyes searched mine with uncertainty as I held him there.

"No going back," I whispered.

His jaw tightened, the muscles flexing as if he were holding something back. Then, slowly, he nodded before closing the space between us as his lips found mine in a firm, claiming, and irrevocable way.

GRACE
forty two

The days that followed blurred into a strange, intoxicating rhythm. Everything had changed since the moment I lost myself to Hunter, and training with him had taken on a whole new meaning. When he wasn't teaching me, he would use any chance he had to steal me while no one was looking.

The first time it happened, we'd been sparring in the forests, where he'd pinned me to the ground, his hands gripping my wrists above my head. I'd expected another remark about my stance or form; instead, his eyes darkened, and before I knew it, his lips crashed on mine. It was reckless and unapologetic.

The following day, when it was Saturday, he surprised me with a packet of condoms he'd bought from a corner shop just a few miles off Celestia. From then on, it became our unspoken routine, finding corners of Celestia where no one would think to look—an empty storage room behind the training grounds and even the armory once again.

During another session, when I was with other Warriors, I

caught sight of the Angelic Council watching from the sidelines. They stood there beside Azrael, their quills scratching against parchment as they jotted down whatever notes they had. My nerves nearly got the best of me, but Hunter's voice steadied me.

"You're fine," he had murmured, his hand brushing against mine under the guise of adjusting my stance.

I nodded, pushing past their stares with the bit of strength I had in me. By the time Azrael dismissed us, the Councils' expressions were unreadable, but their glances towards me felt strange. I was glad Joe wasn't with them during that moment, but I couldn't help my paranoia get the best of me, thinking they somehow knew Hunter and I were doing something behind their backs.

Our stolen moments weren't always so controlled, though, and that stood the test when Hunter came by Marnie's dorm when her roommates weren't there. He'd surprised me by hiding in the shower and grabbing me like I was all his and only his.

"Grace!" Marnie's voice echoed from outside the bathroom. "Are you okay? You've been in there forever."

I bit my lip, trying to suppress the moan threatening to escape as Hunter gripped my thighs tighter. His lips were on my neck, his breath hot against my skin as he moved against me.

"I-I'm fine!" I stammered, my fingers clutching the countertop behind me, desperate to hold on as he pushed me closer to the edge.

"Are you sure?" She didn't sound so convinced, which only worsened when Hunter's movements grew deeper. I almost yelped.

"I said I'm fine!" I practically shouted, earning a low

chuckle from Hunter that vibrated against my chest. His hand slipped lower, and I clenched my teeth, my breathing ragged as Marnie's footsteps faded.

"Are you sure you're fine?" he teased, sounding smug.

"Shut up," I managed to whisper before the words dissolved into a sharp gasp as he made me come undone right there.

One afternoon, though, after I stumbled during training, I felt that familiar panic start clawing at the edges of my mind. Hunter pulled me aside, away from the sight of Warriors around us and handed me a smooth blue stone on a leather cord he had crafted for me.

"What's this?" I asked, staring at the stone like it might come to life.

"It's something to focus on," he said, and my head snapped up at him. He pried it from my fingers and placed it over my head, letting it dangle from my neck. "When it gets too much, hold it and ground yourself. It's a way of distracting your mind."

He was called by Azrael after that, leaving me speechless over his gesture. A sudden warm feeling pricked at my heart as I watched him speak with Azrael off-field, and I struggled to control it. He'd made me something, all the while he played with my ring around his pinky.

By the time the rankings were posted in the common rooms, I was sure I would find Hunter at the top of the list. I'd made my way through Ascendants crowded around, searching for their names as my eyes scanned the list, seeing Hunter and Silas at the top before they landed on number ten—*Grace Martin*—I froze.

"What?" I whispered, blinking as if my name would be gone from the list the next time I opened my eyes.

It hadn't.

Eden appeared beside me, smiling with delight. "Congratulations!" she said. "Keep this up, and you may prove the Council wrong yet."

As she winked at me and walked away to congratulate others on making it into the top ten, the realization sank deep into my stomach.

I caught Matias's glare from across the room, his jaw tight, before I looked back at the list and saw that my name was above his.

Later that evening, once I'd let the reality of being in the top ten sink in, Nadael's voice rang through the canteen.

"Attention, all Ascendants. It is with great pleasure that I say that the competition ball will be reinstated this year—the first in over thirty years, thanks to Eden's proposal of uniting and celebrating you all."

Excited murmurs broke out through the canteen while Marnie clapped beside me. My brows drew together as I searched for the person I wanted to see, but he wasn't there. There was only Brandon and Silas again, though Silas's gaze was fixated on someone else from across the room.

Veronica.

She was alone, opposite him on another table, looking just as irritated as she always looked.

"Now," Nadael continued, and as if Veronica knew I was staring at her, she looked up, and I quickly turned my head. "The ball will take place three weeks from now, where the chosen participants for the competition will be picked."

"Oh, my goodness, do you know what this means?" Marnie leaned into me and whispered. "Dresses! Finally! I'm so tired of wearing the same clothes all the time."

I smiled at her enthusiasm, but as she talked about gowns and accessories, I couldn't help but wonder what I'd wear. I didn't exactly have a closet full of gowns. I'd already risked going out when I wasn't supposed to, so the thought of standing out—*again*—made my stomach twist.

Still, as everyone else broke out into chatter over the ball, I found myself reeling in on the fact that the competition was nearing and things were about to change. I wasn't sure if I was ready; all I was sure about was Hunter, and even then, we were balancing on a thin line.

HUNTER

forty three

I stared at the glowing screen on my desk, scanning articles for what felt like the hundredth time. My mother's name blurred on the page, and the accompanying photograph of her from years ago almost haunted me.

Murder on Crown Lake. It read.

Unsolved.

I dug into the pocket of my hoodie, feeling for the letter my brother had sent me, detailing how he was still alive and ran my fingers along it. I carried it with me almost everywhere. It was sort of a lifeline for me—the only thing that tethered me to him.

But as I was about to take it out and read it for the millionth time, the sound of footsteps made me snap the Google tabs closed, replacing it with a random page on Celestial combat techniques.

"Do you know what Veronica did today?" Silas barged in, his voice immediately grating on my nerves. "Threw a fucking smoothie at me in the canteen. A smoothie! She almost ruined my Warrior jacket."

I leaned back in my chair and stared at him blankly. "Did you provoke her?"

Silas paused, looking genuinely offended. "Me? Provoke her? Do you honestly think—"

"Yes," I said without a doubt. Silas rarely elicited patience from others. I think the closest someone who was ever calm around him was Grace; even then, she had her moments.

"Look." He sighed, dropping himself onto my bed and running a hand through his hair. "All I asked her was if she knew about the demon that killed Lucas being sentenced today to the Hollow by the Council. Obviously, she didn't take it well."

My body stiffened. "Today?"

"Yeah, overheard Nadael telling Azrael."

I nodded slowly, my mind suddenly out of it.

Silas didn't seem to notice. "Anyway—can you believe I actually miss Grace?"

That got my attention. I turned my chair slightly, my gaze narrowing on him. "What?"

"Yeah, I got used to her shampoo." He sniffed dramatically. "It made the dorm smell... I don't know... *nice*. You ever notice that?"

I stared at him. "You're fucked up, you know that?" Though I was well aware of that scent of hers following me everywhere I went. I was no better than him.

"Yeah, yeah." He waved me off. "So how do you feel about her being on the top ten list?Bet Matias is *pissed*."

I leaned back in my chair, a smirk tugging at my lips. "I'm glad she knocked him off." But I wasn't glad she was on the list in the first place.

Silas gave me a look, tilting his head as if he knew something.

"You're not worried she'll make the top five?"

"She doesn't want to do the competition," I said, though my voice was far steadier than my thoughts.

"You sure about that? Because if she does—"

The door opened again, cutting him off as Brandon walked in.

"You know," I said, gesturing to the doorway. "Knocking isn't illegal. You both should try it sometime instead of barging in."

"Relax, it's not as if you were in here jerking off or something," Brandon said, dropping beside Silas on the bed. He winced slightly, rubbing his shoulder. "Had to hit the Healer's Sector after getting absolutely annihilated in training."

Silas perked up, grinning. "Oh yeah? Who took you down?"

"Matias," he muttered, and the name alone angered me. "Marnie patched me up, though."

I didn't miss the way his tone shifted when he said her name or how his cheeks flushed like an embarrassed little kid.

"Wait a second," Silas said, sensing what I was too. He grinned suggestively at Brandon. "Marnie healed you? Are you sure she didn't heal you a little *too* much?"

Brandon threw one of my shirts at him, which Silas dodged with exaggeration. "Shut up, man."

"Can't you two find somewhere else to be annoying?"

"Well, Grace is no longer here to annoy, so it all falls on you now, Cain."

I rolled my eyes at Silas, not bothering to say anything else as I played with Grace's ring and my gaze drifted back to the computer screen.

It was past two in the afternoon. I was meeting Grace in the forest at five.

Time couldn't be moving any slower.

"Looking good, Bambi," I said, pushing off the tree as she came into my line of sight.

Her lips curved into a smile, the kind that managed to knock the air from my lungs no matter how many times I'd seen it. "Not so bad yourself, huntsman," she shot back before breaking out into a run.

I didn't have time to react before she threw her arms around my neck, and her lips crashed into mine. I held her waist, pulling her closer and grounding her to me. I kissed her back with just as much eagerness as I had done the first time at that motel.

When we finally broke apart, she was breathless, her hands still clutching my jacket like she was afraid to let go. Good, because I didn't want her to.

"I was in the library earlier," she said, her voice soft but rushed. "I was trying to find more things on Riftkeeper's."

I raised an eyebrow at that, brushing a stray strand of her curls behind her ear. "And?"

"I didn't find much," she admitted in disappointment, "but it's strange. The more I dig, the more it feels like everyone is hiding something."

My chest tightened. "They always are," I muttered. "Did you hear anything about the demon that killed Lucas?"

Her eyes narrowed slightly. "No, why? What did you hear?"

My grip tightened around her waist. I thought about keeping what I had found out to myself, but it was impossible with her around. "He was sentenced today by the Council."

The air between us stilled, and her small hands holding onto me fell.

"Sentenced?" she whispered.

I nodded; regretting having said it in the first place. "Yeah. Something like that... they don't keep them alive for long."

Her gaze dropped and I hated the sadness that clouded her face.

Pulling her closer, I shook my head. "I'm sorry."

She sighed and closed her eyes. She'd hoped for another answer. I'd hoped for a moment when I didn't have to disappoint her.

"Do you..." she said after a beat. "Do you think about what we're doing? Sneaking around behind Celestials' backs, breaking every rule, they've set? If Joe found out, he'd—"

"Kill me?" I finished with a wry smile. She glowered.

"This is serious." She huffed, pushing me away with her elbows. "Do you regret any of it? Are we any better than that... *demon*?"

I regretted a lot of things in my life. For the first time, this wasn't one of them. "No," I said firmly. "Not a damn thing. Do you?"

Her eyes met mine. Wide and innocent as always. "No."

I nodded, trying to push away the sinking feeling in my chest as she said that. Moments like this were borrowed time, and deep down, I could feel the clock ticking. Whatever we were would eventually come to an end, and I would end up losing in every scenario possible.

But for now, I pulled her toward me and kissed her again like she was the only real thing in this fucked-up world.

HUNTER

forty four

I wasn't used to getting gifts.

Not in the way Grace Martin had just handed me a package with an expectant face, like she was waiting for me to either hate it or have a life-altering epiphany over a piece of cardboard.

"Go on," she said, "open it."

I eyed the package suspiciously, sitting on the edge of my bed. "Is it a pair of handcuffs?"

Grace rolled her eyes, but her lips twitched in amusement. "Just open it."

Sighing, I tore off the brown paper, revealing a small box. When I flipped open the lid, I went still.

A toy model of a '67 Mustang sat neatly inside, a sleek black finish with silver details. My chest tightened slightly.

I had mentioned—*once*—that night we went to the Riftkeeper's, how if I could, I would drive this very car in the future, as far as possible from this place. She remembered. No matter how stupid the idea was.

I lifted the tiny car out of the box, rolling the wheels between my fingers. It was ridiculous. Completely pointless. And yet...

"I know it's not the real thing but think of it as a step closer to your future," she started rambling like she always did when she was nervous. "I thought you'd like it, but if you don't, I can return it, or I can—"

"Come here," I murmured, and Grace blinked, her breath hitching slightly as I set the car aside and grabbed her waist, yanking her onto my lap.

She gasped, hands landing on my shoulders for balance. "That's a strong reaction to a toy car."

"Mm." I smirked, tracing my fingers along her spine. "Guess you just know how to get me at your feet willingly."

I crashed my mouth to hers, swallowing the small gasp she let out. Her fingers curled into my chest as I deepened the kiss, dragging her closer until there was no space left between us.

This girl was ruining me. And I was letting her.

She pulled back for air, eyes glazed over, lips swollen. Fucking perfect. "I didn't know a tiny Mustang could turn you on so much."

I chuckled, dragging my lips down the side of her throat just to feel her shudder. "I'm a man of many pleasures, Bambi." I smirked against her skin before murmuring, "You... and apparently toy models of fast cars."

She laughed breathlessly before kissing me again, more frantic this time. I leaned back, gripping her hips, prepared to forget everything else in the world—

Then the door swung open.

For fuck's sake.

"Fucking shitballs!" Came Silas's voice from the hallway. "Azrael is such a dickhead. I swear if I have to sit through

350

another one of his speeches about discipline, I'm gonna shove that cane of his far up his ass—"

Grace and I froze.

My brain caught up at the same time as hers. We weren't alone anymore.

I barely had time to react before Grace frantically rolled off my lap and straight onto the floor with an undignified thump. I choked on a laugh as she scrambled under the bed like a fucking ninja.

Silas walked into my room without knocking and was still ranting. "I mean, do I look like I care about inner discipline? The only thing I want to discipline is—"

He stopped.

His eyes narrowed on me, more specifically at the *very* obvious issue happening in my lap.

I stared back at him, already fucking done with this entire situation.

Silas blinked. "Bro... are you turned on by my misery or something?"

I dragged a hand down my face and gritted out through clenched teeth, "Get. Out."

He didn't move.

"Because, man, I get some people are into weird shit, but if you—"

I grabbed the nearest object—a pillow—and chucked it at his face.

Silas dodged easily, still smirking. "I'm just saying you should talk to someone about this; I wouldn't want the Celestials finding out."

"Out." I stood and shoved him back into the hallway.

"But Cain, man, I need some advice here—"

I shut the door in his face, locking it—which is what I should have done from the beginning—and the second I heard Silas's mumbled complaints dissipate; a muffled snort of laughter came from under my bed.

I looked down. Grace was still under there, her shoulders shaking with silent laughter.

"Shut up," I muttered, but I couldn't stop the small grin pulling at my lips.

She crawled out, brushing herself off before sitting cross-legged on my bed. "So... we've learned that you have very *specific* triggers."

I scowled at her, picking up the toy Mustang again. "You're lucky I like you."

Grace's eyes widened slightly.

I realized what I said.

Shit.

I cleared my throat, hoping to recover myself from the blunder. "You know, in a tolerable way."

Grace tilted her head, smiling in a way that made my stomach flip. "So, what I'm hearing is that you no longer find me a nuisance?"

"I think we established that a while ago, Grace."

She chuckled, dragging me onto the bed with her. I groaned as she nestled her head into the crook of my neck, and the scent of strawberries filled the space. She was becoming an addiction and that was dangerous. Too fucking dangerous. But I couldn't stop it. I was too far in with her.

I took a deep breath through my nose, staring at the ceiling. Grace's fingers ran circles along my chest before she tilted her head, and I felt her lips smiling against my neck.

"Hunter?"

I hummed, afraid if I looked down at her, I'd lose any

restraint—not that I had any around her.

"I like you too... in a tolerable way, of course."

Yeah... I was done for.

GRACE
forty five

I was making my way out of Sariel's class when I barely
had time to react. Hunter grabbed my wrist and pulled me
down an empty hallway.

His name fell from my lips in a squeak. Rain splattered
against the windows, blurring the outside, as he shoved me
against the wall, pressing his finger to my lips.

"Shh," he warned. "Unless you want Sariel to come here
and lecture us both on moral discipline."

A laugh bubbled up in my chest, but the firm press of
Hunter's finger against my lips had me swallowing it down.

His grey eyes glinted, a smirk curling at the edges of his
mouth. "You think that's funny, Bambi?" he murmured, his
voice low and rough in a way that sent heat up my spine.

"A little," I admitted, my lips brushing against his fingertip
as I spoke.

Hunter inhaled sharply, dropping his hand but not stepping
back. Instead, he braced one arm against the wall beside my

head, caging me in. "You know what's not funny?"

"Let me guess. You?"

His smirk ticked wider, but the look in his eyes darkened. "The fact that I nearly got my ass kicked today in training because you were distracting me."

My stomach fluttered. "Distracting you?"

"Yeah." His gaze flickered to my lips as his voice turned into a lazy drawl. "It's kinda hard to focus when you're standing there, stretching and looking all..." He trailed off as his body pressed in just a little more. I suddenly forgot the meaning of breathing.

"All what?" I whispered.

"Tempting."

My pulse skipped violently.

"That's not my fault," I said, feigning innocence.

Hunter exhaled slowly like he was barely holding himself together. Then, without warning, he gripped my chin, tilting my head up so I was fully caught in his gaze. "How about I show you what happens when you distract me?" he murmured, his breath hot against my lips.

And then he kissed me.

Hard.

Like he was punishing me for every single second he had to spend thinking about me. Like he was staking a claim. Like I was his.

My back hit the cool stone, and Hunter pressed himself against me, his body heat sinking through every layer of my training uniform. His hand slid into my hair, tilting my head as his tongue traced along the seam of my lips.

The worst part?

I let him.

Because I wanted this. I *badly* wanted this.

356

I curled my finger into his jacket, yanking him closer, and he groaned against my mouth.

"Someone could walk by," I whispered, breaking the kiss as I sucked in a shaky breath.

Hunter smirked, dipping his head to trail his lips along my jaw. "I'm willing to take that bet."

"You're impossible," I muttered, even as I tilted my neck to give him better access.

"And yet, here you are, still putting up with me. Interesting."

He wasn't wrong.

My fingers found their way into his hair, tugging him back to my mouth as he kissed me like he'd been starving for it. I melted against him, letting his hands roam beneath my uniform jacket, his fingertips tracing my stomach, then lower.

We were far from a couple. But what were we?

Something dangerous? Something reckless? Or something that would destroy us both...

But I didn't care then. Not when his fingers slipped into my trousers and pressed against me through my underwear.

I gasped, my back arching slightly as he smirked against my lips.

"Keep quiet," he murmured. "Unless you *want* to get caught."

I pressed my forehead against his chest, gripping his jacket as he slipped beneath the fabric and touched me, his fingers slow, teasing, dragging out every ounce of restraint I had left.

It was infuriating.

It was intoxicating.

I bit down on my lip, my breath coming out in short, ragged gasps as pleasure coiled inside me.

Hunter hummed in approval. "You know what I love?"

I shook my head, unable to stop the moans from slipping

out of me.

"That only *I* get to see you like this. No one else."

That almost ruined me on the spot.

I could feel the tension building, the warmth spreading through my limbs like wildfire. My pulse hammered as he worked me to the edge, and just as I was about to come undone, my eyes snapped open at the sound of footsteps approaching.

Oh, no.

Panic flared through me. I shoved at Hunter's chest hard, sending him stumbling backwards into a room opposite the hallway. His eyes lit up in amusement as he smirked at me, and I slammed the door shut in his face right when—

"Grace."

I turned so fast I nearly tripped over my own feet.

Nadael.

I forced my face into something remotely normal.

Nadael raised an eyebrow, her sharp gaze sweeping over me with quiet curiosity. "You're flushed."

"I—I was just in Sariel's class," I blurted. "It gets... hot in there—well, not hot, hot, but something was definitely in the air. Maybe I'm just coming down with something. It's natural for that to happen to humans during this time of year, especially—"

"No need for unnecessary explanations Grace," she cut me off with a frown, and I wanted to slap myself. "Either way, you'll have to excuse me. I'm late for a meeting with the Council."

I nodded, willing her to walk away faster. When she turned to leave, I almost sighed in relief, but then Eden stepped into view.

Why me!

"Grace," she greeted with her usual sweet and effortless

smile. "It's a good thing I've bumped into you. I wanted to ask if you had spoken with Joe since you visited him."

The mention of Joe made my stomach twist uncomfortably. "No," I admitted. "I haven't had the chance."

Eden sighed. "You should. He's... been a little off lately. I think the Council is keeping things from him."

I frowned. "Keeping what from him?"

Eden tilted her head, then shook it like she'd said too much. "Never mind. Just—be careful, okay?"

The words should have sounded reassuring.

But they weren't.

They felt like something else.

Something I was unsure of.

She smiled again before walking off, her heels clicking against the floor.

I exhaled, rubbing a hand over my face as the door behind me creaked open, and Hunter stepped out.

His usual smirk was gone. He looked... tense. Frustrated.

"Are you okay?" I asked, searching his expression.

He nodded slightly, avoiding my gaze. "Yeah. I'll see you tomorrow, Grace."

And just like that, he was gone.

I stared after him, my heart still racing from before.

What the hell was that?

And why did I suddenly feel like I was losing control of something I never really had control over in the first place?

GRACE

forty six

Hunter's dorm was quiet when I stepped in, and I realized none of the boys were there. Hunter's combat jacket was draped over the back of the sofa, and his boots were by the door, but other than that, the place was empty. I pressed my lips together, wondering if we had meant to meet somewhere else and I had just simply forgotten. After Sariel's class the other day, Hunter hadn't necessarily acted like his usual self. Well, he did, and he didn't. It was strange, almost like something was up, but I couldn't quite place if I was the one overthinking it or not.

I stepped back into the hallway, my boots echoing against the wooden floorboards. I was halfway down the long corridor when I heard someone call my name.

I turned to see Matias casually leaning against his door with a smirk plastered across his face. He hadn't spoken to me much since I surpassed him on the ranking list, but that didn't stop me from being set on edge by how he stared at me.

"Matias," I said cautiously. "Are you... okay?"

He nodded. "Oh, I forgot to tell you that Rael had some paperwork for you to complete after you left the class. I have it all in my room. Wanna come in, and I'll go get it for you?" he said, gesturing toward his dorm.

I frowned, not moving from where I was standing.

Matias sighed dramatically. "Come on, Grace. Don't look at me like that. It's just stuff on celestial hierarchies and something about the Reclaimers? We all have to complete it."

Against my better judgment, he seemed genuine for once, so I agreed to go into his dorm. He pushed the door open, motioning for me to enter. I hesitated, but curiosity and foolishness made me step over the threshold.

The room was different from Hunter's. Matias's was far messier, with papers scattered all over and uncleaned plates stacked against the sink.

"Where are your roommates?" I asked, trying to sound casual as I glanced around the living room area. Matias shut the door behind me, and the sound of the lock clicking shivered through me.

I spun around, my fingers shaking slightly. "Why did you lock the door?"

He leaned against it, his eyes trailing over me in a way that made my skin crawl and my stomach churn. "You've been doing well, haven't you? Better than me even."

"Okay... your point?"

His smirk faltered. "My *point is,* do you know how hard I've worked to get where I am? And then you come along—just a human—and suddenly, you're above me."

My unease grew, and I started toward the door. "You know what, I think I'll grab the work from Rael instead; you can keep the others," I tried to say, but Matias blocked my pathway. "You really think you're better than me, don't you? Well, newsflash! You don't belong here, Grace. You never did." I took a step back, but he closed the distance between us, his hand brushing my arm in a way that made me flinch. "Stop," I whispered.

"Don't be like that," he said, his voice dropping into something unsettlingly soft. "I can always show you what it's really like to be part of this world."

I shoved him hard enough to make him stumble. "Don't touch me!"

His expression twisted with anger, and he lunged. I reacted without thinking, remembering every lesson I'd had so far with Hunter. I sidestepped before he could grab me and ran for the door. I managed to reach the lock before I was yanked back by my hair and fell onto the floor.

The side of my face slammed against the corner of the sofa, and I cried out as pain erupted across my eyebrow.

I scrambled to push myself up, the sting of the hit still radiating through my head as my heart raced and I knew I couldn't let fear freeze me now.

Matias towered over me, leaning down as his hand reached toward me again. "Stop pretending you're so innocent, Grace. You're just—"

I didn't let him finish. Summoning every ounce of anger and every lesson Hunter had drilled into me, I swung my leg out and kicked hard against his shin. The impact made him hiss and stumble back, giving me just enough room to roll onto my knees. He lunged again, but this time I was ready. I surged upward, my fist clenched, and landed a solid punch square to his nose. A sickening crunch followed, and he reeled back, clutching his face as blood began to stream down.

"Shit!" he swore, staggering as his other hand flailed to balance himself. My chest heaved as I backed toward the door. My knuckles throbbed, but the satisfaction of seeing him doubled over in pain overpowered it.

"I said don't *touch* me."

He glared up at me as blood dripped onto the floor, and I took the opportunity to twist the lock behind me, yanking the door open.

As I sprinted down the stairs, my heart pounded until I collided with someone solid, the impact nearly knocking me off balance.

"Grace?" Hunter's voice was sharp, his hands steadying me as I gasped for breath.

I looked up, tears burning the corners of my eyes. "I—"

"What happened?" His voice was edged with something sharp as his fingers gently tipped my chin up. His gaze scanned my face before it drifted lower, catching the scratches along my arm and his entire body went still. Then, his voice turned cold. "Who?"

Before I could answer, Matias stumbled onto the top of the stairs, looking disheveled as he held a bloody hand up to his nose.

Hunter didn't need me to say anything as his jaw clenched and his expression darkened. He didn't ask for confirmation. He didn't need it. He just knew.

"Hunter don't—" I started, but it was too late. He stormed up the stairs before his fist connected with Matias's jaw. The sickening crack echoed in the foyer as Matias stumbled back, clutching his face.

Hunter didn't stop as he lunged at him again and they both came tumbling down the stairs, trading blows. Each one more ferocious than the last. Their Warrior powers sparked in flashes of light and sound as furniture splintered and walls cracked, attracting people from their dorms to come down and see what was going on.

I shouted for Hunter to stop, but he seemed so consumed in his rage that he couldn't hear me. I was pushed back into the surrounding crowd of Ascendants, and I desperately tried to reach him.

Silas and Brandon luckily arrived. Their eyes widened as they took in the chaos and realized it was their friend fighting. Without hesitation, they barged through the crowd and joined Hunter just as Matias's friends tried to intervene.

"Stop!" I screamed, but my voice was drowned out by the sound of cheers and fists meeting flesh.

Hunter had Matias pinned against the wall, his fingers digging in as power thrummed beneath his skin, coiling like a predator ready. He looked unrecognizable. Almost primal. "You lay a single hand on her again, and I'll make sure you never get the chance to regret it."

"Hunter, stop!" Something in my voice broke through his fury. His hand faltered, the light dimming as he turned to look at me. His expression was a mix of rage and regret, his chest heaving as he stepped back.

Before anyone could move, Celestial teachers appeared, their wings casting sharp shadows across the wreckage as they sprang out from their backs.

Eden stepped forward, her voice cold and commanding. "Enough!"

Hunter didn't fight back as the Celestials closed in, seizing him, Silas, Brandon, Matias and his friends. Their grips were firm as they began dragging them away but of course, Matias didn't stop for one bit. Even as he was hauled off, his voice rang through the foyer, spitting insults at Hunter and taunting him like a man who had no idea just how close he'd come to being obliterated.

"Where are they taking them?" I asked Eden, my voice breaking.

Her gaze softened slightly. "They will need to speak with the Council."

Hunter turned his head, and his eyes met mine in an instant. There was a quiet resolve in them but also something unspoken—an apology, a promise, a plea.

I watched him be led away, my chest aching, knowing that I might have just ruined *everything*.

GRACE
forty seven

I couldn't sit still.

As I paced the length of the boys' dorm, playing with the stone necklace Hunter had given me, my nerves knotted my stomach. Marnie was sitting on the arm of the sofa, watching me with worried eyes and every second that ticked by felt heavier than the last.

"What if something happens to him?" I asked aloud.

"Grace, you need to breathe," Marnie said gently. "We don't even know what's going on yet."

I stopped and pivoted to face her. "It's my fault. None of this would've happened if I hadn't gone looking for him or gone into Matias's room."

"Stop," she said firmly, blocking my path before I could pace again. "It's not your fault, and you know that the boys wouldn't let you blame yourself."

The door suddenly swung open, and Brandon and Silas walked in. Relief flooded my chest at the sight of them.

"What happened?" I demanded, rushing toward them.

"Where's Hunter? Is he okay?"

Silas's face was grim as he shrugged off his jacket. "Still with the Council," he said. "They're questioning everyone. They'll probably hold him longer because, well, you know."

"Because he nearly killed Matias?" I said quietly, shamefully.

Brandon sighed, rubbing the back of his neck. "They're not thrilled about the fight. But they're also not stupid. They know Matias started it. Luckily Silas and I only got two days off of any training and having to clean the entire canteen after lunch."

I felt like the floor might give out beneath me. "I shouldn't have let it get that far. If I'd just—"

Before I could spiral further, the door flew open again, and Veronica stormed in, her voice echoing through the dorm.

"You asshole! What the hell were you thinking?" she yelled, pointing an accusatory finger at Silas. "Getting in trouble with the Council? Do you have any idea how serious this is?"

Silas groaned, rubbing his temples. "Not now, Ver."

"Oh, yes, now," she shot back, crossing her arms as she glared at him. "I swear, you and your stupidity will drag all of us down with you."

Silas sighed heavily and followed her as she stormed back out, leaving the rest of us in stunned silence.

"What was that about?" I asked, looking at Brandon.

He shook his head, looking just as bewildered. "They've been weird lately. Anyway, Grace…" He hesitated, glancing toward the door. "The Council wanted to speak with you, too."

My stomach dropped. "What?"

"Eden's waiting for you in the main building," he said.

I glanced at Marnie, my pulse racing. "What do I do?"

"You tell them the truth," Marnie said, squeezing my hand. "You didn't do anything wrong. They just want to get the story

370

straight."

Brandon gave me a reassuring nod. "It'll be fine. Just... don't overthink it."

But that was impossible not to do!

Trying to steady my breathing as panic clawed at the edges of my mind, I thought about the Council. They wanted to speak with me. Hunter and I were just as guilty for many things that didn't even deal with Matias.

As I moved toward the door, my legs felt like they were made of lead.

"Grace," Marnie called softly, stepping forward to fix the collar of my jacket. Her smile was warm, but her eyes betrayed her concern. "You'll be fine. I promise."

I nodded, clinging to her words, before pushing the door open and stepping out into the corridor.

When I arrived, the main building was quiet, my footsteps echoing off the polished floors. Eden stood near the entrance; her expression calm but unreadable.

"Don't worry," she said as I approached. "They just want to hear your account of what happened."

I nodded, swallowing the lump in my throat as she led me through several hallways. We stopped in front of a large set of double doors, and Eden pushed them open, revealing a grand hall that resembled a courtroom inside the academy.

The Angelic Council sat at a long table at the far end, their presence overwhelming. Joe stood off to the side with Nadael, his arms crossed tightly over his chest.

"Grace Martin," one of the Council members said, his voice deep and resonant. "Please, come forward."

My legs felt like jelly as I walked toward them, my heart hammering in my chest. They asked me to recount everything that had happened, and I did my best to explain, my voice trembling at first but growing steadier as I went on.

When I finished, the room was silent for a moment before the doors opened again, and Hunter and Matias were brought in.

Matias immediately started defending himself, his voice sharp and defensive. "I didn't do anything! She's lying—"

"Quiet!" Another Council member said, silencing him with a wave of their hand.

Hunter didn't say anything. His gaze flickered to mine briefly, and I felt a rush of emotions I couldn't begin to untangle.

The Council deliberated for what felt like an eternity before their verdict was given.

"For Hunter Cain," Cael this time announced. "You will be suspended from training for this week. Fighting outside of sanctioned sessions cannot be tolerated."

Hunter's expression didn't change, but I saw the flicker of tension in his jaw—the barely perceptible clench that told me just how hard he was holding back.

But Cael wasn't finished. "In addition," he said, eyes sharp with authority, "you are to wear binding chains for two weeks. They are not to restrict your movement but to suppress your power. As a reminder that strength without control is no strength at all."

A ripple of silence moved through the room. My stomach dropped as two Celestials stepped forward, silver chains glowing faintly with runes in their hands. They weren't linked by a chain. Instead, they hovered slightly as they fastened around Hunter's wrists—one on each arm—locking in place with a soft, almost ceremonial click.

Hunter glanced down at them once. Then straight ahead again.

He didn't resist.

Didn't even speak.

But I could see it—the flicker of something behind his eyes. Pain? Rage? Or maybe just the humiliation of it all. Because these weren't just restraints.

They were a message.

And I hated that.

"Now, for Matias Williams," another Council member continued, their tone colder, "Effective immediately, you are hereby stripped of your Ascendant title and your position at Celestia. In accordance with the Seraphim Law, under section nine, your memories along with those of any relative's privy to your role here, will be erased as dictated by protocol."

Matias's face paled. "What? No! You can't do that—" He looked over at me, his eyes pleading for me to intervene. "Tell them, Grace! Tell them you were lying!"

But the Council was unmoved.

When Matias realized no matter what he said wouldn't sway the Council, his expression grew rageful. "This is all your fault!"

I flinched.

"You're a nobody, Grace, you hear me?"

I caught a glimpse of Hunter's hands clenching into fists. He was containing his anger, but for how much longer, I didn't know.

"You're nothing!"

I kept my head held high before one of the Council members stepped forward, their hands glowing faintly as they reached out to touch Matias's forehead.

Matias was prepared to put up a fight, but it was no use as he was grabbed by two Celestials who had taken the boys away in the first place.

He thrashed in their arms, my stomach churning, and a few

moments later, I watched in horror as they took Matias's powers and memories. His body slumped to the floor, unconscious.

"Grace Martin," Cael said, turning to me with a disgusted look. "You may go."

I nodded, barely able to move as I stumbled out of the room. The last thing I saw before the doors closed was Hunter's face; his eyes clung to mine, unwavering, and I knew that this was his way of telling me we would suffer that same fate if the Council found out about us.

HUNTER

forty eight

I slammed the dorm door shut behind me, and I barely registered the sound of Brandon's voice as he jumped up from the sofa.

"Shit, man, you've been gone for hours. What the hell happened?"

Too much to even process.

Silas's voice cut through next. "Matias?"

I clenched my fists—only to feel the cold bite of the Binding Chains tight around my wrists. "Matias," I said, my voice low and flat, "had his memories stripped by the Council."

The room went dead silent. For a second, it was like no one even breathed. Then Silas stepped closer, his dark eyes pinning me like a sharp dagger.

"And the Council?" he asked, but his voice was barely above a whisper. "Do they know about... you and Grace... the kiss?"

My gut twisted, but I forced myself to meet his gaze. I

shook my head. "No."

His lips pressed into a thin line, and I could see in the way his jaw tightened that he didn't believe me.

Brandon scoffed. "Well, did they suspend you or anything?"

I raised my wrists, showing both him and Silas the Binding Chains.

'For fuck's sake, Cain." Silas shook his head. "For how long?"

I didn't answer him. I couldn't. My chest was too tight, my head too full of everything I'd just seen—Matias's blank, hollow stare after they'd taken everything from him. How he fell unconscious to the ground. That could've been Grace. That could still be Grace.

I glanced at Brandon and Silas, then shook my head. "It's been a long day," I said. "We'll talk tomorrow."

Brandon didn't look anywhere done talking, but I didn't give him the chance to speak as I turned toward my room. The second the door shut behind me, I pressed my back against it, dragging a hand down my face. My whole body felt heavy with everything I couldn't feel and couldn't do... couldn't fix. I should've been thinking about Matias, about what his punishment meant for the rest of us. But all I could see was Grace, hurt and bleeding, and the fire in my chest burned hotter than anything I'd ever felt before. I'd risked everything going after Matias. I hadn't even thought twice about it. And the problem wasn't that I'd done it. It was that I knew if I had to, I'd do it again for her.

No one touches her. *No one.*

I walked toward my desk before the door burst open, and Silas stormed in. "You're hiding something, aren't you?"

I kept calm, not answering him. What could I say?

Silas's eyes narrowed as he stared at me, trying to piece it all

378

together. When his expression shifted, I knew he'd figured it out. "Oh," he said, his voice low as he chuckled with disbelief. "You've more than kissed her, haven't you?"

I didn't move. Didn't say a word.

"I knew it. Are you out of your fucking mind, Cain?" he snapped. "Do you even understand what could happen? That what happened to Matias—could happen to you? They'll strip your memories, your powers... you'll be nothing, man. All because you couldn't keep your dick in your pants—"

His words hit a nerve and before I could stop myself, I closed the distance between us and slammed him against the wall. 'And what about you, huh?' I growled, pushing him further up against the wall as he fought me. "Don't think I don't see the way you look at Veronica. You've loved that girl since you were six, so don't test me Dunn."

Silas's eyes flared with anger, but he didn't deny it.

Then, like a switch being flipped, w hite-hot p ain flared up my arms, shooting through my shoulders and chest. The Binding Chains hissed against my skin, burning as the runes lit up. My muscles locked up, and my grip faltered. It was like my power had been sucked out in an instant, leaving me hollowed out and raw.

I staggered back with a strangled breath, clenching my teeth to keep from showing how much it hurt.

Silas clenched his jaw as he straightened his shirt. "Maybe I have. But at least I've never been stupid enough to get caught."

"I didn't get caught!"

"Yet. She's human. She has less to lose than you do."

I laughed bitterly, shaking my head. "You're a fucking hypocrite, Dunn."

"Maybe," Silas shot back, his voice quieter now but no less angry. "But I am someone who doesn't want to watch his best friend destroy himself. I mean, first your brother, now this? Do you really think Grace is worth it? Worth you ending up like Matias?"

I stared at him, my jaw clenched so tight it hurt. "You don't know what's worth it to me."

Silas looked at me for a long time. "Fine," he said finally. "Keep your secrets. But don't expect me to stand by and watch you ruin yourself."

He left without another word, slamming the door behind him.

I smacked a few CDs off my desk and shook my head as I stared at the empty space where he'd been. He thought he knew what I was risking, that he understood, but Silas didn't know the half of it.

There were things I'd done that made a kiss with Grace seem innocent.

I sank onto the edge of my bed with my head in my hands. Grace's face, her voice, and her smile filled my mind again. She was becoming my weakness and my anchor all at once. And the terrifying truth was, I didn't mind risking it all for her.

GRACE
forty nine

Two weeks had passed since Matias's title had been stripped, but the memory of that moment in front of the Angelic Council still haunted me. No one spoke about it—not in Sariel's class, not in the dorms, nowhere. Yet, it replayed in my mind on an endless loop. I couldn't shake the image of Matias collapsing after his essence was ripped from him, leaving him hollow and forgotten.

Hunter and I had barely seen one another since. Both of us were too afraid of drawing attention, too aware of the consequences if anyone suspected what we were doing. The Council's judgment had been a stark warning, and deep down, I knew Joe wouldn't let us get away with breaking the rules. I wasn't even sure if he'd stop the Council from doing the same to me and Hunter if it came to it.

"Grace."

I blinked, snapping out of my thoughts. Veronica was staring at me from the table next to mine, her chin propped on her hand, her eyes sharp. "Are you going to stare into space all day, or are you actually going to contribute?"

"I'm fine," I muttered, brushing her off.

She arched an eyebrow.

I huffed. "Since when do you care if I'm fine or not?"

"Since you wallowing in self-pity is annoying me."

I shot her a glare, but her words stuck. Class ended not long after, and as everyone packed up to leave, I found myself following Veronica into the hallway.

"Veronica, wait," I called after her. She sighed, rolling her eyes but slowed her pace.

"What is it, Martin?"

I hesitated. "Has anyone else... ever had their Ascendant title stripped before? During your time here?"

She stopped walking, her sharp gaze cutting into mine as if weighing whether to entertain my question. "Yeah, loads of times, a few years back even, two Ascendants were caught in a hidden relationship."

My stomach twisted. The knot of tension that had been building over the past two weeks tightened further. "What happened to them?"

"What do you think happened?" she said dryly. "They were stripped of their titles and their memories. Everything was wiped clean. They were sent back to live an ordinary life as humans, and Celestia moved on."

Her words resonated deeply, yet something felt oddly unsettling. "Then... if their memories were gone, couldn't they have just been together as humans? They wouldn't even remember what happened. They could start all over again and—"

Veronica scoffed, her expression twisting into something bitter. "You really think it's that simple, don't you?" She stepped closer, her voice lowering. "Even if an Ascendant's powers, memories, and title are stripped, traces of their Celestial essence remain within their soul. That essence creates an invisible tether to the Celestial hierarchy and laws. Falling in love after losing their status would result in catastrophic consequences for both of them."

"What kind of consequences?" I asked.

Her gaze hardened. "Pain. Illness. Madness. Death, if they're lucky. The Celestial essence clashes with mortal limitations, creating a ripple effect that tears them apart from the inside out."

I felt a cold weight settle in my chest. "So... does that mean they can never fall in love again? Not with anyone?"

Veronica sighed, her tone losing some of its sharpness. 'No. They can fall in love again. But it'll never be with the right person. Not the person they were meant to be with. They'll always feel an emptiness that consumes them, no matter what."

Her words hung heavy in the air between us, and for a moment, I couldn't breathe. The implications of everything she'd just said were suffocating. Even if Hunter and I were to fall in love... even if we lost everything, even if we gave it all up, there would still be no future for us.

"Why are you asking me this, Grace?" Veronica asked, her voice quieter now as a few Celestials passed by with decorations in hand—no doubt, preparing for the ball.

"I... I just wanted to know," I said quickly.

She huffed out a breath and ran her fingers through her blonde locks. "Have you... ever heard about the story of Seorin Yun?"

I shook my head slowly. "No. Should I have?"

"A few years ago, Seorin used to go to Celestia. She was a Warrior and by the look of things, she was on the verge of ascending. That was until she met a guy on one of her free weekends. You can imagine what happened next."

"They fell for each other."

She nodded, her expression tightening.

"Were they caught?"

"No. A Riftkeeper killed him just for being affiliated with Celestials."

The words sent a shockwave down my spine. "What?"

She didn't flinch. "They found out about them before the Council ever did. Riftkeeper's track weaknesses like fucking sharks. Love? That's as good as bleeding in open water."

Everything she was saying... it sounded like a warning—like she knew.

"How do you know all of this?"

"Because I used to look up to her," she admitted softly. "She confided in me, and do you want to know what the worst part of it all is? He didn't even know she was an Ascendant. He thought she was just... normal, yet he was killed for something so mundane in this world."

My legs shook and I desperately tried to stay standing. "What happened to her?"

"She left Celestia after it happened, not wanting her memories to be erased once the Council found out. But... no one has ever heard or seen her since."

"That can't be right. Someone must know where she went—"

Veronica gave me a humorless laugh. "Even the Celestials at this academy don't bring her up. It's like she never existed."

I looked away, whispering, "Why are you telling me this?"

"Because you have the same look in your eyes as she did."

My head swung in her direction. I wanted to open my mouth to argue, but the words caught in my throat. I wasn't even sure what I would be arguing towards. I was the one to come up to her with questions and she saw right through me.

"Whatever you're doing, Grace—" She leaned forward "—Whether it's with an Ascendant or a Celestial themselves... I suggest you stop. I, for one, would hate to have my memories erased or, worse, be killed at the hands of a Riftkeeper over something such as falling in love with the person you weren't supposed to."

I didn't say a word.

I couldn't.

Veronica must have known it too, as she cast me a single warning glance before turning on her heel and walking away.

The evening rain had finally stopped, causing the clouds to part and the sun to stream across the training grounds, casting golden hues over the weapons racks and sparring pits.

I caught sight of Hunter; his broad shoulders turned away from me as he ran his fingers over some of the weapons. He looked focused, his hair curling slightly at the nape of his neck. My pulse quickened, and I hated how my eyes always drifted to him. However, no matter how much I tried, I couldn't stop. And I hated it even more that his gaze immediately found mine when he turned slightly.

And then I noticed it.

The chains were gone.

For the past week, despite us, not able to be together, those iron bindings had clung to his wrist, dimming his power, weighing him down during training. But now—

Now he stood tall. Unchained. Unyielding.

He tilted his head slightly, as if to say *yeah, I noticed you noticing.* That stupid cocky glint returned to his eyes like it had never left, and it made something stir in my chest.

My cheeks heated, and I quickly turned my attention back to Azrael as he paced across the center of the grounds.

"We are days away from the ball and competition." His wings flashed out as if even they were impatient. "Many of you have shown great strength and endurance throughout these months, and I know that myself and Nadael are proud of that." His chest swelled with pride. "That is why today, you'll once again participate in an exercise the Council values highly—the Ecliptic Hunt."

Everyone around me either nodded or fist-bumped one another. I, on the other hand, was nervous about the Ecliptic Hunt. The last time I participated, I was terrible at it.

Azrael continued splitting us into teams, and my heart sank and raced simultaneously when I heard Hunter's name called for the opposing team. Of course, he wasn't with me. We were always on opposite sides, and it felt cruelly poetic in a way.

But it was even worse when Azrael declared my group would be the ones with Celestial Energy this time.

Azrael pried open a chest containing hundreds of glowing orbs and handed us a few each. I placed them in my pockets before he sent us into the woods in scattered directions.

I gripped one of the orbs tightly as I darted between the trees. I remembered the first time I did this, how Lucas had been by my side, always covering for my mistakes, always cheering me on. The ache in my chest tightened, but I swallowed it down.

He wasn't here to cover for me anymore. I had to do that myself. I had to do a lot by myself.

Soon, the first encounter happened quickly. A boy from the

opposing team burst out from behind a bush, and I dodged his first strike as he tried to grab the orbs from me. My movements were faster than I thought possible, as a sharp twist of my body and a sweep of my leg had him tumbling to the ground. Before he could recover, I struck him with the energy beam, and he glowed faintly blue, signaling he was out.

"Good job, Gracie." Silas appeared at my side, throwing an orb in the air before catching it. He winked. "Keep moving."

I nodded to myself and pushed forward, my senses sharper and more alert. The woods became a maze, but I navigated it well enough, knocking out one, two, *and three* more opponents.

On the third, I grinned and tried to stop myself from attempting to perform a happy dance in the middle of the woods.

"Are you kidding me?" The boy on the ground tsked, wiping at the blue smeared on his shirt. "This is going to be a pain to get out."

I chuckled with an apologetic shrug as he stood and marched off, muttering under his breath how annoyed he was.

As I turned in the other direction to find my next victim, I froze.

Hunter.

He emerged from behind a cluster of trees, his expression both amused and dangerous. "You know," he teased. "I'd say you've gotten a bit too comfortable with those energy beams."

I rolled my eyes. "What can I say? I've been training a lot lately."

His eyes flashed playfully. "Really?"

I nodded. "Although the teacher isn't that great, but I guess he will do in the meantime."

His grin widened as he approached, his steps slow and predatory. "Are you saying you're better than him at combat,

Bambi?"

"Definitely, huntsman."

He chuckled, taking that as his cue as he lunged, and we clashed in a series of blows. His strength was overwhelming, as if those chains had suppressed too much from him and he finally had an out. Still, I used my agility to duck and dodge. We traded hits, and for a moment, it felt like the rest of the world disappeared.

I laughed.

He smiled.

And soon enough, he had pinned me to the ground, his weight pressing me into the mud below as his hands caught my wrists. His grey eyes, dark and intense, searched mine as I stared up at him, utterly breathless.

"We need to be careful," I whispered. If anyone saw us, if Azrael saw...

His lips quirked up into a dangerous smile. "I agree."

The tension between us crackled like a live wire, waiting for it to spark at any moment. I refused to let him win this time. As he lowered his lips against mine, I twisted my body, using a move he'd taught me, and managed to flip him, pinning him down with my knees on either side of him.

His head tilted back, exposing the curve of his throat as he exhaled sharply. "This gives me déjà vu. Have we done this before? I think you were even calling out my name during it."

I leaned closer, smiling as the orb glowed faintly in my hand. "If I recall, the only difference was that I didn't have the orb in my hand."

He smirked, and I didn't hesitate. I pressed the orb to his chest, watching as he glowed faintly blue.

"You're out," I whispered, unable to hide the grin on my

face as I leaned inches away from his lips.

The sound of footsteps grew louder, and my head snapped up. Quickly, I scrambled away from Hunter, brushing leaves and mud from my hair in a hurried attempt to look composed. Hunter, however, stayed on the ground, unbothered, as Silas and a few of my teammates appeared through the trees. Their expressions lit up with laughter the moment they saw him.

Silas doubled over, practically wheezing, as he clapped me on the shoulder. "You beat Cain? Fucking finally." He turned to Hunter with a wicked grin. "Gotta admit, this is a good look on you. I'm getting kinda turned on—should I go fetch Jerry?"

Hunter rolled his eyes, extending a hand to let one of my teammates haul him to his feet. His annoyance was there, but it was mild, like it always was around Silas.

"Nice work, Martin," someone from my team called out, their tone genuine for the first time.

My eyes widened in surprise. Had I heard that right? A congratulation? For me?

The disbelief didn't last long. A few more teammates clapped my back in approval, and I couldn't help it as my lips curved into a grin.

They began leading me out of the woods, chatter buzzing around us. Still, I found my gaze drifting back. Hunter stood there, lingering just for a moment longer than the rest as his eyes captured mine. There was no anger in his expression, no sign of frustration or bitterness. Instead, there was pride.

The look sent something sharp and unexpected through my chest. My steps faltered for half a heartbeat before I forced myself to look away, but the damage was already done, and the realization hit me with such clarity that I may as well have been hit with a Celestial beam straight to the heart.

I was in love with Hunter Cain.

Whatever you're doing, Grace, whether it's with an Ascendant or a Celestial themselves... I suggest you stop. I, for one, would hate to be killed at the hands of Riftkeeper over something mundane as falling in love with the person you weren't supposed to.

Veronica's words were there on the back of my mind in an instant like an alarm, trying to wake me up.

But I already knew that I was screwed. I was *beyond* screwed.

GRACE

fifty

I stared at Marnie, who was pacing the dorm room with the same kind of rage people reserved whenever they couldn't find their phones. Except this wasn't about a phone. This was about a tampon.

"I swear, if this thing doesn't go in, I'm dropping out," Marnie huffed, glaring at the tampon in her hand like it had personally insulted her.

I bit back a laugh. "Dropping out over a tampon? That's a bit dramatic, even for you."

She shot me a look. "It's the night of the ball, and I'm on my period, Grace! Why must I have such bad luck." She fell back onto my bed, her arms fanned out at the side as she stared at the ceiling.

"You could just use pads like a normal person."

Marnie gasped, lifting herself onto her elbows to look at me. "*Pads*? What am I, a peasant?"

That did it. I snorted, collapsing beside her in a fit of

laughter.

"This isn't funny!"

"It's a *little* funny."

"No, it's not! If I don't figure this out, I will be waddling around in my dress like a toddler in a diaper."

I sat up, shaking my head. "Okay, okay. Let's just get you to the bathroom first."

I dragged Marnie off the bed, though as soon as the door to the bathroom closed, she began full-on panicking, not knowing how to physically insert said object. After ten minutes of trying to convince her it wasn't the end of the world, I texted for backup without her knowledge. Not even five minutes later, Veronica stormed into the bathroom. "Okay, which one of you is bleeding out?"

Marnie's eyes widened from where she was sitting, legs spread apart on the toilet. "You called Veronica!?"

I gave her a sheepish shrug. "Lily and Dana weren't going to help; they barely speak to us as it is." Not like Veronica was any different, but I wasn't about to text Hunter, Brandon and especially Silas over a girl matter.

Marnie groaned. "Kill me."

Veronica crossed her arms and leaned against the doorway. Her shaggy haircut was in an updo, with strands falling effortlessly around her face. She looked halfway done with makeup for the ball already. "Are you struggling with the angle or the fear of losing it in the void?"

Marnie's mouth dropped open. "I—I—excuse me?"

Veronica sighed. "Scoot over. Let me give you a physics lesson."

"Physics?"

"Yes, now close your legs for a minute. I don't want to see that the whole time."

The next few minutes were a chaotic mix of teaching, instructing, complaining and a lot of swearing.

"Relax your muscles!" Veronica snapped.

"I am relaxed!"

"You're clenching too much."

I was dying.

I didn't know how much longer it took until finally there was a long pause followed by Marnie slowly sitting up, eyes wide.

"Oh, my fudge... it's in."

Veronica clapped. "Only took you about fifty years."

Marnie wiggled her legs and practiced a few unnecessary squats. "I feel like I just gave birth backwards."

I was laughing so hard that I thought I'd need a tampon myself.

Veronica turned to me. "Don't tell anyone I was here. Got it?"

I raised my hands in defense as she narrowed her eyes at me and then turned toward the door. When the door shut behind Veronica, Marnie again relaxed against the toilet seat and exhaled.

"I'm exhausted. And we haven't even made it to the ball yet."

I hesitated, chewing my lip. "Do you think I should even go to the ball?"

Her head snapped toward me. "What are you talking about? Of course, you should. Dress or no dress, we're going."

It wasn't just that.

I stared at my hands.

"What's wrong?"

I didn't meet her eyes as I strolled toward the shower and leaned against the clear pane of glass. "I've done something terrible, Marnie."

That got her attention.

My chest was beating too fast, and I thought about the countless times I'd kept secrets from her. But she'd opened up to me, protected me, and called me her friend when I was hardly a great one at it in return.

"I've—well—"

"Oh, please don't tell me you've gotten yourself involved with someone."

I was dead silent.

She groaned and facepalmed. "Grace, why—"

"It's a natural thing!" I defended. "I'm—ugh—" I ran my hands through my curls, unsure of where to go from here.

She stared at me. "Is it Hunter?"

My chest squeezed. "How—"

"I've had my suspicions ever since he took you to the Healers Sector after your fight with Norah. Also, I found a loose condom packet inside your drawer."

Oh...

My stomach dropped at the thought of her finding those. I should have been more careful—no, *we* should have been more careful.

"I may be innocent most of the time, but I'm not stupid. I was just hoping it wouldn't all be true."

I nodded slowly, my face burning. I wasn't sure whether I felt ashamed or that I kept this from her when part of her already knew. Did that mean that others knew? Could they tell? Were we that obvious?

I was spiraling.

I buried my face in my hands. "I don't know what to do, Marnie. There were moments when I didn't care about risking it all. I just... wanted to be with him. But now..."

"You've fallen in love."

You've fallen in love.

The word *love* drifted through me, slow and steady, seeping into every corner of my mind. I thought about what it truly meant. I thought about the moment I walked away from Hunter after the Ecliptic Hunt, the way his eyes lingered on me like he was proud. Something in me had finally clicked that day.

I had never known what love was before. Not really.

I didn't understand how it could unravel you and hold you together all at once. How it could feel like standing at the edge of a cliff, the wind daring you to jump, but knowing there's no solid ground waiting below.

Until I realized, that love was a little like gravity.

Think of it like gravity. Even the smallest things can pull you under if you're not paying attention.

Hunter's words played in my head. He was right.

Love was silent and invisible but inescapable like gravity. It pulls you in slowly at first, so subtly you barely notice. Then, all at once, it drags you under. It doesn't ask for permission. It doesn't care if you're ready.

And Hunter...

He was my gravity.

"Is he..." Marnie trailed off after I didn't answer, but I knew what she meant.

I shook my head. "I haven't even told him what *I* feel."

Hunter was impossible to read. One moment, he was distant; the next, he was risking everything to protect me. But feelings? I didn't know if he could even let himself feel something like that for me.

"Grace... this isn't just some harmless modern-day romance," Marnie said, her expression softening as she studied me. "You're talking about Hunter—an Ascendant. If anyone finds out, especially the Council—"

"I *know*," I snapped, not meaning to. My shoulders slumped immediately. "I know," I repeated, quieter this time.

Marnie moved closer, leaning against the glass beside me. "You know, despite all the chaos you keep dragging me into, the one thing I'm actually glad about is becoming friends with you."

I blinked, caught off guard.

She gave me a small smile and nudged me with her shoulder. "No, seriously. I know I'm dead set on becoming an Ascendant, but I still have your back. You wanted to be a Warrior? You're crazy but amazing. You wanted to help Hunter find his brother despite how dangerous Riftkeeper's are? You're loyal to a fault. You're in love? Well... I guess I'll just have to tag along with you and your endless emotions. Like I said, Grace, I've got your back. Even if that means dealing with more tampon emergencies."

I let out a small laugh, feeling a lump rise in my throat.

"Thank you," I whispered, leaning my head against her shoulder.

We stayed like that for a moment—quiet, steady—until a knock at the door broke the moment.

One of our roommates peeked in, giving us both a strange look. She'd definitely heard some of the chaos from earlier.

"Uh, Grace? Joe's here to see you."

I sat up straighter, blinking in surprise. "Joe?"

'Marnie raised a brow. "Well, that's my cue then. I'll let you two talk." She pushed herself off the glass and started toward the door. "I'll be in my room, getting ready." She smiled, passing by our roommate before I followed out after a few minutes and found Joe by the kitchenette.

He stood there, looking awkward and unsure as he stared at

the bright pink utensils by the counter.

"Hey," he mumbled, holding a box in his hands.

"Hey." I motioned for him to sit on one of the stools, but he hesitated before dropping onto one.

For a moment, neither of us spoke.

Then Joe sighed. "Grace, I—"

"I know," I said, green eyes snapped my way. "And I'm sorry too." For a lot of things.

"About what happened with Matias..." he added, shaking his head, "I should have known."

A nauseating swirl of anxiety rose in my throat at the thought of him. "Where is he now?" I asked, my trembling voice betraying my ability to act calm and collected.

"London. With his family. They... he doesn't remember any of this. He believes in another life, one where he went to school, university..."

Guilt twisted my stomach, making me stir uncomfortably on my feet. Matias had no idea. No memory of this world. Of what he was. Of what *I* was to him.

Joe cleared his throat and pushed the box toward the end of the counter. "I got you something."

I frowned, walking up to the delicate frill decorating the white box.

"I know it's a crappy way of apologizing, but—"

My breath caught as I opened the box and saw a gown inside. "You didn't."

"I know how hard I've been on you, not letting you go out when others could, forcing you to change dorms. The least I could do was gift you a dress."

I looked at him, the corners of my eyes stinging.

He smiled softly. "You never did get to celebrate your school prom."

"That's because we *had* to move."

He nodded slowly. "Yes, but even then, I had already bought you this dress, just in case."

Oh.

I didn't know what to say.

If I spoke, I might risk crying like an absolute fool in front of him, not that it would be the first time doing so. But this meant a lot... a lot, a lot.

He rose from the stool and leaned in, kissing my forehead softly. "I'll see you down there," he said before quietly slipping out the door.

I stared at the gown, my heart heavy, as I wondered how much disappointment there would be if he knew everything I'd done behind his back.

HUNTER

fifty one

Music echoed through the main hall as Celestials played renditions of songs on harps and violins. The sound was still soft and distant beneath the swell of voices and laughter as gold and silver lights shimmered from the chandeliers onto them.

Silas stood beside me, unmoving, his eyes locked on Veronica as she drifted through the crowd in a midnight gown, its lace details hugging her frame in a way that made Silas freeze.

"You're staring," I said flatly.

"I'm *observing*. There's a difference."

I suppressed a smirk. Silas and I were still feeling tense from when he figured out about Grace and me, but that was the thing with Silas. He could be mad or hurt or feel betrayed and he'd cover it up easily, like nothing happened in the first place.

"Speaking of observing..." Brandon's voice cut in as he elbowed me lightly. "Is Grace coming or what?"

I shifted my weight, my fingers brushing the edge of my

brother's crumpled letter in my pocket. "Doubt it," I said, keeping my voice casual. "She wasn't exactly excited about this whole ball thing." I was going to wait for the competition announcements and then head to her dorm.

I wanted nothing more than to see her, and being in this hall with a bunch of people that I didn't want to see bored me.

"Excuse me," Silas muttered, not having listened one bit, as he straightened his bow tie and waltzed his way up to Veronica.

Before I could roll my eyes and turn to Brandon, he had already been called across the room by someone and excused himself with a wink.

Which left me alone.

I didn't mind.

"I see you are still broody as always, Mr Cain."

That was short-lived.

I turned slightly, just enough to acknowledge Nadael with a tense smile and hoped she would take that as a sign that I did not want to engage in conversation.

She chuckled. "And just as non-talkative as the first day you arrived here."

My jaw clenched as I surveyed the crowd, and my fingers dug into the folded letter in my pocket, crumpling it further. "I had my reasons back then." Still do.

Nadael sighed. I could just about picture her red lips pursed in a way that reminded me of when my mother would be disappointed with me for misbehaving. "You've always been an excellent Ascendant, Mr Cain. I know your brother would be proud."

I saw red for a second, my breath sharp in my chest as memories of Nadael and Council members telling me my brother could not join me at Celestia swirled in my vision. I was ready to tell Nadael, something that I shouldn't, but then—

Someone caught my eye.

Grace had just walked in, and for a moment, the entire room felt like it tilted.

Her timid eyes searched the hall as I stared at her. She wasn't wearing something flashy or overly formal. No, it was something else entirely—*her.*

The gown was golden, deep and rich, fading into darker shades at the hem. Black branches stretched upward like they were reaching for the sunflowers that bloomed across the fabric. The off-the-shoulder design framed her collarbones, the soft curves of her neck and the way the dress hugged her waist before flowing into something *untouchable.*

Her curls were down, untamed and wild—the way I always liked them.

Marnie then trailed beside her in a sparkly green gown, but it didn't matter. No one else mattered.

Nadael was still talking, but her words blurred as my gaze lingered on Grace.

I needed to get away.

"I appreciate what you're telling me, Nadael—" *A fucking lie.* "But if you'll just excuse me."

I didn't wait for her response as I moved, weaving through the crowd, not fast enough but still too fast to be casual.

Grace's eye caught mine halfway across the room, and for a second, I forgot where I was. Forgot why I couldn't just pull her in and kiss her right there in front of everyone.

Instead, I stopped just short of her, my heart beating way too fast for the first time in years. "Grace," I said, quieter than I meant to.

Her lips curved into a small smile, uncertain but radiant.

"You're…" I faltered, searching for something that could match what I was seeing.

Stunning didn't even begin to cover it, but it was all I could manage.

Her bronzed cheeks flushed the faintest pink, and I wanted nothing more than to close the space between us. But before I could, a group of students, voices high with excitement, pulled her away with compliments and questions about her dress.

I stood there, rooted in place, watching as she was whisked away. Yet even while others surrounded her, laughing and chatting, her eyes still found mine.

Then Joe appeared, standing close and saying something in her ear.

Grace wasn't really listening, though. Her eyes were still on me.

The letter in my pocket suddenly felt heavier than ever.

I pictured my brother writing it, but nothing felt real about it. I hadn't even shown Grace the letter when she found out about Aaron, and yet I now realized I didn't need to cling to it. All it was, was a reminder of the unknown.

I pulled the letter out slowly, staring at the messy scrawl for only a second as my grip on it tightened.

Then, I tore it.

Piece by piece.

I watched the fragments flutter into a nearby bin, and without another thought, I moved toward Grace.

I'd found what I was looking for.

Her.

GRACE
fifty two

I stood beside Joe, my fingers brushing against the smooth fabric of the gown he'd given me. No matter how good it felt or how obsessed I was with it, I couldn't shake Joe's sudden silence. He was so happy to see me, but now his posture was stiff, his jaw tight as his eyes watched the crowd like he was preparing for something to go wrong.

I followed his line of sight, and that was when I noticed that he wasn't watching everyone else; he was looking right at Hunter.

Hunter cut through the hall effortlessly, looking utterly unfazed by the glittering chaos around him. His dark suit looked crisp, fitting him perfectly, yet somehow, he looked like he couldn't care less about it.

My stomach was a mess.

"Grace?" Joe's voice snapped me back, but Hunter was already standing in front of us, his hands casually tucked into his pocket while he looked at me with the faintest smirk on his lips.

"Grace," he acknowledged me with my name rather than his usual nickname. "Mind if I steal you for a dance?"

Joe stiffened immediately. "Yeah, actually, I do."

My eyes widened, but Hunter didn't blink. He just tilted his head slightly, completely unbothered.

"Joe," I hissed, turning to him. "It's just a dance. Everyone else is doing it."

Joe's jaw tightened. "Do you remember what happened last time you got too close to him? Or did moving dorms wipe your memory clean?"

I flinched. "It's not like that," I shot back, lowering my voice. "He's still my friend." A friend who was also *not* a friend and one I slept with on a regular basis.

Joe didn't look happy about that remark. After all, he seemed to dislike Hunter after the Riftkeeper situation.

He shook his head, exhaling sharply, and motioned a hand to the rest of the Ascendants dancing. "Fine."

Hunter's smirk deepened. "Glad we settled that, sir."

Joe glared at him as I took Hunter's outstretched hand, his grip warm, steady, and forever welcoming.

Hunter guided me onto the dance floor just as the harp's final notes faded into the air, replaced by something softer—slower. An orchestral version of *With or Without You* began to play, haunting and tender, like the song itself had been made for this moment.

We stopped at the center of the floor, the music curling around us like a secret. Hunter's hands found my waist while my own hands hovered for a second until I finally let them rest on his shoulders.

Everyone else was dancing apart, keeping space between bodies. And then there were us—far too close and aware of each other.

From across the room, I caught Eden staring at us, her eyes narrowed in suspicion. I shook my head as I glanced back at Hunter.

"We should probably try to look less... *couple-y*," I muttered.

"Don't focus on everyone else, Bambi," he said, keeping his gaze fixed on me. "It's just us right now."

I swallowed, feeling that familiar heat creep up my neck.

We swayed slowly to the music, and for a moment, the chatter around us dulled.

"You clean up well," I said, breaking the silence.

You clean up well? Who even said that anymore?

Still, he chuckled. It was so deep, so masculine, it had me shivering. "You think so?"

I nodded. "Don't let it get to your head, though. The last thing I need is for you to become vain too."

Hunter leaned in just enough that I could feel his breath against my ear. "Too late."

I bit the inside of my cheek to hide the smile tugging at my lips.

He pulled back slightly, studying me. Something softer lingered in his eyes. "You're dangerous, you know that?"

I raised a brow. "Shouldn't it be the other way, considering I'm the *helpless* little Bambi and you're the *big bad* huntsman?"

He chuckled under his breath. "You're far from helpless, Grace."

My stomach did a flip. "Oh, but I am. Trust me, I mean, I know. When I was little, I tried to climb this tree in our back garden because I thought if I got high enough, I could touch the clouds—don't laugh, I was like six—and I got stuck halfway up because I didn't think about how I'd get down. Joe ended up having to use his wings just to come get me because

413

I was crying, thinking I'd have to live in the tree forever like some weird forest hermit. And then, in school, I froze during a presentation about dolphins, and I just stood there, staring at my cue cards like they were in another language. So yeah, I have a long and unfortunate history of being helpless in many situations."

I realized I hadn't taken a breath and clamped my mouth shut.

Hunter was staring at me, brow raised with that infuriating smirk tugging at the corner of his mouth.

Heat flooded my face, and I looked away. "Please forget everything I said."

"Never," he whispered, and my breath caught as I glanced his way again. His eyes flickered briefly over my shoulder. "Come with me."

I hesitated. "What?"

"When no one's watching. Slip out."

The music came to a quiet close, and just like that, we stopped dancing, and he was gone, disappearing back into the crowd.

I hesitated for a heartbeat, pulse thundering in my ears, before casting a glance over my shoulder at Joe. His back was to me, deep in conversation with Sariel and a few other Celestials from the Healers' Sector.

I released a slow breath, waiting for the perfect moment. When I was certain no one was watching, I slipped away.

Hunter stood outside the hall, leaning against the stone wall as if he had all the time in the world. "Ready to break a few more rules, Bambi?" he asked, pushing off the wall once he saw me.

I chuckled, taking his hand as I followed him into the night, the cool winter air hitting my skin as we left the warmth and noise of the ball behind. We went past the training grounds and slipped deep into the woods. Hunter moved ahead, leading us to a small clearing. There, he found a few sticks, built a small tinder, and set it alight with a lighter. The flames flickered and danced, casting a soft light against his features and causing something in my chest to tighten.

He turned to me, and I closed the space between us before I could think twice. Our lips met in the middle in a power-hungry kiss.

There was no hesitation this time.

We'd been craving it since we saw each other inside the ball.

His hands slid down my back, pulling me closer. The cold night air seemed to vanish as Hunter's lips moved with purpose—slow, deliberate, yet laced with hunger. His hand found the curve of my hips, gripping me firmly before trailing lower. I bit my lip, and he broke the kiss just enough to rest his forehead against mine, his breath ragged.

"Tell me to stop," he murmured, but there was enough of a rough edge to his voice like he was barely holding himself together.

I didn't hesitate when I said, "Don't."

That was all he needed.

Hunter kissed me again, rougher this time, backing me up against a tree before he slowly lowered himself to his knees in front of me. His hands slipped beneath my gown, but his eyes were fixed on me as I watched him lift the hem of my dress, bunching the soft fabric slowly, teasingly, until the cool air kissed my thighs.

"Hold still." His voice was like pure smoke. I wanted to inhale it.

The next minute, his lips were on me.

The first touch of his mouth was gentle, testing almost, but it sent a sharp jolt of pleasure through me that made my knees nearly buckle.

Hunter's hands gripped my thighs, anchoring me in place as his mouth moved with devastating precision.

Heat instantly bloomed low in my belly, spreading outward in waves.

I gasped, threading my fingers into his hair, tugging lightly, and he groaned against me—a low vibrating sound that only made the tension inside me coil tighter.

Every slow, deliberate stroke of his tongue pushed me closer to the edge, and I couldn't stop the whimpering sounds that escaped my lips.

Hunter pulled back just enough to glance up at me, his lips glistening. "I love it when you fall apart for me."

I didn't have the strength to form a coherent response. My head tipped back, and I was lost in the way he moved against me, relentless and patient all at once.

The fire crackled ahead of us, and as the pleasure finally shattered through me, it was like falling. It was... like gravity.

Hunter didn't let go until I was trembling in his grasp, barely able to stand. Only then did he rise slowly, catching me before I could collapse entirely.

His lips brushed my ear as he held me steady. "I could spend forever learning how to make you feel like that."

The words sank deep, curling around something fragile in my chest.

He wasn't smirking at me when he leaned back just enough to meet my eyes. He wasn't trying to tease me. If anything, he sounded as though he was making me a promise.

I swallowed hard as I leaned into him, completely undone.

The world could have ended at that moment, and I wouldn't

416

have cared.

I almost told him then.

I love you.

The words hovered on my tongue, but I buried them deep.

Not yet.

Instead, I tightened my hold on him and pressed the side of my head against his chest, letting myself fall even harder.

GRACE
fifty three

"We should probably head back," Hunter muttered, clearly not wanting to move after we'd spent the past thirty minutes either talking or him between my legs.

The fire was dying down, its glow flickering low as reality crept back in—the ball, the competition announcements.

I nodded, smoothing out my dress and trying to adjust myself so I didn't look like I'd just—God.

My hair was a lost cause as I raked my fingers through its curls, anyway, hoping it looked somewhat presentable. By the time we slipped back into the ballroom, the warm lights and loud chatter crashed over me, making me wish I was back in the quiet woods with Hunter.

Marnie was straight away in my face, pulling me back from Hunter. "Where the hell have you been?" she hissed. "I looked everywhere!"

I glanced back at Hunter, his eyes on me even as Silas and

Brandon joined him.

"Oh," Marnie muttered, realisation dawning on her. "Oh, Grace, don't tell me you..."

I groaned. "Marnie—"

"Nope! Just because I said I'm with you for anything you need doesn't mean I want details of your sexcapades."

Before I could even try to defend myself, Nadael's voice rose above the crowd, and everyone stilled.

"Attention, everyone!" she called, standing gracefully on a podium, her silver gown glinting in the light. "If you could all please remain where you are. The competition announcements are about to begin!"

The room quieted, and out of the corner of my eye, I noticed Veronica standing alone, her expression distant and almost sad.

I thought about Lucas, and my throat tightened.

She must be missing him so much.

I nudged Marnie. "Come on."

Marnie shot me a look the moment she realized where was heading, but she followed anyway—albeit reluctantly.

She knew just as well as I did, that when no one else, not even our own roommates, had come to her womanly defence... Veronica had.

We sidled up next to her. She didn't look at us, but the slight shift in her posture told me she didn't mind the company.

Nadael then cleared her throat. "As you all know, the Ascension Competition tests our finest Ascendants' strength, skill, and intelligence. For a Healer, this is their chance to show their Ascendant's motto: *Restoration, Life, Purity.*" She took her time, looking at each and every person around her. "For a Messenger, their ability to use *Communication, Speed, Telepathy.* You all have a role, and now is the time to prove that."

420

Marnie squeezed my arm, her excitement palpable compared to how my stomach was in knots.

"...This year's competitors have been carefully selected by the Council after weeks of preparation and assessing your performances." Nadael began to unroll the parchment she had in her hands with dramatic slowness. "First, the *Healers*."

She then spoke carefully as she listed names until—

"Marnie Lewis."

Marnie gasped beside me, clutching my hand until I was sure it'd fall off. "Did she just..."

I grinned, nodding for her to go on, and she looked at me as if she might faint. I nudged her forward and felt immense pride as I watched her walk up to Nadael, shake her hand and stand beside other Healers.

Marnie looked at the crowd, finding me beside Veronica, and waved so enthusiastically that I laughed.

Nadael then continued blurting out names from other sectors, five from each group, before she moved on to the final one.

"For the Warriors... Hunter Cain."

I glanced toward Hunter, who didn't react as applause broke out. Everyone knew he would make it. It was a given.

"Silas Dunn."

Silas let out a sharp breath, and Veronica tensed beside me.

"Sarah Danvers," Nadael continued to call out.

"Brandon Tucker."

He grinned, puffing out his chest and I smiled, clapping as he walked past me. Silas patted his back as he joined them, and once the crowd had settled again, Nadael rolled the parchment lower.

She paused.

Her eyes skimmed the piece of paper again, but the hesitation stretched too long.

The room murmured, whispers rippling through the Ascendants, wondering what was taking her so long to say the last name.

I frowned and glanced at Veronica, who seemed to care less about this moment than everyone else inside the room.

As I looked back at Nadael, her fair skin had turned an even lighter shade of white before she uttered, "Grace Martin."

Silence.

The name barely registered.

Wait.

What?

Every head turned to look at me.

Marnie slapped a hand over her mouth while Eden's face lit up from the other side of the hall. But Joe... Joe was storming toward Nadael, his voice low as he leaned in and whispered something to her.

I looked at Hunter only to see he had gone pale. His hands curled into fists at his sides, his eyes darkening, refusing to even look in my direction.

Nadael cleared her throat and forced a brittle smile that Joe—not even Hunter—could fake. "Grace Martin, if you could please join the others."

My legs moved, but they didn't feel like mine. Each step forward felt heavy, like I was wading through water. The silence in the room pressed in from all sides, thick with judgment. Eyes followed my every move, and by the time I reached the others, I was nearly gasping for air.

I wanted to turn and run away but couldn't as I climbed the steps to stand beside the others. I glanced toward Hunter, silently begging him to look at me.

But he didn't.

My stomach clenched, and I forced my watery gaze on everyone else as Nadael's voice rose again.

"Congratulations to all of you who have been chosen for the Ascension competition!"

Scattered applause followed, the noise feeling distant as everything blurred, and my legs trembled.

I couldn't concentrate. I was barely hanging on by a thread as Nadael began to speak about what would proceed next. We would receive a letter through our dorms ranging from instructions to informing us of a time we had to appear for the competition. She did not specify when that would be; she just said to be prepared at all times.

I moved to step down the moment it was over, but Eden was suddenly in front of me, beaming. "Grace! I knew you could do it! Ascendant or not, the Council clearly saw potential."

They didn't at first, I wanted to say, but my eyes just scanned the hall for Hunter instead.

I barely mumbled a thank you before Joe was in front of me, his expression hard.

"You need to give up your spot," he snapped.

I blinked. "What?"

"This competition isn't for humans. The Council clearly weren't thinking straight when they put you on that list." He sighed, pinching the bridge of his nose. "I'll have to speak with them—"

"If she was chosen, then that means she was worthy in the Council's eyes," Eden defended, and Joe's glare sharpened.

I stepped between them, thankful that Eden saw enough potential in me to argue. But I didn't want her to get in trouble with Joe—not when he was like this. "Isn't this what you wanted?" I said to him. "To prove that a non-Ascendant could be one without the title?"

He didn't answer.

This was more about Joe still wanting to protect me even after telling me he knew he couldn't. He was afraid. He was always afraid for me.

Still, I pushed past him, knowing that I no longer wanted to hear it. Ever since coming here, it was always the excuse he'd give me.

What I needed to do was find Hunter.

I glanced around the hall, spotting as people swarmed around Marnie, congratulating her and other Ascendants. But when Marnie's eyes found mine, the joy on her face faltered. Her brows knitted together in concern, and she tilted her head as if silently asking, *are you okay?*

I shook my head quickly, but I didn't wait to see her reaction as I turned on my heel, and my legs moved before my mind could catch up, half walking, half running toward the exit.

The cool air of the hallway hit me as I came out through the doors. I paused for a split second at the threshold, my heart pulsing against my chest as I scanned the corridor.

I took a left.

It wasn't a decision so much as a pull, an instinct deep in my chest guiding me forward. My heels clattered loudly against the marble floor, and I didn't care. I didn't even care when the sharp stone walls scraped against the delicate fabric of my dress, snagging and ripping at the threads. I didn't care that the noise of the ballroom faded behind me, and I was swallowed by the cold silence of empty hallways and an even emptier canteen.

Call it intuition, but I knew if Hunter had gone anywhere, it wouldn't be back to his dorm or the training grounds, and especially not anywhere crowded.

I approached the canteen kitchen and made my way to the

424

hidden entrance of the armory. My hand skimmed along the familiar groove in the wall, finding the hidden hatch before the stone shifted with a low groan, and I stepped inside.

I was right.

He *was* in the armory all alone as I took the first steps down the stairway. He leaned forward slightly, bracing himself on one of the weapon racks, his shoulders tight.

The first thing that fell from my lips was, "Why did you walk away?"

He slowly looked at me, but the usual warmth in his eyes had turned cold. Just like the first time we had met.

"The competition is dangerous, Grace." He shook his head, more at himself than me. "You shouldn't be in it."

There was a crack in my chest. It was the beginning of something I didn't like. "I thought... I thought you, of all people, would be proud."

Hunter's expression tightened, but he didn't say anything.

I bit the inside of my cheek. It hurt, but it kept me from blurting out something I'd regret. "Maybe this is a good thing. How things are changing around here. How maybe a human can—"

"The competition isn't what you think it is, Grace. You might not even make it past the first part without getting hurt."

The crack in my chest grew.

"Oh." My voice came out smaller than I wanted. "Wow. And here I thought things had changed. That you... never mind."

He opened his mouth, like he wanted to explain, but nothing came.

Frustration swelled inside my throat. "What's the real reason you don't want me to do the competition? Because it's clearly not about whether you care if I get hurt or not."

His eyes flashed with something that resembled anger and

fear mixed in one. "Of course, I fucking care if you get hurt—"

"Then what is it!"

Again, silence.

I've always excused his lack of words because that was just who Hunter was. A guy who didn't like explaining things to anyone, who didn't like sharing his secrets. I respected it to an extent, but now I was confused, hurt and just downright disappointed.

I sighed, defeated. "Why can't you just talk to me properly?"

His jaw worked back and forth as he looked anywhere but at me.

I pursed my lips, feeling the familiar sting of frustrated tears brimming in my eyes, and nodded. "Tonight was a mistake," I whispered, and before he could stop me—if he even would—I turned and walked away.

GRACE
fifty four

The soft rustle of fabric filled my room as I fumbled with the zipper of my dress. I yanked it down with more force than necessary, letting it pool at my feet. I wanted out of it. I wanted so *desperately* to get out of it.

My skin felt too itchy, too uncomfortable, as I clawed at my back and stood there in nothing but my underwear.

This was supposed to be a good night.

It had been.

Until my name was called out from that list.

I was chosen. The Council chose *me*. I should have felt proud and accomplished.

Instead, Hunter's words replayed in my head over and over.

You won't even get past the first stage of the competition.

The sting of his dismissal burned deeper than anything else I had been told in my life.

Maybe... maybe he was right.

I was at a disadvantage. I had never even done the Ascension competition before, unlike thousands of Ascendants.

A soft knock at the door startled me.

"Grace?"

I didn't answer, but the door creaked open anyway.

Marnie peeked in, my eyes softening the moment she saw me standing there, practically half-naked. She closed the door behind her. "Do you need any help?"

I opened my mouth to say 'no'—that I was fine and didn't need anyone right now—but the words never came out.

Marnie sighed and moved past me, anyway, gently picking up the discarded gown and draping it neatly over the chair. "That dress doesn't deserve to be on the floor," she muttered before settling down on my bed. She bunched up her dress and patted the space beside her for me to come over.

I let out a hollow chuckle and sat beside her. "Apparently, neither do I."

"Don't say that."

"I just—maybe I should listen to Joe and ask to be removed from the competition. Let someone more... I don't know; worthy to take my place. I didn't even want to do it at first, anyway."

"You were still chosen for a reason, Grace." Our shoulders touched as she sighed. "You were the one out there wanting to take initiative and be trained to become a better Warrior. You beat Norah in a fight—"

"Yeah, with help."

"Still! You've improved a lot, Grace, and maybe the Council saw that too."

Her words stirred some confidence inside me, but it wasn't enough. I tried to smile at her, but it didn't reach my eyes.

Marnie sighed again and gently placed a hand over my heart. I almost pushed her away, knowing I didn't want her to

430

use her healing since that was all she ever did for me, but it was too late. A soft warmth spread through me, like sunlight filtering through cracks in a wall. I felt the sharp edge of my pain dull, easing me just a little.

I shook my head, smiling. "You need to stop doing that."

"Well, if I don't, all that sadness is just going to build up, and I don't feel like dealing with an emotionally constipated Grace."

I snorted out a laugh, bumping my shoulder with hers.

Her smile softened. "I'd rather see you happy than sad. And I know that Lucas would say the same thing if he were here."

The lump in my throat threatened to rise again, but I swallowed it down. "I just... I thought Hunter would be proud of me," I whispered. It looked like he was the other day of the Ecliptic Hunt, but maybe that was just an illusion on my part.

"He should be."

I nodded slowly, staring down at my hands.

"But even if he's not," she continued, "I am, and that's all that should matter."

I exhaled. "Thanks, Marnie." I was so glad to have met her, to have someone not judge me from the beginning.

"Don't thank me; thank my healing abilities." She wiggled her fingers, and I chuckled once again before we slipped into an endless conversation about music and food.

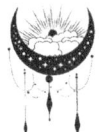

Two days after the ball, a sharp knock rattled the door to our dorm at the crack of dawn.

Groaning, I sat up and rubbed my eyes, the cold air biting at my skin. Across the other side of the living room, Marnie was

431

already half-dressed, her hair a tangled mess.

"At least one of us is semi-ready," I croaked as Marnie yanked the door open to find one of the Messenger Celestials standing at our doorway with two crisp envelopes in her hand and bagged clothing.

She passed the letter over to us, and we didn't make any sound or movement to return to the dorm as my fingers traced the wax seal of a wing from the Council. My stomach flipped.

I broke the seal, unfolding the letter at the same time Marnie did.

Dear Competitor,

You have been selected to participate in this year's Ascension Competition. Enclosed is your assigned uniform. Wear it during all stages of the competition.

Right at that moment, the Celestial handed Marnie and me the bagged clothing.

The competition will commence at midnight in the west wing of the academy.

Further instructions will be given upon arrival.
Failure to appear will result in immediate disqualification.
—The Angelic Council

I stared at the words, and the letters blurred for a moment. *Midnight.*

I ran my fingers over the uniform, concealed in a clear plastic bag. It was heavier than expected and darker than the royal blue Celestia usually made us wear.

The Council clearly wasn't wasting any time with us.

432

Marnie and I shared a wary look, and by lunchtime, the canteen was buzzing with low voices as I sat opposite Marnie, playing with my bowl of soup.

I was too nervous to eat.

"So, what do you think the competition is going to be like?" Marnie asked. I looked up at her.

"I thought you'd know more than me or would have asked others who have previously done it."

"No one tells me anything; besides, it's always changing. Who knows what this one will be like?"

I nodded in agreement, but a shadow loomed over our table just as I was about to tell her that we should be more prepared for tonight.

My head snapped up.

Norah.

"You didn't deserve that spot in the competition," she outright spat, eyes narrowed on me as she leaned across the table. "If you hadn't gotten Matias kicked out, he'd be on the list. Not you."

I tensed.

That wasn't true...

"Norah."

All heads looked past Norah to where Hunter stood behind her with his usual unbothered expression.

My breath hitched.

I hadn't spoken to Hunter since the night of the ball. I had actively avoided him throughout the weekend, but now that it was Monday and the competition was among us, I couldn't no longer.

Norah turned to him. "Defending her now, are we? Wouldn't be the first time."

Hunter's eyes narrowed. "No. I'm just tired of always

hearing your voice. Do everyone a favour and shut up before you embarrass yourself."

Marnie's fork clanged against the table, her eyes widening as she looked between Hunter and Norah.

Great.

I hated the part of me that felt satisfied hearing him shut her down. But I was still annoyed. And when Hunter gave me a pointed look, silently telling me to just walk away, I listened. I grabbed my tray and stood, even as Norah's jeering voice followed me as I walked past her.

"Enjoy your spot while it lasts, Grace. We both know your *fake angel daddy* pulled some strings to get you in."

Something snapped.

Without even so much as a thought, I spun on my heel, ready to charge straight for her, but before I could, Hunter rushed toward me, strong hands wrapping around my waist, and turned me away from Norah.

His grip was firm as I tried to yank myself free from him. "Don't," he warned against my ear. "Unless you want to get disqualified."

I ripped my arm from his hold, the sting of his touch lingering as I spun to face him. "Isn't that what you want?"

Hunter's jaw tightened, but he didn't answer.

Just like always.

Marnie came beside me, tugging at my sleeve. "Come on, let's just go back to our room."

I turned with her, stalking away as my pulse hammered against my ears.

I got only as far as the entrance before a loud shriek of disgust echoed through the canteen.

"What the fuck is wrong with you, creep!"

I glanced over my shoulder just in time to see Norah

434

standing frozen, covered in what looked like soup and bread, dripping from her shoulders down to her training clothes.

Veronica stood beside her, holding an empty tray with an expression of pure indifference.

"Sorry, didn't see you there."

But she *definitely* had.

Marnie let out a quiet snort, barely containing her laughter.

I didn't smile. Not fully.

But it helped.

Just a little.

HUNTER

fifty five

I was ready to go after Grace, but I knew she didn't want to hear what I had to say.

"Of course you saw me! You did this on purpose."

Norah's shrill voice stung my eardrums as I glanced behind me to where Veronica stood calmly, staring at Norah, now drenched in soup. She was holding an empty tray with that same flat expression she always had on.

Seeing Norah in this state should've amused me, but I wasn't.

Grace was already gone, and the way she snapped back at me a few minutes ago didn't make things any better.

I rubbed my hand over my face, feeling like fucking shit.

"Hunter Cain?"

I turned sharply at the sound of my name.

A Celestial stood stiffly before me. "Azrael has requested your presence in his office. Immediately."

Of course, he had.

I didn't waste time responding; I just pushed past the

Celestial, leaving a screaming Norah in Veronica's hands and headed straight to Azrael's office.

He didn't look up as I entered. He was sitting behind his desk, back straight and suit dark, blending with the velvet high-backed chair.

Azrael barely ever summoned me to his office, but when he did, it was always something I didn't care about.

The stained-glass windows of his office bled fractured light across the stone walls, casting jagged patterns against the floor. The air, on the other hand, smelt like old parchment and metal. It always made me feel restless in here.

"You wanted to see me?" I asked, hoping he dismissed me soon enough.

He raised his head slowly, studying me with those pale green eyes. "I want you to win tonight," he said plainly, not wasting any time.

I scoffed. "Not that I'm honored or anything, but why?"

Azrael leaned back in his chair, fingers steepled across his abdomen. "Because I believe you'd make an exceptional Authority."

Ah, there it was.

Authority. Heaven's military kings. The *enforcers*.

I let out a short, humorless laugh. He wasn't trying to be kind or even motivating.

He was being strategic.

This wasn't about me. It was about control. Ever since I arrived here, Azrael took it upon himself to mold me into exactly what he wanted. Another weapon in his arsenal.

Azrael stared at me as I shook my head with amusement. Then, slowly, he stood and moved toward an iron safe embedded in the stone wall. He turned the lock before reaching inside and pulling out a thin, sealed envelope.

438

Without a word, he walked back to the desk and dropped it in front of me.

"What's this?" I asked, eyeing it warily. The stamp on it told me it was from the Council.

"Open it."

I snatched it from his desk and broke the seal in record timing. My eyes skimmed the Council's emblem of a wing, then the words that followed.

In light of recent events and ongoing concerns regarding the stability of the Ascendant ranks, the Council has reached a decision regarding the upcoming Ascension Competition.

It has been deemed necessary to include Grace Martin in this year's selection of competitors.

This decision is not founded on her merit, skill, or potential but rather serves a greater purpose: to show the first order of the Angelic Hierarchy, the inherent divide between Ascendants and humans.

Her inclusion will provide undeniable evidence that mortals—regardless of training or circumstance—cannot endure the demands required of our kind. Let her participation stand as a public testament to the Council's unwavering belief that ascending is not something granted through effort but by divine birthright.

We trust that this demonstration will silence further discourse regarding non-Ascendants' integration into Celestial ranks.

This matter is to remain confidential. No other members of the faculty, including Celestial Nadael, are to be informed. We expect you to monitor this situation closely.

Her inevitable failure will serve its purpose.

By Order of the Angelic Council,

Archangel Seraphiel

High commander of the Authorities
Archangel Meriel
Council overseer of all Celestia Academies
Archangel Cael
Advisor of Celestial Doctrine
Dated 6th of October

My grip on the letter tightened, the edges crumbling beneath my fingers.

Inevitable failure.

They didn't choose her because they saw potential.

They chose her to watch her *break*. To prove that humans could never stand beside Ascendants.

"Is this why she made the list instead of Matias?" My voice was low and fucking dangerous, but my heart split, just remembering how Grace's face lit up one time as she told me how great it felt to finally be in the top five of something.

Azrael nodded. "The Council directly sent it to me. They knew Nadael and Joe would oppose."

"Why are you showing me this?" I snapped.

Azrael's gaze sharpened as he sat down. "Because I know you didn't want her here to begin with."

I clenched my teeth. "Grace has done more without powers than half the people here. She *earned* her place to stay here."

His expression didn't change. "She shouldn't be here at all, Cain. She's useless to us."

The words triggered a memory. One where Nadael didn't allow my brother to come here with me.

Because Hunter... humans are useless to us in this place. You'll learn to realize that in time.

My fists clenched, anger swarming my vision.

"Nadael has become too soft over the years. She excuses

everything regarding Joe because she sees him as a son. She doesn't realise how much danger she is putting us in by having Grace here."

I stared at Azrael. "What do you mean?"

Azrael's silence stretched just long enough to twist something in my gut.

"Grace didn't just appear on Joe's doorstep by chance," he said finally. "She was brought here for a reason."

My gaze narrowed on his.

"Her mother was a Riftkeeper. A powerful one. Until she betrayed their kind."

Her mother was a Riftkeeper.

My pulse pounded in my ears over Azrael's revelation.

How—

"Supposedly, instead of killing Joe, she fell in love with him. But when Grace's father—another Riftkeeper—found out, he killed her."

The room tilted.

"But not before her mother gave Grace to Joe for protection."

My hands were shaking.

That's why they were always moving. Why Joe was so desperate to keep her hidden.

Why she was here.

And I had inadvertently put her in danger, taking her into the den of Riftkeeper's.

"And Joe..." I said quietly. "Was he—"

"No." Azrael shook his head. "He wouldn't be here if he had fallen for her. But that didn't mean he didn't care for Grace's mother." He sighed. "Like I said before... Grace shouldn't be here. She's dangerous. More than anyone realises. But the Council is too blinded by other threats to see it."

I needed to get out of here.

441

I needed to *think*.

I stormed toward the door, my hand hovering over the doorknob.

"I suggest you think carefully before running to tell her."

I stilled.

"Especially since I know how much you've come to care for her, too."

The room felt ice-cold.

Slowly, I turned back to face him.

"I've noticed it for weeks," he said casually, like it wasn't a fucking blade twisting in my chest. "Although I'd say the armory is a terrible place to... well, you know."

My hands curled into fists.

He knew.

He saw us.

"Why haven't you told anyone?" I managed to ask, but my voice came out strangled.

A thin smile ghosted across Azrael's face. "Because Hunter..." He paused, "You're my favorite student. Whatever it is with her, it'll pass. But for now, I'll be rooting for you tonight."

I hadn't thought this through. Not properly.

Which was stupid because this was the most important thing I'd ever done.

After leaving Azrael's office, my head was a mess, which explained why I stood outside Grace's dorm, fist hovering over the door when Azrael had told me not to run after her.

I shook my head and knocked regardless.

A beat of silence. Then, muffled footsteps. Then—

The door cracked open, and Grace's head peeked through. She blinked up at me, eyebrows furrowing in confusion.

"Hunter?"

I cut to the chase. "I don't know how to do this."

Her eyes flickered with something unreadable. "Do what?"

"This," I gestured vaguely between us. "I don't know how to say what I'm thinking without fucking it up. I don't know how to... be that kind of guy you probably deserve."

Her eyes widened slightly as she glanced behind her before quickly shutting the door and stepping out into the corridor. I didn't care that her roommates could have heard all of that at that moment in time, not one fucking bit.

She exhaled sharply, but I didn't let her get a word out.

"I tell myself that it doesn't matter. That you don't matter. That I could walk away and be fine. But that's a lie. Because you are everywhere. You're in my damn head when I wake up, when I try to sleep, when I step into a room and expect to see you. It's—" I dragged a hand down my face, frustrated at myself. "It's fucking annoying."

A small breath of laughter escaped her, barely there, but it was enough to make something shift in my chest.

I swallowed. "And then, when you're not there, when I don't see you—it's worse. It feels like something is missing. Like I'm missing something I didn't even know I needed."

Her lips parted slightly, but she said nothing.

So, I took a step closer. "I don't deserve you. You know that. I've screwed up more times than I can count, and I will screw up a thousand times more. But if there's even a single part of you that wants me, that feels the same—" my voice dropped lower, rougher, more desperate than I meant it to be "—I need you tell me."

443

I just wanted to hear her say it.

I needed it because I was slowly losing my mind.

Her lips parted, and my whole world narrowed in on her. But before she could speak, a voice cut through us, slicing that moment between us to ribbons.

"Mr Cain."

Grace flinched slightly, snapping her head to where a Celestial stood, arms crossed, and his gaze locked firmly on me.

"You're out of your sector," he said coolly. "You're in the competition. You should be preparing instead of playing visiting hours."

Grace took a small step back. No. Not now.

I clenched my fists. "I—"

"Now, Cain."

I clenched my teeth as Grace looked between us. I wanted to tell her to wait. To tell her this conversation wasn't over. But instead, I did what I always did: I swallowed it down, shoved it deep into the part of me that never got to have good things, and stepped back.

Her expression fell, but she quickly masked it.

I took one last look at her before turning and following the Celestial out of the Healers Sector.

I didn't get to tell her anything else. And she didn't get to say whatever the hell she was about to say.

And something in me whispered that we'd just run out of time.

GRACE

fifty six

I stood by the window, staring out into the dark expanse of the academy grounds. Tonight, the moon hung low, casting silver light over the frost-laced grass and training grounds. It was almost midnight.

My stomach twisted with endless nerves.

Behind me, Marnie moved around my room, pulling on the last pieces of the uniform we'd been given in the morning.

"How do I look?" Her black combat boots scuffed against the floor as she struck a mock battled pose.

At least one of us was excited.

I managed a weak smile. "Like you're about to win this entire competition."

"Damn right, I am." She grinned before her expression softened. "Are you... okay?"

My fingers tugged at the hem of my jacket.

"I don't know," I admitted. It seemed like the only answer I ever responded with.

"You're going to be fine," Marnie said, grabbing my arm.

"You've trained for this. Well... sort of." She gave me a sheepish smile. "But hey, you're about to prove to a whole group of angels that you're worth becoming one."

I let out a shaky laugh. "Come on," I said. "We're late."

She nodded, and soon we slipped out into the cold, boots crunching against the frostbitten ground as we made our way through the silent academy. Torches flickered as we passed corridors, and with every step closer we took toward the west wing, my stomach twisted tighter.

When we got there, the other competitors were already gathered, while others, such as Azrael and Sariel, stood in front of the towering wall of ancient paintings.

My gaze immediately landed on Hunter, and the sight of him sent a jolt through me.

He was beside Silas and Brandon with his arms crossed, eyes distant and shadowed.

He looked... far away. Not just physically but *gone* in a way I couldn't explain. But before I could decide on what to do, a familiar voice spoke from behind.

"Grace."

I turned to see Joe approaching. He looked me over, his gaze lingering on my uniform.

"Be careful," was all he said, but his voice was tight.

I sighed. "Joe—"

"Just... be careful, please?"

My first instinct was to wrap my arms around his neck, not caring how much of a toll our relationship had taken ever since I came here. "I will be," I whispered. "I promise."

He hugged me back tighter, and when we separated, I saw Eden approaching us.

"Grace!" She smiled. "I just wanted to say... I'm rooting for you," she said earnestly. "You deserve to be here."

I believed she meant it. "Thank you, Eden, that... means a lot."

Joe glanced at her, but Eden never even looked him in the eye. Before she could say anything more, the crowd shifted as Nadael stepped forward, standing in front of the paintings. Her presence silenced us instantly.

"Competitors," she began as we gathered around her. "Thank you for all your patience while we prepare everything." Her gaze swept over us. "Most of you know that this competition consists of three rounds. Each is designed to test not only your skill but also your judgment."

My heart thundered against my chest.

"Council members will be observing from their headquarters, using Guardian magic. Which means every action you take will be watched."

A heavy silence settled, and I glanced at Marnie, wanting that reassurance she always gave me. But she was too engrossed, too excited by everything Nadael was saying. This was her chance to make it as an Ascendant and she wanted it desperately.

"This year's competition scenario is called *the Hunt and the Hunted.* For each sector, you may use your powers to showcase your skills. Warriors, however, will not be given any weapons. This is to enforce your skills in weapons crafting from natural objects.'

A chill slid down my spine.

"Now," she said. "Your objective is simple: collect three sigil stones scattered through the glade before sunrise and make it out of there in time. Those who do not will have to wait, hide, survive until Celestials come to your aid."

A murmur rippled through the competitors; meanwhile, my eyes widened at Nadael mentioning sunrise.

"These stones," she continued, "are ancient, enchanted, and heavily guarded. Shadow beasts—born from the very first creations of hell—prowl the glade. They have been released from their homes, and they are *merciless*."

I struggled to swallow.

"But be warned. Some stones are cursed."

Joe stiffened from where he stood on the other side.

"Touch the wrong stone, and you will face visions of your worst fears. Loved ones in danger. Enemies begging for mercy. These lies and half-truths are designed to break your focus. You must decide whether to trust what you see or leave it behind." Nadael turned toward the massive painting on the stone wall—a vast glade bathed in pale moonlight. She raised a hand, her palm glowing faintly as she pressed it against the canvas.

The surface rippled like water, and the glade inside the painting seemed to sway as if alive.

Hunter shifted slightly, and his eyes finally met mine for a brief second, but there was something raw and distant in them.

"Good luck," I mouthed, and his jaw tightened before he looked away.

Disappointment crashed into my chest, and I wanted nothing more than for him to look back at me.

"Competitors," Nadael called, but I couldn't physically bring myself to glance at her when I was so focused on Hunter. "Prepare yourself."

But I couldn't prepare myself.

"Deep breaths, deep breaths," Marnie was muttering to herself just as everyone surrounding Nadael flexed their hands and pumped themselves up with energy. Brandon was jogging on the spot as if this were just a race and nothing more, while Silas was already tying his hair into a low ponytail.

450

My gaze found Hunter again. It always did, even when I didn't mean for it to. I should have looked away.

But I didn't.

And for the briefest moment, neither did he.

The space between us seemed to stretch and shrink at once as we slowly moved closer towards one another until we stood side by side. Nadael kept talking, but it was a distant hum to me. Then, barely noticeable, Hunter's hand shifted—ever so slightly, so deliberately that I might have thought I imagined it if not for the warmth that brushed my skin.

Our pinkies touched, and the world stopped turning.

Neither of us pulled away.

Neither of us breathed.

Neither of us looked at each other.

His fingers twitched, like he wanted to grab my hand, but he knew he shouldn't. Knew he couldn't.

I should have pulled away. I should have stepped back and created distance before it swallowed me whole. But... I stayed.

And so did he.

Until the moment shattered, and Nadael's hand lifted toward the painting. "Competitors," she said as the glade shimmered brighter. "You may begin."

I could no longer feel Hunter's touch as everyone went for it, all running towards the painting and letting it swallow them whole.

Marnie tugged at me, and my legs barely moved as I stumbled forward, letting the cold air of the glade slam into my face.

I was no longer staring at a painting.

I was inside of it.

It was real. Just like the day I went to the Council's headquarters.

The wind howled through the dark trees and the moon was covered by fog as the scent of damp earth filled my lungs.

I didn't have time to think because everyone was already running, and I was right behind them.

As I sprinted forward, branches clawed at my arms, weaving through the dense trees. The cold air stung my face, but thankfully, it kept me awake and alert.

The glade was massive, stretching endlessly in every direction as shadows shifted between the trees.

Marnie was ahead of me, her slim, shadowed figure slipping through the underbrush easily while others had scattered in different directions, disappearing into the dark.

Hunter was nowhere near in sight. Of course, he wouldn't be. He was always too fast and agile.

I pushed the thought away and focused on the path ahead when a flicker of movement to my left caught my eye. I turned sharply, body tensed, but it was just another competitor darting between the trees.

But something was wrong.

I could tell.

I could sense it.

That was when I heard it.

A low guttural growl curled through the dark.

Shadow beasts.

The hairs on the back of my neck rose, and I didn't even think before I ran with every fibre of my being.

I kept running until I couldn't breathe anymore, and only then did I slow down.

Pressing my palm against the trunk of a tree, I tried keeping my breath shallow, but it was impossible. "Come on, Grace, come on," I whispered. "Find the stones and—"

The branches above creaked.

I froze.

Slowly, I looked up.

Eyes.

Glowing, pale eyes stared down at me from the branches, unblinking.

Before I could scream, it lunged.

Instinct took over.

I threw myself to the ground as claws swiped through the air where my throat had been a second before.

It hit the earth hard, snarling—a beast made of shadows and bone, limbs too long and its mouth full of jagged dark teeth.

I scrambled backwards, heart pounding in my throat.

How were we supposed to outrun these with no weapons?

The creature slowly moved towards me, its movements unnatural, as if its bones were constantly stiff and breaking.

My breaths came in ragged gasps, cold air burning my lungs.

Move, Grace. Move!

The creature's head tilted in slow motion; those glowing eyes fixed on me as it stalked forward.

Run!

My body finally listened to my mind as I scrambled to my feet, boots slipping on the damp forest floor, and bolted.

Branches whipped at my face as I tore through the trees, but the beast was faster. I could hear it crashing through the undergrowth behind me, snarling low and closer with every second.

I spotted a thick fallen tree ahead, its trunk half rotted and split open. Without thinking, I dove behind it, landing hard on the cold ground.

I clamped a hand over my mouth, chest heaving as it all went silent.

Then—I heard the sound of heavy footfalls.

My eyes darted around the dark forest floor, searching for anything to defend myself with before my fingers brushed against something cold.

A rock.

Not much, but better than nothing.

I tightened my grip on it, muscles coiled.

But right when I was about to fight back, something slammed into the creature with a sickening crack.

I rose to my feet, and that was when I saw Hunter, with a spear made of wood, standing between me and the beast.

"Grace, run!" He barked, digging the spear further into the creature.

But I didn't move.

I couldn't.

The beast lunged, and Hunter met it head-on, slamming his spear through its shoulder.

A shriek tore from its throat, and it reared back. Shadows rippled across its skin before it vanished into the dark like smoke drawn into a vacuum. Gone. As if it had never been there in the first place.

Silence fell except for the sharp sound of Hunter's breathing.

He stumbled back a step, blood dripping from a shallow cut on his arm. The spear clattered to the ground beside him.

I blinked. My body finally unlocked, and my lungs caught air in one desperate gasp.

"You didn't run," he said, turning toward me. There was no anger in his voice—just disbelief.

"I—" My voice broke. "I couldn't."

His eyes met mine. "You can't freeze like that again, Grace. Next time, I might not be fast enough."

He reached out, brushing his fingers over my sleeve before

they dropped away. The contact was brief, but it grounded me.

"I know," I whispered.

He shook his head, jaw tight. He reached into his pocket, pulling out a blade made of stone and tossing it over to me. "Just stay alive."

I stared at the blade, then back at Hunter as he turned to retrieve the spear, leaving my heart hammering in my chest before he disappeared into the woods.

HUNTER

fifty seven

The glade felt endless as my boots hit the hard ground, and mud kicked beneath me as I wove between trunks. The last competition involved simulations, but this time, the Council involved actual creatures that had been stored away for centuries. They were doing everything possible so that Grace failed.

I caught movement ahead. I slowed, crouching low, my fingers tightening around the spear. As I moved closer, muffled voices reached my ears.

"If you keep stumbling like that, we're not going to make it past sunrise," Silas hissed.

"Me?" Brandon shot back. "Maybe if you weren't fucking whining every five seconds, we'd actually make progress."

I stepped out of the shadows, glaring at both of them. "Are you two shitheads seriously arguing right now?"

They spun to face me, Brandon clutching a makeshift spear like mine and Silas holding what looked like a broken tree branch.

Rule number one: Never depend on these two for strategy.

"Cain." Brandon lowered his weapon. "We were just—"

"Getting nowhere," Silas interrupted.

I shook my head. "Guessing neither of you have found a stone yet."

They exchanged a sheepish glance, and I sighed.

Of course not.

I shook my head, stepping past them. But before I could get far, I stopped, turning back slightly. "Grace," I said, "make sure to look out for her."

Silas blinked. "Grace?"

Brandon tilted his head. "She's capable, isn't she? I mean, she did get chosen, so—"

"Just do it," I said sharply, the edge of my voice cutting off any protest.

I started moving again, but Silas's voice stopped me.

"Hey," he said, tipping his chin up at me. "What's wrong with you tonight?"

My jaw tightened. "Nothing."

Silas stared at me; his eyes narrowed like he didn't believe me one bit. I didn't say anything else and instead focused on the path ahead because I already knew what was wrong. And the last thing I needed was to involve anyone else in my problems.

GRACE

I decided that I hated any type of running.

Not just physically but mentally, too.

I was tired, craved sleep, and desperately needed to sit

down, but all I did was run and run and run. I didn't know where I was going; I just knew I was heading forward.

The ground was uneven as I slowed down, and my lungs stung with the lack of air. I pressed my hand to a tree trunk to steady myself, my breath shaky and my hair damp from sweat.

I leaned my head against the bark, closing my eyes as I tried to focus on getting my heart rate back to normal.

That's when I heard a whimper come from nearby, and my heart jumped into my throat.

My eyes snapped open as I scanned the forest. Slowly, I pushed myself off the tree and crept towards the sound.

That's when I saw it.

A girl—someone from the Guardian Sector.

She was slumped against a tree, her arm bent at an impossible angle that made my stomach churn.

I swallowed hard, stepping closer until her head snapped toward me, eyes narrowing with distrust. I raised my hands and glanced skyward, wondering if the Council were *really* watching me like this was all a reality TV show for them.

I shook my head at the thought.

"It's okay. I'm—" My gaze lowered to meet with the girls. "I'm here to help."

She didn't move as I approached, though her fingers twitched like she was deciding whether to strike. Kneeling beside her, I reached out towards her arm, but she lunged the second my hand touched her.

I barely had time to react before she knocked me back. I hit the ground hard and watched as she stumbled to her feet, running off in another direction.

"Shit. Grace!" Brandon yelled out as he and Silas burst through the trees. Helping me to my feet, his eyes scanned my face and blew a breath of relief. "What happened?"

I nodded, brushing dirt off my uniform. "I was just trying to help her."

"Molly doesn't take any help from anyone." Silas snorted, then muttered under his breath. "Guardians."

Right.

"I need to find Marnie," I said, glancing at the tall trees. "She might be hurt—"

I didn't finish as a deep, guttural growl sounded behind us.

Brandon's and Silas's eyes widened comically as I slowly turned around.

It was another beast, this one larger than the last. Its body rippled with dark energy as its glowing eyes locked onto us.

Silas raised a branch.

Oh, he had to be kidding me.

"Seriously?" I hissed. "You're one of the best Warriors out there, yet you choose a branch as a weapon?"

Silas's eyes never left the beast. "Trust me, a branch can be just as effective as a regular weapon."

The creature growled again, the sound rumbling through the air as it stepped forward, setting every single one of my nerves on fire.

My hand shook as I gripped the blade Hunter had given me earlier.

"Maybe we should run," Brandon whispered, but before I could scold him, a branch snapped behind us, and I spun around.

Marnie stumbled through the underbrush, her uniform torn as she clutched her side, her hands glowing faintly with healing energy.

Relief and worry crashed into me at once, but she waved me off, wincing. "Got caught by some Messenger earlier, but I'm fine. Where did you get the dagger?"

"Hunter," I said quickly, glancing back at the monster. Its eyes locked on us as it crouched low, preparing to strike.

"Shit," Silas whispered before the creature lunged at us, and Brandon shoved me to the side, his spear raised to intercept it.

"Go!" he shouted, and for once, we all agreed.

We scattered, tearing through the forest in different directions, and the creature's growls faded slightly behind me.

Marnie caught up to me, her breath ragged but steady. "What's the plan?" she gasped.

"I don't know," I admitted shamefully. "Find the sigil stones? Hope we don't run into more of those shadow creatures?"

"Well," she panted. "It's better than nothing."

I agreed.

We slowed down slightly as the forest opened into a clearing, and moonlight spilt onto the ground in pale patches. In the center of the clearing was a tall, sleek pillar with a sigil stone atop it.

"What the hell is this place?" I whispered, not intending to get an answer out of it, but Marnie had already opened her mouth to explain.

"Different realms, I think. I heard this is the hardest competition we've done so far."

Just my luck to get stuck with the hardest competition of all.

I stared at the stone as it pulsed faintly with golden light. However, the sight of it didn't give me any hope.

Some stones are cursed.

Nadael's warning flickered through my mind, and I shuddered. I thought about what we could do and our next move, but someone else had already beaten us there. A tall and broad-shouldered boy from one of the other teams. His hand hovered over the stone as if he were hesitant to touch it.

Marnie grabbed my arm. "Wait," she whispered.

I nodded, watching closely.

The boy finally reached out, his fingers brushing the surface of the stone. The light changed instantly, shifting from gold to a sickly green.

He froze.

A second later, a bloodcurdling scream tore from his throat. He stumbled back, clutching his head, his body writhing as if invisible hands were pulling him apart from the inside.

I felt vomit rise in my throat, and I did everything not to spill whatever contents I had in my stomach all over the ground.

"It's a cursed one," Marnie whispered, her voice shaking.

The boy kept screaming before he ran as if something imaginary was chasing him and disappeared deep into the forest.

Marnie and I stayed frozen for a long moment, neither of us wanting to move or speak. Then, from somewhere to my left, Silas and Brandon appeared, both breathing hard. I couldn't help but search for Hunter, wondering where he was. Whether he was okay or hurt or fending off one of those monsters alone.

Brandon was the first to spot the sigil stone and started towards it when Marnie pressed a hand to his chest, stopping him from going any further.

"It's not one of the real stones. It's a cursed one," Marnie said, and Silas raised an eyebrow.

"And we're still standing here because...?"

I ignored him, my eyes locked on the now glowing green stone. "There might be more stones nearby."

"Then we should move," Brandon said. "That thing from earlier could still be tracking us."

I nodded before we stepped forward and headed into the forest, where the trees closed in on us again.

GRACE

fifty eight

"**D**oes anyone else feel like we've been walking in circles?" Brandon muttered, glancing at the identical trees surrounding us.

"Told you," Silas said. "This forest is messing with us on purpose."

Brandon snorted. "Or maybe you're just shit at directions."

"Tucker, you're getting on my last nerve, I swear—"

"Guys," I interrupted, exhaling sharply. "Can we focus? You know, on *getting* the sigils?"

Marnie chuckled beside me. "I honestly don't know how you survived living in the same dorm with them for so long."

I didn't know *how*, either. "I barely did," I said dryly, earning a smirk from her.

Behind us, Silas was still grumbling, "I feel wildly unappreciated right now."

"You'll live," I called over my shoulder, and the exchange between us brought me a flicker of warmth, easing the anxiety clawing at me since the competition began.

Except it was short-lived.

The deeper we went into the forest, the heavier the air felt. Shadows stretched for too long under the night sky, and the trees only seemed to close in tighter with every step we took.

"You know," Brandon said after a while, "we should really come up with a way to mark where we've been."

Marnie raised an eyebrow at him. "And how exactly do you plan to do that? Leave a trail of breadcrumbs behind?"

"Maybe carve something into the trees," he suggested, ignoring her sarcasm.

Silas snickered. "With what? Your stick?"

"It's a spear."

"No, it's a glorified stick."

"You have a fucking branch to defend yourself with; stop talking."

Marnie stifled a laugh at both Brandon and Silas, and I couldn't help but crack a small smile. Sometimes, I wished— no, I *always* hoped for a moment like this where everything felt normal, like we were just a group of friends out for a walk in the woods instead of being hunted by monsters and Celestial judgment. But that wasn't the case. Not for me. Not ever.

A sudden rustling sound had us all stop.

I tightened my grip on my blade, my pulse so loud it drowned out the words Brandon was muttering.

"Relax," a familiar voice drawled from somewhere to the left.

Hunter stepped into view with his spear hanging loosely at his side, and relief shot through me, seeing him again, even if it was under different circumstances.

"Finally!" Silas said.

Hunter rolled his eyes at him before they locked on me, his

focus so intense it felt almost tangible. "Any luck?"

I shook my head, though I was finding it impossible to breathe. "Nothing yet."

His gaze lingered on me for a moment too long, reminding me of how much was still left unspoken between us.

My chest tightened, and everyone around us seemed to notice. Marnie cleared her throat loudly, and I tore my gaze away.

Suddenly, the ground became the most fascinating thing in the world as I stared at it. Unlike everything else, it wasn't threatening to tip me over the edge. It was solid, steady— something I could rely on when the rest of me felt like I was free-falling.

Gravity couldn't pull me under as long as my focus stayed there.

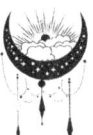

The five of us moved together this time, as the earlier humor had drained from our group. The only sounds were the crunch of leaves and the occasional twig snap as we stalked through the forest. Hunter took the lead, guiding us through paths like he knew exactly where he was going.

"Does anyone else feel like we're being watched?" Marnie whispered, glancing over her shoulder as she shuddered.

"We're always being watched," Silas muttered. "The Council are probably having a good laugh at us right now from the comfort of their headquarters."

"Either that or the monster from earlier is watching us, too," Brandon added.

I opened my mouth to say something reassuring, but

honestly, I wasn't sure I could come up with anything worth comforting.

"Wait, stop." Hunter held up a hand, and we all came to a standstill beside him. My gaze tracked his, and that was when I saw a faint golden glow peeking out from beneath the roots of a gnarled tree. It was barely visible through the dense underbrush. Still, there was no mistaking what it was.

"Another stone," I whispered.

"Thank fuck," Silas said, stepping forward, but Hunter slapped a hand against Silas's chest, stopping him in his tracks.

Hunter approached it cautiously, the group spreading out in a loose circle around the tree. The sigil stone pulsed faintly, just as the last one had done before we realized it was cursed. Up close, I stared at its intricate carvings that seemed to shift the longer I kept my eyes on it.

It looked small and harmless—an object I would gladly collect just for how beautiful it looked. However, the memory of the boy screaming earlier was still fresh in my mind, and I knew that this could just as well be deadly.

"It doesn't look... cursed?" Marnie said, though there was doubt in her voice.

Hunter crouched by the tree, his spear resting across his knee as he studied the stone. "Looks can be deceiving."

I knelt beside him, trying to get a closer look at the stone. It was impossible to tell which was the real stone and which wasn't.

My fingers trembled slightly as I reached for it, but Hunter gripped my wrist, pulling it back. I glanced up at him, and the warning look in his eyes sent an unexpected pulse to my core. Swallowing, I stared right back at him with as much conviction as I could muster. "I can handle myself."

His jaw flexed. "I know." A pause. "But that doesn't mean

I want you to."

I pulled my wrist back. "Then, who else will do it? You?"

"If it means that you're not the one risking it, then yeah," he shot back without hesitation.

Sometimes, I wanted to punch him and kiss him all at once. It was a baffling thought.

"You don't get to decide for me." I have had too much of that in my life.

"I'm not—"

Before he could fight me on this, I slapped my hand over the stone's smooth surface just as he yelled my name not to.

For a moment, nothing happened.

Then, the ground beneath us trembled.

The golden light from the stone spread outward in a wave, illuminating the glade as the trees groaned and their branches curled unnaturally toward the sky.

I stood with the stone in my hand, staring at everyone else as the light continued to spread, swallowing the clearing in its glow.

"What's happening?" Marnie called out in panic, but I could barely hold myself up. I grabbed Hunter's arm as he held me, ensuring I didn't fall.

The ground shifted, cracked, and splintered, and the blade Hunter had given me slipped from my grip, disappearing into the cracks below us.

"It's changing!" Brandon cried out as the glade went silently still, and then branches twisted together, forming thick, impenetrable walls.

My wide eyes shot to Hunter before another branch came between us, separating me from him, from everyone.

"Grace!" His voice sounded urgent, but I could no longer see him as the world fractured. Everything around me became an endless maze that stretched as far as I could see.

Mist crept in through the branches, and everything became colder, heavier, and still. The only sound was the faint hiss of the sigil stone pulsing in my hand. I looked down at it, its angelic carvings glowing faintly in the dimness.

I was alone.

Fear settled in my chest, and my breaths turned shallow as I whirled around. Everything started spinning, and I couldn't focus. Pressing a hand to my chest, I could feel each thump of my heart pounding against it, almost as if it were trying to escape its confines. Much how *I* felt right now.

Trapped and alone.

My fingers curled into the fabric of my uniform, and nails dug into my palms as the edges of my vision blurred.

Stop, I tried to tell my mind, but the panic didn't lessen for one second. My legs felt even more unsteady than before, and I stumbled forward, bracing myself against the rough bark of the maze-like wall.

I started clawing at my neck, wanting to breathe, but then my fingers brushed something cool and smooth.

Hunter's necklace.

I closed my eyes, gripping the small charm between my fingers as its familiar shape grounded me.

I could still hear his voice from the day he'd given it to me.

What's this?

It's something to focus on. When it gets too much, hold it and ground yourself.

I clung to those words, now holding the blue charm stone like it was the last piece of sanity I had left in me.

My breathing slowed just a little as I pressed the charm against my chest, letting the cold surface sink into my skin.

One breath in. One breath out.

The maze was still there, surrounding me, but the necklace anchored me, pulling me back from it all.

I wasn't out of the labyrinth yet, but at least I wasn't lost in my head anymore.

"I can do this," I whispered, my voice breaking the silence. "I can figure this out."

I wasn't going to let this place win.

Not now. Not when I still had time to prove myself to others.

With the sigil stone in my other hand, I straightened, stepping forward—and then another. I didn't know where I was going, but I wasn't frozen anymore, and for now, that was enough to keep me going.

HUNTER

fifty nine

"Grace!" My voice echoed through the maze but was quickly swallowed by the twisting walls of branches and dense mist curling around my feet.

I couldn't see her.

I couldn't see anyone.

The thought gnawed at me as I stalked forward, intent on finding her, but every pathway I took and every section I turned looked identical to the last.

"Grace!" I shouted again, the word cracking in my throat.

Only silence answered.

I swore under my breath, and I forced myself to keep moving. Why didn't I stop her before she touched the stone? My jaw clenched at the memory of it all despite my warning. She rarely listened, and why should she after I had angered her the night of the ball?

"Fuck," I whispered, annoyed at myself, before a faint sound reached my ears—footsteps, hurried and uneven.

I stilled, my muscles bunching up as I gripped the edge of my spear tighter. The steps grew louder and closer, accompanied by the sound of heavy breathing. The footsteps were practically on top of me now as I rounded the next corner and collided with something solid, the force knocking me back a step.

The other figure hit the ground with a grunt, scrambling back as they looked up at me.

It wasn't Grace.

It was just Matt from the Healers Sector. He was younger than me, with wiry limbs and wide, panicked eyes. His uniform was torn, and dirt was smeared across his face.

"I—I'm sorry!" His hands raised defensively. "I don't want to fight, okay? I don't even know where I am going—I just—" His gaze darted around like he was expecting something to leap out at him.

Poor guy must have encountered one too many of those shadow beasts.

I took a step closer, but he shook his head, whimpering. Before I could say anything, he staggered to his feet and bolted down another path.

I stood there for a moment, watching the empty space where he'd been, but he no longer mattered to me. What mattered was finding Grace.

Her name burned on my tongue as I shouted it again into the silence and was met with nothing.

GRACE

I forced my legs to keep moving, even as my lungs burned, and my muscles ached. Somewhere out there was another sigil stone, the real one, and I desperately wanted to find it.

That thought was the only thing keeping me moving, even as exhaustion started consuming me with every step.

"Grace."

I came to an abrupt stop and turned in all directions to where the voice had come from. "Hunter?" I whispered, but there was nothing. I went to say his name again, but that was when I heard it. My name once more, and the faintest whispers followed close behind. I froze, my ears straining to hear more, but what they were saying wasn't clear.

Whatever it was, my feet began moving without warning. I couldn't help it as I followed the sound, anyway, weaving through the maze as the whispers grew louder and more insistent.

I sucked in a sharp breath as I rounded a corner, and there it was. Another sigil stone, this time embedded into the maze's wall. Except this one didn't look like the one I'd found before. It was pale, almost silver.

I hesitated.

It could be a cursed one.

Every instinct in me screamed for me to turn around, to leave it alone, but I couldn't move. It was as though my feet were stuck in quicksand. I couldn't escape it. There was something so magnetic about the stone. It was pulling me toward it, an invisible force that wrapped around my mind and body.

"No," I whispered, shaking my head, but my feet finally moved as if they were no longer my own. I reached out, my fingers trembling as they hovered over the stone. *Don't touch it. Don't touch it.*

I couldn't stop myself.

The moment my fingers brushed the surface, shadows swarmed me, and I stumbled back, feeling the darkness wrap around me like a shroud. The maze disappeared before me, and I couldn't see anything except figures.

I turned to see Hunter standing before me. His expression was twisted and cruel, resembling the hatred in his eyes whenever he used to look at me—before everything happened, before I... fell for him.

"Why are you here, Grace?" he asked, though his voice lacked any warmth.

I tried to speak, but my words were stuck somewhere between my mind and mouth.

He stepped closer, and something in him changed.

His eyes.

They weren't grey anymore.

They were black, an endless void that seemed to pull the light from the air around them.

A chill swept through me as his darkened gaze penetrated my soul, slicing every single one of our memories.

"Did you really think I was the hero?" he whispered, smiling a slow, sinister smile. "You're so naive, Grace. You always have been."

"No," I choked out, shaking my head. "You're not real. This isn't real."

But that hatred never faded from his eyes as more versions of Hunter appeared around me, each one worse than the last—his hands covered in blood, his laughter sharp and cruel, his voice whispering things I couldn't understand but knew were just harsh words, tormenting me.

It's not real. It's not real.

I clutched at the necklace around my neck. I focused on that instead and squeezed my eyes shut.

"Open your eyes, Grace." Hunter's voice sounded like it was coming from behind me.

I shook my head.

476

"Open your eyes!"

"This isn't real!" I screamed, the sound tearing from my throat as I fell to my knees, and everything went silent.

My breaths came in sharp, ragged gasps, and I slowly opened my eyes to the maze, snapping back into focus around me. The cursed stone lay in front of me, its glow fading to nothing.

"Grace!"

I looked up, my vision blurry, but there he was.

Hunter.

Please be real, please be real.

As soon as he saw the state of me, he crouched in front of me and cupped my face. "Hey," he said, looking around him as if cautious that the Council could be watching this moment. "You're okay."

I swallowed hard, nodding shakily.

He couldn't stop himself as he pulled me into his embrace, and I held onto him, his chin resting atop my head.

"You're okay," he whispered again, but the image of his black eyes lingered in my mind, and I wasn't sure if I would be.

GRACE
sixty

The maze shifted and groaned as Hunter, and I ran through its tangled corridors. Each turn felt like a gamble, and another dead end was waiting on every path.

"Where do you think they are?" I asked, my breath hitching as I kept pace beside him.

"We'll find them," he said tightly, and I caught a glimpse of his face as we turned another corner. His jaw was clenched, and his eyes were swirling with something I couldn't quite place.

"Hunter?" I started, but he stopped, grabbed my arm, and turned me to face him. I stumbled slightly. "What? We have to keep moving—"

"There's something I need to tell you."

I blinked. "Now? Are you serious? We're in the middle of—"

"Grace, just listen to me first. If something happens—if this—"

"Stop—"

"Would you still stick by me?" he asked, his voice dropping lower, almost into a whisper.

"What?" I breathed, staring at him. Had he been affected by the stone, too? I didn't understand any of this.

His eyes searched mine with something raw and unguarded in them. "If you knew something about me—something that could change everything. Would you still... stay?"

I opened my mouth to answer, wary of the Council, but when I saw that vulnerability that I wasn't used to seeing in him, I couldn't help what came out: "Yes but... what are you trying to—" before I could finish, a deep groan echoed through the maze. The ground trembled beneath us as I looked to my left. The sharp scent of damp earth filled the air before thick, gnarled vines snaked from the stone and lashed out at us like tendrils. One barely missed my shoulder before Hunter yanked me back.

"Fuck," he hissed and grabbed me by the arm again as we ran. My boots pounded against the uneven ground as vines whipped at our legs and thorns slashed at my arms.

With every turn we took, more vines would come spiralling toward us before we skidded to a stop, and the path ahead disappeared. Another wall rose behind us as Hunter pulled me into another turn.

The maze wanted us lost.

Branches clawed at my clothes, the roots beneath us shifting unnaturally while the walls twisted and groaned, reshaping the corridors before our eyes.

We couldn't outrun it forever. We needed to find the sigil and move on.

A sudden voice echoed through the maze.

I recognized it immediately and skidded to a halt.

"Marnie!"

480

Hunter cursed under his breath, eyes darting to where the sound came from.

"That was her," I gasped, my heart pounding as I ran down the maze corridor.

"Grace—" Hunter called after me, but I was already forcing my way through vines. I knew he was right behind me even as I sprinted toward the distant cries.

We rounded a corner, and there, half entangled in vines, was Marnie.

Silas and Brandon were with her, slashing wildly at the vines wrapping around them. The tendrils had sneaked up their arms, coiling around their waists, pulling them toward the walls as if the maze was trying to consume them.

"Fuck—" Hunter lunged forward, tearing a vine away from Brandon before it could wrap around his throat.

I scrambled to Marnie's side, grabbing the tendrils and holding her. "Okay, just hold on!"

Marnie coughed, her fingers clawing at the vines constricting her ribs. "Grace—the sigil—it's in the roots—it's—"

My eyes widened as I glanced at the ground in search of it. "Hunter—" I hardly got his name out before another vine lashed toward my throat. I stumbled back, dodging just in time before slamming my boot down on it. The tendril coiled violently, like a severed limb writhing in pain.

Hunter was already at my side, his expression focused. "Keep them off me."

He didn't wait for a response before dropping to his knees, shoving his hands deep into the mass of writhing roots. The moment his fingers dug into them, the vines screamed.

I didn't have time to process how unnatural it sounded before the walls closed in.

A thick vine struck Silas across the chest, knocking him

flat on his back and causing Hunter to look over his shoulder. In that one second, a vine lashed out at him. I reacted on instinct. I dove toward him, shoving his body aside as a thick root snapped towards his face. Pain seared my arm as thorns slashed through fabric and skin alike, but I bit down the cry that tore through me.

Hunter's arms tried to catch me before I could collapse, but the vines wrapped around his wrists, pulling him back.

I gritted my teeth against the pain when another vine circled my ankle, and I grabbed onto a trunk, holding myself in place before I could be dragged.

"Grace!" Hunter shouted, fighting off the vines. "The sigil!"

I nodded and used my other hand as I reached inside the roots, searching for the sigil. A strangled scream slipped past my lips. I couldn't help it.

"Come on," I whimpered in desperation. I could feel the smooth exterior of the sigil, but it was too far out of my reach.

I kicked at the vine, holding onto my leg, and placed all my strength on grabbing that sigil.

Marnie was still struggling to breathe, her body growing limp by the second.

Shit, shit, shit.

Determination pushed against my chest, and I pulled myself up. Another tendril wrapped around my waist, and I knew now was my only chance. With a pained cry, I stretched my arm until my fingers could close around the sigil.

Everything stilled.

Then, something ancient and enraged groaned from within the walls. The vines loosened their grip on all of us at once before recoiling back into the walls, and a shockwave of golden light exploded outward. Marnie fell beside me as Brandon raced to catch her. Hunter rushed toward me, cupping my face as I

482

shielded my eyes, and the walls dissolved around us, melting into nothingness. The air shimmered, and the maze around us transformed into something surreal and otherworldly.

Hunter helped me stand as the ground beneath me wavered again, sending a ripple through my body as if I were standing on water instead of land. Fragments of floating paths and patches of grass hovered in the air, breaking off and reforming.

Brandon muttered something about getting high, and Marnie nudged him hard enough to make him stumble, but even then, Marnie was struck by awe as she looked around at the swirling colors of reds and golds bleeding into the sky.

A storm churned in the distance, its crackling energy throwing shadows against mountains and hills before I noticed the other competitors standing in different parts of the glade, looking just as confused as us. Some were already moving, hopping across the unstable paths toward something in the distance.

I looked at where they were heading and saw the unmistakable glowing orb hovering in the center of the landscape. Two other stones were on each side of it.

"Well, that's subtle," Silas said as all of us spotted the sigil stones floating in midair.

"It's the last part of the competition," Hunter said grimly. "And we're not the only ones who can tell either."

He was right.

A Guardian to our left raised her hands as her fingers traced glowing patterns in the air. A vision flickered to life in front of her, showing a clearer path to the stones.

"That's cheating," Silas mumbled. "I thought they couldn't control their visions."

"It's called strategy," Hunter corrected. "Now move."

We lunged forward, leaping across fragments of floating

paths. Each step felt unsteady as every competitor who hadn't been affected by a cursed stone or beast moved closer to the sigil stones like we were predators circling their prey.

A Messenger on another path stopped, her eyes glowing faintly as she focused on someone else from her sector. She wasn't speaking, but her silent telepathy directed the person toward the stone with precision, guiding him through the chaotic shift in paths.

"Messengers have it easy," Silas grumbled, narrowly dodging a crack in the ground as it split open beneath his feet.

"They're not the only ones," I said, pointing toward a Healer who had crouched near a fallen friend. Her hands glowed with golden light as she quickly patched up the competitor's twisted ankle.

"Hey, we don't always have it easy. Sometimes it's too late to heal," Marnie said, clutching onto Brandon as he helped her from further back.

At least everyone was using their strengths—that's what the Council wanted to see: that the Ascendants could use their gifts to their advantage.

I had nothing to show for it, but I had the will to compete and win, at least.

A Guardian suddenly surged toward the sigil, clearing the gaps in the floating paths with impossible ease.

I gritted my teeth and pushed forward, my boots skidding on the unstable ground as I ran.

Hunter was ahead of me as he leapt across crumbling platforms and intercepted the Guardian with a fist swing. The Guardian staggered back, but not before grabbing Hunter by the collar of his jacket and dragging him off one of the moving platforms. They both fell to the ground, and I panicked, wanting to run to him, but he looked over his shoulder, telling me to just go as he fought off the Ascendant.

My feet faltered, and I debated whether to listen to him or not.

"Grace," Silas said. "Marine, both of you go. We'll be there soon." Him and Brandon jumped onto other platforms, trying to get to Hunter while Marnie looked at me and without needing to say anything, we raced toward the sigil stone.

We dodged cracks in the ground and bursts of energy from platforms as we manoeuvred through the glade. I tried to look back to where Hunter was, but Marnie kept me steady before someone appeared in front of us, her hands glowing as she conjured another vision. The image flickered for a moment, showing an alternate path to the stone, but before she could finish, Marnie struck back.

Her glowing hands lashed out, disrupting the Guardian's concentration and breaking the vision. The Guardian stumbled, and Marnie grabbed my arm, pulling me forward.

Leaping over a cracked platform, I landed without much effort, but Marnie slipped and fell onto a lower piece of land.

"Marnie!" I yelled, but the storm nearly drowned out my voice.

"I'm fine!" She coughed, lifting herself from the ground and scanning the glade. "You're closer to them; grab whichever you feel is right!"

My brows furrowed as I looked over my shoulder at the sigil stones just ahead.

"Grace, just *get* the stone!" Marnie yelled, and a groan slipped past my lips as I jumped onto the next platform, the stones glowing a bright blue with every second I got closer to it. But as I reached for the one in the middle, the air around me changed. The storm above crackled louder, and a bolt of lightning struck the platform I was on. It cracked into pieces, and I fell, hitting one platform, then another, then another.

Pain shot up my entire body as I landed on my back and fought to open my eyes.

Everything around me began to fade, and suddenly, I was no longer on the ground. Instead, I was standing in a small, cosy flat—the same one Joe and I used to live in when I was younger. Joe was sitting at the kitchen table with a cup of tea in his hand as he glanced up and saw me.

"Welcome back home," he said, "You've been gone so long, I was beginning to think you'd never come back at all."

A pang rippled through my chest, seeing him there, smiling at me warmly as if nothing had ever changed between us.

The sigil stone and competition were gone. There was only Joe, the smell of freshly baked bread, and the warmth of the sunlight streaming through the windows.

"You don't have to do this anymore, Grace," Joe said, his smile softening. "You can stay here where you'll be safe."

For a moment, I wanted to believe him.

But even back then, I was never safe. We were always running, hiding, searching.

"I don't want to stay."

Joe sighed. "You're not ready for what is out there, Grace. You never will be."

I stilled.

No.

I wanted to be ready. I believed I could be.

If not now, then maybe someday.

Slowly, I raised my eyes to meet his. He was smiling again, waiting expectantly for me to take a seat beside him and *stay*.

"This isn't real," I whispered, my voice shaking.

Joe's smile faltered. "What did you say?"

"You're not really here. You never were."

"Grace—"

I ran towards the door to our apartment, Joe's voice calling my name over and over again. I didn't listen, and I didn't stop once. But every corner I turned, the door didn't seem to be there. Shadows appeared around me, whispering, taunting me, and manifesting into people like Matias, Norah... Lucas.

Pushing through all of them, I rushed toward the end of the hallway where my old bedroom used to be and pushed through the doorway. When I stepped out, I wasn't in my bedroom. Instead, I found myself falling, falling, *falling*.

I jolted awake with a sharp gasp, my eyes snapping open to the swirling sky above me. The air was cold and sharp against my skin, grounding me in the reality of it all as I lay sprawled on the uneven ground.

Every muscle in my body protested as I pushed myself upright, and pain radiated through my limbs. A fierce determination bloomed in my chest, steadying me as my gaze locked on the other two glowing stones hovering just out of reach.

One pulsed brighter than the other, flickering with an almost hypnotic glow. For a moment, I thought the answer was obvious. The middle stone seemed unassuming, waiting—safe. So, I reached for it. And I fell.

But the last two stones...

The one on the left glowed in the darkness like an ember. It was inviting and powerful. Which was exactly why I knew that it wasn't the right one.

Sometimes the most powerful things were those that could only be witnessed from the inside.

Taking a deep breath, I steadied myself and leapt toward the nearest platform. My hands caught the edge, but my legs dangled beneath me as I tried to haul myself up and managed to scramble onto the platform. I didn't stop to catch my breath. I didn't want to.

I lunged for the next platform, then the next, each leap carrying me higher.

The stone was right there within reach, and my hands trembled as I focused on nothing but the goal ahead.

Somewhere from below, I heard Hunter's voice calling my name, but I had already reached out and grabbed the sigil stone, its light spilling over my fingers as the storm above us crackled again.

GRACE

sixty one

The moment my fingers closed around the sigil stone, the floating platform beneath me cracked like glass, and I dropped onto the other platforms. Everything else started to fall away, revealing the forest again as sunrise began to loom over the glade. Then came the sound—a guttural, bone-chilling growl that echoed through the trees.

The shadow beasts were back.

Hunter rushed toward me, and I stumbled forward, clutching onto the stone tightly as I leapt off the last crumbling platform. He managed to grab me by the waist in time and lowered me to the ground before Marnie came over, frantically trying to heal my cuts and bruises.

I shook her off, hearing another distant growl. "We need to get back before we get stuck here." I glanced at Silas and Brandon. They didn't hesitate as we all sprinted through the dense forest, some of the other competitors fighting to get back themselves.

Silas was ahead this time, his breathing labored but

determined while Brandon kept pace beside him. Hunter stayed close to me, his spear drawn at the side, ready to fight off anyone and anything who tried attacking.

"Keep moving!" he yelled as one of the monsters lunged from the darkness, and Brandon turned to help Hunter fend it off.

Once struck, the creature dissolved into black mist, but another took its place, snarling as it chased after Marnie.

"Behind you!" I warned her, and she turned, her hands glowing faintly. She threw a burst of light at the beast, and it screeched, retreating into the shadows.

"We're almost there!" Silas yelled, his voice strained as he pointed at a shimmering oval of light carved into the forest, separating the glade from the academy.

I could feel the creature's presence pressing against our backs, urging me to run faster. But as I reached the portal, I hesitated.

My hands shook as I stared at the three sigil stones in my grip.

I'd won.

And yet, I felt nothing.

"Grace?" Marnie's voice wavered with confusion as she stopped by me.

I looked at her as the boys paused and turned to us. "Marnie," I said quietly. "You should be the one to take these."

"What? No. Grace, you earned those. You—"

"You are the one who said it was your dream to ascend," I cut her off. "You've wanted it your whole life. This is your chance."

"Grace, no. I can't—"

"You can," I said firmly, pressing the stones into her hands. She stared at me, stunned.

"You deserve this," I whispered. "Take them."

For a moment, she didn't move. Then she nodded, her arms wrapping around me in one of her fierce embraces.

"Thank you," she whispered, her voice breaking as my eyes stung.

I nodded as we broke apart and watched her step through the portal, clutching the sigils tightly. Brandon and Silas followed, both sparing me a brief glance before disappearing.

Hunter then came to my side as we shared one final look that tore through my heart.

I wanted to say many things but now was not the right time. So, with a smile, I stared up at him as we stepped through and emerged on the other side of what was the painting.

But straight away, something was wrong.

Something was very, *very* wrong.

As soon as everything refocused, blaring alarms echoed in the distance.

My blood froze.

More Ascendants came through the painting, all clattering onto the ground, panting and chests heaving before panic settled into them at the sounding alarms.

Around us, there was no one, no Joe, no Azrael, no Nadael, nothing but emptiness.

"Where is everyone?" Marnie stepped forward, but no one answered her.

I glanced at Hunter, then at Brandon and Silas, who gave Hunter a single nod.

Hunter's fingers interlaced with mine as his eyes scanned the area. He told everyone to stay there but neither Brandon, Silas, nor I listened to him like the rest did.

All four of us cautiously headed towards the corridors, with Marnie deciding to follow as we walked through the empty academy. A metallic tang of blood lingered in the air, the kind of scent that clung to your skin and made it hard to breathe, think, and function.

My stomach twisted with dread, and I wasn't prepared for what I saw next as we pushed through the hall doors.

The first body I saw was sprawled near the edge of the doorway, its shadow wings bent at unnatural angles as a pool of blood surrounded them.

Marnie gasped, her hand flying to her mouth. "Eriel."

But it wasn't just one Celestial.

More bodies were scattered across the hall, like fallen leaves. Celestials and Ascendants, young, older... so many of them lay there lifeless, their faces pale and their eyes empty.

Brandon swore under his breath. "It's Norah."

I whipped around and saw him looking down at Norah, her face pale as she stared at the ceiling with empty eyes.

Oh god...

Where was everyone else? Were the other younger Ascendants safe? Was Joe—

My heart dropped as my gaze locked on Nadael among the deceased.

She was at the center of the hall, her hand still gripping a staff, its light flickering weakly as though refusing to fade entirely.

I shook my head. "No..." The words slipped from my lips, but they were barely a whisper.

I stumbled forward, my legs trembling as I knelt beside her. Her usually stern face was soft now, her features peaceful in a way that made the reality of her like this even harder to grasp.

Marnie clutched Brandon's arm for support while Silas knelt beside bodies, his usual sarcasm replaced by a grimace as he inspected the wounds and searched for the one person he hoped wouldn't be here among the deceased.

Hunter came beside me, his knuckles turning white as they clenched at his side. "Looks like it was demons," he said, and my blood turned to ash. "The barriers were weakening for a long time. They must have got in that way."

I couldn't even muster a response. This... this all happened while we were inside the glade. The whole academy was attacked, and we weren't even here.

"Joe," my voice cracked. "I need to find Joe." I got up on unsteady legs, but Hunter caught me upright. "I need to—"

Hunter's grip on my arm tightened, and I looked up at him, expecting the same determination I always saw in his eyes. Instead, I saw something dark and conflicting, like he was fighting some invisible battle I couldn't see.

"Grace—" he started, but the words seemed to fail him.

"What?" I snapped, frustration and worry clawing its way through my chest. "What is it?"

He went to answer, but the words that came weren't from him.

"You don't need to go looking for him, Grace. He already took the pleasure upon himself to evacuate as many Ascendants out of here."

I turned as Eden stepped into view. Her usual air of poise and smile were intact, but there was something different this time. It was colder, more ruthless.

Her gaze swept over us, looking almost amused. "Sorry, I missed the finale of the competition. Who won?"

My stomach twisted. "What—"

She chuckled, but it no longer sounded like the soft tone I was accustomed to. "Right, my bad. You must all be so confused right now! Let me just set it all straight for you." She stepped closer, her heels clicking against the bloodied ground.

"This attack, the demons breaching the walls, the deaths? It was *my* plan."

This couldn't be happening right now. "You... did this?"

Eden tilted her head, a smile tugging at the corner of her red-painted lips. "Well, not entirely. Let's just say I gave the demons the opportunity they needed."

"Why?" Brandon asked, glaring at her.

Eden's eyes flicked to him, her smile faltering. "Why? Because the Celestials are hypocrites. They preach virtue and justice, but all they do is destroy anything that doesn't fit their perfect little narrative." She jerked her head up, raising her voice. "But Joe knows that better than anyone, don't you, Joe?"

I frowned as Joe suddenly walked into the hall; his face grim as blood coated his shirt.

Despite it all, I was relieved to see him.

"Eden," he said, his tone filled with an exhaustion I'd never heard from him before. "What have you done?"

Eden's smile vanished, replaced by a sneer as she spun to face him. "What have *I* done? No, Joe. What did *you* do? You abandoned everything we believed in. You left me, left *us*, all to side with them!"

My mind was racing in all directions. All my thoughts weren't processing, and I could only keep wondering, *why, why, why?*

"Eden... you wanted a world without rules just because you didn't agree with the Council's methods."

"No, *you* didn't agree either, and you knew that. But then, you ascended, and once Grace came into the picture, of course, you only cared about her, even going as far as to work with *them*."

My head cut toward Joe, shock slamming right into me.

"The Council, even the Celestials, are using you, and now

they're using her." she pointed at me, her eyes flashing with unrestrained anger. "They sent her into that competition to prove humans are worthless. You think they care about her? About you? You're both just pawns to them. We all are."

I jolted back in surprise.

They... sent me into that competition to prove I was worthless?

Hunter tensed beside me, and when I looked up at him, something a lot like guilt crossed his eyes.

Realisation sunk in hard and fast.

He already knew that.

How...

"The Celestial system is broken," Eden said, her voice sharp yet strangely weary. She let out a sigh, her expression cold and distant. "It's just disappointing how useless that information was at the time when I let Malcolm into the academy."

Her words struck me like a hammer, shattering everything around me. The room blurred, and her voice echoed endlessly in my mind, with each syllable carving deeper into my chest.

"What?" I whispered.

When Eden turned her head in my direction, sinister amusement danced in her eyes.

"You... you're the one that let that demon in—the one that killed Lucas."

"Ding, ding, ding!" she sang. "It was more of an accident, though. Malcolm was only meant to go in as a form of distraction while I checked to see what that *interesting* letter Azrael received from the Council was. You can imagine my disappointment when I opened Azrael's safe and found it was just about you. Although I guess it worked in my favor since it only proved how much the Council manipulates." She sighed, shaking her head. "It's a shame, though, that Malcolm had to die. He sacrificed so much for me without any questions. Something that the Council could never do."

My throat burned. Everything did. "You killed innocent people—people who trusted you."

"Innocent?" Eden scoffed. 'You're so stupid, Grace. None of them are innocent. Not the Council, not the Celestials. And *certainly* not him." She turned her gaze to Hunter, and everything collapsed around me.

"What does she mean by that?" I asked him, trying to keep the quiver in my voice at bay.

Hunter didn't meet my eyes.

"Hunter," I said again, his silence only feeding further into my fear.

Eden's laugh was bitter and cruel. "Go on, Hunter, tell her."

A muscle ticked beneath his jaw.

"Tell her," Eden goaded him. "Tell her how you're just as corrupted as I am. That your soul was marked by a demon the moment you realized the Celestials failed you and your brother."

"No," I whispered, shaking my head. "That's not true."

Hunter finally looked at me, his grey eyes filled with desperation. "Grace," he started, but I stepped back, my heart splintering.

"Cain..." came Silas's voice, looking just as hurt as everyone else.

Hunter's gaze never left mine, not for one second. The longer I stared at him, the longer I felt I would break.

When that balance shifts—when demons gain too much power, or there is corruption within Celestials and Ascendants—the barriers weaken.

The memory of that day Lucas died rang so clear in my mind. Hunter knew the barriers were weakening. He was one

498

of the reasons why. He and Eden—two corrupted souls.

"When you'd sneak off, telling us you were training. It wasn't true, was it?"

He tried reaching me, but I pulled my hands back as if his touch would burn me.

"When you came back, beaten, making us think it was the Riftkeeper's... it wasn't really them, was it?"

He didn't deny it.

And that was the worst part.

"Ah," Eden chuckled. "Is that what he made you all think? That it was the Riftkeeper's? Oh, Hunter, we both know those times were only for your lack of work. The demons don't like it when you waste their time."

Betrayal pounded against my chest.

Hunter could only look at me with sorrow and pain flashing across his face.

But I didn't care in that moment. I didn't care because I was officially broken.

"And *you*." Eden turned to Joe with a vicious smile plastered on her lips. "You know what I'm going to say." Her gaze drifted towards me and her smile grew. "But maybe Grace, should hear it come from you first."

I froze but there was only silence for those few seconds before the faint sound of a weapon unsheathing clashed in the distance, and I turned to see as Joe lunged toward Eden before she could say anything else.

She was faster, already drawing out a weapon of her own as the boys reacted, rushing to intercept her, but it was Marnie who was closest to Eden.

She threw herself between the boys and Eden, her hands glowing as she tried to blind Eden.

Yet Eden's blade sank into her abdomen, and time seemed

to freeze.

"No!" The scream tore from my throat as she crumpled to the ground. My legs nearly buckled beneath me as I dove forward, catching her before she could collapse completely.

Blood. So much of it.

My shaking hands pressed against the wound at her abdomen, desperately, frantically.

"Marnie—" My voice trembled. "You're going to be okay. Just—just heal yourself. You can heal yourself."

I grabbed her hand and pressed it over the wound, waiting and pleading for the familiar golden glow to bloom beneath her fingertips.

Nothing happened.

Her breath shuddered in her chest. "Grace..." She coughed, red staining her lips. "I can't—it won't—it won't heal—"

"No, no, no, that's not true—just try again, okay? Just concentrate." My vision blurred, tears welling and slipping past my lashes. "You always fix things. You always fix *me*."

I glanced back at the boys. My voice cracked as I choked out, "Go get help!"

They hesitated.

"Please!" I screamed, barely recognising the sound of my own voice. "Somebody—just get someone! Please!"

At my urgency, Brandon and Silas ran, leaving Hunter behind. I heard their hurried footsteps disappear into the wreckage of Celestia and somewhere in the distance, Eden's retreating heels clicked against the stone. Joe's voice shouted after her, but it all faded into nothing.

Because Marnie was looking at me like she already knew.

She gripped my wrist, her fingers sticky with her own blood. "I don't want to go," she rasped. "Please don't let me—

don't—"

"You're not going anywhere. Just breathe in and out, yeah? You're okay; you're going to be okay—"

She gasped one final time, her hand falling limp as the sigil stones tumbled from her grip, clattering softly against the cold floor.

Her eyes fluttered shut.

And I knew.

Everything inside me shattered at once. I couldn't breathe. I couldn't move.

"Marnie?" I whispered, pressing her hand against her wound in hopes it would finally work, and she would be healed.

"No," my voice broke. I looked up for help, but Hunter was the only person I found staring at me with the same pained look. "No." I shook my head as grief swallowed me whole and sobs wracked my whole body. They sounded like I was screaming. "I—I can't —" I gasped for air. "I can't do this without you. Please... *please* don't leave me."

But she already had, and there was no one left to fix me.

HUNTER

sixty two

Grace held Marnie's lifeless body in her arms. The weight of her cries was tearing me apart from the inside out, and it felt as though my chest was going to collapse in at any moment.

I moved closer to her and muttered, "Grace." I was uncertain about whether I should reach for her, and I was also uncertain about whether I had the right to do so.

She didn't raise her head as her shoulders shook furiously, and her sobs soaked the fabric of her uniform. The sound of her anguish hurt more than any injury I'd ever endured.

I crouched down next to her and took a deep breath. "Grace," I said, this time in a quiet voice, as if uttering her name could somehow bring her broken pieces back together.

I was completely unprepared for the look that she gave me when her head suddenly snapped up. A mixture of grief and rage contorted her face, and for a brief moment, she appeared to be someone else.

"Don't," she snapped, her voice breaking as she spoke.

"Don't you *dare*."

I froze, my hand hovering in the air before I slowly pulled it back. "I'm just trying to—"

"To what?" she cut me off, her voice rising. "To make me feel better? To tell me that everything's going to be okay? Because it's not, Hunter. *Nothing* is okay."

Her rage struck me with more force than any weapon could ever have the ability to deliver.

"I'm not going anywhere," I said firmly, my voice steady despite the storm raging in my chest.

She stood abruptly, her hands trembling as she wiped her tear-streaked face with shaking fingers, smearing blood across her cheeks. Her movements were sharp, almost frantic.

"Don't," she said again, her voice quieter but laced with venom. "You don't get to say that to me."

I rose slowly, towering over her as she shook and sobbed, her grief pouring out in waves. For the first time, I understood what it meant to truly hate myself. To hate what I'd become.

"Grace, I—"

"Was it Eden?" The question came out of nowhere as I blinked, caught off guard.

"Was it her?" she repeated, her hands curling into fists at her sides. "Did you have something with Eden? Was she the one that you lost your...?" Her voice broke, and I saw the realization dawn on her face.

I couldn't answer that at this moment in time.

Because the truth was a poison I couldn't force out of my throat. How was I supposed to tell her that her whole life had been a lie, that the Riftkeeper's—her actual mother, me...

'Do you realize how insane that is?"

'I was—"

"She manipulated you, Hunter! Do you not see that?"

I didn't at the time. Even now, I struggle often to see it that way.

"You lied to me," she whispered, her voice thick with betrayal. "You lied, and I let myself trust you."

Her breath hitched, her chest rising and falling unevenly as tears fell down her cheeks. She took a step closer, her fists trembling.

"Grace—" Before I could say anything else, her fists smashed into my chest. They were not strong enough to cause me physical harm, but they still tore me apart in ways that I had not previously considered they were capable of doing.

"I trusted you!" she cried, her voice breaking with every word. "I cared for you! I—I—"

I caught her wrists gently, trying to still her, but she yanked them away. Her glare pierced through me, filled with so much pain it made my soul ache.

"I never wanted to hurt you," I said, my voice cracking for the first time. "You have to believe me."

Her tears fell harder as she shook her head. "How did it happen?"

"What?" I asked, confused and desperate.

"How were you corrupted?" she demanded, her voice rising. "Why did you even stay here, knowing you would never be worthy of ascending? Why did you let me get so close to you!"

I tried to speak, but the words lodged in my throat. I couldn't tell her how Eden had found me at my lowest, how she had whispered lies that I was too desperate to question, how I had let her pull me into the darkness when I thought there was nothing left to save.

Grace's lips trembled as she watched my silence. She nodded slowly; her voice hollow when she spoke again. "You knew, didn't you? About Lucas. About that demon that infiltrated the academy. About the Council wanting me to fail. You knew, and you said nothing."

I stepped toward her, my hand outstretched, but she stepped back, shaking her head.

"Grace," I pleaded, my voice raw and broken. "I tried to change. Once I met you, I tried. I thought if I stayed away from Eden if I distanced myself, I could—"

"Redeem yourself?" she finished, her voice bitter.

I faltered, the weight of her words crushing me.

"I told you I'd always be here, no matter what, right?" she interrupted, her voice trembling. "I lied. See how easy it is for me to do that, too?"

I flinched as the words sliced through me, repeating in my head like a cruel mantra.

I lied. I lied. I lied.

"Leave," she whispered, her tone cold and final.

I didn't move; my feet were rooted to the ground despite the crushing weight of her gaze.

"Leave!" she screamed, her voice cracking. "Just fucking leave me alone!"

I stared at her, my chest hollow and aching, knowing I couldn't fight her anymore. She looked at me like I was the monster she always feared I'd become. And maybe I was.

She came up to me and shoved me hard, Marnie's blood painting my uniform. "Go," she whispered brokenly this time.

My heart was burning and aching, and there was nothing to soothe it. So, I did what I should have done from the moment Grace came into my life. Turned and walked away.

Every step felt heavier than the last, her sobs following me like ghosts, breaking me apart piece by piece.

And for the first time, I didn't think there was anything left of me to save.

506

GRACE
sixty three

I felt cold... dead even. It was a feeling that penetrated my bones and that refused to leave. The only thing that seemed to be able to prevent me from falling further apart was the fact that I was sitting against the wall with my knees pulled in close to my chest and my arms wrapped around them.

Marnie lay a few feet away, her body still and silent. Her blood had dried on the stone floor, leaving a dark stain that I knew, no matter what happened, would remain there forever.

I couldn't bring myself to look at her for too long.

The boys had tried to get me to move. When they returned without a Healer in sight, knowing it was already too late for any kind of help, they began pleading with me to leave this place. Silas had crouched in front of me, trying to coax me out of my stupor. But even I could tell how hurt he was, how he wondered where Hunter was, and how he could fail him when they were friends.

I thought the same. I *grieved* the same way as him.

Brandon hovered nearby, his face pale, muttering something

about needing to move Marnie.

But I didn't want them to do anything.

I wanted them to go and get the rest of the competitors, make sure they were fine and find somewhere they could all be safe.

So that was exactly what I told them to do.

They argued, of course, but when I didn't respond—when I just sat there, staring at nothing—they finally gave in. One by one, they left, their footsteps echoing as they disappeared down the bloodstained halls.

And now, it was just me.

I had no idea how long it had been. It could have been hours or minutes that I stayed there like that, and the only sound accompanying me was the distant wail of the alarms.

I stared at the wall in front of me, its smooth surface blurred by unshed tears. My mind was empty yet so full that it felt like it was about to burst open. I couldn't stop replaying the scene —the look on Marnie's face as she trembled, telling me she didn't want to go.

I had let her down.

The one person that was there for me from the start. The one person who deserved to ascend more than anyone else.

The thought lodged itself deep, carving a hollow space in my chest that I could not shake. I couldn't even heal her myself. I couldn't do *anything*.

Footsteps broke through the silence, but I didn't look up. I was too tired to care who it was.

"Grace," Joe said.

A slight tilt of my head was all that was required to catch a glimpse of him standing a few feet away. His face was etched with lines of exhaustion and grief as he stared at me.

He crouched beside me, his movements slow, almost

cautious, like he feared I might shatter if he got too close.

What he didn't realize was that I had already shattered long ago.

"I'm so sorry," he whispered, but the words felt like they weren't meant for me.

I nodded numbly. *Bring her back,* I wanted to say. I didn't care whether it disrupted the equilibrium or if her soul had found peace. I wanted Marnie *back.*

Instead, all that came out of me was, "Are there still any demons out there?"

Joe let out a slow breath, rubbing a hand over his face. "No. They attacked not long after the second part of the competition. They tried infiltrating the Council quarters but luckily, we managed to put barriers up for that, and once they fed from the chaos they inflicted, they left on Eden's orders."

"So, Eden planned it all," I said what we already knew. What she'd already told us.

A brief pause. "Yes," he admitted quietly. "She waited until the Council were too focused on the competition to notice what was happening outside. It was all too late by the time enforcement came. We evacuated as many Ascendants as we could, but..."

My heart was torn to shreds.

There were children here, Celestials...

"Why?" was all I could whisper.

"She wanted control. Eden demanded that Nadael give over her position as the leader of Celestia. She thought she could use the chaos to force her hand."

"But Nadael refused," I said, already knowing what came next.

Joe nodded, his mouth set in a grim line. "Nadael refused, and Eden... she didn't take it well."

511

I glanced toward Marnie's body, and something sharp and horrific twisted in my gut. "Did you get her?"

Joe's silence told me everything I needed to know.

"No," he said. "She got away."

As much as I wanted to scream and cry at that moment, I still couldn't help but feel empty inside. It was the kind of emptiness that was just as bad as being able to feel everything.

Joe's gaze searched mine. "Where's Hunter?" he asked, but there was a bite to his words.

My jaw tightened suddenly, and every bit of emptiness I felt became an anvil, pressing down on me like the world itself was trying to break me. "It doesn't matter where he is."

"Grace—"

"You were right about him. About all of it." I looked at him, my throat tight. "And I'm sorry, I didn't listen to you when you were just trying to help." My lower lip trembled. "I know... I know that there is so much I have yet to ask, to find out but you're also the only person now left in this world who actually cares about me, so please don't leave me, Joe. I don't think I could handle another loss."

He didn't respond right away. His brows furrowed as he studied me for seconds, maybe minutes. Then, he reached out, hesitating momentarily before placing a hand on my shoulder and wrapping his other hand around me.

I clung onto him, gripping the back of his jacket as I pressed my face to his chest and let out a shaky breath.

"We'll fix all of this, Grace," he said quietly. "I promise."

I nodded, but I couldn't bring myself to believe him.

Not when Lucas was gone.

Not when Marnie risked herself for all of us.

And not when everything around me had fallen apart, and the one person I'd come to trust had proven me wrong.

512

Eden was right. I was so stupid. I had always been.

I made a promise to myself then. A promise that I would never let anyone have that kind of power over me. Never again would I let my guard down.

Because doing so cost me everything. And I refused for that to be my undoing.

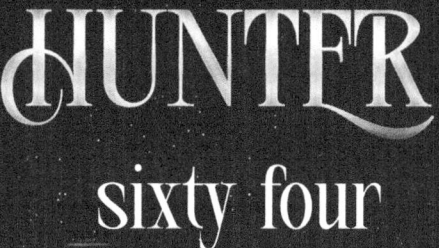

HUNTER
sixty four

The tires screeched as I yanked the wheel hard, the car skidding to a stop in a cloud of dust and gravel. I didn't wait for the engine to cut off—I was already throwing the door open before the car had even fully stopped.

The door hung open, creaking on its hinges like it might fall off, but I didn't care. All I could focus on was the building in front of me—the rotting, hollowed-out skeleton of what was once a hotel.

I didn't hesitate. My hands curled into fists at my sides, and I barrelled toward the door, shoving it open without a second thought. It groaned in protest, but I was already inside when the stench of alcohol and cigarettes permeated the air. My breathing was harsh, my chest tight with anger, but I forced myself to stay steady.

A few flickering torches dimly lit the lobby, and laughter sprang through one of the rooms. I entered and saw that the space was filled with demons I'd been associated with for a while.

One sat sprawled on a broken sofa, flexing his tattoos at others. Another leaned against a collapsed pillar, blowing out puffs of smoke as he grinned at what someone else was saying.

But the only person I wanted to find was Eden. I pushed past a few girls before finding Eden laughing and holding a glass of wine. She looked almost unchanged from the Eden I had known at Celestia—still poised, still sickly beautiful—but there was something even darker now, something unhinged. Her eyes gleamed with malice, and her smile was a weapon of glee.

The laughter died down as I stormed toward her and roughly turned her to face me. Drops of wine spilled across the dusted floor, but that didn't matter to her as she looked up at me with that lustful smile, she'd always given me.

I felt sick.

"If it isn't the golden boy," she chuckled, setting her glass down on a broken table. "Or should I say the tarnished boy?"

"Stop," I said through gritted teeth. "This isn't a fucking game, Eden."

"Isn't it? Because I think it's been a spectacular game so far. And you, Hunter, have played your part beautifully."

I stared at her, disgusted by everything that fell from her mouth. "What are you talking about?"

Eden stepped closer, and internally I squirmed. "Don't act like you don't know. I thought placing Grace in your dorm would prompt you to fall deeper into corruption. The human girl and the Ascendant, who hated the idea of one ever coming after his brother, were rejected." She scoffed. "I mean, you did so well, making Grace like you. I didn't even have to tell you to do anything, and she *still* fell for you. See, I knew something was off with you both when you no longer looked at her like

516

you despised her. I figured it out the night of the ball, watching you two... it was priceless. Imagine how the Council... *Joe* will feel knowing little Grace was charmed by someone like you. A corrupted soul."

I grabbed her upper arm and shook her hard. "You went too far. All of it. Killing Celestials, Nadael, destroying everything, all for what? Because you were bored?"

She laughed, a harsh, grating sound. "Don't act like you're so noble, *Cain*. No one in power is truly good; that included Nadael. Have you forgotten that? Or have you forgotten who you were before Grace came into the picture?"

My jaw tightened as she smirked, adept at manipulating me. She had allied herself with demons, preyed on me at my lowest, and dragged us both into damnation by selling our souls to them. But whatever she'd once been, she wasn't anymore. Eden had officially lost her grip on reality.

"Or perhaps you have forgotten all about Aaron."

I stiffened. "Don't bring him into this."

"Why not?" she said. "Isn't that why you're here? Still clinging to the hope that you'll find him? That the *letter* he sent you means he's out there somewhere."

I swallowed what felt like glass. "I haven't found him. The letter... it must've come too late. I've looked everywhere—"

Eden burst out laughing, causing others inside the room to chuckle along with her. "Oh, I can't—" Amused tears welled in her eyes as she clutched her stomach. "I tried to keep it in for a bit longer, but—" She sighed dramatically. "The look on your face... oh, Hunter. I should probably tell you that the letter you received wasn't actually from your brother."

My blood ran cold. "What?"

"It was me," she said, her look turning into a pitiful mock. *"I* forged it. It wasn't hard, really. All it took was finding a few

517

scraps of his handwriting hidden in your notebooks, copying it, and making sure you found it. It was incredibly easy how you fell for it."

"Why?" I couldn't stop the crack that tore from my throat. "Why would you do that?"

"To break you, silly," she said simply. "You were so distant from us that I needed to reel you back in. To corrupt you further. And look at you now, Hunter. You're everything I wanted you to be." Her smirk returned, and she gestured to the shadows. "But enough reminiscing. It's time for you to embrace what you've become. For both of us to embrace it. Just how we had spoken of it in the past, remember?" She touched my shoulder, and I flinched away from her touch as she circled me.

From the darkness, a figure stepped forward.

Seorin Yun.

An ex-alumnus at Celestia. She'd suffered the same fate from the Riftkeeper's, and now, only recently, had she become a full-fledged demon.

I barely saw her whenever I came here, but she was still striking. Her midnight-black hair reached up to her shoulders, and her wispy fringe framed her pale face and golden eyes.

Despite how beautiful she was, there was still a coldness about her, a detachment from that reality that no one ever dared question.

"Shall we?" I heard Eden say before realization dawned on me.

"Eden don't—" I turned, but it was too late as Seorin came at me with a blade in her hand and plunged the cool steel into my side.

Pain exploded through me, sharp and blinding, as I staggered back and Seorin smiled at me, my own blood dripping from the blade in her hand.

The room then blurred as I pressed my hand against the wound and looked up at everyone else, staring.

I took two steps forward before I collapsed onto the ground, and Eden crouched beside me.

"Have I ever told you how a corrupted soul becomes a full demon, Hunter?" Her voice was soft... taunting.

Blood bubbled in my throat as I tried to get up but failed and fell again.

"When a corrupted soul dies..." she whispered, and I could no longer breathe. "They don't pass on, Cain. They transform, awakening as their true selves."

No.

"I'll see you again in a few hours. We'll talk about what to do next then. I already have *so* many things planned."

I reached out, wanting to fucking strangle her, but darkness suddenly consumed me, and the only person I could think of was Grace.

Her face flashed across my mind. The hurt in her eyes turned to pure hate.

I whispered her name, hoping she would somehow come to me, but Eden's shrill laughter was the last thing I heard before everything went black.

Acknowledgements

Mum & Dad – Thank you for always supporting me through all the book ideas I tell you about. I love that you're my mum but also my best friend. We laugh, we cry and most of all we share the same passion for writing books. Dad, you're my favourite person in the world. I feel sorry for those that don't get to experience you all the time with your jokes, your kindness and your meme pictures! Thank you for being the first man in my life to show me what love is. I look up to you and mum as the inspiration for all my books.

Noelia & Eddy – To my siblings, you both are chaotic— include me and we're unstoppable. Noelia, you have followed me through this journey with Hunter and Grace since you were twelve years old and now, you're going to be eighteen and forever my fangirl for these characters. Eddy, you may not read a single thing unless it is a comic, but you've always been the best brother in the world to me, supporting me through everything. I love you both for that.

George – To my best friend and my everything, you have witnessed every momentum within my writing journey. You have seen my highs and my lows and never once put me down for it. You've endured my crazy nights of telling you all about the story ideas I had, the plot twists I wanted to try out and

520

of course, the swoon-worthy romance. I'm forever grateful to have you by my side, no matter how much I may annoy you.

To my readers – Thank you for being my biggest support for every book I have written so far. You've all kept me going even when I wasn't sure I could. I hope you enjoyed this book as much as I have loved writing it and I hope you will all stick around for what is to come of this series.

Para mi familia en España - Me duele no poder estar con ustedes para celebrar estos momentos. Siempre me han querido y han creído en mí desde que era pequeña. No importaba qué quería ser de grande o quién quería ser, siempre estuvieron ahí para apoyarme. Los quiero a todos, sin importar la distancia que nos separe.

Yaya – Nunca superaré que ya no estés con nosotros. Te extraño cada día con la esperanza de verte otra vez. Pero sé que estás aquí, cuidando de todos nosotros, porque para ti, tu familia lo era todo. Te seguiré esperando, Yaya, hasta que pueda contarte mis historias y lo que he logrado. Mientras tanto, miraré al cielo y sonreiré, porque sé que, de alguna manera, me estás viendo.

Solaris & Crello Trilogy

A City of Flames
A Kingdom of Shadows
A World of Ruins

Made in United States
North Haven, CT
23 June 2025

70042752R00290